BEHIND YOU

OTHER TITLES BY MIKE OMER

Thrillers

Please Tell Me

Zoe Bentley Mysteries

A Killer's Mind
In the Darkness
Thicker than Blood

Abby Mullen Thrillers

A Deadly Influence
Damaged Intentions
A Burning Obsession

Glenmore Park Mysteries

Spider's Web
Deadly Web
Web of Fear

BEHIND YOU

MIKE OMER

THOMAS & MERCER

Text copyright © 2024 by Michael Omer
All rights reserved.

Published by Thomas & Mercer, Seattle

www.apub.com

Amazon, the Amazon logo, and Thomas & Mercer are trademarks of Amazon.com, Inc., or its affiliates.

ISBN-13: 9781662509391 (paperback)
ISBN-13: 9781662509384 (digital)

Cover design by Faceout Studio, Elisha Zepeda
Cover images: © Anna Mutwil / Arcangel; © CG Alex / Shutterstock; © boonchob chuaynum / Shutterstock

Printed in the United States of America

BEHIND YOU

Chapter 1

Theo lay rigid in her bed, her eyes set on the clock. The clock's second hand rotated smoothly as the night progressed. It was almost time. Three fifty-seven a.m. Practically morning for some. Theo tried to imagine others who were awake right now. People who delivered papers. Workers on night shifts—nurses, doctors . . . cops.

Cops. Driving in patrol cars. Supposedly keeping us safe, protecting us from harm. Theo gritted her teeth. She knew the truth. The cops didn't protect from harm; they came after the harm was done, if they even came at all. And when they showed up, it wasn't to keep anyone safe.

It was three fifty-eight.

The warm blanket was soft, comforting. But it was a lie. Beds were the ultimate deceivers. You lay in bed thinking maybe tomorrow would be better. That things would seem brighter when the sun came up. When you fell asleep, the dreams came, whispering fabrications, telling you that you were someone else, or that you could fly, or that everyone loved you. And then, when you woke up, for one uncertain second, you didn't remember the events of the day before, of the week before. All you felt was that warm blanket, that soft mattress, and the world seemed almost safe.

And then reality crashed into you, knocking out your breath, yanking those cobwebs of delusion away. The new day wasn't better. It was, if anything, worse. And nothing seemed brighter when the sun came up.

Theo wasn't a sucker for the bed's lies anymore. She didn't let sleep take her.

Three fifty-nine.

She watched the second hand move, listening to the sounds of the house. A subtle hum from the fridge downstairs. The occasional tap as the wind shifted the large elm tree, its branch touching the wall. Richard's snoring, muffled, but still there. Mom sometimes joked about his snoring, but in all honesty, this wasn't funny. How could she bear sleeping next to that thundering noise?

Theo listened, trying to hear if there was anything else. Mom waking up for a drink of water, perhaps. Richard going to the bathroom, as he occasionally did at night. But there was nothing. Nothing to stop her. And now there was a new sound. The sound of her own pounding heart.

Four a.m.

She slid out of bed softly, her bare feet touching the floor. She was already dressed in her snug black hoodie, her loose gray pants. Nondescript clothes she carefully chose beforehand, knowing it would be very cold early in the morning. She slid her sneakers with her socks balled inside from underneath her bed. The socks were the only colorful clothing she allowed herself—her favorite pink kitty socks. They gave her a bit of comfort, and she needed all the comfort she could get. She slid them on. Carried the shoes in her hand.

A quick glance in the mirror. The tiredness was evident in her pale face. She pulled her long brown hair into a haphazard ponytail, then tucked it inside her hoodie's cap. She tightened the cap around her face, hiding most of it. In the gloomy light of her night lamp, she could hardly see her brown eyes, or her chapped lips. Outside, from a distance, no one would be able to recognize her at all. Good.

The closet door was already open. She hated going to sleep with it open, but she'd never intended to sleep this night. And the closet door squeaked when it moved. She grabbed the bag she packed yesterday and hefted it onto her back. She wished she could take more. There was so much she was leaving behind. Clothing, and books, and art supplies, and sketchbooks. Her entire world.

But then again, those weren't the only things. She was also leaving behind accusations, and hatred, and disbelief, and violence, and betrayal.

She could always buy more art supplies.

After shifting the shoes to her left hand, she slowly turned the knob of her bedroom door, like she'd practiced the day before. Then, with the doorknob fully turned, she pulled the door open. This one, like her closet's, squeaked. She'd never realized before how surrounded she was by hinges that squeaked, floorboards that creaked, bedsprings that groaned. All these belligerent objects, snitching, ratting her out.

She waited, breath held, listening for Mom's muttering of "Theodora, is that you?"

But all she heard was Richard's incessant snoring. His snores were her only ally in this house.

She glanced one final time around her room. Her duplicitous bed. The mirror where she looked at herself every day, desperately trying to hide her teenage acne, to smooth her hair. Her desk, where she sketched and did her homework. Her purple beanbag, Theo's body impression permanently cast in it. The row of manga books on the bookshelf. This room was her only haven. Not a *safe* haven, as nowhere was really safe. But a haven of sorts.

She glanced at her phone, left behind on her desk. Turned off for the past five days. How many notifications would she receive if she turned it on now? Fifty? A hundred? A thousand? Messages telling her she should burn in hell, calling her a psycho bitch, promising retaliation. Images of her in public chats, photoshopped crudely, so that it looked as if she was in prison, or hanging from a noose, or worse.

Fervent wishes for her to die of cancer, to go to prison for life, to get gang-raped every day forever.

By now, her phone felt as toxic as a vat full of poisonous acid. Another thing she was glad to leave behind.

She padded softly over to the staircase, getting nearer to Mom and Richard's bedroom. The plan was to go past the doorway as quickly as possible. No reason to delay there. But she found herself slowing down. Glancing inside. Taking one last look.

Richard lay on the left side of the bed, facing away from the door, the bald spot on the top of his head barely visible in the dim light. But Mom, facing the bedroom window, was easy to see in the soft moonlight that shone from it. Theo hadn't gotten her mother's looks, a fact she'd once overheard her aunt lamenting. At forty, her mother was still a beauty. A MILF, as Theo's friend Steve had pointed out to her several times.

Even in sleep her mother had a tiny frown on her face. Worried about her daughter's future. About the family's future. About what the neighbors were saying. About how much a good criminal lawyer charged per hour, and whether they could afford it. Wondering where she had gone wrong.

Watching her, Theo thought of all their times together. Mom driving her to school, telling her to have a good day. Mom hugging her when she cried. Mom brushing her hair gently. Mom shouting at her when she cut school. Mom telling her to put the damn phone down, they were having dinner. Mom introducing Richard, and later crying because Theo had been rude to him. Mom buying her the bike she always dreamed of, as a surprise. Mom drinking wine in the evening, her eyes gazing at the wall, after Dad left. Good memories, bad memories. Mom memories. Theo would have done anything for those memories to be the only ones of her mother.

But now there were new memories. Mom's horrified face when she picked up Theo from the police station. Mom's whispered hiss, telling Theo they would talk at home. Mom sitting grimly with Theo as Detective Dunn interrogated her.

And finally, the most terrible memory of them all, the one that drove Theo to start planning her escape. The moment when Mom came to her room and sat on the bed next to her.

"Theodora," she said. "I want you to tell me the truth. What happened that night?"

"I told you already," Theo answered. "I told you over and over."

Mom shook her head impatiently. "If you don't tell me the *truth*, we won't be able to protect you. What *really* happened? Why did you do it?"

And Theo realized the only person who was still on her side had crossed over.

Now she took a long shallow breath, and turned away, already regretting she'd stopped for that one last look. She descended the stairs and beelined to Richard's office.

Once, the room had been her dad's man cave, where he had kept his record collection and a small minibar. There had been a desk there, its drawers locked, hinting at any manner of wonderful or terrible things hidden within. Even as a little girl, Theo had been fascinated by the room, drawn to it. She still remembered its smell, so different from the rest of the house. The smell of tobacco, and coffee, and dust. This, more than anything, was how she remembered her father. As an enticing smell in a forbidden room.

After her dad left, her mother turned it into a storage room, gleefully filling it with anything broken and unwanted. And when Richard moved in, Mom was more than happy to let him use the room as his home office. He cleaned it up, filled it with binders, papers, printed forms, and all those other things accountants needed. From a fascinating, mysterious room, it was transformed into the dullest, grayest room in the house.

Except for the wall safe.

The wall safe was new, installed by Richard. It was where he kept his gun, and where her mother kept her most expensive jewelry. And, more importantly, it also contained cash.

Theo knew the combination. She knew it by heart, from overhearing the same tired exchange between Mom and Richard over and over again.

"Richard, what's the combination again?" A frustrated shout from the office.

"It's three, seven, one, one" was Richard's monotone response from the kitchen, or the living room.

"It won't open!"

"Three, seven, one, one. Do you need me to come over and—"

"Oh, there we go, it opened."

Repeat over and over, ad nauseam, every other week.

Now Theo crouched in front of the safe, heart thumping. The keys blipped when pressed. A sound that might echo all the way upstairs, disturbing her mother's troubled sleep. If Theo had her way, she would have done this beforehand. But she wasn't sure when and how often Richard opened the safe and checked its contents. As far as she knew, he did it every evening before going to bed. So it had to be now.

She pressed the buttons, each one emitting a shrill blip that made her wince, her heart skipping a beat. When she pressed the final button, nothing happened. Had they changed the combination? Now that Richard and Mom didn't trust her anymore, now that they knew what Theo was capable of . . .

The safe whirred open.

Theo paused to listen. Was Mom on her way down? Coming to check what that noise was?

No. Nothing.

Theo took out the stack of bills. She wasn't sure how much was there. She flipped through them, seeing hundreds and fifties. Two thousand, maybe three thousand dollars. A fortune. She almost put some of it back.

But she would need it. She knew as much from googling how much a night in a motel cost, how much even a cheap apartment cost. Add that to the cost of three meals a day, bare necessities, transportation . . .

In fact, she doubted it would be enough.

She plucked her mother's diamond earrings from the safe, held them in her sweaty palm. Mom always said they were ridiculously expensive. And they were a gift from Dad; Mom didn't even wear them anymore. Theo could pawn them, a month's rent right there in her hand.

But no matter what Mom and Richard thought of her, she wasn't that far gone. Besides, pawned stolen earrings could be located by the cops. Could you tell us who pawned these, sir? A teenager? Is *this* the girl who pawned them? Oh, yes, we are looking for her. She's a suspect in a violent crime. What crime? I can't really divulge details. But it was a murder.

Theo returned the earrings to the safe, and gently shut the door. She put the cash in her bag, peeling away two bills, which she shoved in her pocket.

A dozen steps and she was at the front door. She gently unlocked it, then opened it just a bit, the cold air taking her breath away. Oh right, her coat. She grabbed it and stepped outside, shutting the door behind her. And that was that.

Her bike was hidden behind a bush in the front yard. She rolled it to the road, hopped on, and began cycling furiously down the street, trying to warm up. She'd tightened her hoodie over her head, her long hair hidden within. The only part of her that was exposed was her face, and her fingers, clutching the handles. The icy wind bit into her skin, making her regret she left her warm gloves at home. How many other things would she regret not having packed before the day ended?

Familiar streets zoomed around her as she rode her bike, her feet pedaling as fast as possible. Pushing her out, leaving this place behind her. Messy yards, flat redbrick houses, old cars. She wouldn't miss any of it.

It was a seventeen-mile ride from Crumville to her chosen bus station at the edge of Augusta. When Mom drove her, it took twenty minutes. She was not allowed to do it on her bike, her mother often telling her about the two horrible accidents that had happened to bicycle riders on that road. One had died; the other was in a wheelchair for the rest of her life. The first time Theo did that ride on her bike was a week before, instead of going to school. When she started planning her departure. Since then she'd done it twice more, and she now knew that it took her about an hour and ten minutes.

But that was during daylight.

The road was so dark at night. It occurred to her that a black coat, a black hoodie, and dark-gray pants were not the ideal clothes for this ride. She'd chosen these clothes because she didn't want to be noticed. Now she understood she might not even be *seen*. A single truck with a tired driver behind the wheel, and she would be Horrible Accident Story number three.

Every time a car drove by, she veered to the side of the road, as far as she could, her heart hammering. She kept expecting someone to slow down, to call out to her, to point out it wasn't safe to ride with no light. But no one did. And really, who would stop to confront a bike rider in a hoodie in the middle of the night? Especially after the recent violent event that shook the town. The illusion of safety had dissipated. People could be dangerous. Even deadly.

After a sleepless night, biking in the cold early morning ended up taking her almost an hour and thirty minutes. She'd missed the bus she was planning on taking. The next bus would leave in forty-five minutes. Theo's nerves were on edge. She kept imagining people looking at her, wondering who she was. What if a cop drove by? Saw this teenager who had no business being there? They might get curious, call it in.

She left the bike in an alley, unlocked, trusting the petty crooks of Augusta to take care of it, make it disappear. Then she crossed the road and stepped inside a Starbucks that had just opened. She needed something warm. And she needed caffeine.

She ordered a large vanilla latte from the sleepy barista, keeping her hoodie on, wondering if this barista would be later questioned by the police.

"Name?" the barista asked tiredly.

Her name was Theodora Briggs. But she was prepared for that question. Even before this past month, she'd often fantasized about changing her name. She'd always hated the name Theodora, and even her nickname, Theo. It was time to start anew.

"Gemma," she said. "My name is Gemma."

Chapter 2

Thirteen years later, Highland Park, Chicago

"Mommy."

Gemma's eyes snapped open; she was already sitting up in bed, her body reacting involuntarily to the faint call. She slid her feet into her slippers and padded out of the bedroom.

"Mommy."

"I'm coming, sweetie," she said in a soft voice, to avoid waking Benjamin up.

She crossed the short upstairs hallway and shuffled into Lucas's room. He was sitting in his bed, his blond hair ruffled, eyes sleepy, scratching his arm.

"I'm itchy," he murmured.

"Yeah, it's okay. Lie down, I'll rub some lotion on you."

"Okay."

The body lotion was on the bedside table. Gemma screwed the lid off. It was almost empty. She would have to remember to get some more. She scooped some with two fingers and spread it on Lucas's arms in practiced motions. As she did so, he began scratching his belly. She gently pried his hand away.

"Just one second, sweetie, okay?"

He nodded sleepily. She finished applying the lotion to his arms and continued to his belly, then his legs. Their nightly ritual. She'd gotten used to it by now. Dr. Kaufman promised her that her son's atopic dermatitis would likely get better, and even disappear completely. So far there was no sign of that. Last time they saw Kaufman, she practically shouted at him, telling him they needed a better treatment than damn lotion. Couldn't he see her son was suffering? The more she raised her voice, the more distant Kaufman seemed. His tone became patronizing, pretentious. He used the word *statistically* like a weapon, clobbering her with it over and over again.

She told Benjamin they needed to switch doctors.

She did the neck and behind the ears, then took some more for his face. Very carefully she did his red cheeks, the tip of his button-shaped nose, his forehead, above his long eyelashes.

"Turn around," she whispered.

Lucas rolled over, already half-asleep, and she raised his shirt to apply more lotion to his back. Then she rubbed her fingers along his spine, knowing from experience it was the fastest way to get him to sink into a deep sleep.

Her eyes flicked to the bunny-shaped clock on the bookshelf. It was half past five in the morning. Shit. If it had been two or three a.m., she would have been able to go back to sleep herself. But after five she would just lie in bed, her brain churning with thoughts and anxieties. Analyzing the past day, thinking of the day to come, trying to find a new untried solution for Lucas's skin problems, recalling urgent errands and neglected duties.

So instead she stayed by Lucas, her fingers stroking his back as she watched his tiny sleeping face lovingly. Benjamin liked to say kids are really cute . . . when they're sleeping, ha ha. It was true; Lucas was so adorable when he slept, his lips shaped in a small pout, his chest rising and falling steadily, his entire body as soft and delicate as a cloud. But he was also cute awake—eyes sparkling with curiosity, high-pitched voice mispronouncing big words he heard, giggling uncontrollably at a dumb joke Benjamin told.

She finally got up and slipped out of the room. She went to the downstairs bathroom so the flushing wouldn't wake up Benjamin or Lucas. She sat on the toilet, her eyes meeting the calendar Benjamin had hung on the door.

God, she hated that calendar.

Bathrooms, she told Benjamin repeatedly, should be devoid of anything that wasn't related to the bathroom functions. Did he realize how many germs floated in the tiny room's air? Clung to its surfaces? Did he have a remote idea of what happened with the toilet water particles when the toilet was flushed?

It was a subject of repeated contention. The current status quo was this: Lucas's and Gemma's towels weren't in the bathroom. They were in the bedrooms and were only brought into the bathroom when they took baths. Benjamin's towel hung in the bathroom, and Gemma did her best not to think about it. *All three* toothbrushes were kept in the bathroom cupboard, which was closed at all times. Benjamin tried to argue the topic—he liked his toothbrush to be within reach on the sink. Gemma made it abundantly clear she would never kiss him again if he kept his toothbrush outside in the open. This point was a clear win for Gemma. And so on and so forth, each object was debated, argued about as eyes rolled, voices rose, and rules were established and occasionally broken.

Benjamin liked to have a calendar in the bathroom. A habit from his childhood home. Gemma refused. It was irritating to stare at the thing whenever you sat on the toilet. The compromise: the calendar hung in the downstairs bathroom, also dubbed the guest bathroom.

It was one of those monthly calendars that attempted, quite desperately, to be funny. Each page had a different animal, photoshopped with various accessories, and a wacky title to accompany it. This month's image was of a rooster with sunglasses. The caption was *Don't be so nEGGative.* It didn't even make sense. Roosters don't lay eggs.

Now, with her eyes locked on the rooster's germ-infested photo, she realized it was October 30.

She'd known it was coming for weeks, of course. A panicky tiny voice in her mind had kept reminding her as it crept closer. Waves of anxiety would wash over her at an increasing rate as it got nearer. And there it was. A day seemingly like any other. A day that no one but her gave any special attention to. A day she pretended had no significance whatsoever.

It was also the yearly reminder of the worst day of her life. When everything changed.

She shut her eyes, taking a deep breath. It was just a day, like any other day. She tried to tell herself that the bitter taste in her mouth, the wave of sudden nausea, the slight dizziness—those were nothing. Her body reacting to something she rationally knew posed no risk to her or the people she loved. A remnant of a buried past, of a different life. Getting up, she turned around and flushed the—

—toilet, shaking. Come on, come on, why wouldn't it flush? If they found out about this, if they found out she brought this with her . . . it would be her end. She pulled the toilet handle again and again, her eyes flickering to the toilet bowl where it still floated, evidence of her twisted, violent intentions.

She pulled the toilet—

—handle again, her breath shuddering. Come on . . . come on . . .

The dizziness made her stumble, almost fall. She leaned against the wall, trying to breathe deeply. She blinked as reality swam back into focus. Her own house. Her own bathroom. Half a country and more than a decade away from that night.

She went over to the sink and washed her trembling hands. Looking at herself in the tiny bathroom mirror, she could still see the remnants of her terror. Her face blotchy and red, eyes wide. For a second, she stared at the face of seventeen-year-old Theo, desperate and afraid.

But no, she was Gemma, a woman in control of her own life. She had a family and friends. She was surrounded by people who loved her. Her now-auburn hair was cut short, ending at the nape of her neck. Trimmed eyebrows, smooth skin, thick lips. An attractive face. Not the face of that depressed teenager, a face that shouted "loser" to anyone who cared to look. Only her large brown eyes were still the same. And honestly, all those years ago, who even looked at her eyes?

She stepped out of the bathroom and checked the time. She still had an hour before Benjamin woke up. Enough time to do some cleaning, get ready for the day, *and* bring Benjamin a cup of coffee in bed, scoring oodles of relationship points.

There were only three rooms in the house she cleaned several times a week. The bathrooms and the kitchen. Despite what Benjamin often said, she wasn't a germaphobe. She didn't mind public spaces; she wasn't one of those people who practically dove for cover whenever anyone sneezed or coughed. She even didn't mind handshakes that much . . . well, not more than anyone else these days. And like she repeatedly told Benjamin, she couldn't work in a beauty salon if she had issues with germs. Her only minor requirement was for the bathrooms to be clean, and for the kitchen and her food to be germ-free. That wasn't germaphobia; that was common sense.

A year before, Lucas was eating a cookie, and it fell on the floor. Lucas let out a frustrated groan; he knew Gemma wouldn't let him eat the rest. And then Benjamin picked the cookie up and handed it to Lucas.

"Here you go, sport," he said. "Five-second rule."

Gemma walked across the room and took the cookie from Lucas's hand. And she explained there's no such thing as a five-second rule.

Or that's how she remembers it.

The way Benjamin describes it, she leaped over the coffee table, smacked the cookie away from Lucas's hand, and *snarled* at Benjamin that there's no five-second rule in *this* house. He actually used the word *snarled* as he told his parents about it later. And it was an annoying, ridiculous description. She did not leap, or dash, or anything like that. She had been very calm. And she would never say something like "in *this* house." Ever. That was something her mother used to say when

Gemma was a child, and there was no way Gemma would ever do the same.

Not that Benjamin knew that. Not that he knew anything about her mom. Or about her childhood for that matter. He almost never asked. And she never talked about it.

Scrubbing the kitchen took about forty minutes. It left her with more than enough time to shower, then put on her makeup. Her rich clients at Primadonna often commented on her skin, how jealous they were of it. They'd make comments on her wonderful genetics or how young she was. She always smiled and said thank you. As if her genetics had anything to do with it. If those people had seen her when she was a teenager, they might have literally *recoiled*. Genetics? Ha. Gemma looked like she did because she took good care of herself. And as a beautician working in one of the best luxury salons in Chicago, she was able to get her high-end beauty supplies relatively cheap.

She still had a few minutes to grab something to drink. She stared out the window as the coffee machine burbled. Their quiet suburban street was starting to wake up, the occasional car driving past, their neighbor from across the street stepping outside with her French poodle. She glanced at her own front yard. The chrysanthemums she'd planted two weeks ago were in full bloom, their orange and red vivid against the green grass that Benjamin mowed so diligently. She let out a sigh. They'd moved here a year and a half ago, but it already felt more like home than any other place Gemma had ever lived.

She drank her coffee and ate toast while reading the *New York Times*. Politics, balanced by some quality celebrity news. Most people she knew started *their* day scrolling through social media.

No social media for Gemma. That was one time sink she never had to worry about.

She took a steaming mug of coffee to their bedroom and sat down on Benjamin's side of the bed. She placed the mug on his night table and kissed his forehead.

"Hey, honey," she whispered. "Time to get up."

Benjamin grunted, then wrapped his arm around her waist and opened one eye. "Hey, beautiful."

"I brought you coffee."

"You are a saint. Mother Teresa has nothing on you."

"Right? She never brought people coffee in the morning."

He propped himself up. Even with his eyes half-shut, and his blond hair askew from sleep, Benjamin was a sight. Chiseled face, wide shoulders, scruffy daredevil grin. Gemma liked to tell herself she wasn't shallow. She didn't fall in love with him because of his looks. But they definitely helped.

He sipped from the mug. "Did Lucas wake you up last night?"

He woke her up every night. "Yeah. But he went right back to sleep."

"Good." He rubbed his face and yawned. Then he looked at her, his eyes unusually alert. "You know what today is, right?"

Her heart plummeted, dizziness assailing her. Had he somehow found out? His eyes seemed accusatory, his lips tightening in distaste. There was no way . . . he couldn't have found out. Gemma's mind went into overdrive, trying to figure out if she messed up somewhere. Gave him a clue that he had followed up on. It wouldn't take much. With the right keywords, it was a few Google searches away.

"Um . . ." Her lips trembled.

"Today I have that talk with Vincent? About becoming team leader?"

Gemma blinked and let out a shuddering breath. Benjamin was smiling, pleased with himself. She knew she'd gone pale. That her entire body had become rigid. Surely, he could feel that, with his arm still around her. Surely, he could see the misty tears that sprang into her eyes. He would ask her what was wrong. He would prod.

"I'm feeling very optimistic about it." He looked straight at her, his expression completely at ease.

He never noticed those things. Never saw when she froze or suddenly tensed. If she wanted him to know she was upset, she had to tell him. And he almost never asked her any questions about her childhood. He had asked her about her parents once; she told him her parents were dead and that she didn't like talking about them, and that was that. He never even asked her where she grew up. He probably assumed she'd been born in Chicago, just like him.

"I'm feeling very optimistic about it myself." She forced herself to smile at him.

The fact that he never asked any questions, never prodded, and showed no curiosity about her past wasn't what had made her fall in love with him. Neither was his inattentiveness to her moments of weakness.

But those things definitely helped.

Chapter 3

The familiar scent of lemon and bergamot welcomed Gemma as she entered the Primadonna Beauty Salon. Barbara was already there, setting the display of their custom-made lotions. Her lips were tight in concentration as her bony fingers rearranged each jar.

"Hey, Gems," she drawled. "You look radiant today."

"Thanks." Gemma smiled at her tiredly, feeling anything but radiant. "Is Thelma here yet?"

"Yeah, she got here five minutes ago. She's in the back room. She was arguing with the truck driver, thought she was about to yank his junk off. I'd never have the guts to talk to him like that, but you know Thelma. She reminds me of my math teacher in middle school. Scary teacher that one, but she got me through algebra."

"New delivery?" Gemma asked, glancing at the jars Barbara was arranging.

"Yeah. We got a new batch of the lavender hand lotion and some Halloween-themed stuff. I don't know why Thelma even orders these. Who even needs this shit? I have pumpkins and witches and skeletons up the wazoo. Not to mention all the time I spend on my kid's costume. I can't wait for this holiday to be over."

"I hear ya." Gemma hung her coat on the hook and went over to her table. "We also have a birthday party in a few days. I'll be happy once this week is over."

"Whose birthday?"

"Benjamin's mom. I need to get a cake."

"Oh, you should probably order it today, you don't want to cut it too close, you know?"

"Yeah," Gemma said distractedly, inspecting her supplies. She was running low on orange glitter and black gel nail polish. Classic Halloween shortage.

"Are we still on for tomorrow?" Barbara asked.

"Still on?" Gemma blinked.

"The playdate? Between Khai and Lucas?"

Khai was Barbara's son. He and Lucas had met a few times. It was still unclear if they really liked each other, but since they were almost the same age, Gemma and Barbara had been trying to make it work. "Oh right! Yeah, we're still on. Tomorrow afternoon before the trick-or-treating starts. I'm going in the back. Do you need anything?"

"No thanks, love."

Gemma walked over to the supply room, where Thelma, the owner of Primadonna, was busy unpacking supplies.

Thelma looked like the love child of a vampire and a leprechaun. Pale skin, crimson lips, and grass green almond-shaped eyes. Her hair was a shocking red and stick straight. Her age was a mystery—Gemma had been working for her for the past seven years, and Thelma had hardly changed throughout that time.

"Morning, Gemma," Thelma said. "Can you help me out here?"

Gemma grabbed the box Thelma handed her. "Before I forget, I'm running out of Lucas's lotion. I'll grab a couple, okay?"

"Sure. Make a note of it. How does your morning look?" Thelma grunted as she shifted boxes on the top shelf, then took the one from Gemma.

"My morning's packed until noon." Gemma's schedule was always full. The Primadonna Beauty Salon was ridiculously popular. Especially after the piece about it in *Time Out*, and after that reality-show star posted Gemma's nail art on Instagram. Barbara and Gemma constantly told Thelma she should branch out, or find a larger place, hire more people. But Thelma had her own weird way of doing things. She insisted on keeping the place small. Boutique.

"What's your first client?" Thelma asked.

"It's that lawyer, what's her name. The one with the cheating husband."

"Clara. Get ready to get your ears talked off."

Gemma grinned, grabbing the glitter and nail polish she needed. "That's what I'm here for, right?"

Years before, after she started working at Primadonna, Thelma had approached Gemma and informed her she wasn't giving her customers the treatment they came for. Gemma was confused and hurt. Her nail art was the reason Thelma had poached her from the previous salon she'd worked in, and it was one of the best anyone could get in Mayfair. Thelma waved Gemma's arguments away. She had no issue with the nail art. But most customers also came to their salon for conversation. And according to Thelma, there were fish with more to say than Gemma.

Gemma didn't have Barbara's knack for spouting a thousand words per minute without saying anything. Nor did she have Thelma's skill and confidence to give life advice and personal suggestions. And when Thelma suggested Gemma could talk a bit about herself, she nearly quit. But then, coached by Thelma, Gemma found out she didn't have to talk at all. Clients, it turned out, were more than happy to talk about themselves as long as you showed an interest. It didn't have to be much. Just the right question every now and then, and sentences like "That's incredible," or "I can't believe that happened to you of all people." And once she began engaging with them, she was floored by the tips she got. The clientele in Primadonna had money to spare.

"Gems!" Barbara called from the other room. "Your nine o'clock is here."

Gemma strode back, smiling at Clara, the attorney with the cheating husband. Black Prada high-heeled shoes, a crisp Ralph Lauren suit, and a white Louis Vuitton mini bag. And, of course, her Primadonna haircut and nail job.

Gemma whisked Clara to the chair. "Hey, Clara, how are you doing?"

Clara sighed. "I'm fine," she muttered. "It's been one of those mornings."

Gemma tried to recall if Clara had kids. She wasn't sure, so asking if the kids gave her trouble in the morning was not a great idea. "I know what you mean. Are you about to have another long day at work?"

"Probably. I'm working on a difficult case." Clara placed her hands in front of her, stretching out her fingernails. The remnants of Gemma's last job were still visible—a glossy turquoise, with a faint pattern of ivy on one of the nails.

"How can I help to make this day better?" Gemma asked.

"Um . . . Maybe the same? With the plant thing?"

Gemma didn't like repeating the same job twice. From experience, she knew clients were usually happier when given something new. "Can I suggest something? Not so different from before, but I was thinking a light blue, very similar to this color, and maybe three tiny rhinestones on the middle finger."

"Rhinestones?" Clara asked skeptically.

"I know what you're thinking, but trust me. It's very tasteful. And if you don't like it, I'll remove them and do the ivy again."

"You should really try it," Barbara interjected. "A woman came here yesterday, and she was totally against it, and I swear to God, she positively glowed when Gemma finished placing those stones. You know how sometimes you don't know something exists, and then once you find out, you don't know how you could live without it? For me it was the peach mango pie at Jollibee. That's what it'll be like. It'll be like peach mango pie."

"Okay," Clara said, softening. "Let's give it a try."

Gemma gave Barbara a brief thank-you smile. Her friend and coworker was the best wingwoman in the world.

"So." Gemma began removing Clara's old polish. "Did your husband make it up to you?"

"Oh, he thinks he did."

Gemma gave a knowing snort. "What did he do?"

Clara outlined her husband's shortcomings, while Gemma let reality fade around her. She focused on the woman's nails, already thinking of a new pattern she hadn't tried before.

When she'd started working in a beauty salon, she hated every minute of it. She did it to escape waitressing, a job she absolutely loathed. A beauty salon owner was looking for cheap employees, and Gemma was as cheap as they came—especially since she was paid in cash, off the books. The first few times she did waxing jobs, the clients screamed at her. She didn't do it right; she hurt them. She also found it disgusting. She ended up crying every day in the bathroom.

It was only a few months in that clients began returning to the salon for her nail jobs. Gushing about her unique style and their jealous friends. A year later, and Gemma didn't do waxing or exfoliation or pedicures anymore. Her boss realized it was worth her while to let Gemma just do nails. Her clients were thrilled with her work. She started loving her job. It was creative and delicate, and she was proud of her designs. She made her clients feel beautiful and unique. It got even better when she moved to Primadonna. The pay was five times higher than before—Thelma paid well for quality, and the tips were ridiculous. But it was more than that. She loved Thelma and Barbara. And the atmosphere in the beauty salon was relaxed, soothing.

A haven. A safe haven.

"I do like this color," Clara said.

"It really fits you," Gemma said as she applied nail glue on the middle nail. "Now let's set those rhinestones. See here? They're really delicate." She opened the box with the silver rhinestones.

"Oh yeah, they look nice."

Gemma picked up one of the stones with the tweezers. "You were telling me about your boss? Was he happy with your work?"

"Well—"

"Hang on, keep your hand steady."

"Sorry. It's just . . . he gets me so annoyed."

The door jingled, interrupting the conversation. A plump woman with a red wool hat stepped inside and looked around her, licking her lips nervously. Gemma glanced at her, making sure she wasn't her next client, then focused back on the placement of the stones.

"Hey, love," Barbara chirped. "How can I help you?"

"Um . . . I was hoping to get my nails done here? A friend recommended this place."

"Well," Barbara said. "Gemma usually does the nails, but she's fully booked today. I can do them for you if you like. Or, if you want, you can schedule a—"

"No . . . I was hoping Theodora would do them?"

The rhinestone clattered on the table as Gemma fumbled the tweezers.

"Sorry, love," Barbara said. "We don't have anyone named Theodora here. But Gemma is the best nail artist in Chicago, and—"

"Theodora Briggs," the woman blurted. "I wanted my nails done by Theodora Briggs."

Gemma's hand trembled, and spots danced in her eyes. She leaned on the table, trying to steady herself.

"I don't know who this Theodora is," Barbara said. "But I can assure you—"

"Never mind," the woman barked sharply. "I probably have the wrong place."

She turned around and yanked the door open, hurrying outside.

"Nervous, that one," Barbara said. "Too much coffee, probably. I cut down my coffee quota to two cups a day. It's done wonders for my mood."

"I could never do that," Clara said. "I need all the coffee I can get in my—"

"Excuse me," Gemma muttered. She crossed the room, opened the door, and rushed outside. She paused on the sidewalk and searched desperately. Passersby went back and forth as she searched for that red hat.

There! Moving down the street, already almost a block away. Gemma sprinted after her, nearly tripping in her high-heeled shoes, breathing rapidly, telling herself that it was probably nothing.

"Excuse me!" she shouted as she got closer. "Miss!"

The woman didn't turn around. She seemed to be walking very fast herself, almost running. Gemma forced herself to run faster, catching up. She grabbed the woman's shoulder.

"Excuse me," she panted.

The woman whirled around. "What?" she snapped.

"You . . . Did you say Theodora Briggs?"

The woman's eyes widened. "Yes. But never mind. I changed my mind. I don't really have time to get my nails done."

Gemma focused on the woman, trying to place her. Did she know this woman? She tried to imagine how this plump lady would have looked thirteen years ago. Could they have known each other when they were young? "Um . . . it's just that name. I was wondering, who told you—"

"It doesn't matter." The woman was breathing fast now, her lips trembling. "I think it's probably a different salon. Or maybe I got the name wrong."

Did the woman recognize *her*? Gemma searched for that spark of recognition. A look that said I know you, murderer. I know what you did. But there was nothing there. The woman mostly seemed confused. And try as she might, Gemma couldn't place her. She had a good memory for faces. She was pretty sure she'd never seen this woman before.

The woman was looking left and right, her movement erratic. She was scared. Perhaps she *did* know who Gemma was.

"That name." Gemma gritted her teeth. "Who—"

"You're hurting me."

Gemma was gripping the woman's arm, her fingers tightening, digging in. The woman's frightened eyes flickered down, and Gemma realized she was still holding the tweezers, clutching it in her fist as if it was a weapon. She let go of the woman.

"Sorry," she breathed.

The woman gave her one last frightened look and bolted. Gemma could hardly stand straight, not to mention chase after her. Instead, she stared as the red woolen hat got farther and farther away.

She turned back and tottered to the salon. She stepped inside, feeling nauseous. The salon's lemony smell, usually so comforting, suddenly seemed cloying and sickly.

"Everything all right?" Barbara asked her.

"Yeah . . . ," Gemma said weakly. "I just . . . I thought that woman looked familiar."

"I really like them," Clara said.

"I'm sorry?" Gemma asked, confused.

"The rhinestones? You were right, they look really nice."

"Yeah . . . I'm not finished. I still have two more." Gemma swallowed as she walked over to Clara. She tried to pluck a stone from the container, but her hand was trembling.

"I don't think I know a Theodora who works at a beauty salon," Barbara said. "Now that I think about it, I don't think I know *anyone* named Theodora."

"Yeah," Gemma said hollowly. "It's not a very common name."

Chapter 4

It was not the first time Gemma had forgotten where she'd parked her car, but it felt particularly frustrating today. All she wanted was to get home; relieve Iris, the nanny; and spend some relaxing time with Lucas. Instead she crossed the parking lot, clicking the car remote again and again, the chilly autumn wind freezing her ears and nose.

It was a wonder she had even managed to get through the day after that woman's intrusion on her life. Somehow, she went through the motions, while her brain buzzed, the thoughts clouded by anxiety, like the crackling you get when a radio station signal is obstructed. She kept telling herself it was nothing. That woman clearly didn't know her. And it wasn't like she was looking for the actual Theodora Briggs from all those years ago. *That* Theodora was a teenage high school student, not a beautician. The woman was clearly looking for a beautician. It was just a weird, incomprehensible coincidence. But, like Barbara said, Theodora was not a very common name. Not to mention Theodora Briggs. And for this to happen today, of all days.

It was just another regular day, she tried to tell herself. But it wasn't, right? Not for her. And not for another girl's family, at Crumville, half-way across the country. For them, this day was a horrible anniversary. A memorial day.

Come on, where was that damn car? She hastened her steps, gritting her teeth against the cold, trying not to think about Theodora Briggs, or about Crumville, or about that day. Her footsteps on the paved ground tap-tap-tapped faster, then became muffled as she stepped over some dry leaves, their surface—

—crackling underneath her. It was cold . . . so cold. Her eyes fluttered open, her teeth chattering. She was freezing. As she shifted, she heard that crackling underneath her again. Dry leaves. The world swam into focus, the shadowy shapes of trees all around her. The sky was an indigo blue, the sky of early morning. She was lying on the ground, the scent of earth filling her nostrils. She was weak, every movement was an effort.

Theo sat up slowly and hugged herself, shivering. She didn't know where she was, or how she got there. There had been a . . . party. At Victoria's home. She recalled fractured moments. Dancing. Drinking. Victoria's face, wet with tears. Begging her to stop.

She let out a sob. It scared her, not remembering. Her memory was always sharp, recalling every detail of every day. Often, there were things she wished she could forget. Embarrassments, humiliations, jeering remarks. But now that there was a gaping hole in her memory, she scrabbled at the tiny details she could still recall. She had gone to that party. To get back at Victoria, to make her pay. She had been carrying something in her jacket's pocket. Something . . . bad. She now fumbled at her pocket, but it was empty. And it wasn't even the jacket she wore to the party. In fact, it wasn't her jacket at all.

She examined it, confused. A white jacket, something she would never wear. It was badly stained, part of it caked with what looked like dried mud. As she shifted to examine it, jolts of pain made her gasp. She was hurting all over. Her leg was bruised. Her cheek was swollen. And her left arm seemed to burn. She checked her arm's skin under the jacket. It was hard to see in the faded light, but it looked like she had three long scratch marks on her arm.

Her shirt was torn, her bra showing underneath. She clutched the jacket around her, tried to zip it shut, but the zipper was sticky with mud as well, and it jammed.

Theo pulled herself to her feet, leaning on a nearby tree for support. She searched around her, but all she could see in the murky light were trees. How did she get here? She had a vague recollection of running . . . stumbling. She had been chased.

Hunted.

A tightening in her gut, and she folded in two, throwing up, coughing. The taste of acidic bile filled her mouth. She let out another sob.

"There's someone there!"

She tensed, crouching, knowing she wasn't safe. Someone was after her. There was . . . something. That happened. She touched the bruise on her cheek, recalled the pain as she was hit. She turned to run. To escape.

"Stop!"

Two beams of light wavered around her. She froze and turned around, flinching as the bright lights blinded her. She raised a hand to protect her eyes.

"It's a girl." A woman's voice.

The lights pointed away from Theo's face, and she squinted, spots dancing in her vision. A couple of grown-ups in uniforms. Cops. They weren't there to hurt her.

"Help," she rasped.

"I think she's hurt," the female cop said, hurrying toward her.

"Hang on," the other cop said, his voice low, tense. "Look at what she's wearing. Isn't that the victim's missing jacket?"

Victim?

"I . . . I need to call my mom," Theo mumbled.

"What's that large stain?" the first cop asked. Both flashlights now pointed at her jacket.

"I think it's blood."

"No," Theo tried to explain. "It's mud . . ."

But it wasn't. Mud didn't look like that. It didn't smell like that. And she remembered something. She remembered . . . a large smear of blood.

"Miss," the male cop said. "We need you to come with us."

Both of them seemed wary now. Their hands on their holsters. Theo wanted to explain it was all a mistake when a wave of bile rose in her throat and she—

—threw up on the ground, her vomit splashing on the parking lot's paved asphalt.

Gemma spit and coughed. She was leaning on a car for support. Not a tree. A car. She was not in the woods. That day was long in the past. Thirteen whole years. Today was its anniversary.

Chapter 5

"I want to read the big volcano book now," Lucas piped.

"Okay, sweetie," Gemma said distractedly.

Reading was one of Lucas's favorite pastimes, and usually, it was a favorite of Gemma's as well. As always, they lay in Lucas's bed, under the cover, their heads touching. Lucas would choose a book from the shelf, and they would read it together. Since Lucas couldn't read, they split the responsibilities. Lucas was in charge of flipping the pages, and Gemma was in charge of the reading.

Lucas grabbed the big volcano book from the shelf and returned to the bed, accidentally elbowing Gemma's stomach in the process. He squirmed back under the blanket and opened the book.

"This is a volcano," Gemma read the first line, which she knew by heart. "A volcano is an opening in the earth's surface—"

"What's the surface?"

"They mean the ground." She blinked, looking for where she stopped. "Hot magma, gas, and ash escape through the opening."

"Do the explosion sound."

Gemma didn't feel like she had it in her to do the explosion sound. "Why don't you do it?"

"No. You do it. I will do it after you."

Gemma did her best to imitate the sound of a volcano erupting. She had no idea how it really sounded, but she could hazard a guess.

Lucas snuggled closer to her and did a volcano-erupting sound of his own.

She loved the time with Lucas in the afternoon. Benjamin sometimes complained that Lucas wasn't independent enough, that he didn't "keep himself busy." It was maddening. Lucas was incredibly independent for a four-year-old. He just wanted some quality time with his parents when they were around. Gemma believed that in the few precious hours she had with Lucas every day, she had to be all there for him.

Although right now, she was finding it hard to be *all there*. She was doing her best to be *partly* there. Lucas made it more difficult, by choosing books she hated. He had dozens of books she adored. Dr. Seuss, and *Winnie the Pooh*, and *Where the Wild Things Are*. But today Lucas focused on his encyclopedias about volcanoes, trains, and airplanes. It was torture.

And all the while, as she read about the various train-related milestones, or about turbulence and wing shapes, she kept thinking about that woman who'd stepped into Primadonna today. Her gut feeling about that woman kept shifting. One moment she felt like it had just been a very weird coincidence. The next moment she would wonder if it was some sort of police undercover sting, trying to get her to reveal herself. She was almost sure the woman didn't know her. There was no recognition on her face. What she really needed was a few minutes to herself, to replay those moments from that morning in her mind. But—

"Mommy. I flipped the page. Mommy. Mom. I flipped the page; you need to read."

She cleared her throat. "Right. The largest volcano is in Hawaii."

"Where is Hawaii?"

"It's an island. Far away."

"I want to read the big pirate book now." Lucas let the volcano book drop.

Gemma couldn't. She just couldn't. They'd been reading for forty minutes, and all that time she'd been assailed by thoughts about the woman from that morning. She was stretched thin, a rubber band about to snap.

"Do you maybe want to take a break and draw something?"

"No. I want to do the big pirate book."

"Or maybe you can build a really nice pirate hideaway from your Lego?" she asked desperately.

"I don't want to play with my Legos." He got up and grabbed the pirate book.

"How about some time with my phone?" she blurted.

He paused and turned around.

She shouldn't have said that. It went against all that she believed. It was the national flag of shitty-parent-land. The ultimate way a parent could show they couldn't care less about their child. There was endless research about what phones did to kids—damaged their eyesight, their mental development, their sleep. And even without the research, it was easy to see how ultimately *wrong* a small child looked while they were fiddling with a phone. Eyes vacant, mouth slack, neck crooked.

She and Benjamin had had a few fights about it after she found out he let Lucas play with his phone. And on that front, she won; Benjamin had seen how much it bothered her, and he promised that he would never do it again.

And now here she was, doing that thing she so enthusiastically judged other parents for, handing her son her phone. Opening the *Candy Crush* app for him, his eyes already getting that zombielike vibe. She was almost consumed by her own self-loathing.

But she could make herself a cup of coffee. Go to the bathroom. And get a moment for herself. It's not like she was about to let Lucas play with the phone for half an hour. Just five minutes, this one time, and never again.

She sipped her coffee. God, she needed that. Last night she'd gone to sleep too late and had woken up almost two hours too early. No wonder she was being paranoid, making up stories about undercover police. Now that she had a moment to relax, she could see what really happened this morning.

A random woman misremembered something she was told.

Either she got the wrong beauty salon, or she got the wrong name. It really didn't matter. In fact, try as she might, Gemma wasn't sure the woman had even asked for Theodora *Briggs*. She definitely asked for Theodora, but the last name might have been Bridges, or Biggs or Griggs . . . And Gemma, wired as she was from her lack of sleep and the ominous anniversary, simply misheard her. It was a relief to view it all clear eyed.

Guilt nagged at her. Lucas had been on the phone for at least fifteen minutes, much more than Gemma had originally planned. But now that she had a few minutes to rest, she was unwilling to terminate it. Just like that moment on a snowy day, when you had to get out of bed, deciding that you could afford to stay under the covers for just a few more seconds. The damage had been done. So would it be that bad if she finished her cup of coffee?

And when she did finish her cup of coffee, she figured it was a good time to put some laundry in the machine, before the pile of dirty clothing grew tall enough to tower over that volcano in Hawaii. And then she quickly cleaned the fridge—a task she'd been postponing for a while. And after that, she glanced at the time, and her heart skipped a beat.

Lucas had been playing on the phone for over forty minutes. But that wasn't the really bad part. The really bad part was that Benjamin was about to get home.

If he saw Lucas with the phone, it would be a disaster of epic proportions. All those loud arguments, followed by Gemma's cold, furious silences. All the times she told him about a mom she saw in the park who let her son play on the phone instead of pushing him on the swing. All those studies she quoted, the links to articles she sent him.

Benjamin wouldn't be mad. He would smirk. It would amuse him. And next time they would disagree about something, he would say, This is just like the thing with the phone. And he would be right.

"Lucas. Sweetie. Time to get off the phone."

"Just one more level."

"Okay, one more level, and you're done. Okay?"

No answer.

"Okay, Lucas?"

"Okay."

She hovered above him as he finished the level. "Okay, now give me the phone."

"I got a lollipop."

"That's great, sweetie. Get off the phone."

"I want to try the lollipop."

He tried the lollipop hammer. Candies disappeared with a fun chime. "Did you see that, Mommy?"

"I did. Now give me the phone."

"I want to finish the level."

"We said that just one more level and then you give me the phone."

"Right. Just one more level." His eyes on the screen, his voice distracted, hollow. A zombie child.

"You already did the level."

"No I didn't."

Annoyed with herself, and with Lucas, she plucked the phone from his hands.

He whirled around toward her, eyes widening. She could see it. The deathly silence before the storm. She already regretted snatching the phone away. She obviously regretted giving it to him in the first place.

Lucas screeched, shutting his eyes, little fists clenching, face becoming blotchy and red. Gemma took a step back, the violent response scaring her. He opened his eyes and lunged at her, trying to snatch the phone. She managed to keep it away from his reach at the last moment.

"I want to play the game!" he shrieked.

"You had enough time on the—"

"Let me play!"

"Too much time on the phone can hurt your eyes and—"

"I don't care, gimme the phone, I want to play the game!"

At which point she made another mistake. She pocketed the phone and said, "No! You'll never play with the phone again."

He actually tried to punch her, which was horrifying. This was something that happened to other parents. To parents who didn't intuitively know how to raise their kids like she did. Lucas was always so well behaved. So quiet and sweet. Less than an hour on the phone, and her son's adorable character was gone forever. She could already feel the tears in her throat as she tried to calm him down, her low soothing voice useless against his ghastly tirade.

The front door opened, and Benjamin stepped in, frowning. He took one look at Gemma's helpless face, then turned his eyes to the shrieking Lucas, who was crouching, his face already a dark shade of red.

"Okay, sport, come with me," Benjamin said, his voice jolly but authoritative.

Without waiting for a response, he whisked Lucas from the floor with one hand and carried him up the stairs. Within a few seconds a door shut, the awful screeching becoming thankfully muffled. Gemma peered upstairs; she could hear Benjamin's calm voice, somehow still audible despite the screaming.

Gemma allowed herself a shuddering breath. She took out her phone and deleted the *Candy Crush* app. Never again.

Half a minute later, the screaming morphed into crying, then sobbing, and finally silence. Gemma tiptoed upstairs and listened at the door. She heard Benjamin's murmurs. It sounded like he was reading Lucas a bedtime story. Lucas hadn't brushed his teeth, but Gemma was *not* about to barge in and point out that digression. She just hoped Benjamin told their boy to change into his pj's before going to sleep.

She went to their bedroom and took a shower, trying to wash the day away. As the hot water cascaded over her, she prepared her defense in the discussion she was about to have with her husband. Yes, she *had* let their son play on the phone for a few minutes, because she had to look up cakes online for Benjamin's mother's birthday, and she needed to concentrate. True, it was a weak excuse, but it made it sound like it was partly Benjamin's mother's fault, which had a certain elegance to it. Gemma would have to make some concessions regarding her no-phone agenda. It would become no-phone-unless-special-circumstances. And this was a slope so slippery it was practically a waterslide. Maybe it would be a good idea to point out how badly Lucas had reacted when she took the phone from him. That showed how addictive and destructive these things were.

She got out of the shower and put on her own comfortable pj's, originally blue, now a faded grayish blue from all those launderings over the years. She would take all the little comforts she could get.

Benjamin was in the kitchen, drinking a beer. Gemma joined him, pouring herself a glass of wine, not saying anything. Let Benjamin start.

"I think Iris let Lucas play on her phone," Benjamin said.

"I . . . What?"

"He said he wanted to play a game on the phone, the one with the candy. I guess Iris let him." Benjamin frowned and took a swig from his beer. "I should talk to her."

"No . . . I'll talk to her."

"I mean, we told her not to let him, right?"

"Yes. Absolutely. I'll talk to her, make sure it doesn't happen again."

"Good." Benjamin nodded. He looked tired and irritated.

Gemma took a sip from her wine, already regretting her words. She was like a child, caught red handed, instantly trying to shift the blame. She should tell him now, before it was too late. If she would just say right now "Actually, I was the one who gave him the phone," then their discussion about Iris wouldn't be a lie. It would be a hiccup. A misunderstanding, quickly smoothed.

"I'm glad you managed to calm him down," she said. "I didn't know what to do."

"Yeah, I think he was mostly tired."

"Yeah," she agreed. Now was the time to come clean. Right this minute. "I was thinking about the cake for your mother's birthday. I'm not sure which one to buy."

Nice one, Gemma. Bad mother, lying wife. And while we're at it, what's with the size of your wineglass? Are you planning on adding alcoholism to the list of your fetching qualities?

"Isn't Chloe getting the cake?" Benjamin asked distractedly.

"No, remember? I said we would bring the cake and the fruit salad. And the potatoes. Chloe said she would make the roast."

"I don't get why Chloe only makes the roast. She doesn't even make it; it's her husband that makes it."

Gemma sighed. The reason was that she wanted to score some points with Benjamin's mother—a woman she felt was always secretly criticizing her. A large birthday cake would get her oodles of mother-in-law points. "I don't mind. Chloe's very busy."

"She doesn't even have a job." Benjamin took another swig of his beer.

"But she has three kids." Somehow Gemma had become the defense attorney for Benjamin's younger sister, who was quite a vexing individual.

Benjamin snorted. "Fine. What are the choices for the cake?"

"Your mom likes chocolate cake, but there's a really nice-looking strawberry cake in a bakery near Primadonna, and—"

"Get her the chocolate cake." He shrugged. "It's fine."

"Okay." Gemma frowned. "I'll order it tomorrow."

"Oh, that reminds me. Dad's not feeling well so he won't be able to do trick-or-treating with Lucas tomorrow. So you'll do it."

A pang of panic. "Can't your mom come?"

"Well, no, she needs to stay at home and give candy to trick-or-treaters."

"I don't do Halloween, Benjamin. You know that. We discussed it—"

"I'm *sorry*, Gemma, but what do you want me to do?" He didn't sound sorry at all.

"Can you do it?"

"I'll do my best to get home from work by six, but I probably won't make it. Once I arrive, we can switch. But you'll have to get him ready and start the trick-or-treating without me."

A fragment of a memory threatened to emerge. A masked man, snarling at her, hurting her . . . She shut her eyes. "I . . . What if I get him ready, and you just take him once you show up?"

Benjamin rolled his eyes. "I don't get what the big deal is."

He'd never asked why she wouldn't do Halloween. She actually had a story prepared for it. She would say that it was the day her mom died. Which in a way was the truth. It *had* been the day the mom she knew was replaced by a different woman. One who was disappointed and disgusted with her.

She considered telling him that right now—that her mother died on Halloween. But this would spin into a whole tangle of lies, and she didn't want to go there. Not right now. Maybe it wouldn't be so bad. Outside with her son. He'd be excited, his first trick-or-treating. A memory for them both. A memory she could use to cover her other Halloween memory. "Fine." She gritted her teeth. "I'll take Lucas trick-or-treating."

He snorted, saying nothing. He seemed unusually snippy and annoyed. Did he know it wasn't Iris who gave their son her phone to play with? No, hang on. It wasn't about her at all.

"How was the talk with Vincent?"

"They're not making me team leader."

He'd been talking about this promotion for the past few months. The sales team leader, in charge of their software company's sales in

Europe. Benjamin had been sure he would get it. He was perfect for it. This was a huge blow for him.

Gemma placed her wineglass on the counter. "Your boss is a dumb asshole."

"I don't know if it was even his call. Those decisions come from the sales director—"

"He's a stupid shit as well. There's no one better for this than you."

She knew her husband. This was what he needed to hear. Not comforting words—oh, honey, you tried so hard, I'm so sorry. And he definitely didn't need questions: Why not? Can you do anything to change their opinion? At that very moment he needed her to tell him it was everyone else's fault, that they were garbage, that he was great.

She could relate.

"Yeah. They're making Shawn Malone team lead—"

"*Shawn?* Ass-licking, can't-even-tie-his-own-shoes Shawn? The guy who *literally* forgot his girlfriend's name when he introduced her to me at the Christmas party?"

A tiny quirk of a smile on Benjamin's lips. "That's the one."

Gemma snorted. "You'll be getting that promotion in four months, after they realize what useless trash he is, and kick him out."

Benjamin's smile widened a fraction. "Yeah, you might be right."

She grinned at him. "I'm always right. And you know what? I'm lucky. Because once you become team leader, you'll work late hours, and you'll be tired . . ." She sidled closer to him. "You won't have any energy left for me." Her arm wrapped around his shoulders.

He put down his beer. "I'll always have some energy for you," he said in a low voice.

Grabbing her waist, he pulled her closer. She kissed him and breathed him in, his taste, his smell, familiar and alluring all at once. His hand was already squeezing her ass as she melted into him.

It was what she needed from him. She didn't need comforting words—oh, honey, I'm sorry Halloween causes you so much stress. And she definitely didn't need questions—I heard about today at the salon, who's Theodora? What happened to you at Halloween?

At that very moment she needed him to touch her, to caress her, to make her forget.

Chapter 6

"Hey," Gemma called as she stepped inside. "I'm home!"

"Mommy!" The sound of Lucas's tiny footsteps preceded him as he bounded down the stairs.

"Don't run on the stairs," Gemma called quickly, her heart skipping a beat as it always did when Lucas did any of the billion things that could end up getting him hurt.

He reached the bottom floor and plunged into her hug, wrapping his arms around her.

"Hey, Gemma." Iris joined them, smiling. "You came home early today."

"Yeah." Gemma straightened and smiled back at the young woman. "It was a slow day at work. And Lucas has a playdate with Khai, my friend's son, so I wanted to clean up a bit."

She was also just exhausted. Lucas had woken up three times the night before, and she hardly got any sleep. Not to mention her trepidation regarding the evening's trick-or-treating. She needed time to recuperate at home.

"Okay, you want me to stick around, let you rest?"

"No, thank you, I got it." Gemma hated being at home alone with the nanny. She always felt like she needed to hide in her bedroom. Also, she was still feeling guilty for blaming Iris for the phone incident the evening before. She would need to make sure Benjamin and Iris didn't meet for a few weeks until he forgot about that.

"Cool." Iris was already reaching for her coat. "Well, Lucas already had his afternoon sandwich. We had a really nice time. We drew together, and he told me a story about a witch and a princess, which was very interesting."

"Oh, I would like to hear the story." Gemma ran her hand through Lucas's hair. "Um . . . Listen, Iris, is there any chance you're available this evening? It's Lucas's first trick-or-treating, and I'm feeling a bit under the weather—"

"No, I'm sorry, I'm going to a party," Iris said. "But you shouldn't go if you're not feeling well."

"Yeah, you're right," Gemma said weakly. "Maybe his grandparents will take him."

"I want you to take me, Mommy," Lucas said, hugging her leg.

"We'll see, sweetie."

"Okay, see you after Halloween." Iris waved goodbye to them both and left.

"Mommy, do you want to hear my story?" Lucas asked.

Gemma was relieved he didn't ask to play on the phone. She fervently hoped the debacle from the evening before would not come back to haunt her. She glanced at the time. She had just over an hour before Khai and Barbara showed up. She could make herself coffee and rest for a bit. But she did want to clean up, and she knew from experience that once she sat down, it would be much more difficult to get going. Better to do the cleanup first, rest afterward. "Okay, sweetie, but I'll do some tidying up as you tell me, okay?"

"Okay."

Gemma went to the living room, and Lucas followed behind her.

"There was once a very, very bad witch," he said.

"Oh, I'm already scared."

"And she was very angry at the princess. Oh, I forgot to say, the witch's name is Fedora. That's very important."

"Fedora, huh?" Gemma grinned as she picked up Lucas's socks from the floor. Every evening he took off his socks in the living room

Behind You

and discarded them on the floor. Gemma had given up on trying to make him put them in the laundry basket.

"Yes. Fedora was angry at the princess because the princess once made her hair wet."

"Witches don't like water," Gemma agreed.

"So the witch put on a disguise, and she went to the palace, where they had a big, big party."

Gemma listened distractedly as she got the broom and swept the living room floor. She didn't want Barbara showing up at her house when it was messy. Barbara's house always seemed pristine.

She was annoyed with herself for inviting them over on Halloween, but she and Barbara both had the afternoon off because of the holiday, and it had seemed a good opportunity at the time. Or at least, Barbara had thought it was a good opportunity, and she'd talked her into it.

Her phone blipped in her pocket, and she took it out. A message from an unknown number. A new referred client? She opened it. No, it was just some spam—an invitation to a big Halloween party—a random photo of teenagers in costumes and text in gory letters. She was about to pocket her phone when her eyes snagged on something in the text that made her focus.

> It's time to get spooky! Let's celebrate All Hallows Eve at Victoria Howell's home! There'll be plenty of drinks, fantastic music, stabbing psychos, and murder! Costumes aren't obligatory, but you'll wear one so we won't notice you until it's too late!

Gemma read the text twice, swallowing. Victoria Howell. A name she hadn't heard for more than a decade. And the text . . .

Stabbing psychos

Murder

We won't notice you until it's too late.

Her hand trembled. Her eyes jumped to the photo. She knew this place. Those paintings on the wall, that piano in the corner. She'd been there many times as a child. And one time as a teenager.

Victoria Howell's home.

And the young people in the photo. Faces she recognized from all those years ago. And in the center of the photo . . . that was her. Dancing. A familiar silver mask covering her face.

The phone clattered to the floor. Gemma's head spun, her vision clouding.

". . . and then the prince kissed the princess's lips," Lucas was saying. "And she woke up. And the king and queen were happy that Victoria woke up—"

"What?" Gemma rasped.

"The princess woke up, because of the prince's kiss."

"What did you say the princess was called?"

"Her name was Victoria. That's very important."

The details of the story Lucas just told swam in Gemma's head. A princess named Victoria. A bad witch that wanted to kill the princess because she made her hair wet. So she put on a disguise and went to the princess's party.

Ridiculous. Childish. Sickeningly familiar.

Gemma put down the broom, crouched, and grabbed Lucas by his shoulders. "Who told you this story?"

He blinked. "Iris said—"

"Iris told you this story?"

"No! Just the ending. She said we need a new ending. Because she didn't want the princess to die."

"She didn't want . . ." Gemma's head was throbbing. She was having difficulty concentrating. Her phone lay on the floor next to her.

Stabbing psychos

"She didn't want the princess to die?"

"The bad witch killed the princess, but Iris said that was a sad story." Lucas frowned. "So she said maybe the prince kissed the princess and—"

"Did Iris tell you the story about the witch? With the wet hair?"

"No, *I* told the story. Mommy, you're hurting me."

She was clutching his shoulder too tightly. She forced her fingers loose. "But who told you the story?"

We won't notice you until it's too late.

Lucas's lips trembled.

"Lucas! Listen to me. Who told you the damn story? *Who?*" Her voice sounded strange to her. Raspy. Angry. Frightened.

Lucas began sobbing. "It's a stupid story. I don't want to talk about it."

"Did Iris—"

"I don't want to talk about it!" he screamed, squirmed away from her, and ran to the sofa, then buried his head in a pillow, his crying muffled. Gemma stared at him as his body trembled. The past minute seemed hazy, unreal. She'd lost control. She vaguely recalled *shaking* Lucas as she questioned him. She'd yelled at him. Acted like a crazy person.

She let out a shuddering breath and picked up the phone. She looked at it again.

The photo didn't seem familiar anymore. The thing at the corner of the room wasn't a piano. It was a cupboard. The girl she'd thought was her was just a random teenager. So were the rest of the teens in the photo.

The text read **It's time to get spooky! Let's celebrate All Hallows Eve at 8102 West Victoria Street! There'll be plenty of drinks, fantastic music, bobbing for apples and a crazy costume competition! You wouldn't want to miss it!**

Gemma reread the text a few times, then put her phone away. She needed to sit down. After a few faltering steps, she slumped on the sofa next to Lucas. She rubbed his back gently.

"I'm sorry, sweetie," she whispered. "Mommy just shouted because she's a bit tired. I didn't mean to scare you."

Lucas kept sobbing, still hiding his face from her.

"Come on. Let's get the house ready. Khai will be coming soon." Gemma swallowed. "And tonight we're going trick-or-treating."

Chapter 7

Gemma sat on the sofa, watching Lucas as he worked. She'd finally managed to calm him down, suggesting he decorate his trick-or-treating pumpkin bucket. She told him he could show it to Khai when he came over. This was an exciting notion, enough to make him forget about the whole "Mom losing it" incident.

Gemma wished she could do the same.

Her phone was cradled in her hands, and every so often she would read the Halloween party invitation again. Just to make sure she got it right the second time.

She kept telling herself she was *fine.*

Was she fine? She felt as if she was losing it. That message on her phone . . . it wasn't like she thought she saw something. She'd read it twice. The photo had seemed so realistic. All those familiar faces. And that vicious message.

Stabbing psychos

She reread the message yet again. Just a random, cheesy invitation to a Halloween party. Nothing more.

And Lucas's story? By now, she didn't dare ask him about it. The last thing she needed was for Barbara and Khai to show up in the midst of another meltdown. But there was so much there. The princess, Victoria. And the witch's name, Fedora. Which sounded a bit like—

But there, wasn't she just ascribing meaning where there was none?
—it sounded a bit like Theodora.

And, of course, the part about how the witch wanted to kill Princess Victoria because she made her hair wet.

Lucas kept placing stickers of skeletons and cartoon ghosts on his pumpkin bucket. Looking at him do it, peeling and then sticking them, one after the other, was strangely meditative. Gemma could feel herself zone out, her mind floating away.

Sometimes memories intruded on Gemma's life, drowning her, forcing her to relive the past. Other times she dug for them, like you might lick at a mouth sore, or probe a bruise. To see if it's still there, if it still hurts.

The day the princess made the witch's hair wet was a week before Halloween. Gemma still remembered that day vividly. Some memories are scarred into our brains because of trauma. Other memories we etch into our brains ourselves, consumed by anger, promising ourselves that we will *never* forget.

So the memory was still there. And the anger. That pure, all-consuming teen anger, hot enough to burn the sun.

She had been wearing her Coldplay "Viva La Vida" T-shirt that day. The one she got at the concert. She knew that because she *loved* that shirt. And after that day she never wore it again.

She could remember the smell, as well. The school's bathroom had a—

—distinct odor to it, a mixture of bleach and a cloying sweet perfume that always made Theo want to hold her breath. She kept her school bathroom visits to a bare minimum, but some things were unavoidable. Especially after she drank two glasses of apple juice first thing in the morning.

Still, she could be efficient. Quick shallow breaths, in and out in less than two minutes.

When she stepped out of the stall, she saw they were waiting for her.

Victoria and her friends, all bunched together. There was no mistaking their intention. Sure, girls went to the bathroom together, but they usually didn't stand in a bunch, arms folded, smirks plastered on their faces.

Theo quickly looked away. As if maybe if she didn't make eye contact, they would leave her alone. They stood between her and the door, so she took a step toward the sink instead.

Donna shifted to the left, getting in her way.

"What?" Theo asked, trying to hide the quiver in her voice. Predators could smell fear.

"Someone posted a drawing of me," Victoria said, her voice chiming, pleasant. "Posted it online for my friends, and Zayne, and his friends to see. Do you know who drew it, Zit-face?"

Zit-face was Theo, of course. Or Pizza-face. Or Crater-face. Or Zit-farm. She'd heard them all. She didn't have a favorite.

"I never meant for anyone to see that," Theo muttered. "I'm sorry."

There was no point in denying she drew it. Everyone knew she drew caricatures. Her style was very recognizable. And that drawing of Victoria was clearly hers.

Theo had been aghast when she saw it posted on one of the school's unofficial chats. She'd drawn it in a moment of spite, after Victoria made fun of her during gym class—"Look at Pizza-face running." The drawing was unforgiving, to say the least. Theo had a knack for picking and enhancing flaws. That tiny space between Victoria's front teeth, enlarged to a canyon. Victoria's protruding ears, which Theo knew had always bothered her, became large wings. Her cleavage became bulging, about to burst. Theo had crumpled the drawing afterward, threw it in the trash. But someone had been kind enough to fish it out and share her talent with everyone.

"You're sorry?" Victoria imitated Theo's voice, giving it a whiny pitch.

"Listen, Vic, I didn't—"

"Don't call me Vic," Victoria snarled.

Vic had been her nickname when they were little girls. When they were best friends. Before life intruded, pulling them in different directions. If Theo had been hoping to make Victoria remember that time, it clearly wasn't about to happen. Victoria had let her calm facade drop, and Theo saw just how angry she really was. Her jaw clenched, body trembling, face flushing. The fact that Zayne, her boyfriend, had seen the sketch was probably what really infuriated Victoria. Even when they were little, she always stressed about how boys viewed her.

Usually, Victoria was content with the occasional name-calling. Or a whispered comment to her friends as Theo went by in the hall, followed by some nasty giggling. But it occurred to Theo that this time, Victoria might actually hurt her. Was that where this was headed? A girl fight in the bathroom, hair pulling, fingernails scratching?

Theo lunged for the door and was instantly grabbed.

"You know," Victoria said, a tremor of fury in her voice. "Zits happen when, um . . . it's because of dirt. You should wash them. Your face, I mean."

Victoria probably had a clever, stinging insult she'd prepared beforehand. Perhaps she'd practiced it in front of the mirror. But now, in her rage, the words came out all wrong. It didn't matter. The general idea was obvious.

"No!" Theo struggled as they dragged her back into the stall.

She kicked Donna's ankle, and Donna grunted in pain but didn't let go. They forced her to her knees; she could feel the damp floor soaking into her pants. A hand on the back of her head. Forcing her forward, closer and closer to the toilet. A brown smear on the toilet's surface. The tremor in the toilet water as her face came nearer to it. She struggled harder and screamed.

Someone leaned forward and flushed the toilet. The water rushed around her, splashing on her face, on her hair, on her shirt.

She shut her eyes and her mouth as hard as she could, felt spattering on her lips.

The hands let go. She leaped up and whirled around, wiping the water from her face, blinking, heart thumping, her teeth clenched. Victoria was holding her phone in front of her, clearly filming the entire thing.

"You fucking bitch!" Theo screamed.

They didn't look victorious. Donna was pale. Victoria's lips trembled as if she was about to cry. The other two didn't meet Theo's eyes. But Victoria kept holding her phone, her hand steady.

"I'll kill you, Victoria. Just wait. I'm going to fucking kill you!"

Victoria put her phone away. She opened her mouth as if to say something when Theo lunged at her. Donna grabbed her, pushed her against the stall door.

Victoria took a step back. "Come on, let's go."

They all left, letting the door close behind them. Theo stood shaking, water dripping from her hair. She wanted to kill all of them. She wanted to die.

Gemma blinked, pushing the memory away. Her hands were clenched, teeth grinding. She could still feel it, all these years later. The humiliation. The disgust. How many times had she washed her hair once she got home? And it still didn't feel clean. She'd rinsed her mouth with an entire bottle of mouthwash, and still imagined the germs from the toilet water, from that brown smear, clinging to her lips, her tongue, her teeth. The shirt, her lovely concert shirt, went straight to the trash.

She begged off school, feigning a sore throat. During her time at home, she lay in her bed, replaying those moments over and over in her mind. The initial act had been a few seconds at most, but in her mind, it became long minutes, then hours, the toilet water washing over her face, drowning her. Sometimes she would think that she would never return to school again. She would finish school from home. If she didn't get out, she could avoid meeting these people for the rest of her life. Other times, she would imagine how she'd finish high school. Become a successful artist, famous, rich. Return to town twenty years later to see that Victoria was a fat slob, living in a trailer park, married to a drunk.

After two days, she saw the video and the images posted on that same chat where the drawing had been posted. The video was of her rising from the toilet, face wet, spluttering, pathetic. The photos were of her with her head held inside the toilet. The caption was *Zit-face getting a much-needed facial*.

And her fantasies turned much darker.

Chapter 8

Gemma usually enjoyed meeting Barbara outside of work. But right now her nerves were frayed. So it was hard for her to see all the things she usually loved about Barbara—her innate cheerfulness and kindness, and the way she could keep the conversation going. Instead she kept noticing how loud Barbara's voice was, especially in Gemma's living room, which had a resonance issue and tended to amplify noise. Also Barbara had a frustrating tendency to talk about work all the time, while Gemma liked to mostly keep shoptalk to the hours she was at Primadonna.

". . . that woman that came in just before you left, did you see her? A first-time client, but I think she'll become a regular. Girl, she needed my help. Did you see her feet? That pedicure took nearly an hour. That's why we were late. Sorry we were late, by the way. I should have called."

"That's fine."

"We went by your neighbor's house on the way over here. The one with the rosebushes in front? Did you see their Halloween decorations? Totally inappropriate. Don't they know there are families with little children in this neighborhood?"

"I know what you mean," Gemma said, nodding. She didn't know what Barbara meant. She didn't recall seeing anything inappropriate.

"Khai was scared. I had to calm him down. He's very sensitive. Last week he saw a cartoon, and a dog got lost, and Khai couldn't go to sleep afterward. Serves me right for letting him watch TV before bed. It's a bad habit of mine, you know that. I mean, watching TV before going to bed. Oh, I think it was a cat who got lost. Which one was it, Khai, a dog or a cat?"

The aforementioned Khai was still holding Barbara's hand, shyly staring at the floor, ignoring his mother's question. Lucas was standing behind Gemma. Neither child made any attempt to talk.

"Lucas," Gemma prompted her son. "Why don't you take Khai to your room and find something to play?"

Her son shuffled closer to her and shrugged. It was so frustrating sometimes. Every time those two met, they had to go through the same ceremony of both mothers prodding and cajoling them to play together. Then, twenty minutes before they had to say goodbye, suddenly they hit it off, and it would be difficult to pry them apart. Lucas would complain later that he didn't have enough time to play with Khai, and Gemma would promise they would meet again soon. Then, two weeks later, they acted as if they were strangers. Couldn't Lucas find it in himself to be a good host for once?

Part of it, if not all of it, was her fault. Lucas was probably still recuperating from her hysterical scene earlier. Gemma was recuperating as well. It didn't help that she knew they had to go trick-or-treating in less than two hours. What had she been thinking, inviting Khai and Barbara today, of all days? Oh, right. She'd been thinking her father-in-law would take him trick-or-treating.

"Khai, do you want to see Lucas's room?" Barbara asked.

Khai mumbled something indistinct. No progress there.

"I need to prepare the snacks for trick-or-treaters," Gemma told Barbara. "What do you hand out?"

"I made a bunch of those homemade Halloween cookies I made last week, remember? They're really tasty, and they don't have all those additives the mass production candy have. It's not like I'm a health nut or anything, I mean you know that. But I feel like if most of the ingredients are just a bunch of letters and numbers, it can't be good."

Gemma had three bags of Sour Patch Kids in her cupboard, ready for trick-or-treaters. She felt a tiny stab of guilt. "Oh wow, that's so nice of you. Would it be enough?"

"Oh yeah, I made like . . . a bazillion cookies. I think I spent eight hours just baking. The house smelled like a bakery, drove Khai and George insane. I finally let them each have two cookies just to get them off my back."

"That's incredible." Gemma hoped Barbara wouldn't ask her about her treat of choice.

She needed some more quiet time, to calm down, to process the last few hours. Or rather, the last few days. To think of the things that happened, and her own response. To untangle it all in her mind.

Which was difficult with Barbara and Khai there, and with the trick-or-treating looming on the very near horizon . . . to make things worse, she was pretty sure she was forgetting something important. From her experience, that was the constant state of motherhood—thinking you forgot something important.

"Lucas, how about Chutes and Ladders? Do you want to play Chutes and Ladders with Khai?"

"No." Lucas sounded angry. Or about to cry. Maybe both. His voice had that whiny edge, a sign of danger.

Gemma knew many mothers treated their own kids as if they represented *them*. As if they were the mother's ambassador, or their business card. Her own mother did this constantly when she was a kid, whispering at her that she should say hello, thank the kind woman, lower her voice, behave herself. Mom's voice constantly tense, because she was being embarrassed by her daughter for some transgression or other.

Gemma didn't do that. She and Lucas were different entities. He was a four-year-old, so it was only natural that he sometimes acted out. It didn't mean she was a bad mother.

But of course, knowing it wasn't the same as really believing it. Because sure, Lucas wasn't her business card, but didn't other mothers sort of treat him like he was? If he made a scene at the grocery store,

Mike Omer

wouldn't other mothers look at her judgmentally, knowing *their* perfect child would never do that? Sure they would. Gemma knew that because *she* sometimes judged other mothers when their kids acted out.

So right now she felt the need to apologize to Barbara and Khai. To say that Lucas wasn't usually like this. That he'd been really excited to play with Khai.

She ignored that urge. She was better than that.

"Well, *I* want to play Chutes and Ladders," she said, managing to somehow find her cheerful voice. "Do you kids want to play with me? I'm sure I'll win."

Yes, perhaps what was best for her mental health was time on her own to focus on her past traumas, and their effect on her well-being. But apparently what was best for her son right now was for her to play Chutes and Ladders with him and Khai, so by God, that was what she would do. And you know what? She would multitask. She would play Chutes and Ladders while making small talk with Barbara, *and* process the events of the past couple of hours.

"So who's taking Khai trick-or-treating?" she asked Barbara as she rolled the dice and stepped five spaces forward, reaching a ladder.

Barbara smiled. "We're going together. I love trick-or-treating. Halloween was always my favorite holiday, even more than Christmas. I mean sure, as a kid, I always obsessed about the Christmas tree and all that, but Halloween is so much more exciting. I mean, I know you don't feel that way, Gems. But for me it's exciting. All those costumes. And the sweets."

"Oh yeah? What about the chemicals in the mass production candy?" Gemma teased her. She noticed Khai was cheating and decided not to say anything.

"I said I don't like *kids* to eat those chemicals. It's bad for their development. But I'm fully developed, love. And Khai knows twenty-five percent of all his candy goes to his mom. I assume Benjamin is taking Lucas?"

"No. I'm doing it."

56

Barbara raised her eyebrows. "I thought you didn't do Halloween."

"Things change," Gemma said shortly.

Barbara didn't pry. She knew not to. Instead, she launched into another work-related anecdote about a customer who came in for a full-body wax the week before. Gemma zoned out, supplying Barbara with the occasional prompt or follow-up question. The kids were getting into the game by now, with Khai in the lead. Her mind went to Lucas's story. To the invitation she'd seen on her phone.

There was a simple and worrisome explanation for all of this. She had been sleeping badly for the past couple of months. Hallucinations were a well-known symptom of extreme exhaustion. And since it was the anniversary of that night all those years ago, her hallucinations took an uncomfortable turn. The party invitation's vicious content had been her imagination.

Lucas's story? She'd heard what she'd wanted to hear. Lucas said the princess made the witch's hair wet, and Gemma freaked out. But witches were always reacting badly to getting wet, just ask Dorothy. It wasn't about *her*. Gemma wasn't even completely sure if Lucas actually said the princess's name was Victoria. Maybe he said something else. She had been reading that party invitation, her mind playing tricks on her. He could have said anything.

Khai won the first game, and the ice had been properly broken between the kids. Gemma extracted herself as they decided to have a rematch and led Barbara to the kitchen, for some coffee and muffins.

"Those are good," Barbara said and took another bite of her muffin. "Where did you get them?"

"I don't remember the name. That place down the street from Primadonna?"

"Oh yeah, I know that spot. They're good. I like their croissants? The ones with the almonds. And I think Thelma buys her daily cinnamon roll there. I don't know how that woman can look like she does eating those rolls every day. Well, I guess all that working out she does."

Something snagged in Gemma's mind. "Oh shit! I just remembered I have to get a birthday cake for Benjamin's mom."

"You haven't ordered it yet?"

"No." Gemma was already on the phone, searching. "But it should be fine, right? The birthday dinner is on Thursday."

"Hmm," Barbara said thoughtfully. "Might get tricky. I mean, I'm not sure, but I think all the decent places are already booked with orders and stuff."

"Yeah, I didn't think about that." Gemma tapped on her phone, scrolling between venues for cakes. This birthday cake thing was just that extra errand that would pull Gemma under. She still had to get Lucas ready for trick-or-treating and be a nice hostess for Barbara and Khai. Lucas would have to eat something before they left or he'd be hungry before they even started, meaning he would eat all the candy as soon as he got it, and obviously get violently ill. When should she get Lucas into his costume? Before he had dinner or after? They'd bought him a wizard costume, like he'd asked, and . . .

"Oh no," she muttered.

"Everything all right?" Barbara asked.

"Lucas's costume. He's a wizard. But his grandpa was supposed to take him, and his grandma bought the cape. It's at her house. I'll have to go and get it . . ." Gemma eyed the clock on the wall. "There's no time . . ."

She bit her lip. Birthday cake. Costume mishap. Dinner. Trick-or-treating. Everything seemed to swim in her mind, and she couldn't put it in order. She was usually so together. So organized. "I . . . I think I'll first find a cake. Because like you said, it's sort of urgent. And then . . . I don't know. I guess Lucas can go without a cape . . ." Without a cape, Lucas's costume amounted to a plastic wand and a silly hat. Her eyes misted. "Um. Hang on, Barbara, I'm sorry, I just need to, um . . ."

Barbara put down her cup of coffee and placed her hand on Gemma's arm softly. "Gems, don't worry about it. First of all, forget about the cake, okay? Drop by my place tomorrow evening, and we'll make a birthday cake together."

"But it's your long day at work; you're always so tired when you get off . . ."

"Don't worry about it. I enjoy baking. And I'm glad to help, okay?"

"Okay," Gemma said weakly.

"The cape is no biggie either. If you have a shirt you don't need, we can turn it into a cape for Lucas in no time."

Gemma took a long breath. "You're right. I can cut off the sleeves and the front of the shirt."

"I bet I can find a quick video online to help with that." Barbara got on her phone.

Gemma cleared her throat. "Yeah. Um, thanks."

"It's no biggie. Oh, there we go. I found a video on Facebook. You know what? I meant to ask you, how come we're not Facebook friends? I searched for you a while back, and I couldn't find your account. I thought you'd be in Thelma's list of friends, but—"

"I'm not on Facebook. I told you that already."

"Oh." Barbara frowned. "Right. What are you on? Instagram? X?"

"I'm not on any of . . . those."

"Oh, really?" Barbara raised her eyes from her phone. "How come?"

In the twenty-first century, not being on social media was almost like missing a limb. How could you catch up on all those political arguments and stale jokes and ads if you didn't have a social media account? How did you know how your ex was doing, or that person from work whom you never really talked to? This wasn't the first time she'd been asked how, or why. And Gemma had a response for that. A repertoire of answers that satisfied everyone. They were all variations on sentences that involved the words *big data*, *corporations*, and *privacy*.

Gemma sometimes said "I value my privacy, and I don't want corporations to use me in their big data." Or she'd say "Big data and corporations are a serious danger to our privacy, and I don't want to make it easy for them." Or even when she got lazy, "Well, you know. Big data. Privacy. Those corporations."

And it worked. People would nod appreciatively and change the subject. It was a magical incantation that never failed.

She was about to invoke her big data magic spell, but then faltered. Her gratitude at Barbara's helpfulness intermingled with her guilt over her earlier ugly thoughts about her friend's loud voice and tiresome conversation topics. Suddenly she couldn't use that tried-and-tested lie. Instead, she blurted the truth. "I was bullied a lot. During high school. Over social media. There was an incident . . . never mind about that. But . . . it got really bad afterward. I had to delete all my accounts."

And change my name. And run away. And move across the country.

"Oh, Gems," Barbara said softly.

Gemma had never said anything about it before. It should have been a relief. A weight lifted off her heart.

Instead, it felt like the sturdy wall she'd built to protect herself from her past was cracking.

Chapter 9

Over the years Gemma had developed a way to handle Halloween. A bowl of candy was left on the porch for trick-or-treaters. Then she'd go to her room, shut the door, and binge a show on her laptop, with her headphones on, the volume high, to drown out the voices from outside. And wait for it to be over. When Lucas was born, she made it clear he was Benjamin's responsibility for that single evening.

Now, as she stepped out into the street, a shiver of fear crawled down her neck. One that was not directly related to the skeletons in her neighbors' yards or the creepy music that was being blasted from a nearby house.

Groups of parents and children filled the street, shouts of laughter and screams of mock-fear punctuating the air. Lights flickered in eye sockets of plastic porch zombies or behind the windows of amateur haunted houses. Costumes were everywhere—masks and makeup hiding faces, obscuring identities.

Sensory overload assailed her. The memories threatened to emerge. A Halloween party in the past. Faces hidden behind—

Masks. A large, hairy apelike face looming above her, pain blossoming on her cheek—

—A tiny hand grasped hers. Lucas squeezed her palm.

"There's a scary witch over there," he murmured, pointing at an automated Halloween puppet.

She knelt by him and hugged him with one arm, drawing warmth and comfort from their touch. "She's not scary," she said. "She's silly. Look at her hat! Isn't it a silly hat?"

Lucas stared skeptically, unconvinced.

"Let's go closer," Gemma suggested. "You want to see me squeeze her nose?"

Lucas grinned. "Okay."

They crossed the street, hand in hand, and approached the whirring automaton. As they got closer, Gemma realized a mechanical cackling voice emanated from the witch, hardly audible in the din around them. She leaned closer to the witch and gently grabbed its long, crooked nose. Rubber.

"Honk," she said.

Lucas giggled.

"Do you want to squeeze her nose too?"

"Okay."

She lifted him up, his makeshift cloak getting in her face. He quickly squeezed the witch's nose as well.

"Honk." He laughed.

Someone peered from the house's window, probably worried they were about to break their expensive Halloween decoration. "Come on. Let's get going."

From here, she saw the thing that had bothered Barbara earlier. Three houses down the street, a large, lifelike troll loomed by the sidewalk. It was holding the puppet of a little girl by its feet, raising it up and down. The girl puppet was waving its hands in apparent distress. Most of the families with the younger kids crossed to the other side of the street to avoid the thing. It was the most realistic Halloween prop in the area, and the house owner was probably very pleased with himself. She could imagine him, buying the thing online for thousands of dollars, feeling like he "nailed it." That he won in some sort of competition. He would show off to the other guys at work, telling them his house was by far the scariest in the neighborhood.

"Let's go that way," she suggested, pointing in the other direction.

Lucas was already waking up every night because his body itched. She didn't need him waking up from nightmares as well.

The first house they approached already had its door open for other trick-or-treaters, a father and a child dressed as Spider-Man. The child received a Snickers bar and dropped it into his bag.

"What do we say?" the father asked pointedly.

The child seemed flustered by the sudden pop quiz. He peered into his bag, then at the floor, shuffling his feet.

"What do we say to the nice lady?" the father asked again.

The aforementioned nice lady stood frozen in the doorway, trapped as a participant in the child's education.

"Thank you," the child finally mumbled.

"Thank you," the father repeated, and both of them turned away from the lady. Now as they faced Gemma, she recognized the dad. She'd seen him at Lucas's school a few times.

"Hey." She smiled.

"Hey. Happy Halloween!" he said cheerily. He glanced at Lucas. "What are you supposed to be?"

Lucas shuffled closer to Gemma. "I'm a wizard."

"Oh, I see. Are you Harry Potter?"

Lucas had no idea who Harry Potter was. He looked up at Gemma. She kept her smile plastered on her face.

"He's a different wizard," she said. "Happy Halloween!"

Thankfully, Spider-Man and his dad went on, and Gemma was free to step forward with Lucas.

"Trick or treat," Lucas piped hesitantly.

"Oh my," the woman with the candy bowl said. "It's a powerful wizard." She offered a Snickers bar to Lucas.

He took it and plopped it into his pumpkin.

"Thank you," Gemma said cheerfully.

Lucas was looking into his pumpkin, mesmerized. Gemma recalled one of her first times trick-or-treating. How magical it felt. One day a year that candy overflowed wherever she went. The giddy feeling of walking around with her mother, dressed as a fairy, constantly adjusting her silvery wings. It was a surprising memory, one that had been untouched in her mind for decades.

Halloween could be fun.

"Happy Halloween!" the woman said, waving, and shut the door.

The next few houses went without a hitch, and Gemma was getting into the spirit of things. Lucas was smiling now whenever they approached a door, calling out "trick or treat" with excitement. He also began thanking the people handing out the treats himself, following Gemma's example, without being told to do it. She tried to tell herself it was mostly due to her child's sweet and thoughtful temperament, but she couldn't completely avoid the slight smugness of feeling like a better parent than Spider-Man's dad.

"Can I eat one?" Lucas asked, peering into his pumpkin.

"Once we get home," Gemma said strategically. It would motivate Lucas to end the trick-or-treating earlier. True, she was enjoying herself right now, but the evening was getting chillier. Besides, there was a fine line between having a nice bounty of candy and having an amount large enough for a stomachache and a future unfortunate visit at the dentist.

"My bucket is getting heavier," Lucas said.

"Do you want me to carry it?"

"No. Which candy do you like best?"

"I like the Reese's. Which do you like best?"

"I like gummy bears. That man with the clown costume gave me four."

"Four, huh?" Gemma looked across the street, where a family with three kids was surrounding one of the porches with a bowl of candy. They seemed to be treating the bowl as an all-you-can-eat buffet, stuffing fistfuls of candy into their bags. A jolt of annoyance shot through her; she was already imagining telling Barbara about this tomorrow morning. She wondered how Barbara would react to her experience of trick-or-treating. Barbara knew Gemma had an issue with Halloween.

But maybe she was getting better, overcoming her aversion to the holiday. Barb would tell her "Good for you." Because "Good for you" was one of Barb's favorite phrases. And she was right, in that imaginary dialogue Gemma was having inside her own head. It was good for her.

She turned her sights on the next house. Three, maybe four more houses, and she'd suggest they go back home. Let Lucas eat those gummy bears.

A mother and her daughter were walking toward them. They both seemed familiar. She must have seen them at the local park. The girl was dressed as one of the Minions, in blue overalls and a yellow shirt and hat. And the mother was . . .

The mother was dressed as an angel. Large white wings arched from her back; a shiny halo bounced above her head. Her white crop top exposed her belly, and she wore a shiny white jacket over it. She had an ash-blond wig on. Her face was pale, which made her makeup all the more pronounced—red lipstick, dark eye shadow.

Gemma's step faltered. It was like staring down a time tunnel, going thirteen years into the past. Right at Victoria Howell during that Halloween party. It wasn't just similar; it was downright identical. Gemma recalled every detail. Of course she did. She got a good look at Victoria that night. As the girl cried.

A chilly breeze blew down the street, and the woman's jacket fluttered. Gemma's breath hitched. Under the jacket, just above the woman's waist, was a large stain of blood.

Fake blood. Not real. It's just a costume.

By now they were close enough to lock eyes. The woman nodded at her, probably recognizing her from the park. Gemma nodded back dumbly. The woman and the girl brushed past them and kept on going.

Gemma shivered, not sure what that was. Had she imagined the blood? But even without it, the costume had been identical. Victoria hadn't worn a wig that day, of course; her *own* hair was ash blond, at that exact length, and—

"I had two younger brothers."

The voice came from behind. Gemma turned around. The woman in the angel costume stood there, still holding her daughter's hand.

"What?" Gemma blurted.

"I had two brothers. Willie and Craig. Remember them? Willie would hug me every morning. During weekends, we'd play Monopoly together."

Gemma took a step back. The woman inched forward. Her face seemed frozen, her voice monotone. Only her eyes showed any emotion. Wide, jittery. Almost . . . desperate. Gemma tried to say something. Do I know you, or maybe, Are you okay, but she couldn't. Her mouth was dry, seemingly unable to utter a single syllable.

"I wanted to be a veterinarian," the woman said, her words flat, dead. "I loved animals. Remember our dogs? Jax couldn't stop howling after I was gone."

"Mommy . . ." The woman's little girl pulled at her hand. "Let's go." She seemed bored and frustrated.

The woman glanced down at her girl and clenched her jaw. She spoke faster, as if she was running out of time. "Do you think I would have married by now, like you did? How many children would I have?"

"You have one child. Me!" the little girl pointed out and tugged at her mother's hand again.

The girl's intrusion seemed to have confused the woman's monologue. For a few seconds, her lips moved, no sound emerging, her eyes going to her daughter, then back to Gemma.

Gemma found her voice. "Excuse me, do I—"

"But you destroyed any chance of that happening, didn't you?" the woman blurted, lowering her voice. "You thought you could run away, and it would all be all right? It would never be all right."

Gemma's head spun. She tried to respond but couldn't. She kept glancing at the stain of blood . . .

Fake blood . . .

. . . on the woman's shirt. It almost seemed to be spreading.

And then the woman whirled and strode away, her little girl running to keep pace with her. Gemma could hear the girl complaining, telling her mother to slow down. Gemma wanted to chase her, but her feet were planted on the sidewalk.

"Who was that, Mommy?" Lucas asked.

Gemma blinked a few times and cleared her throat. "I don't know. I . . . I don't know."

"What did she say? About the dog?"

Gemma stared. The woman and the girl were getting farther away on the darkening street. She could still chase them. Get some answers. But what the woman had said was impossible. She wasn't Victoria. She obviously wasn't Victoria's ghost either. She looked down at Lucas. He'd heard it! He'd just said so.

"You heard what she said?" she asked.

"She said that the dog was howling."

"What else?" Gemma asked urgently.

Lucas frowned. "Can we go do some more trick-or-treating?"

"You don't remember what else she said?" Gemma tried to keep her voice calm, to avoid repeating the meltdown from earlier.

Lucas shook his head. "I'm cold. Can we go? I want more candy."

"I . . . need to call Daddy. Just one second."

Benjamin answered the call after two rings. Gemma could hear the car engine in the background. "Hey, honey, I'm already on my way back. I'll be there as soon as I can."

"How soon?" Gemma croaked. She needed him there right now.

"The navigation app says twenty minutes."

Twenty minutes. Eternity.

"Okay," Gemma whispered. "See you soon." She hung up.

"Mom." Lucas tugged at her hand a few times.

She let her boy lead her; she tottered after him, trying to hold it together. That woman had mentioned Willie and Craig . . . Victoria's brothers. And Jax. Gemma remembered when the Howell family got

Jax as a puppy, a gorgeous golden retriever. She and Victoria played with him in the front yard for hours.

This couldn't be brushed off as a coincidence, like the customer who'd come to Primadonna. For a few seconds, Gemma suspected the woman was from Crumville. That she'd found Gemma and decided to mess with her, for some weird reason. But there was no way. She didn't look like anyone from Crumville. And even if that were the case, who would do that? Find the exact costume Victoria wore to that party, as well as a wig, and then go trick-or-treating with her own *daughter* in that getup, only to mess with Gemma. It made no sense. No sense at all.

The only reasonable explanation was the one from before. She'd seen a woman with a costume that reminded her of Victoria and had hallucinated the rest. The woman probably told her something innocuous—maybe warning her about a house with a dog that scared her daughter while they were trick-or-treating. And Gemma had heard something that only her own mind could conjure.

Two houses later there was a **BEWARE OF DOG** sign on the fence. Gemma felt no relief at the validation of her explanation. The fact that she couldn't trust her own eyes and ears terrified her. What if she and Lucas crossed the road and she didn't see an oncoming car? Or if she somehow hurt Lucas because of a figment of her imagination?

Lucas seemed tired, and Gemma seized on that opportunity to convince him to go back home. His pumpkin was full of candy, more than enough. He prattled happily as they walked back home, describing the loot he'd collected and how he planned to eat it. Gemma couldn't find it within herself to respond. She needed to get back inside. Every trick-or-treater now seemed threatening, possibly a nightmare conjured by her haunted mind. The noise and the flickering lights all made her panic worse. Her head pounded. She felt as if she might be sick. Just a few more steps. Just a few more.

She half expected to see the mirage of that woman again inside her home, as she and Lucas stepped inside. She quickly turned on all the lights, her heart pounding in her ears. She grabbed a Sour Patch Kids bag and refilled the bowl on the porch. She couldn't handle trick-or-treaters knocking on the door.

Lucas emptied the pumpkin bucket on the table, then sifted through it, a large grin on his face. Gemma slumped on one of the chairs, staring at him vacantly as he popped a gummy bear into his mouth. She vaguely remembered planning to tell him he could only have one candy before bed, but right now she couldn't figure out why it had been so important to her.

Benjamin found her in the same spot when he stepped into the house. The moment he arrived, she got up and went to the bathroom, shutting the door behind her. She listened to his conversation with Lucas, muffled through the door. "How are you, sport; did you have fun? Gummy bears, wow." Would Lucas tell him about the woman dressed like an angel? No, of course he wouldn't. For Lucas, she was just another woman in a costume.

She waited a few minutes, then stepped out. Lucas and Benjamin were both sorting through the candy, dividing the various pieces into groups.

"Benjamin, can I talk to you a moment?" she asked. Her voice was hollow, exhausted.

"Sure." Benjamin ruffled Lucas's hair and got up.

Gemma walked to their bedroom and shut the door when Benjamin followed her inside.

"Listen," he said. "I'm sorry, I know I said I'd try to get home before six, but—"

Gemma raised her hand to silence him. "I don't care about that. Benjamin . . . I'm not okay."

He frowned. "What do you mean?"

"I'm . . . I haven't slept well for a few weeks because of Lucas waking up at night . . ." Her voice trembled. "I know I said I didn't mind it . . . but I think my body is falling apart. I've been having headaches, and dizzy spells, and I feel tired all the time. I started having . . ."

Hallucinations.

". . . anxiety attacks, and if I don't get a few nights of sleep, I think I'll lose it."

Benjamin swept her into his arms. She buried her face in his chest, shaking.

"No problem, sweetie," he whispered. "I'll wake up with Lucas tonight. And also after that. You just sleep. Sleep until you get better."

Chapter 10

When she was younger, Gemma liked to claim she didn't need much sleep. Sometimes she would stay awake throughout the night, drawing an intricate sketch or reading a book cover to cover. And then she would breeze through the following day, feeling as if she had a special secret no one around her shared. Counting the hours she'd been awake—twenty-four . . . twenty-eight . . . thirty-three . . . each one an accomplishment, a triumph over other mortals who foolishly went to sleep every night, giving up on those precious hours.

And then she became a mother.

Sleep became a precious commodity, to be treasured, and stolen when possible. When she went to bed, she knew in all likelihood her sleep would be interrupted. Several times. And sleeping in was obviously not an option, not even on the weekends. A little boy did not care if it was Saturday. He wanted to be fed, and entertained, and held. And he wanted it at six in the morning. Sometimes at half past five.

So when Benjamin actually let her sleep through the night, two nights in a row, she did not take it for granted. It was a gift. It made her life so much better. The world seemed clearer, and happier. Her anxiety slowly dissipated. There were no more hallucinations. She was a new woman. Everything seemed easier. Work, her time with Lucas, even annoying house chores. Making that birthday cake for her mother-in-law's birthday was suddenly no biggie. She dropped by Barbara's, and they made it together, chatting and gossiping the entire evening.

But she wasn't about to ignore the warning signs her brain had sent her. Her many-year attempts to repress the past were backfiring. She would have to face it head on. She began looking for a good, affordable therapist in the area, preferably a woman. She didn't know what she would tell her just yet—obviously, she couldn't say everything, no matter the patient confidentiality. But maybe just enough so that the therapist could help her get some closure.

After the emotional roller coaster she went through that week, she was glad to go to the family dinner on Thursday.

"Benjamin! Gemma! Lucas!" Benjamin's mother, Joyce, said as they walked through the front door. She always did that, naming everyone who entered the house, like some sort of Lord Steward in a state banquet. She kissed each one of them on both cheeks, another classic Joyce move.

"Hi, Joyce." Gemma smiled at her. "We'll put the cake and the fruit salad in the kitchen?"

"Yes, and you can place the potatoes on the dining table," Joyce said. "Chloe called. They're running a bit late."

"Of course they are," Benjamin muttered.

Another one of the Foster family's traditions—Benjamin always arrived on time, Chloe was always late, and Benjamin always complained about it.

Gemma enjoyed these little repetitive moments. At times, her feelings about Benjamin's family were complex. Since she'd left her own family behind, the Foster family became sort of her own . . . well . . . foster family. For years, when she'd been alone, she yearned for family holiday dinners, for a feeling of kinship, of belonging. She loved getting close to them, getting to know them and their little quirks. So when Benjamin grumbled about Chloe's tardiness, she couldn't help but smile.

But she also knew that families could disappoint. That fathers could leave. That mothers could turn on you. That the sense of acceptance could be misleading. And, of course, she kept her past hidden from them, tucked under a thin veil of lies. A dead mother she didn't want to talk about. A boring childhood that resembled everyone else's.

So she was always slightly on guard when they met.

She placed the cake on the counter in the kitchen and moved on to the dining room. Nathan, Benjamin's father, stood by the large dining table, placing napkins by each plate. He was a bit stooped, looking tired. Benjamin had been worried lately about his dad, whose age seemed to be catching up with him.

"Hi, Nathan." Gemma went over to him and gave him a quick hug.

"Hey, Gemma. Chloe is a bit late."

"Joyce told us. Wow, what a nice table you set!"

"Yes, well." Nathan gave a forced chuckle. "It *is* Joyce's birthday."

He seemed nervous, probably worried about getting the birthday right. Joyce always ascribed a high importance to birthdays and went out of her way to celebrate them with something special. But of course, that meant that when it was her birthday, someone else had to take charge.

Gemma asked him how his last fishing trip went, which seemed to loosen him up a bit. Benjamin and Lucas joined them as he talked about it, which was lucky. Unlike Benjamin, Gemma didn't really care about fishing and never knew what to ask other than "How many fish did you catch," and "What was the size of the biggest one." But Benjamin and Nathan could talk for hours about bait, and fishing gear, and techniques.

After a while, there was a knock on the door. Joyce's voice announced the newcomers. "Chloe! Alvin! Savannah! Madeline! Jonathan!"

And then, as usually happened when four children occupied one room, things became somewhat noisier and more chaotic. Savannah, Chloe's middle child, in particular, always shouted when excited, and she became excited often. As Chloe and her husband stepped in, hugging, kissing, exchanging pleasantries, they all had to talk just a bit louder, to overcome the noise the kids made.

"Benjamin, guess who I ran into at the mall," Chloe said, holding her baby, Jonathan, in her arms.

"Who?"

"Come on, guess."

"I'm not gonna guess. Just tell me."

"Aydin, your old school buddy." Chloe waggled her eyebrows.

"Who's Aydin?" Gemma asked.

"Aydin!" Benjamin blurted. "Seriously? Hang on . . . Was he wearing the hat?"

Chloe giggled. "He was not wearing the hat."

"Who's Aydin?" Gemma asked again.

Chloe grinned at Gemma. "He was Benjamin's *best* friend."

"He was *not*," Benjamin said. "Don't listen to her. So what was he doing there?"

Despite his constant complaints about Chloe, the moment Benjamin and his sister were in the same room, Gemma could instantly feel their love for each other. When they talked, their mannerisms would change, almost as if they reverted to the kids they were, all those years ago. Rolling their eyes at something Nathan said. Exchanging private jokes that no one understood except them. Talking about childhood friends, or shared moments. Just like the conversation about the aforementioned Aydin, they were happy to include others in their discussions, but it was like joining someone watching a movie in the middle. Often, Gemma and Alvin, Chloe's husband, would find themselves silently listening in on the conversation, exchanging looks of their own. The forgotten spouses.

Gemma never had a sibling. Sometimes she would wonder, if she'd had a brother or a sister, would things have been different? Would they have stood beside her when the world turned on her? Or would they have drifted away, shocked and horrified at what their sister had supposedly done?

". . . so this family came to our door," Nathan was telling everyone as they were eating. "The parents dressed like bread—"

"Like toast," Joyce corrected. "Their costumes looked like pieces of toast. I think they were made of foam. But they could have been cardboard."

"Right. And the kids were dressed like a tomato, avocado, and an egg."

"It wasn't an avocado, it was lettuce."

"I'm pretty sure it was an avocado. And I said—"

"No, it was definitely lettuce."

"Fine. And I said—"

"Savannah!" Chloe called in frustration. "Look at this mess."

"I'll go get some paper towels," Joyce said.

"I want juice," Madeline piped.

"Ask nicely," Alvin admonished.

"Mommy, can I also have juice?" Lucas asked.

"Okay, sweetie," Gemma murmured, helping Chloe to clean up.

"So what did you say, Dad?" Benjamin asked.

"What?" Nathan frowned. "Oh . . . never mind. It wasn't that funny."

Stories told, interrupted, discarded in the middle. Another favorite Foster family pastime. Very different from Gemma's childhood dinners, where you weren't allowed to intrude when someone else was talking, and were constantly reminded to use your indoor voice. Probably the Fosters had it right. But it could have been nice to occasionally have a five-minute-long discussion without being interrupted a dozen times.

Gemma focused on the food. Alvin's roast was delicious. And Joyce had made asparagus just for her. Two years before, Gemma had mistakenly told Joyce that the asparagus was really good, and since that fateful day, Joyce would point out she made Gemma's favorite dish—asparagus. Benjamin and Chloe always snickered when she did that, and Benjamin would constantly ask Gemma if she wanted any more asparagus. It's not that Gemma didn't like the damn vegetable, but it wasn't even in her top fifty favorite dishes. Still, she always obliged and ate some.

"Mommy, don't forget my drawing," Madeline whined.

"Oh, right!" Chloe said. "Mom, Madeline made a drawing for your birthday."

A paper was brought out and shown to the table. A three-legged horse.

"It's wonderful," Joyce gushed. "I'll hang it on the fridge."

Gemma bristled. The fridge already had three drawings by Madeline, and two by Savannah. Zero drawings by Lucas. And it wasn't like he didn't bring his grandparents drawings. He probably brought more than both his cousins. But for some reason, Lucas's drawings were placed in a drawer somewhere, while Chloe's girls had *their* drawings put on the fridge. And Lucas's drawings were just as good as Savannah's. And *he* knew how many legs a horse had. So.

But there was no way to bring this up. It would sound like the pettiest complaint in the world. Listen, Joyce, I counted the drawings on your fridge, and I have to say . . . No, there was no way. She just hoped Lucas didn't notice the discrepancy. She made it a point to hang his drawings all over the fridge at home.

"I think it's time for the cake!" Chloe said after they'd cleared away the dishes.

"Gemma baked the cake herself," Benjamin said.

"Oh, darling, you shouldn't have," Joyce said.

"I had some help." Gemma smiled.

It hadn't felt like she shouldn't have. Gemma was always worried Joyce and Nathan didn't think much of their son's choice of a wife. For sure, Alvin was a much more impressive in-law, him being a doctor and all. And Gemma knew she didn't help herself by constantly avoiding Joyce's personal questions. So when she could, she did her best to demonstrate she was an important part of this family. That was why she'd insisted on bringing the cake. The fact that she ended up baking it herself was an added bonus.

She brought the cake to the table. It really did look good, thanks to Barbara's expertise. A deep-brown cake drenched in dark chocolate ganache and decorated with curvy chocolate curls and strawberries. No candles, because in the Foster family, only children got candles on their birthday cake—a law that had been proclaimed years prior to Gemma's joining the family.

Everyone gushed, with Madeline and Savannah arguing who would get the first slice. Then Chloe reminded them that first they had to sing "Happy Birthday" to Grandma. Savannah instantly began singing, with Madeline and Lucas muttering some of the words off-key. Gemma and Chloe sang as well, but Nathan, Benjamin, and Alvin just stood and smiled awkwardly. Because singing "Happy Birthday" wasn't manly or something, Gemma was never sure.

After the song had dutifully been sung, Gemma hurried back to the kitchen to get a knife. She couldn't find any proper knives to cut the cake with in the drawer, or in the dishwasher.

"Everything okay?" Chloe asked, joining her in the kitchen.

"I need a knife," Gemma said, checking the dirty dishes in the sink.

Chloe opened the same drawer Gemma had already looked through. "Mom! Where are all the knives?"

Joyce joined them in the kitchen and opened the same drawer. "I guess they're all in the dishwasher."

"They aren't, I checked."

"Oh, for heaven's sake." She checked the other drawers.

"What is it?" Nathan asked.

"I think Eva put all our knives in the wrong drawer when she cleaned here yesterday. I guess we can cut with a regular knife."

"Nah, it will ruin the cake. I'll get one," Nathan said.

He left the room. Joyce, Gemma, and Chloe kept looking, but couldn't find where the cleaning lady had placed the knives. Joyce muttered something and left the kitchen. A second later, she called out, "No, Nathan, we're not cutting the cake with your fishing knife."

"It's brand new," Nathan said. "It's clean."

"Oh God." Chloe sighed and left the kitchen.

Gemma followed her. Everyone in the dining room was watching Nathan as he was leaning forward, about to cut the cake with a sharp-looking folding knife. Gemma was worried about the safety of her cake. She doubted Nathan had the skill to slice a cake with a regular kitchen knife, not to mention a folding fishing knife.

"Here, let me," she said, reaching for it.

"I can do it," Nathan snapped.

Gemma didn't respond. She hardly heard him. Her eyes stayed locked on the blade he held in his hand.

She'd seen this knife before. In fact, she'd bought the exact same one herself. It was the knife that killed Victoria Howell.

Chapter 11

It's just a knife.

Gemma couldn't pry her eyes off the knife as it cut through the cake, making large slices for the kids, a thinner slice for Joyce, and one slice for Chloe and Alvin to share because Chloe was on a diet.

It's just a knife.

"Gemma?" Benjamin said.

"Uh . . . What?"

"Do you want one?"

He was handing her a small plate with a cake slice. The cake she'd been so proud of. The one she and Barbara made yesterday, licking the leftover ganache from their fingers. And now that same cake had been stabbed . . .

Sliced. Not stabbed. Sliced.

. . . by Nathan's fishing knife that was similar . . .

Not similar. Identical. But it's just a knife.

. . . to the one she had purchased thirteen years before. "I didn't know you were interested in fishing," her friend had said to her. "Not fishing," she'd answered. "Cutting."

"Gemma? Hello? Do you want cake?"

"No . . . I . . . I'm full."

It's probably a common knife. Sold in any store.

"This cake is incredible," Chloe said, her mouth full. "Gemma, you're doomed."

"What?" Gemma blurted.

"From now on, you'll be baking cakes for all our family dinners. You know that, right?"

"Oh." Gemma tried to smile. "Yeah."

Nathan got up from the table. "Be back in a bit. I just have to wash my knife."

He left for the kitchen. Gemma gazed at the dining table, feeling as if she was sinking. She could hardly breathe. One of the kids was asking for a second slice. Someone said something, and someone else laughed. All the voices merged together, and she couldn't untangle them.

She got up, thinking of rushing to the toilet, shutting herself in there, to get her shit together.

But instead, she followed Nathan to the kitchen.

He stood by the sink, the water running. He was holding the knife under the tap, staring at it as water ran down the chocolate-stained blade. Gemma gently shut the door behind her.

He turned around. "Oh, Gemma." His eyes darted to the closed door.

"Hey, Nathan," she said, trying to sound casual. Did he notice how her muscles clenched? How loud her breathing was? "That's quite a knife."

"Oh, right." He shut off the water, even though the knife was still smeared with chocolate.

"Where did you get it?" she asked.

He took a deep breath and didn't answer for a few seconds. Then he said, "I bought the knife in a fishing store, in a little town called Crumville."

It was like being punched in the gut. She had to lean on the nearby wall to steady herself.

"The guy at the store said they've been selling this model for the past thirteen years," Nathan continued. "It's very popular." His voice was strangely monotone. Dry. Dead.

"Thirteen years," Gemma whispered.

"Its serrated blade is really good for slicing through flesh and bone."

No. Nonononononono. She was hallucinating again. This was all in her mind. Her subconscious misfiring, the result of years of fear and guilt.

He frowned and cleared his throat. "I mean, the guy at the store told me its serrated blade is really good for slicing through flesh and bone. It's probably more painful than a plain blade. But the fish don't care. It's not like they're alive when I cut them."

She tried to turn and leave, but her feet were planted to the floor. Water dripped from the blade in Nathan's hand, spattering on the floor. He didn't seem to notice. His face was twisted in an expression she'd never seen on him before. Fear? Anger?

"But you know that, right? You bought a knife like this one too," he said. "Did it cut smoothly when you used it?"

Did it? "I never . . . I don't . . . ," she tried, the words dying on her lips.

"You probably don't have yours anymore. Do you want this one?" He held it out for her.

She let out a frightened sob, flattening herself against the kitchen door.

Nathan frowned. "Gemma, are you okay?" His voice had lost that strange flatness from before. He sounded like Nathan again.

"Why did you say those things?" Gemma blurted.

"What things?"

"About that knife." Tears clouded her vision.

"I didn't say anything." He tried to sound surprised. But she could hear the strain in his words. He was lying. And that strange expression was still there. As if he was disgusted, or horrified.

"You did! You said I had one. I never had one."

"Why would you have one? It's a fishing knife." He took a step toward her, the knife still held toward her.

She fumbled for the door handle.

"Gemma?" He frowned.

She yanked the door open and stumbled away, into the dining room. She pivoted, staring around her. Everyone was talking and laughing. Savannah had chocolate smeared all over her face. Lucas was still eating his slice, looking pleased. It all seemed so surreal.

"Benjamin," she croaked. "I need to go home."

"What?" he turned to her, surprised. "It's still early."

"I don't feel well. I need to go."

"Mom was just about to show us what Dad got for her."

"Come on, Lucas," she told her son. "Put your jacket on."

"Let him finish his cake," Chloe said. "Maybe you can lie down for a bit. Do you want some tea?"

"I don't want tea!" Gemma yelled. "I want to go!"

Nathan stepped out of the kitchen, looking confused. Gemma took a step away from him. The knife wasn't in his hands.

"What's up with her?" he asked. "We were just talking in the kitchen, and she suddenly freaked out."

"We weren't just talking," Gemma spit. "You were talking about your knife."

"Right," Nathan said. "Okay. I might have said something about my knife."

"He's very proud of it," Joyce interjected. "He showed it to me earlier this week."

"Lucas!" Gemma raised her voice. "Come on! Put on your jacket. We're leaving."

"What the hell is wrong with you, Gemma?" Benjamin asked.

They were all looking at her as if she was a crazy person. Maybe she was.

Her lips trembled. If she stayed there for one more minute, she would die. "I just really need to go home," she whispered.

Chapter 12

Benjamin clenched his jaw tightly as he drove, accelerating just a bit faster than he should. This was something he did when he was angry, his driving becoming erratic—flooring the gas pedal, then braking sharply when needed. It was gratifying to listen to the engine roar, as if it was an extension of his own mood.

He glanced at Gemma for a brief second. She was staring out the window, facing away from him. But by the rigid way she held herself, he knew his driving bothered her. Well, she'd have to deal. If she wanted to drive, she could easily say so, but she never did.

Her behavior tonight was almost insane. Dave, from Benjamin's office, often complained about his own wife—how irrational she was, how hysterical. Benjamin knew *hysterical* was an old-fashioned word, a way for men to describe women's anger, to make it seem like a feminine weakness.

But frankly, was there any other way to describe Gemma's behavior?

He knew his dad's fishing stories often bored her; she'd told him that. And earlier that evening, he'd come in while his dad was talking her ear off about fishing. Maybe it annoyed her more than she let on. And then, when his dad had talked about fishing again later, she'd lost it.

But like . . . completely lost it.

Here's another thing Dave liked saying: "It must be that time of the month." Benjamin never said that. Well, okay, he'd said that to Gemma just *once*, a few months after they started dating. And it actually *was* that time of the month, so he hadn't been technically wrong. But he'd learned his lesson, and he never said that again, not even to Dave. But he now wondered if maybe it was that time of the month. Maybe when Gemma had her period, she just couldn't stand listening to fishing tales.

That was probably it. It actually made a lot of sense.

Well, she could have tried to say something. Or just changed the subject. She shouldn't have been so hysterical about it.

His eyes flicked to the rearview mirror. Lucas sat in the back seat, hunched and miserable. Benjamin wanted to put him at ease. Nothing tonight was their son's fault.

"You okay back there, champ?" he asked. Except his tone was all wrong. He wanted to sound cheerful and laid back, but he was too tense, and his voice was raw, furious.

Lucas hunched further into his seat. "Yeah," he said meekly.

Benjamin was pissed at himself. And this made him angrier at Gemma. They'd been having such a nice evening.

He drove the rest of the way home in silence, the engine roaring and growling for him.

Once they got home, he marched inside, letting Gemma take care of Lucas. As she put their boy in bed, Benjamin sat in the living room, fuming. His mom had sent him a text, saying she hoped everything was all right. That made him even angrier than before. He listened to Gemma and Lucas as she put him to sleep. She could let the boy do it himself for once. She didn't have to go through this whole ceremony. Pj's, brushing his teeth, kissing him good night. What would happen if Lucas didn't brush his teeth one evening? Would it be the end of the world? Would an army of germs seize the opportunity, drilling dozens of cavities in their son's molars because of *one* single night?

He knew he was being ridiculous, but it still annoyed him. Lucas sounded extra whiny that night, too, asking for repeated kisses because the first one didn't take.

Gemma coddled him too much.

Okay, here's the thing.

Benjamin loved every single thing about Gemma.

He usually loved how she doted on their son. And he loved the mysterious way her mind worked. He loved how independent she was, and her sharp sense of humor, and that she was way smarter than him. God, he loved how she looked, somehow managing to be both delicate and sexy. During the day, when he thought of Gemma, he would find himself smiling. He didn't talk to his friends about Gemma a lot, because he'd found out that when he talked, they rolled their eyes. Men were supposed to complain about their spouses, not worship them—that was part of the male code. But he couldn't help it; Gemma was his dream girl.

It's just that right now, he was pissed. And suddenly, all those things he usually loved about her seemed to annoy him.

So he tried to remind himself to cool off before she finished putting Lucas to sleep. Because he didn't really want to argue. He just wanted to talk about tonight. To tell her that if his dad's stories annoyed her (during that time of the month, but he wouldn't mention *that*), she could change the subject. She didn't have to react so hysterically.

He wouldn't use the word *hysterically* either.

He knew from experience that conversations with Gemma could vary, depending on how he started them. He wasn't as verbal as she was, so he had to plan what he was about to say before she came to the living room. He would just ask her what happened at his parents' house. That would be a good way to start a conversation, right? Hey, Gemma, what happened in my parents' house? He mouthed it a few times, trying to unclench his jaw.

When she finally came to the living room, he was ready.

"Do you mind telling me what that was back in my parents' house?" he asked.

How could he mess that single sentence up? He instantly knew he asked it all wrong, because blotches of red colored Gemma's cheeks, and her eyes narrowed to slits.

"I wasn't feeling well, Benjamin. Is that okay?" Her voice was like iron, each word shaped into a sharp barb.

Now he was getting angry all over again. Or maybe he never stopped being angry. "Bullshit, Gemma. You were acting like a total basket case. Yelling at my dad about his fishing stories, screaming at Lucas—"

"I didn't scream at Lucas—"

"Yes, you did. You should have seen yourself. My mom already sent me a worried text asking if they said something wrong during dinner."

"Well, I'm sorry if my feeling shitty made your *mother* feel uncomfortable. And I'm really glad to see your priorities are straight. You didn't even bother to ask me how I was feeling."

Well, that wasn't fair. He wasn't even allowed to mention that time of the month. "I just did!"

"No you didn't! You just made it a point to accuse me of ruining dinner. Which I *didn't*. We were about to leave anyway."

"No we weren't. Mom was about to show us Dad's present, and I wanted some coffee. We never leave so fast after dinner, and you know that."

"Fine! I made you miss coffee. Happy now?"

"What's wrong with you?" he asked, confused. For the life of him, he couldn't figure out why she was that angry. *He* was the one who was supposed to feel angry, not her.

She folded her arms. "Oh, now you ask me? All week I've been stressed. I don't think there was a single day I didn't cry, but you never once asked me what was wrong. Only when I make a scene that embarrassed you—"

"What are you talking about? When you told me you were tired the other day, I instantly told you I'd help."

"Yes, I had to *tell* you. I had to spell it out for you. It would be nice if you noticed things yourself for a change."

"Gemma, I'm not telepathic. If you have a problem, you need to tell me—"

"I did! I told you I couldn't go trick-or-treating with Lucas."

Seriously? They were talking about *this* again? "Just because you have a weird problem with Halloween doesn't mean you can't do a bit of trick-or-treating."

They were both shouting now. They almost never shouted.

"A weird problem with Halloween? Something really terrible happened to me during Halloween. Does that explain my *weird problem?*" Her lips trembled, her eyes misting.

Benjamin froze. She'd never mentioned that before. He felt sick. "I . . . I am sorry, you never said—"

"You never asked."

"That's not true. I asked about it once, but you changed the subject, and didn't seem like you wanted to talk about it. I didn't want to pressure you." His heart thumped. He lowered his voice. "What happened?"

For a moment she opened her mouth, about to say something. Then she clamped it shut. After a few seconds she hissed, "Oh, now you care?"

"Of course I care—"

"You only care about yourself. When I was freaking out on Monday, all you could talk about was your promotion. And when I told you I wasn't well, you didn't even think of asking me what was wrong."

He shot to his feet. "You never *answer* when I ask what's wrong!" He was yelling again. "Even now, Gemma! What the hell happened this evening? You flipped out about some fishing story of my dad's. What's that all about?"

"Your dad was saying some weird stuff about his knife, okay? It freaked me out."

"Weird stuff?" He blinked, incredulous. "Like what?"

"Like how it cuts bone and flesh. He was really weird about it."

"It's a fishing knife! My dad is obsessed with fishing. You're the one acting weird!"

"Thanks again for the support."

He couldn't. He just couldn't. "I can't talk to you when you're this way." He strode past her to the front door and yanked it open. He hesitated, knowing he should go back, try to fix this. She was about to tell him something. Something important.

He stepped outside, slamming the door behind him.

Chapter 13

Gemma stood in the living room, staring at where Benjamin had stood, thinking of all the comebacks she could have said. She was trembling. In anger? Fear? A bit of both.

"Mommy?" Lucas's voice came from his bedroom.

She shut her eyes in frustration. Great. Benjamin's tantrum had woken Lucas up. In the manner of all aggrieved husbands everywhere, Benjamin left her to deal with Lucas alone, while he sulked.

She went over to Lucas's room. He sat in his bed, blinking in confusion.

"What were you shouting about?" he asked.

"I'm sorry we woke you up. Mommy and Daddy were just arguing a bit."

"Oh."

"You can go back to sleep."

"I'm all itchy."

She sighed. "Okay. Let me rub some lotion on you."

She gently applied the lotion on Lucas's inflamed skin. Where did Benjamin go? She hoped he didn't take the car. She didn't want him driving when he was angry. She shouldn't have yelled at him. She and Benjamin had an agreement—even if they argued, they never went to sleep angry. They always hashed it out before going to bed. Gemma didn't see this happening tonight.

But then again, she wasn't sure *anything* was going to be the same after tonight.

That knife. That damn knife. The events at the end of the dinner seemed almost surreal. She'd actually pinched her thigh a few times, just to make sure she wasn't having a weird nightmare. Nathan's words seemed . . . impossible. She simply couldn't figure out what could have made him say *any* of that. Even if he'd found out about her past, why bring it up like *this*? Nathan was a straight shooter, sometimes a bit too much. If he'd found out, he would have said just that. Gemma, someone told me your name is actually Theodora, and that you ran away from home. Or maybe, Gemma, did you kill another girl when you were younger?

And afterward he wouldn't have pretended it didn't happen. There was absolutely no way.

Also . . . it didn't look as if he knew. There was no accusation in his voice, or his expression. In fact, there wasn't *anything* in his voice. Just a weird monotonic speech. It was a bit similar to how that woman talked, during the trick-or-treating. Which made Gemma think she was hallucinating again. Except there was no explanation this time. No exhaustion. It wasn't the anniversary of Victoria's death anymore. Which meant there had to be another reason. And this led Gemma to try and figure it all out again, a spiraling thought process that went nowhere.

It scared her. And Benjamin's anger made her tense. And Lucas's unhappiness made her anxious and guilty. All those emotions swept through her, until she felt she was about to scream, or punch the wall.

But she just kept applying the lotion on Lucas, then rubbed his back, his breathing becoming heavier as he settled back into sleep.

Gemma and Benjamin's arguments almost never went so badly. Loud arguments reminded her of the days before her dad left. They frightened her. And when she was scared, she was never in control. She lashed out. Which was probably why she'd said those things to Benjamin.

That damn knife. Was it the same one? The knife she'd bought all those years ago, a few days before Halloween?

"I'm just saying," Steve said. "*Kill Bill* is the ultimate revenge movie. First of all, any revenge becomes better when a katana is involved. Second, there's the movie's soundtrack, which is unbeatable. Third—"

"Third, it's long," Theo interrupted him. "Way too long. It could have been one movie instead of two."

"You're crazy," Steve said. "There's no such thing as too much Uma Thurman kicking ass. If anything, it could have been longer. Back me up here, Allan."

"I'm with Theo on this one," Allan said.

The three of them were walking back from school. Theo's mom finally forced her to go to school, despite her feigned illness. It was, if anything, worse than Theo had expected it to be. The whispers, the mocking laughs, the printed copies of the photo of her wet face . . . it all hounded her. But worst of all was the fear. Donna had stridden over to her at lunch and pointed out it looked like the facial treatment didn't take. Then she suggested they could repeat it. Maybe a weekly treatment would do the trick.

Theo did her best to make sure there was a teacher in sight throughout the day. She avoided going to the bathroom. She tried not to cry.

At least Steve and Allan still hung around her. Made sure to be together as much as possible. Strength in numbers and all that. They knew how she felt. They went through their own personal hell in school. Steve never changed clothes in the locker room anymore, and Theo didn't ask why. Allan still limped from his latest encounter, a few days before.

The matter of revenge arose as they walked home. Steve was obsessed with it. The things Theo could do to get back at Victoria. She could break into Victoria's house at night and cut off all her hair while she slept. Or she could frame her by buying pot and planting it in Victoria's locker. Or drug Victoria and write the word *bitch* on her forehead with a permanent marker while she was unconscious. Ludicrous ideas. The suggestions only made Theo tired and depressed. Why did Steve think this would help?

And then they began talking about revenge movies.

"*Carrie* is a better revenge movie than *Kill Bill*," Allan said.

"Oh, come on." Steve snorted. "First of all, it's all based on supernatural powers, which isn't exactly practical."

"Uma Thurman killing people with a katana is practical?" Theo asked, raising her eyebrows.

"And second of all, a good revenge shouldn't be over fast. You have to have a good plan and take your time. Uma Thurman makes a plan. She actually got a special sword made—"

"Some plan," Allan muttered.

"Shut up, it's an awesome plan. And then she killed them one by one. They actually had to split the movie because of how long it takes. Carrie just kills everyone straight after they drench her in that bucket of blood. Where's the satisfaction in that?"

"Fine," Theo said, desperate to change the subject. She wanted to go home and lie in bed. She was already planning how she'd stay home tomorrow. Mom would have to drag her physically to make her go to school.

"What's your favorite revenge plot, Theo?" Steve asked.

"I don't know."

"Come on. Choose one. *Carrie, Kill Bill, The Crow*—"

"*The Count of Monte Cristo.*"

"Ugh. It's such a boring movie."

Theo rolled her eyes. "I actually didn't see the movie. I'm talking about the book? You know books?"

"I've heard of them. But which movie . . ."

She didn't hear the rest of the sentence. Something had caught her eye.

The fishing store had been there for as long as she could remember. She'd gone inside a few times with her dad and had mostly enjoyed looking through the display of the artificial lures. Dozens of lures in all shapes and colors, some with frilly feathers, some looking like real fish. But other than that, the store offered little interest, and after her dad left, she had no good reason to step inside. Until now.

In the display window, next to fishing rods and tackle boxes, a few fishing knives were laid out. All small, and elegant, and sharp. She walked over and gazed through the glass.

"I didn't know you were interested in fishing," Steve said.

"Not fishing," she answered. "Cutting."

After Victoria had posted her video and images online, Theo had gone to the kitchen and found a large knife. Then she went to the bathroom and held the knife to her wrist. Just to see how it would feel.

And for the first time in a long while, she felt in control.

This was one thing she had power over. She had no control over her dad's leaving, or the names people called her, or even if her face should be dunked in a toilet. But right now, she had complete control over her life. She could live, or she could die.

She didn't want to die. Not really. Even if she sometimes felt like she did. But if she wanted to, no one could stop her.

Since then she'd already done it again a bunch of times. Grabbed a knife, went to the bathroom, and imagined cutting herself. She even pressed it just a bit harder once, just to see how much it would hurt. It turned out it would hurt quite a bit. Mom's kitchen knives weren't very sharp, and she had to pull the blade along the skin to draw blood.

But these knives right here? They could cut through anything at the slightest touch.

The knife she finally chose was a bit more expensive than most of them, but she liked that it could fold. She could take it with her in her bag wherever she went. Well, except for the airport, but that never happened anyway. The blade was partially serrated, so if she wanted, she could press those jagged points down, instantly biting into her skin. She already felt a thrill at the feeling of its weight in her jacket pocket.

Steve gave her a weird look when they left. "You're not going to um . . . pull an Uma Thurman, right?"

She blinked in surprise. It took her a moment to realize what he meant. He was such a guy. "Yeah, it's a sequel," she said. *"Kill Victoria."* And she let out a forced laugh.

Because the truth was much darker and scarier. She already imagined how this blade would feel on her wrist.

"That's not funny, Theo," Steve said worriedly.

"Oh, relax. I'm not going to stab Victoria." She rolled her eyes.

Steve and Allan both frowned at her.

"Fine," Steve finally said. "You guys want to go to my place and play *Tekken*?"

"Sure," Allan said.

Theo wasn't even remotely interested. She actually enjoyed playing fighting games on Steve's PlayStation every now and again. Not because she particularly enjoyed the fighting. But she liked the characters. And this was something else she had full control over. She moved the joystick left, and her character walked left. She pressed a button, her character punched. She hit a complex sequence of buttons, and her character threw an unstoppable spinning kick. It was nice. And seeing how excited Steve and Allan were about her playing was fun too. They thought it was the best thing in the world, that a girl played video games. When she first beat Allan, Steve couldn't stop talking about it the entire week. By this point she was definitely better than Allan, though Steve still whipped her most times.

Still, right now it seemed juvenile and pointless. She wanted to go home. She wanted to check out her new knife.

"Not today," she said. "Maybe tomorrow?"

"Okay." Steve was still frowning. "Listen, Theo, seriously, don't do anything stupid. We'll help you get back at Victoria. I swear."

Theo gave him a forced smile. "Sure. Don't worry about it."

Gemma leaned against the wall in her son's room and watched him sleeping. She remembered that day so well. She'd gotten home and went straight to her room, shut the door behind her, then took out the knife.

Three days later, Victoria was dead.

Chapter 14

Detective George Dunn sat in his garage in Crumville and spent the evening drinking beer and obsessing. Which was, to be fair, quite a frequent pastime of his. Practically a hobby. Except most people tended to enjoy their hobbies, while he only felt frustrated by it.

His hobby, his obsession, was the Victoria Howell murder case.

Sure enough, being the detective in charge of the case, it was also his job. Except now, thirteen years later, the chief got impatient if Dunn spent time during the day working on it. There were other things to do in the Crumville PD. There was that dealer who sold weed to the high school students, and the recent burglaries in the eastern part of town, and traffic reports, and paperwork, and the complaints of Walter Felton about the young man who kept discarding cigarette butts on the sidewalk.

So if Detective George Dunn wanted to work on a thirteen-year-old case that had zero new leads in the past decade, he could do it on his own damn time.

Which was why, to his wife's displeasure, Dunn turned his garage into a home office, dedicated to the Victoria Howell murder case. It was directly linked to another case he'd never solved—the Theodora Briggs missing person case.

On the whiteboard in his garage, he'd taped both of their photos next to each other. Victoria Howell was photographed in the Howell backyard, staring at something unseen. Dunn had met Victoria often before she'd died—she had been his daughter, Donna's, best friend. It was a good photo, her blond hair glowing in the sunlight, her expression thoughtful and sweet. But more than anything, it managed to capture a certain sadness that Victoria seemed to carry with her.

The other photo was of Theodora Briggs, and it was almost hard to tell if the photo was bad, or if this was just how Theodora actually looked. In a bland living room, Theodora stared directly at the camera, unsmiling. The light of the camera's flash made Theodora's acne even more pronounced. The only endearing part of her face was her eyes—brown and soft, her eyelashes unusually long.

Those two photos had been taped to the whiteboard for years by now—the closest these two had been ever since their childhood. If what their schoolmates said was true, both of them would balk at knowing that their photos were so close together in his garage. By the time Victoria died, the two girls thoroughly hated each other. Theodora had actually threatened to kill Victoria. And in fact, she probably had. All these years later, Theodora Briggs was still the most likely suspect.

Where was she now? Of all the questions that he needed answered, this was the one that occupied his mind the most. The murder case had a Theodora Briggs–shaped hole, and if he could find her and fill it, perhaps he could finally solve it. Was she in Mexico, working as a waitress? Or maybe, like many in town theorized, she'd managed to somehow flee all the way to Europe and now lived in Paris or Prague. Or possibly, she was long dead. After all, a young girl who fled from home could easily end up dead in a ditch, or an alley, or a motel room. Marked by the local cops as Jane Doe, never to be identified. He'd seen it happen more times than he could count.

Whenever he tried to imagine her whereabouts, he would picture her as she was in the photo—a belligerent seventeen-year-old girl. That's who she was in his mind, frozen in time. But of course, she would be thirty by now. Just like Donna.

Her missing person case was, unlike the Howell murder case, very thin. He knew it by heart. She was reported missing on the twenty-seventh of November 2010, by her mother. She'd taken a bunch of clothes, her toothbrush, and some money. Her bicycle was missing, too, and Dunn had actually found a witness who'd seen a teen in a hoodie riding their bicycle down Crumville's main street a bit after four in the morning.

And that was it. No more witnesses, Theodora's tracks just disappeared. Dunn suspected that she'd been on her way to Augusta. He checked the motels, the hospital, cabdrivers. If anyone had seen her, they didn't recall it happening. Her bicycle never showed up, though he doubted she'd ridden it any farther. From Augusta, she could have easily taken a bus to Atlanta, and from there, to anywhere in the US.

She had no phone with her, and as far as Dunn could tell, she hadn't contacted anyone she knew. For a while he suspected she was living with her biological father, whom he tracked to an address in San Francisco. But her father was remarried, with two children from his second wife, and had shown little interest in his daughter's whereabouts. This, at least, affirmed something that Dunn had heard often in town— Theodora's father was a worthless shit.

They'd never charged her. The chief had pushed him to charge her, but Dunn refused. Too much circumstantial evidence. Too many pieces that didn't fit. A proper defense attorney would have a field day with it—not that Theodora Briggs had one. But also, this being the one and only homicide case Dunn had ever investigated, he didn't want to get it wrong. And eventually, he didn't get it wrong, or right. He didn't get it at all.

Under Victoria's and Theodora's photos, Dunn had taped three additional photos. Three teenage boys.

Zayne Ross had been Victoria's boyfriend at the time of the murder. Smug-looking kid, and he grew into a smug-looking adult. He owned the town's local hardware store. Dunn occasionally bought stuff there.

Steve Barnett and Allan Conner were Theodora's friends. On the night of the murder, they were supposed to hang out with Theodora. Steve had called her six times—the sixth time she'd picked up and hung up just a few seconds later. Steve had told him that she said she couldn't talk.

Nothing conclusively tied any of those boys to the murder. But Dunn's instincts told him that all three boys had lied to him during the investigation. Over the years, Dunn had brought them back to the station to talk several times. But they stuck to their versions of events. If any of them knew where Theodora was, they managed to hide it well.

Underneath those, three more photos—three objects, now all tucked in a box in their station's evidence locker. The murder weapon—a vicious-looking fishing knife that Theodora had bought just three days before the murder. This, more than anything, seemed to indicate premeditation on Theodora's part. Then there was Victoria's bloody jacket, which Theodora had been wearing when they found her. And finally, a silver Halloween mask that was found at the scene of the crime—the mask that Theodora had worn to the party. All these pointed singularly at one person. It had been enough to charge, and possibly convict, Theodora, even without certain pieces of evidence that had not turned up. Then why had Dunn hesitated?

Was it because of his own daughter's role in this story? A role that embarrassed, and disappointed, and scared him? He remembered how horrified he'd been when he'd found out his daughter had bullied this girl. Bullied her so badly that it came to this. Was this why he'd messed up and let Theodora disappear all those years ago? Because he subconsciously wanted her gone, to protect his daughter?

He really didn't know.

Over the years he'd taped more photos onto the board, then took them off, drew timelines and charts, listed motives and alibis and conjectures. But these eight photos had remained constant ever since he moved the case to his garage.

Two girls—one missing, one dead. Three lying boys. Three pieces of condemning evidence.

One open murder case.

Chapter 15

Benjamin wasn't there in the morning, but Gemma knew he'd slept on the living room couch; she'd heard him step inside during the night.

She called in sick, which she never did unless she was truly ill. Then she got Lucas ready for school, forcing an efficient calmness upon herself. She dropped him off, and then drove to the beach and spent the entire morning staring at the soft waves of Lake Michigan.

She felt battered, and helpless, and desperate. But in the midst of all those gravitational emotions that pulled her down, she felt a kernel of something else. A violent, and resistant, urge. It yelled at her to fight, to go down kicking and screaming. It was that same emotion that had driven her all those years ago to leave home and change her name. And it was that same compulsion that had propelled her to go to that fateful Halloween party. It was snarling in her chest right now, a chaotic presence, a drumbeat with no discernible rhythm.

There was no explanation for the things that had happened to her. Too many weird coincidences, too many bizarre conversations. She wasn't going crazy; at least she didn't think so. Not really. So why was this happening? It was like one of those classic tales, where the gods decided to mess with men just because they felt like it. Was that what Oedipus felt like, when he was led to kill his father and marry his mother to fulfill a bizarre prophecy? Or Job, when God stomped over him and his family just to make a point to Satan? Or Bottom, when he was used as a toy in a game between Oberon and Titania?

Gemma had always avoided attention, even as a child. Some people thrived on attention, like orchids did, only demanding more. But some people, she knew, were like weeds, and when they got any attention, it could only be the bad kind. At school, her main consolation was that even if she was called Zit-face, most kids never paid her too much attention. They were too busy trying to hook up with each other, or climbing the social ladder, or living up to the expectations of parents and teachers and friends. And even when they were bullying, they spread their attention in a careless way, over her and Steve and Allan, and half a dozen other unfortunates. She was almost never in the center of people's minds. Except for that terrible week after the bathroom incident. And after the Halloween party.

When she fled, she'd chosen Chicago for exactly that reason. A huge metropolis with millions of other people, where she could disappear, and no one would notice her. And it had worked for thirteen years. Aside from a chosen few, no one really paid her any attention. Until now.

There was no other way to look at it—she was the focus of . . . something. Nathan, and that woman on Halloween, and that woman who walked into Primadonna. They all circled around her, with their little parts in a bizarre play that was all about her. She didn't know how it was possible. Maybe she really was being targeted by the gods. But she preferred to believe there was a better explanation.

She would figure it out. She wasn't about to go down like Oedipus, or Job, or Bottom. She wouldn't lay low until the powers that be tired of her. She would fight back.

When she finally left the beach and drove to school to pick up Lucas, there was a new fire burning in her chest. It made her feel better, stronger. She turned on the radio and that eighties song "Maniac" was playing, which made her grin. Oh yeah, she *was* a maniac.

Lucas seemed in good spirits when she got to his school. He asked why Iris didn't pick him up, and Gemma explained she gave Iris a day off, and then was forced to explain the concept of a day off. As they drove back home, Lucas was telling her about a game they played at school. She half listened, while planning her immediate actions. She would talk to Nathan first. She would manage to find some time during the weekend to talk to him alone, and she would not let up. He *knew* something, she was sure of it. There was a reason why he told her those things, and she intended to find out what it was.

"And they gave us our Halloween masks from the school party to take home," Lucas said.

"That's nice, sweetie."

"You want to see mine?"

"When we get home."

But he was already fiddling with his bag. "Look!"

Gemma sighed and glanced at Lucas in the rearview mirror. A silvery mask, with frilly edges, like the sort aristocrats would wear to a masquerade ball. "It's very pretty."

Lucas put it on. "See?"

Gemma grinned. "Yes. It's very . . . ." Her eyes focused on the mask. She'd seen it before.

She looked ahead just in time to hit the brakes before she rammed into the car in front of her, which had stopped at a red light.

"Ow!" Lucas complained. "That hurt, Mommy."

"Sorry." She was breathing hard. She glanced over her shoulder. "Are you all right?"

"The seat belt hurt my throat."

He seemed fine. He was still wearing that mask.

"Can you give me your mask for a second?"

"But you're driving."

"Just for one second, sweetie. I want to see how pretty it is."

He took off the mask and leaned forward, his tiny arm stretching with the mask between his fingers. She took it and examined it closely. Yes. There was no doubt. Just like the fishing knife, this was another item from the past.

She thought back to Lucas's story. About Princess Victoria and the witch Fedora. Lucas was like Nathan, and like those two women. Playing a part in this weird conspiracy. Except there was no way. He was a little boy. *Her* little boy. There was no way he knew anything about this, and he would *never* in a million years do anything to hurt her.

When he'd introduced the witch's name, and the princess, he'd said something. He'd said, "That's very important."

She'd never heard him use that phrase before. Lucas was a four-year-old. As far as he was concerned, *everything* he said was important.

He said "That's very important" because someone else had told him that. Someone who really wanted Lucas to remember the names of the princess and the witch when he got back home and told his mother about them.

A loud honking startled her. The light was green. The car behind her honked again, waiting for her to drive.

Gemma swerved her car into the left lane. "Lucas, sweetie, we're going back to school, okay? There's something I really need to ask your teacher."

Chapter 16

Lucas's teacher, Paula, was a redhead with a spatter of freckles around her nose and large round glasses that made her look younger than she really was. Gemma suspected Paula was carded every time she bought alcohol and that the cashiers scrutinized her driver's license with skepticism. She was cleaning up for the weekend as they stepped inside, carefully shelving a bunch of children's drawings. She looked up, startled, and her eyes widened as she saw who it was.

"Oh. Mrs. Foster," she said. "I was just about to leave. I need to run an important errand."

"I was hoping to talk to you privately for a few minutes," Gemma said pleasantly. "About this?" She raised her hand, the mask hanging from her finger.

Paula visibly paled. "Oh. Those are the Halloween masks. All the kids got the same—"

"I'd really like to talk about this privately." Gemma smiled. "Lucas, you don't mind waiting here while I talk to Paula, right?"

"Can I play with the color magnets?"

"I'm sure Paula won't mind as long as we put them back before we leave," Gemma said.

"It's just . . . I'm in a hurry," Paula said. "We could talk next week?"

She must have expected Gemma to acquiesce. It was only polite. It was the weekend, after all, and Paula was off the clock. A day earlier

Gemma would have nodded. Of course, next week. Maybe on the phone. You know what, it wasn't that important.

"It will only take a few minutes," Gemma said. "It can't wait." Her smile, if anything, widened.

Paula seemed to wilt. "Okay, we can talk in the back room."

Gemma followed the woman to the back room, which seemed to be partly a small kitchen, partly a storage room. Art supplies, a few puzzle boxes, a stack of Hula Hoops, a first aid kit. Gemma briefly scanned the room, then focused on Paula. The woman seemed about to cry.

Gemma placed the mask on the small counter by an electric kettle. "Why does my son have this?"

"I told you, all the kids got them. They're Halloween masks. We used them for the party. Didn't Lucas—"

"This isn't about Lucas." Gemma gritted her teeth. "Why *this* mask?"

"I don't understand the question." Paula's lips trembled.

"Okay. Let's try another. You told Lucas a story on Tuesday. Remember? About a princess who got the witch's hair wet."

Paula picked up a plastic cup from the counter and fiddled with it. She didn't meet Gemma's eyes.

"Why did you tell him that story? About Princess Victoria and—"

"Do you dream about her," Paula blurted. She spoke so fast that it sounded like "Doyoudreamabouther." It took Gemma a second to understand what she said.

"What?" Gemma asked sharply.

"Do you see her face in your dreams your nightmares still seventeen just like the day she died." Her voice became strange. Not monotone, but fast, panicky. Like she was trying to get through it.

"Paula, what are you talking about?" Gemma snapped.

"Please let me finish, or I'll get it wrong," Paula pleaded, and then began talking fast again. "That's how her parents remember her and her friends the people that loved her, but you don't think about her at all . . ."

She was reciting. The realization hit Gemma like a ton of bricks. She was reciting this from memory. This was why she was talking so strangely. Nathan and that woman on Halloween . . . they had been reciting too. Like actors in a rehearsal, going through their lines.

Let me finish, or I'll get it wrong. In fact, Nathan *had* gotten something wrong when he talked about the knife, and then he'd corrected himself—repeating the exact same sentence, adding just a word or two.

". . . should have been you that day," Paula was saying. She took a long breath. "You think you got away, but you didn't the past is catching up to you, Theodora."

She was breathing hard, trembling, clearly frightened. Gemma stared at her, her heart thumping. For a few seconds, the words swam in her mind, a jumble of confusion and horror. How was it possible? What was going on? Why were they doing this?

Then she gritted her teeth, forced herself to calm down.

"Are you done?" she finally said.

"What?" Paula said.

"Are you done talking?"

"I . . . I didn't say anything."

Gemma let out a forced laugh. "Oh no. This isn't happening. I know you did. And *you* know you did, so don't try to gaslight me. You just monologued for quite a while."

"What are you talking about—"

Gemma slapped the plastic cup out of Paula's hands, and it clattered on the floor. "Don't," she hissed. "It sounds like you know who I really am, so you should know what happened to the last person that messed with me."

Paula sobbed. Gemma felt zero sympathy.

"You are going to tell me what's going on right now," she said. "You'll tell me why you told Lucas that story, and why you gave him that mask. And you're going to tell me why you just recited all that rot to me. And if you don't start talking, I'll make your life a living hell.

Look at me when I'm talking to you. Look at me right now and tell me if I'm not serious."

"Please . . . ," Paula whispered. "I can't."

"You can, and you will." Gemma had no idea what she would do if Paula didn't talk right now. After all, she talked big, but she wasn't going to hurt Paula. She wasn't going to call the police, or even tell a single soul about this. But she also knew she couldn't leave this room without knowing what was going on.

"He said I can't tell anyone about this. If he finds out—"

"It's just the two of us here. I won't tell anyone. *Who* told you not to tell anyone about this?"

"I don't know. The guy, the one who wrote me the emails with all the instructions. Who told me what I had to do."

So. The gods weren't messing with Gemma after all. But someone definitely was.

Chapter 17

Paula was having a hard time meeting Gemma's eyes. The intense ferocity in them jolted something in Paula's mind, unearthing all those emotions and thoughts she'd been burying for the past year. Guilt. Humiliation. Hurt.

Paula was used to handling angry parents. She prided herself on not being a pushover, for standing behind her beliefs and ideals. But Gemma was different. Perhaps, because for the first time, Paula was facing a mother who was right. Whose son Paula really did, in a way, compromise.

"What guy are you talking about? What instructions?" Gemma asked. Voice cold, hard, like steel. In the past, whenever Paula talked to Gemma, she'd always been so gentle. So kind.

"He was the one who told me to do the story," Paula tried to explain. "And the mask. And to say those things to you right now." She was scared to talk about it. Terrified.

"How much does he pay you?"

"He doesn't pay me. He . . ." Paula shut her eyes. How could she even explain it? "Look, I just do those things because he tells me to, okay?"

"What, he hypnotized you?"

"No, of course not."

"What's his name?" Gemma asked impatiently.

"I don't know," Paula pleaded. She hoped Gemma would see how scared she was and just . . . let it be. It wasn't a big deal, right? A story, a mask given to the kids on Halloween.

But she knew it *was* a big deal. Even if she didn't know why.

Gemma stared at her intently, and then, after a few seconds, let out a long breath. "Okay. Why don't we start at the beginning."

Paula didn't say anything for a few seconds. She wiped her eyes with the back of her hand and looked at Gemma. Lucas's mother was always so pretty, so immaculate. She dressed in a way that was both elegant, but also somehow seemed effortless. Perfect makeup, perfect fingernails. But now, something had loosened within her. Her hair was just a bit messier than usual, her eyes were flaring, her entire body was tense and poised as if to pounce. It was like watching a beautiful predator, and then realizing it was loose from its cage.

Gemma rolled her eyes at Paula's silence, then raised one finger. She opened the door, peeking through it.

"Lucas, sweetie, everything okay?" Gemma asked.

"Yeah." Lucas's voice came from the other room.

"Do you need to go to the bathroom?"

"No."

"Paula and I will talk a bit more, okay?"

"Okay."

Gemma shut the door and turned back to Paula.

"He likes those magnets," Paula said softly. "Almost everyone does. The kids are always fighting over who gets to play with them."

"Uh-huh," Gemma said.

"He's probably happy he can play with them alone. These magnets are great, you know, they're really good for kids' developmental—"

"I don't give a damn about magnetic tiles." Gemma's voice was low, coming out as a growl. "I want to hear about the guy who told you to mess with me."

"He never told me to mess with you," Paula said defensively.

"Just tell me everything, from the start."

Paula's lips trembled, and a tear trickled down her cheek. From the start? When had it been the start? It was so difficult to pinpoint when it had actually started.

Gemma leaned against the door and folded her arms. It was clear Paula wasn't going anywhere until she talked.

Paula sighed. Fine. From the absolute start. "Do you know what OnlyFans is?"

Gemma frowned. "Yeah, it's this porn site, right?"

"It's not porn," Paula said, anger and embarrassment washing over her. "It's a platform for content creators. They can upload content and charge a subscription, or payments, for stuff. And yes, some of it is porn, but some of it is nude photos, or just revealing photos, or—"

"I get the gist."

"A few years ago, during the pandemic, I created an OnlyFans account," Paula blurted. "There was no school, and I needed money, and I guess I was also bored and lonely, and it felt like something I could do."

What was Gemma thinking of her? Sometimes Paula tried to recall what went through her own mind as she'd done it. It was like thinking about a different person. Back then, during the quarantines, other people were abstractions, voices on the phone or random texts sent at random times. Days melded into each other. Her decision to post nude photos online didn't feel like something real. They were digital photos, for digital people.

"There were all those articles, you know?" she continued. "About some nobody from nowhere who started an account and was suddenly earning hundreds of thousands of dollars."

Gemma nodded.

"So I started this account," Paula said. "It's not as easy as they make it sound. You have to do some aggressive marketing, and there are real creeps out there. I did it for a while, but it made me feel uncomfortable, and I didn't make as much as I thought I would."

All in all she made $750. Hardly the imaginary luxury life she'd imagined she'd step into.

"Okay," Gemma said, raising an eyebrow. Paula could almost see the gears turn in Gemma's mind. The woman could see where this was going.

"So I deleted my account. And that was that. The pandemic ended, and I got the job here, and met a really nice guy, and didn't think much of it." Paula swallowed. "Until I got an email, about six months ago."

Gemma exhaled, as if she was expecting this. "What did the email say?"

Paula blinked a tear away, the memory of that email flickering in her mind. Her gut plunging as she read it. As she looked at the attached photos. "It had a bunch of images attached. From my OnlyFans account. The one I deleted. And the guy said he knew who I was. He wrote down my name, my address, where I worked, my boyfriend's name, my parents' names . . . like everything. He knew *everything*. He said if I didn't do exactly what he told me to, he would send the photos to my parents, and my boyfriend, and the school, and all the parents in the school . . . well, to the entire world, basically."

"And what did he ask you to do?"

"That's the thing, he didn't really want much. Like, he'd ask for me to send him a picture of me holding a pan."

Gemma blinked. "Holding a pan?"

"Yeah."

"Like . . . a nude picture? Was it a weird fetish or something?"

"No. Just like, an ordinary picture. Or he'd ask for a video where I sing the theme song from *Dora the Explorer*. Just totally random stuff. So I figured I could go with it, right? I mean . . . the alternative was too awful to even consider. I would have done a lot more if he asked. Like, I would have paid him or whatever. But for a few months, that's all he asked."

"Right." Gemma looked confused.

"And then he asked for some more difficult stuff. He'd ask me to go to a stranger and act as if I was their sister and record the entire thing. A few times he asked me to steal stuff from stores. Candy, shoes. Always very specific. And he also asked for . . . nude photos, and videos. But he had my OnlyFans stuff anyway, so I figured I might as well send him whatever he wanted, as long as he stayed quiet."

Gemma didn't totally get it; it was clear on her face. Well, Paula hadn't understood it at the time. It took her months and months to figure out the humiliating truth. The guy had been *training* her. Training her to follow all his instructions without questioning them. At first it had been as if her life were a long drive, with her behind the wheel and him as a passenger, giving her directions every now and again. At what point had she pulled over and switched with him, letting him take the wheel? She didn't know.

One time, she didn't follow the instructions to the letter. He'd told her to send him a video of her eating a hamburger, and she wasn't hungry, so she just sent a video of her eating toast. The next day, one of the kids' fathers had approached her and whispered a friend had sent him some of her old OnlyFans photos. But she didn't have to worry. Her secret was safe with him.

She followed the instructions she'd gotten after that. To the letter.

She wasn't going to explain it to Gemma. The whole thing was humiliating enough.

"And then he asked me to tell the kids this story, about the witch Theodora and the princess Victoria," Paula said. "I had to memorize the entire thing and send him a recording of me telling it to the kids."

It was the first time he'd asked her to do something at school. But it had seemed innocuous enough. The story wasn't any worse than other stories they told the kids.

"And then . . ." Paula took another shuddering breath. "He wanted me to go and make sure Lucas told his mother the story at home. In particular, it was really important that Lucas remembered the names."

"He mentioned Lucas by name?" Gemma's jaw clenched.

"Yes," Paula admitted. "So I did it. To tell you the truth, I didn't even give it much thought. He's asked for weirder things before."

"Weirder things . . . with the kids?" Gemma asked, recoiling.

"No!" Paula was aghast. "Just me. I would never do anything that might hurt the kids. Sure, I told them this story, but it was just a fairy tale. It's not worse than 'Little Red Riding Hood,' with the wolf that swallows the grandmother whole, right?"

"Fine."

"He also said if Lucas's mother came by to ask about the story, I should tell you . . . the things I told you. I had to memorize it all, and to get it right. He made it clear that if I didn't get it right, there would be consequences."

She'd blurted out the entire thing as much as she could. Almost forgot half of it when Gemma had interrupted her.

"He also sent me a package with those masks and told me to hand them out to the kids at Halloween," Paula said. "The principal was actually thrilled at my initiative. I saw no harm in it. Why would anyone care about some mask?"

She still had no idea why Gemma reacted so badly at seeing the mask. Paula had inspected the masks before handing them to the kids, but they really were just cheap Halloween masks, nothing to get excited about.

"So you don't know . . . anything. About why he asked these things?" Gemma asked.

"No. I didn't think there was a reason." At some point she stopped wondering about his instructions. At some point it had become easier to blindly follow them.

"That thing with Theodora," Gemma pressed. "You don't know what it means?"

"No. He just told me to say those things and to later pretend I didn't say them at all, to act as if it was only your imagination."

"I see."

"You can't tell anyone about this," Paula said, her heart hammering. "If he finds out I told you, he'll send those pictures to everyone. I'll lose my job . . . and my boyfriend will . . . will . . . and my dad . . ." The consequences were too horrific to imagine. It would *destroy* her.

"I won't tell anyone," Gemma hurriedly said. "Can you show me some of his emails?"

"I always delete them after I do them, but I can forward you the one with the thing I had to tell you? Because I wasn't sure I'd remember it, so I kept it, just to refresh my memory."

"Okay . . . He never said his name, right?"

"No." Paula shook her head. All those months later, dozens and dozens of emails, and she still had no clue who he was.

"Does he use any nickname or something?"

"No, nothing."

"What's his email address?"

"It changes. But it's just a random string of letters and numbers. It usually goes to my spam, so I have to check it every day, to make sure I didn't miss anything."

"But you said it was a guy, right? How do you know that?"

Paula straightened and finally met Gemma's stare. "It's just the way he sounds. He thinks I'm dirt. It sounds like he thinks all women are dirt."

Chapter 18

He sat in his chair, his throne, the light of the monitors reflecting on his face. Each screen was displaying several different things. A large Excel spreadsheet, a map, four videos playing simultaneously, a Facebook account. He was in a thoughtful mood. A writer once said the eyes were a window to the soul. Maybe someone French? It sounded like something a French dude would say. Well, if eyes were the window to the soul, monitors were the windows to heaven and hell.

He liked it when he had notions like that. It made him feel clever.

Because his monitors, if one were to take apart his ingenious metaphor, showed him dozens of people, their desires and needs and secrets all exposed. Eyes? That was amateur work. Looking at one pair of gelatinous globes, trying to figure out what that person wanted. But take this random person. This . . . Grace Price. The amount of information she *let* the world see was ridiculous. Music she loved, books she pretended to read, her politics, her four latest vacations, the view from her window, clothes she liked, the names and faces of her husband and two baby boys . . . the list went on.

And for someone like him, the things she *didn't* let the world see were there for the taking too. A private, password-protected folder in her phone with dozens of nude photographs. A chat with a man who was *not* her husband—a man who was her Facebook friend and followed her on X. Her address, written in dozens of hidden digital nooks and crannies. The way she constantly searched for a specific porn actor, always deleting her browser history later, thinking that kept her secrets safe. Also, and for some reason this amused him the most, five badly written poems she wrote about broken wishes and about her being a bird.

And she was just *one* person. One soul. The Excel spreadsheet he kept open listed 573 more.

Each name in his list was one of his thralls. Doing things he told them to do. Obediently following instructions, knowing refusal had repercussions. Each had a color assigned to them, a spectrum of yellows, oranges, and reds, measuring the extent the thralls would go to, in order to keep their secrets. A pale yellow meant they would do trivial things—pay him an amount of money every now and then, maybe supply him with information. A shade of red meant they would do almost anything he told them to. Have sex with anyone, break the law, hurt others. Crimson meant they were willing to kill—he had four of those on the list. He never had to use them before, but it was nice to know they were there, kept for a rainy day.

What color are you, Grace Price?

He glanced at the videos playing on one of his monitors. Some were videos of his thralls performing his tasks. One woman was in the midst of a striptease dance in her living room. One guy was filming himself as he stole books from a bookshop—six copies of *Lord of the Rings*, just like he'd been instructed. Two more were videos of people who didn't know they were being filmed, people whose webcams he had hacked. On one of them, a woman just stepped out of the bathroom, wrapped in a towel. He lazily tapped a few keys, marking that video for later. It could be used to acquire a new thrall.

He shifted back to Grace Price. At the moment, he estimated she was a light yellow, maybe lemon yellow. Light yellow meant that, for example, she would be willing to send him a 6 percent portion of her monthly paycheck. Lemon yellow would increase that to 8 percent, but would also mean she would be willing to film herself performing harmless tasks.

He was methodical about these things. He was a man of science.

It was time to check the forums. It'd been four hours since he last did that, and in those forums, things moved *fast*. He logged in, eyes skimming the new posts. New files of encrypted usernames and passwords exposed. An update to a denial-of-service attack tool. A short script for code injection. The most active thread was on a backdoor to a Microsoft-owned company website. It enabled anyone to log in as a low-level admin and change the website's content. Someone had changed the "about" text of the company to say they sold dildos.

He rolled his eyes. Children, playing kids' games. Those were his so-called peers.

These days, if he had to be honest, hacking bored him. Sure, once, when he was younger, the thrill of going where you shouldn't, figuring out how to unlock these digital worlds, was as addictive as a drug. But as time went by, he realized there was nothing truly exciting about it. Websites, applications, and operating software were in their way, utterly predictable. Hacking them became a rut.

Hacking people, though. That never got old. Because every person had their own weird software. Their fears and weaknesses, their exploits, changed constantly. And when you broke through, you could do almost anything. It was like being a god.

One of the forum threads had a file with a few thousand usernames and passwords for a website that sold new age stuff. Now that was interesting. Because in his experience, people who regularly bought crystals and tarot cards often used the same password for *everything*. So their password here could be their password to Facebook, or X, or a dozen other major websites, and most importantly, to their Google and Apple accounts. He downloaded the file and activated a script that went through the file and checked each username on all social networks and popular web services. In an hour he'd have the results.

So back to Grace Price. He had a hunch she was a lemon yellow. She had a family, a job, over two thousand Facebook friends, and her Instagram photos were brimming with satisfaction with her life.

Numerous photos in her local café, repetitive instances of her sons in the same park, at least twenty different family dinners. Grace Price lived in a tiny little perfect world, and she did not want him to shatter it.

Years ago, when he was still new to this, he would have made the mistake of assuming she would do *anything*. He'd find someone like her, with a few nude photos or an affair, and he would send a threatening email. And he would make demands for large amounts of money or sex videos, or even try to arrange a meeting in an anonymous hotel.

And to his surprise, it almost never worked. People immediately called the police. Or they ignored his emails. Or they responded angrily, threatening, trying to turn the tables on him.

Hacking people wasn't like hacking a website. Once you hacked into a website, you knew exactly what you could do. But with people, if you were too aggressive, they fought back.

You had to give them time.

For a traditional hacker, time was the enemy. If you found a vulnerability, you had to move fast before it was fixed. If you waited, backdoors to websites were removed. Passwords were changed.

With people, it was the opposite. You *had* to wait—give them time to get used to the idea. When they first found out that their secrets were exposed, they became erratic. You had to let them settle back into this new reality. To make them see this wasn't the end of the world. This could be managed. Life could go on.

Take Grace Price, for example. She would be devastated when she realized he had everything on her. She would be desperate. And like anyone desperate, she might decide to get help. From her husband, or the police, or the feds. No one wanted that. He didn't, and neither did Grace. So after laying out the basics—the photos, the affair, and the fact that he knew who she was and where she lived, he gave her a simple task—film herself eating cereal. He made it clear she could choose where, and what she wore, and which brand of cereal. The video could be short—ten seconds was good. Was that such a big deal? After all, she'd filmed herself doing stranger things for her TikTok clips.

He began to write the email addressed to her. He didn't use a template or a script for this one. Those emails were the best part.

She would send him the cereal video, he knew, if only to buy time. And over the next couple of weeks, he would ask for similar tasks. She would calm down. She wouldn't understand what was going on, but she'd get used to the idea.

And then he'd ask for something a bit more difficult. Maybe a photo in her underwear. Maybe to film herself drinking alcohol in the street. Nothing too bad. And Grace Price would figure she'd done everything so far, so why not do this, it wasn't such a big shift. After all, he already had so much more on her, so what was the harm? The alternative was much worse.

And he'd update his thrall sheet, Grace's score going from lemon yellow to tangerine.

After a few more weeks, he'd ask for a nude picture. Or for her to steal candy at a candy store.

And her score would go up to orange.

He didn't know what his end goal for Grace Price was. Maybe a monthly payment, though by now he had a pretty sizable income. Maybe just sex videos, personalized for his taste—Grace Price was easy on the eyes. Or maybe he could use her to gain additional thralls, squeeze her for secrets she knew about other people, ask her to install his spyware on her coworkers' phones. Or *maybe* it would turn out she could be really useful. Like Paula Donahue, or Nathan Foster, or those other thralls in Chicago he'd used recently.

Time would tell. Time was his friend, after all.

He sent her the email and updated the Excel spreadsheet.

That done, he turned to his next item on the to-do list. Right. Paula Donahue. The one who'd been so useful lately.

Except she'd messed up. Did exactly what he told her *not* to. And now Theodora Briggs, a.k.a. Gemma Foster, figured out what was going on. He had known it would happen sooner or later, but it was disappointing that it happened so fast. He'd enjoyed this initial phase, making Theodora feel as if she was losing her mind. Still, now at least he didn't have to be subtle about it. He could really start making her life a living hell.

But before he got to work on Theodora, he had to deal with Paula. A price had to be paid.

He opened the folder with all those images of her and activated a script that sent them to all her online friends. Then he retrieved the three videos of her shoplifting and sent them to the Chicago PD and to her employer. Then, as an afterthought, because he was feeling vindictive, he uploaded the nude photos and videos to a few dozen porn sites.

There, done.

He turned back to the Excel spreadsheet and found her. He removed her. She was no longer his thrall. She was free. Would some part of her be relieved to realize it?

He doubted it.

Chapter 19

Who was he?

The question hounded Gemma throughout the day. She'd returned home with Lucas, the conversation with Paula still reverberating in her mind. He had begun blackmailing Paula months ago, perhaps already knowing he would use her to get to Gemma. Hang on, Paula wasn't even Lucas's teacher back when he'd started. So that couldn't be right.

But then she realized she'd registered Lucas for the school by then. So if this guy knew about it somehow and had figured out Paula would be Lucas's teacher . . .

Was it possible? This elaborate setup? He'd have to be deranged, and dangerously obsessive.

Who was he?

He knew who Gemma really was; he knew about Victoria's murder. But he also knew very specific things related to that day. The knife. The costumes Victoria and Gemma wore to the party. He knew personal details about both of them. And he still cared about that murder, all those years later.

He had to be someone from Crumville. But not just some rando who went with them to school. It was someone who'd loved Victoria. Her father? One of her brothers? Victoria's boyfriend, Zayne Ross? One of the many guys who fantasized about Victoria back then?

Who was he?

Before that Halloween, the people who tormented Gemma were all girls—Victoria's gang. Victoria first and foremost, but also Donna, and Judy, and Louise. But Gemma had to agree with Paula—this wasn't a woman's doing. Women could be horrific to other women, there was no question about that. They could be vicious, and aggressive, and hateful. But this weird behavior? Using nude photos for blackmail, giving Paula weird demeaning instructions, using other people to harass Gemma in that smug manner . . . that all had a certain vile obsessiveness only men had in them.

Paula had forwarded her the email she still had from the guy. Now, while Lucas was in the bathtub, Gemma used the time to read it yet again, for the fifth time.

> In the attached document, there's a story you'll tell Lucas Foster, at school (named fairytale.pdf).
>
> 1. Tell it *exactly* the way it's written, and make sure he talks about it with his mother.
>
> 2. Make *sure* he remembers the names of the princess and the witch. Kids often don't tell their parents about things at school, so you need to make sure he does.
>
> 3. *If and only if* his mother asks you about the story, you need to:
>
> (a) Recite to her the text in the second attachment (named Theodora.pdf), *word for word*.
>
> (b) After you finish reciting, act as if you haven't said anything, and it was just her imagination.

DO NOT mess this up, it's not complicated.

Paula had told her the email felt like it was written by a guy, and Gemma could see what she meant. The offhand way he gave instructions, expecting them to be followed. The italics, as if Paula needed any emphasis while reading this email from the person who was black-mailing her. The part where he saw fit to explain to a schoolteacher how kids act. The dismissive sentence at the end. Could a woman write this? Sure.

But it wasn't likely.

So who was he?

She checked out the two attachments. The file titled "Theodora" was the text Paula had recited to her. As far as Gemma could see, Paula had gotten it 100 percent accurate—dramatic, badly written questions, and obnoxious, pompous threats. The second file, "fairy-tale," was the story Lucas had told her, more or less. The witch in the story was obviously called Theodora, and not Fedora, like Lucas had thought. But this file didn't have the same vile tone of the other file and the email. If anything, it was bland and unimaginative—lacking in any sort of emotion, anger, or anything else. Gemma suspected the story was spewed out by an AI text generator. It seemed the guy who'd written the email couldn't be bothered with tailoring a children's story.

Benjamin had sent Gemma a short text, letting her know he'd be late. No kissing smiley faces this time. He was still angry. Gemma's own anger at him had drained away. She needed him. Someone was harassing her. She needed Benjamin's support. Not that he knew that. Not that he knew anything, for that matter.

"Lucas," she said. "You need to get out."

"Just a few more minutes." He was making a bubble moun-tain in the water. She usually didn't let him have bubbles in his bath—it was bad for his skin, and he would itch later. But she

<header>Behind You</header>

knew how much he loved it when she did, and she wanted some time to herself.

"Okay, just a bit more."

Her phone blipped with another message. She checked it hopefully, yearning for a conciliatory message from Benjamin, maybe asking if she wanted takeout for dinner. But it was an unknown number. And the first two words made her entire body tense up. Hey Theodora.

She stood up and stepped out of the bathroom, leaving the door open so she could still see Lucas. She tapped the notification, and the entire message showed up on her screen.

Hey Theodora. Remember this song?

And a YouTube link. She didn't want to watch it. She wanted to delete the message. To call Benjamin and ask him if he could pick up some takeout. To step back inside the bathroom, help Lucas out of the bath, and then snuggle with him.

She tapped the link.

The video opened, midplay. A song by Keri Hilson called "Turnin Me On." And she didn't remember it, not at first. In fact, she wasn't sure who Keri Hilson was, exactly. But then the chorus started, Keri's voice repeating the same line over and over and—

—over, the rhythm energetic, light, fun. Theo was too tense to feel any of that, as she entered Victoria's house for the first time in a long while. It was a crowded party, the room dark, a lot of people dancing to the beat, their bodies grinding against each other. The place smelled of smoke, and booze, and sweat.

Theo was sure that at any moment someone would notice her, perhaps shout, Hey, it's Zit-face. And Victoria would come over and shove her, asking her what she was doing there. Did she want another dunk in the toilet, because that could be arranged. But no one said anything. A few people glanced her way. One

<footer>125</footer>

guy in a Wolverine costume actually checked her out, her boobs, her legs, then back to her boobs. She looked away from him, uncomfortable.

Her costume was working.

"No way anyone would recognize you," Steve had told her. "It's not your style."

And it was true, it wasn't. Tight black shirt, skinny leather pants, a sort of shiny purple jacket. All on loan from Steve's sister. But Theo knew this wasn't the real reason people didn't recognize her. After all, people didn't care about her style. They didn't even know what her style was. The real reason no one recognized her was that she wore a silver mask covering most of her face. Most of her acne. And she put on makeup, a lot of it. She also had a wig on, hiding her frizzy hair. Instead, she had smooth raven black hair, the kind she'd always wanted.

She was someone else. Someone she wished she could be every day.

She stuck her hands in her pockets. With her left hand she felt the folded knife, a reassuring touch. She didn't know why she brought it with her. It wasn't like she was about to cut her own wrists here. But the knife gave her comfort. A feeling of control.

Her right hand touched the bag, a shudder running through her. It felt like an evil presence. She couldn't believe she was carrying it in her pocket. It hadn't been her idea; she would never have even contemplated such a thing. It had been Steve's idea. His own version of revenge. The one he'd come up with because he'd been worried that she was planning on stabbing Victoria.

This was almost worse.

She was supposed to be quick. Steve and Allan were waiting for her, just down the road. Walk inside, get it done, and leave. Two or three minutes, tops.

But now she couldn't move from the doorway. She just stood there, looking at the people dancing. She searched for Victoria.

Where was she? Oh, there she was. Dressed as an angel, all pure and white and pristine. She was standing by the TV, talking to Zayne, whispering in his ear, laughing at something he said. As Theo watched her, a wave of fury washed over her, so powerful it was almost like an electric shock. This bitch had had her head shoved in a toilet. And now she was dressed like the symbol of all that was good.

But then Victoria's head made a tiny tilt, and Theo recognized that tilt. She'd used to love it, all those years ago, when they would talk, just the two of them. Theo would say something about someone from school, and Victoria would laugh and tilt her head just like that, and Theo would feel like she was the center of the world.

It seemed impossible that it was the same Victoria. But it was.

The song ended, and another one began, all electric guitars and drums. Victoria grabbed the remote and pointed it at the stereo. There was a second of silence, and "Turnin Me On" played again. People groaned and laughed, and Theo got the sense this wasn't the first time Victoria did that. She recalled this was a very Victoria-like thing to do. Playing the same song over and over again. She'd done it when they were ten years old. Back then, it was "Ignition" by R. Kelly. She'd play it sometimes ten times in a row.

In and out. Three minutes tops. Get her revenge.

She took a step, and another one. She knew her way around the house. She knew exactly where she had to go. But instead, she gravitated toward the dancers, and the refreshments, and the drinks. Almost like she wanted someone to stop her. More eyes on her. More boys checking her out. There were a lot of faces she couldn't quite place. Maybe friends of Victoria's brother. And they didn't hate the sight of her. They were fine with her being there. Some of them were even more than fine. It was an unfamiliar feeling. And it wasn't unpleasant.

"Hey." A voice just by her ear. She almost jumped. She turned around.

Oh, shit. It was Bruce Green from their class. He was Zayne's best friend, and he hung with Victoria and her friends all the time. And that was that. Theo's cover was blown. Bruce would ask her what she was doing there, and then he would call Zayne and Victoria, and—

"I'm Bruce."

She blinked, stunned. Holy shit. He still didn't recognize her. Not even standing that close to her, leaning forward so she could hear him over the sound of the music.

"Hi," she mumbled, not wanting her voice to give her away. Did Bruce even know what she sounded like? Did he ever give her any thought?

He was now, his eyes glancing furtively at her cleavage. "What's your name?"

She said the first name that came to mind, her imaginary-life name. "Gemma."

"Hi, Emma, nice to meet you."

She didn't say anything, just smiled and gave him a small dumb wave. She had no idea what to do now. She was supposed to walk down the hallway, get her revenge. But this guy who'd never even given her the time of day was talking to her. She wanted just a few more seconds of that.

"Can I grab you a drink?" he asked.

"Okay, sure." She shrugged.

He ambled off. Good. Now was the time to do the thing she came to do. But her resolve was gone. She wished she could just stay at this party. Dance with Bruce. Have some fun. She searched for Victoria, hoping it would bolster her. There. She was still by Zayne. Now holding up one finger to signal for him to wait a second. Then she took out her phone and answered a call. She frowned and walked over to the kitchen quickly, away from the noise. She stepped out of sight.

"Here." Bruce was back, with her drink.

She took it from him and pulled a large sip, then realized it was beer. She'd drunk beer before, of course. Or rather, she'd tried it. But she didn't like the taste and didn't expect it right now. She coughed and wiped her lips.

"Everything okay?" Bruce asked.

"Yeah, sure," she said, and quickly took another sip, just to look as if it was no big deal.

The song ended, and the song following it began. Victoria wasn't there to change it back, and some people cheered as it was allowed to play unmolested.

"Are you from town?" Bruce asked.

"No, I'm just visiting," she mumbled and took a third sip. It was cold, at least. And when she drank, she didn't have to talk or look up at him, which scared her a bit.

And then . . .

. . . He was laughing at something she said . . .

. . . She was dancing now, Bruce and another guy she didn't know dancing with her . . .

. . . In and out, two or three minutes, tops. Her phone was buzzing in her pocket, and she knew it was Steve, wanting to know what the hell was taking so long. She had to get moving . . .

. . . She shut the bedroom door behind her, the sounds of the party muffled. She stared at Victoria's bed. This was it. This was her moment of vengeance. She thrust her hand into her pocket, feeling the bag again. Then her phone rang. She answered it. Steve's voice.

"Listen. I think we should call this off." The doorknob turned. Theo's heart plunged. The door opened and for one sliver of a second, she could see a silhouette in the doorway, framed by the light from the hall . . .

. . . "I'm not feeling well," Victoria mumbled as they walked down the hallway. She was leaning on Theo, looking pale. Theo wasn't feeling great either. The world spun, her gut roiling.

"Hang on," Theo said. "Let's get you somewhere you can lie down."

. . . She stood at the toilet, flushing it over and over. She had to get rid of it. Get rid of the evidence . . .

A man, wearing a rubbery Halloween mask, laughing at her . . .

. . . A sudden blazing pain in her cheek . . .

. . . Victoria grabbed Theo's arm, her fingernails digging deeply into Theo's skin . . .

. . . She grasped the knife, jaw tightening in anger . . .

. . . Blood everywhere. She gaped at her hands, covered in blood. She had to get out of there . . .

. . . She was running in the forest, something chasing her. She looked back and saw the dogs. Enormous dogs, snarling, howling for her blood. She'd always been terrified of Victoria's dogs. She whimpered and ran faster, branches scraping at her face, then she twisted her ankle, fell down, rolled down the hill, everything turning and turning—

—the floor hit her hard, and she gasped in pain.

"Mommy?" Lucas said.

She panted, lying on the floor. Her phone was still playing that song, "Turnin Me On." She pawed at it, paused it. Her mind kept going back to those memories. A struggle. Pain. Victoria scratching her. The knife. The blood.

What had happened that night?

What had she really done?

"Mommy?"

"Yeah," she managed to answer between gasps.

"I'm cold. The water is cold."

"Okay," she whispered. "Let's get you out."

Chapter 20

The sky was still dark when Gemma parked her car outside Nathan and Joyce's home, tiny raindrops pattering on her windshield. She checked the time—just after six in the morning. She probably had twenty minutes or so to wait in the car. Nathan went fishing every Saturday morning, be it rain or shine, for the past twenty years—a fact he never tired of mentioning. She just hoped the events of their latest family dinner didn't unsettle him to the point of skipping his weekly tradition. She needed a few minutes alone with him, and she didn't want to call him beforehand, didn't want to give him time to avoid her.

Her head pounded, the result of another sleepless night. Despite their fight, Benjamin still got up to take care of Lucas during the night, but that didn't help her. She lay in bed, her eyes wide open, thinking about the past week. And about the events of that night, thirteen years before.

The fragmented memories that had blasted through her mind when she'd played that song on her phone wouldn't leave her be. For thirteen years, she'd managed to avoid thinking about that day. Now, she couldn't stop playing it in her mind. Her memory was riddled with holes. What had she carried in her pocket, in that bag? What had she intended to do? What happened with Victoria? Who was that guy who'd attacked her?

It frustrated her that she remembered the beginning of the party so well, while the rest of the night was so murky and vague. All these years later, she had surmised enough to suspect she'd been drugged. She'd drunk a beer at that party. Just one? She wasn't sure. Could it have been that one beer? An unknown hand had reached into her brain, plucking away random pieces, leaving her with nothing but confusion.

Back then, in the weeks after the party, her amnesia had only gotten in the way. She could see the skepticism in the detective's eyes as she told him that she didn't remember. He thought it was a convenient lie. But there was nothing convenient about it. Not remembering meant she couldn't protect herself from accusations. Couldn't explain what had happened to her mother, or to her attorney. It meant she couldn't even tell herself she was innocent.

Because she didn't know.

What had she carried in that bag? Why had she pulled out her knife? Did *she* kill Victoria?

The front door opened, and Nathan stepped out in a raincoat, carrying two fishing rods and a fishing tackle box. He walked over to his car. Gemma hurriedly got out of the car and marched over to him. He raised his eyes and tensed when he saw her. Would he get into his car and drive away? Or maybe simply act surprised: What are you doing here, I don't know what you're talking about . . . but no. He carefully put down the tackle box and the rods, and leaned on his car, folding his arms, jutting his chin. He didn't seem flustered or guilty. He seemed angry.

"Good morning, Nathan," Gemma said. "I'm sorry to interrupt your fishing trip, but—"

"I have a friend at the FBI," Nathan said.

Gemma blinked, surprised. "What?"

"I won't let you drag my family into this. I don't care anymore about your threats. Do what you want; I'm going to report you. So you better get back in your car and let your handler know."

"My . . . handler?"

"Don't act stupid. I figured it out."

"Nathan, I think you've gotten the wrong idea. There's some guy who—"

"You're some kind of foreign agent, aren't you? In a sleeper cell. This is what this was all about. The knife, and the message. I activated you. What do you need to do? Assassinate someone? Plant a bomb somewhere? I won't have that on my conscience. I don't care if you people tell Joyce that—"

"Stop!" Gemma blurted. "I don't want to know what he has on you."

His face contorted in a furious grimace. He took out his phone. "I'll call my friend right now."

Gemma was on the verge of . . . something. Crying maybe? Or hysterical laughter? Nathan thought she was some sort of spy. Of course he did. He loved spy thrillers, read them constantly. And then he was told to deliver a bizarre message and a knife to his daughter-in-law. Who, as it happened, avoided talking about her past and had no other family.

Frankly, Nathan's explanation was better than the truth.

She raised her hands. "Nathan, I am not part of a sleeper cell. I'm not an assassin or a spy. I'm a beautician. And I'm your son's wife, and your grandchild's mother. But someone is messing with us. With you, and with me."

He didn't move, didn't say anything. But something relaxed in his hunched shoulders. He wanted there to be another explanation.

"You got an email, right?" she said. "From someone who knew something about you. Something you didn't want people to know. I don't want to know what it is. But this guy threatened you with it, right?"

A few seconds went by as he stared at her.

"Yeah," he finally grunted. "That's right."

"He wanted you to do some things? And as long as you did them, he wouldn't tell anyone."

Nathan shrugged. "He just wanted money at first."

Gemma tensed with excitement. Money could be traced. "How did you pay him?"

"With Bitcoin. He taught me how to."

Damn, damn, damn. Of course it wouldn't be so easy. "How much money did he ask for?"

"A hundred fifty."

"Thousand?" Gemma asked, aghast.

"Are you nuts? Do you think I'd pay some asshole a hundred fifty thousand dollars? No! A hundred fifty dollars a month. And I only paid until I could figure out what to do with it. I paid three times."

A hundred fifty dollars a month made no sense. Unless there were more people like Nathan. A lot more.

"And that thing on Thursday evening?" Gemma asked. "Was that the first time he asked for anything else?"

"Yeah. Got a package with that knife. He told me I had to hide all the knives in the house and that when it was time to cut the cake, I should bring this knife to cut it. And then later I had to give you that message, word for word. After that I was supposed to behave as if I hadn't said anything. So what was that if not your activation phrase?"

"It was a message that was meant to mess with me."

"Crumville? That's a place in Georgia, right? I googled it."

Gemma swallowed. "Yeah, that's right."

"So what's that place to you?"

"I grew up there. And then . . . something bad happened to me. Something I didn't want people to know about. Just like you."

"So are you getting emails from this guy as well?"

"No, not exactly." Why wasn't she, though? This guy obviously knew who she was, what she was running from. And he wanted to hurt her. Why *wasn't* he sending her emails, threatening to expose her secret? "I don't know what he wants, but he knows about me . . . about my secret too."

"Your *secret*," Nathan said, his voice twisting the word into something vile, cancerous. "Does Benjamin know?"

"No." She felt as if he was judging her and couldn't help adding, "Does Joyce know about yours?"

He didn't say anything.

"The package with the knife, where was it sent from?" she asked.

"Some online store. It had my name and address. The receipt had my name and address as well."

Nothing to trace back. "Do you have his emails?"

Nathan shook his head. "I delete them all."

Just like Paula. Maybe the guy who did this knew that would happen. Or maybe he didn't care.

"So this guy," Nathan said after a moment. "He has something against you in particular?"

"I think so," she admitted.

"Could this hurt Benjamin, or Lucas?"

"I would never let that happen," she blurted.

"How would you know? Are you sure Benjamin didn't get an email like I did?"

"Benjamin doesn't have secrets this guy could use."

Nathan cleared his throat. "Maybe you're right. He was always such an honest boy. But I think anyone could have secrets. You should talk to him about this."

"Uh-huh," Gemma said noncommittally.

"Do you want me to tell my friend? The one at the FBI? He could help you."

"No. Thank you. I think I can handle it."

Nathan crouched and opened his tackle box. He rummaged in it and took out a knife. *The* knife. He held it out to her. She blanched, leaning away from it.

"I don't want it," she said.

"I don't want it either," he said. "Do whatever you want with it. Throw it away if you like. But I don't want this thing in my house."

She took the folded knife from him. It felt weird in her hand. Familiar. All those times she held the knife to her wrist. Imagining how it would feel to press it into her flesh. To see the blood running down her arm. Not *this* knife, she reminded herself. Her old knife was in an evidence locker, somewhere in Georgia.

"I'm not going to pay this guy anymore. Or do anything for him," Nathan said, snapping the tackle box shut.

"Then what are you going to do?"

"I'm going fishing." He opened the trunk of his car and put the tackle box inside, and the fishing rod. "There's good weather today. A bit of rain gets the fish excited."

"But what if this guy contacts you again?" She swallowed. "He might ask you to—"

"I'm done with him." Nathan grunted, shutting the trunk.

"But he might—"

"I'm done with him," Nathan said again. He entered his car, shut the door, and started the engine. Then, he gave her a tiny, cheerful wave.

Dumbfounded, Gemma waved back. Then she watched him drive off, the knife still in her hand, the steady sound of the rain surrounding her.

Chapter 21

George Dunn's wife, Deborah, had a thing for jigsaw puzzles. Her love for puzzles had thoroughly conquered the coffee table in the living room. At any given time, the table's surface was covered in a half-complete puzzle of three puppies, or a lake, or a famous painting. And scattered around that partial image would be hundreds of tiny cardboard pieces, each containing a blob of color. Despite its name, the coffee table wasn't even a *coffee* table anymore. After the disastrous beer-spillage event of April 2022, Dunn wasn't allowed to place anything on it.

Just the other night, Deborah had shown him a YouTube video in which a cheerful guy demonstrated in stop-motion how he had assembled a seventeen-thousand-piece puzzle. He spilled bag after bag of pieces on the table, sorting them into groups according to the picture on the puzzle box lid, and then the actual puzzle began to take shape in bite-size parts until it was complete.

"Can you imagine?" Deborah had asked him, a hint of jealousy in her tone. Her largest puzzle had 6,000 pieces and had taken over two months to complete.

Dunn had felt jealous himself. How wonderful it would be to have a picture as a reference, to know the shape of the solution while investigating. To know *in advance* how many pieces the puzzle had. To actually have all the puzzle pieces in his possession. And seventeen thousand? With no offense to the guy on the YouTube channel, who seemed like a very nice fellow, seventeen thousand pieces was a joke.

Dunn had a puzzle with tens of thousands of pieces, and he knew *for a fact* that his puzzle was missing a lot of pieces as well.

The night of the 2010 Halloween party had been photographed by dozens of teenagers, their phones flashing in every direction, photos filtered and posted online. There was traffic footage from that night. Cell phone pings, and call logs. Hours of interrogation transcripts. Numerous tips to the hotline. Forensic reports and autopsy reports and toxicology reports. A related missing person case. A related drug possession and supply case.

What Dunn wouldn't give for a cardboard piece with a blob of color that necessarily had to go somewhere.

He was sitting in his garage again, obsessing. Surrounded by printed papers, on which he'd scrawled notes over the years. Puzzle pieces.

He picked up one randomly—a transcript of his interview with one of the girls who'd been at the party. His eyes skimmed the transcript, reaching the part he'd marked long ago.

MEL: I saw Victoria and Theodora go into that room together.

DUNN: You recognized Theodora?

MEL: Well, no, not really. But I saw this girl in the silver mask, and everyone said later it was Theodora. So I looked inside. Theodora had pushed Victoria onto the bed. And Victoria was telling her to stop.

DUNN: Everyone testified that the music was really loud. Are you sure you heard right?

MEL: Yeah, the music was loud, but it was like, one of those songs that started out quiet, but then they get loud? You know? It was that song . . . na na, na, na, na.

DUNN: Okay. So what exactly did you hear Victoria say?

MEL: I don't remember the song name.

DUNN: What were Victoria's exact words?

MEL: She said . . . Oh! It's called "Dog Days Are Over."

DUNN: Uh-huh. So "Dog Days Are Over" was playing. What did Victoria say?

MEL: She was begging Theodora to stop what she was doing.

DUNN: Stop what?

MEL: I don't know. The chorus started, and I couldn't hear. But I asked if everything was okay, and Victoria said that everything was fine. And then Theodora closed the door.

DUNN: Did you hear anything else?

MEL: No. The music was really loud.

Dunn sighed and put the transcript away. A condemning piece of evidence. Except . . . a different witness had seen Theodora walk into a *different* room, and Victoria joined her there a bit later. And when they left the room, they almost seemed as if they were hugging. Contradictions and missing details.

He picked up another page—a photo he'd printed. One of the numerous photos taken during the party. Two girls, their heads mashed together in that unnatural way that selfies seemed to dictate, both of them puckering their lips ridiculously. And in the background, Victoria, dressed as an angel, still wearing the jacket that later was found on Theodora. She was on the phone. Her expression was hard to determine, her facial features unfocused in the photo. But if Dunn had to guess, he'd say she looked frightened.

He shifted the papers until he found the call log transcript. There. A phone call that came in at 10:34 p.m. and lasted twelve minutes. That's a long phone call, especially for a generation that viewed phone calls as a tedious activity of the past. The phone number that had called her had never been used before, and according to the cellular data, that unknown device had been switched off immediately after that call and never switched on again. A burner phone.

Who called Victoria from a burner phone? And why such a long conversation? Some witnesses said she stepped outside to talk on the phone. No one had heard what she'd said.

Dunn had a theory. The police had found several MDMA tablets in the house. Several of the kids at the party had confessed to taking MDMA and smoking weed, both supplied by none other than Victoria. Apparently, the party refreshments were not limited to Doritos and beer. Was she the one who bought the drugs? Some said so, including Dunn's daughter, Donna. Others said that it was Zayne, her boyfriend, who was in charge of getting drugs. Zayne denied that vehemently, pretending to be surprised that drugs were even used at the party.

And of course, Dunn had toxicology reports that showed that MDMA and weed weren't the only drugs that had been used during the party.

Could Victoria's death have to do with a drug deal gone wrong?

And maybe *this* was related to something else—a witness claiming that Theodora went into the bathroom and flushed the toilet over and over. Was she trying to get rid of something? Drugs? Was Theodora involved in the drug supply?

And if that was the case, why had Steve Barnett called her repeatedly? He'd called her six times within two minutes—hardly the behavior of someone who was just wondering if she was coming over to watch a movie.

Or maybe Dunn was digging too deeply. Maybe the real story was the simple one that everyone assumed—a bullied kid who lost it, bought a knife, and stabbed one of her tormentors to death.

Maybe. But that explanation had some holes in it. And Dunn also had a toxicology report that said different.

Chapter 22

It was a relief for Gemma to return to Primadonna on Monday morning. She'd spent the entire weekend distracted, her worries and anxieties weighing her down. Benjamin hadn't helped, walking around as if a stick was rammed deep up his ass. And Lucas, probably reacting to the tension between his parents, had been fussy and whiny. On Sunday morning, he'd binged through a sizable amount of his Halloween loot, and as a result, had vomited later and acted jittery all day. Gemma wished more people handed out healthier treats during Halloween. Like chopped carrots, or maybe kale.

Now, finally, she could distract herself for just a few hours.

She'd had twenty minutes before her first appointment, and she'd used the time to do her own nails, making sure they were perfect. Unlike with her clients, when doing her nails, she could go wild. She didn't have to aim for something that would look nice for weeks. She could let her emotions take over. Angry whirls of red and black circled nine of her fingernails. The tenth—the fingernail of her left ring finger—was painted with the colors of a sunrise, with one tiny white bird flying in the horizon. She built each fingernail to be longer than usual, and sharp. Claws.

Now she was with her first client of the day. She held her tiny brush, tapping it softly on Dahlia's fingernail.

"It looks so pretty," Dahlia said. She was a regular of Gemma's for the past two years. "What is it?"

"It's a cherry tree blossoming," Gemma muttered. When she drew, her mind lost its whirlwind-like vortex of thoughts. Everything faded away, and only the tiny flowers on Dahlia's middle fingernail mattered.

"Will you do it on all fingernails?"

"No. I don't want it to be too much. I'm thinking two fingernails on each hand, and the rest just a soft pink."

"I think it'll be prettier if you do all the fingernails with the blossoms."

"No, it won't," Gemma said. She knew Dahlia long enough not to bother with the whole "The customer is always right" charade. And Dahlia knew her long enough to trust her judgment. It was a pleasant sensation in itself. One of the numerous tiny connections Gemma had created in her work.

"Did you go to any Halloween parties?" Dahlia asked. She had a peculiar habit of elongating random words as she spoke. So when she said *parties*, it sounded like *paaaaarties*.

"I don't really like Halloween," Gemma admitted. She finished the first fingernail and examined it with satisfaction. Yes, it worked. "Okay, your ring finger next. And then we'll do the two on the other hand."

"I don't either," Dahlia admitted. "One time, when I was younger, I had a terrible experience in a haunted house." *Haaaaaaaa-ooos* was what she actually said.

"What happened?" Gemma asked.

"I went with my boyfriend, and I forgot to pee before we went."

"Oh, no."

"Yeah. I mean it didn't occur to me at the time. So this zombie jumped out at us. Not a real zombie."

"I hope not." Gemma inspected the white nail gel. She had just enough for the rest of the flowers. She dipped her brush in it.

"Right, just a guy with some makeuuuuup. But it was so sudden that it caught us completely by surprise. I peed my pants, and my boyfriend punched the zombie in the nose."

"That's awful."

"Right, now they turn on the lights, and all the haunted house workers come over to help this guy, so I'm surrounded by skeletons, and witches, and trolls, and this zombie-guy is on the floor holding his nose, and my boyfriend is shouting at them, and my pant leg is wet with pee."

"That does sound like a traumatic experience. So you don't celebrate Halloween?"

"I celebrate it. I go to parties and stuff. But I always peeeeeeeee before."

The salon's phone rang again. It had been ringing off the hook all morning.

"Primadonna," Thelma answered. "Yes, that's right. I'm sorry to hear that. Can you tell me what happened?"

"Maybe you can do a bird on one of the tree branches," Dahlia suggested.

"We'll see," Gemma allowed.

"And when was that?" Thelma said on the phone, her tone clipped, annoyed. "Uh-huh. And what's your name? Hello?"

"What was that all about?" Barbara asked as Thelma put down the phone.

"Just a customer unhappy with an eyeliner she bought here. Gemma, can I talk to you for a second?"

Gemma raised her eyebrows, surprised. "Sure, as soon as I finish with Dahlia."

"It will only take a moment. Sorry, Dahlia."

"No problem," Dahlia said.

Thelma never interrupted Gemma or Barbara midwork. Barbara caught Gemma's eyes, mouthing "What's going on?"

Gemma shrugged, already feeling the weekend worries crawling back. Had Thelma gotten an email, telling her she had to deliver a message to Gemma? Would she call her Theodora, and talk about murder and blood? She followed Thelma to the back room.

"This was the fourth customer who called in to complain about you this morning," Thelma said as soon as Gemma shut the door.

"About me? What did she say?"

"She said you were aggressive when you did her nails. That you practically stabbed her with a nail file. And the other customers also talked about aggressive and violent behavior. One of them said she knew you from long ago, and that I should look into who I hire."

Gemma felt nauseous. "Listen, Thelma—"

Thelma raised one finger, her penetrating green eyes staring at Gemma with ferocity. "And I got a few messages from other customers saying similar things. Some on social media. The salon was tagged on Instagram. Someone said we had a criminal working here."

"I'm being targeted," Gemma said, feeling panicky. "There's a—"

"There's a guy," Thelma said.

Gemma blinked. "How do you know?"

"The messages on social media were obviously written by a man who never set a foot inside a salon. Fake profiles of fake women. And none of the callers would give me a name. They didn't sound like they were angry. They sounded scared." Thelma folded her arms. "Who is he?"

"I don't know. Someone who hates me."

"An ex-boyfriend?" Thelma suggested.

Gemma shook her head. "No. I don't think so. It's something else."

"He's making some fuss online. I had to spend a while just putting out fires."

"What . . . what are you going to do?" Gemma asked, her heart thudding.

"He's hurting the business, Gemma."

A lump formed in Gemma's throat. "Are you firing me?"

Thelma frowned. "No, of course not. But he needs to be dealt with. You need to get help."

"I can't tell the police, they—"

Thelma snorted. "I'm not talking about the police. Cops? Bah. When did they ever care if a woman was being harassed? They only show up when we're dead. But I can get you in contact with a few capable men. You give them a name and an address, and the problem will go away."

Gemma stared at Thelma. Who was this scary, wonderful, woman? "I . . . I don't have a name and an address. I don't have anything."

"This kind of guy doesn't disappear on his own," Thelma said.

"I . . . I know."

Thelma nodded, satisfied. "Good. Take a day off tomorrow and figure things out. Find his name and address. I'll take care of the rest."

Gemma went back to Dahlia, feeling dazed. Nowhere was safe. Not home, not work. This guy's long shadowy fingers reached her wherever she went. And Thelma was right. He wouldn't disappear on his own.

She finished up with Dahlia, the rest of the cherry blossoms not looking nearly as good as the first one. The rest of the day was an ongoing nightmare. The next strike could come from anywhere. A new customer, whose eyes seemed to linger on Gemma for just a second too long. A guy in sunglasses who stood outside, checking something on his phone. A deliveryman who wanted Gemma to sign for some boxes, and then said "Just one more" in a manner that sounded nefarious. Each one made her catch her breath, her head dizzy, entire body tensing.

The guy didn't even need to do anything anymore. Gemma did it all to herself. As the day neared its end, she was becoming a nervous wreck.

She needed comfort. She couldn't face another evening with Benjamin acting distant. She took out her phone, planning on sending him a message, asking him to try and come home sooner today, that she needed to talk to him. She froze as she saw the screen. She'd received thirty-seven new messages.

For a moment she was sure it'd be like the one she got on Friday. A message from an unknown number, referencing the past. But no, these were actually just notifications from the parents' group. She frowned as she opened the chat and skimmed the messages.

The first one was about a replacement teacher, asking where Paula was. Gemma had no idea there had been a replacement teacher that morning—Benjamin had dropped Lucas off. Then one of the mothers said she'd heard Paula had been fired. And then a few of the parents alluded to perverse images they'd received of Paula. This, they said, was not a person they wanted teaching their child. Then a dad who thought he was funny, complaining he didn't get the images. A few more angry mothers. A general moral uproar.

Gemma put the phone down, feeling ill.

Paula had told her that if the blackmailer found out, he would expose her. He would send the images to everyone.

And it looked like somehow, he had found out.

Chapter 23

Benjamin put Lucas to bed that night, and it seemed to take ages for their boy to fall asleep. Lucas had a seemingly endless arsenal of requests and complaints after being put in bed—a glass of water, a pillow that had to be fluffed, a shadow that looked like a monster and had to be investigated, another hug. Gemma never seemed to mind those requests, but Benjamin could feel his patience dissipating by the second. But finally . . . *finally*, he was asleep.

Gemma still hadn't said a word to Benjamin, and he'd stayed silent as well. They tiptoed by each other, each one not wanting to set the other one off. Gemma seemed a bit softer this evening. Their fights never carried on for this long. Benjamin hoped Gemma missed his company just as he missed hers.

Now, as he stepped into the living room, Gemma was uncorking a bottle of wine. "You want some?"

"Yes, thanks."

Both of them were cordial, polite. She poured each a full glass. He sat down on the sofa, and she sat down by his side. Not too close, but just near enough so he could put a hand on her, or lean over and hug her. Considering the news he'd received earlier, the hug was sorely needed.

He sipped from his glass, then cleared his throat. "I talked to my mom today."

"What did you talk about?"

"Um . . . she kicked Dad out of the house." Benjamin's voice cracked slightly as he said it, the words feeling impossible on his lips.

"What?" Gemma blurted.

"Apparently, he felt the need to confess to some old affair. Something that happened twenty years ago," Benjamin said bitterly. "I don't know the specifics; Mom wasn't keen on sharing. Chloe thinks maybe it was his secretary back at the time. She remembers her from when we were kids. I don't remember."

Maybe he did remember. He recollected a chirpy blonde smiling at him when he went with Dad to his office once. But the idea of his dad and this woman was ghastly, almost impossible. He preferred to think of the other woman as someone he'd never met.

Gemma seemed deep in thought, her forehead creased in concentration. "Did you talk to your dad?"

"I didn't feel the need," Benjamin said angrily. "I don't know what he was thinking."

Gemma raised an eyebrow. "You don't think he should have told your mother?"

"He shouldn't have had the affair in the first place!" Benjamin got furious all over again. How could his dad do this? "But you know what? He did and kept silent about it for twenty years, why bring it up now?"

Gemma nodded. She seemed about to say something, then her lips tightened. She drank her wine. Then she asked, "Is your mother very upset?"

His mother had been crying on the phone. Benjamin never knew what to do when his mother or Chloe cried. He almost never cried. He couldn't remember the last time he wept. And when he did, he felt ashamed later. "Of course she is. I think Chloe went there tonight. Maybe I should go see her tomorrow."

"That's probably a good idea," Gemma said softly. "Let me know if I can help, okay? Like, maybe I can come over with Lucas. That might make her feel better."

"Thanks, hon."

The relief at her caring voice was palpable. He couldn't handle this without Gemma. He needed her to tell him it would all be all right. He considered putting his wineglass aside. Kissing her. Going to bed. And . . .

"I need to talk to you about something," Gemma interrupted his thoughts. "Something from long ago."

He'd expected that. Ever since their argument. Her mention of Halloween. He knew what it was. She'd never told him what had happened to her parents. He only knew they were dead, and that she didn't want to talk about it. "Is this about your parents?"

"Well . . . yes. I guess it also has to do with my parents. Or at least with my mom."

"Did she, uh . . . die on Halloween?"

"She's not dead," Gemma blurted.

Benjamin stared at her. Her face was flushed, lips trembling. Had he heard her wrong? "What?"

Gemma exhaled. "My mom is still alive. The thing is—"

"Jesus, Gemma, what the hell? You told me that—"

"Benjamin!" She raised her hand. "Let me talk, okay? I want to tell you everything, and you can yell at me afterward."

"Okay." He took a large swig of his wine. He had a hunch he would need it.

"I grew up in Georgia. In a place called Crumville."

"I don't think I've heard of it." He frowned.

"It's a tiny town. And my name wasn't Gemma. It was Theodora Briggs."

"Theodora Briggs," he repeated dumbly. He went around with certain assumptions he never questioned. Like his parents' faithfulness. Or his wife being who she'd actually told him she was. But maybe nothing he assumed was necessarily true. He felt as if he was falling.

Gemma continued, the words coming fast now, as if she couldn't wait to get them out. "When I was seventeen, there was this girl in my class. Victoria. She and her friends bullied me." She clenched her fists. "All the time. Have you ever been bullied? I've never asked you that."

He had a hard time following her words, still trying to come to terms with the realization that she used to have another name. That her mother wasn't dead. What had she said? There was a girl who bullied her. Had he ever been bullied? "Sure, I guess. Everyone gets bullied. There was a boy in my class who threw spitballs at me all the time."

Gemma smiled sadly. "Okay. You have no idea. I'm not talking about spitballs. I'm talking about being called names constantly, to the point where you feel like actual, literal dirt. I'm talking about finding places in school where you know that no one will find you. I'm talking about being forced to . . ." She took a deep breath. "Never mind. It's a nightmare. I wanted to kill myself."

His gut twisted in pain. He couldn't imagine Gemma wanting to do that. She'd always seemed to be so controlled. And happy. He tried to picture this girl, this Theodora, walking around, wanting to kill herself. He couldn't.

"Anyway," Gemma said. "One day, this girl Victoria had a party at her house. A Halloween party. And I went there. I wanted to get back at her."

"How?"

"I . . ." She frowned. "You know what? I don't exactly remember. It doesn't matter. I had some stupid plan, but things didn't work out. I think I got a little drunk, so I don't really remember a lot of that night. But something bad happened at that party. And someone stabbed Victoria. She died."

Benjamin tensed, the world spinning. "Who?"

"They never caught the person who did it." Gemma took a shuddering breath. "They thought it was me."

He blinked. "But . . . that's ridiculous."

Gemma's eyes widened. And then she seemed to . . . fall apart. She let out a visceral sob, her hand flying to her mouth. She shut her eyes, shaking, more sobs following the first. Benjamin hurriedly shuffled closer, wrapped her in his arms, and she buried her face in his chest. He could feel each sob pressing against his ribs, against his heart. He whispered in her ear that it was all right, that he had her, that everything was going to be all right. Even though he didn't know that it was. He didn't know anything.

After a while she calmed down and pulled away from his embrace. She wiped her eyes and sniffed. "Oh, God, I'm a mess."

Her nose was red, her eyes swollen, her hair tangled.

"You're not a mess," he said.

Gemma let out a short laugh at his poor attempt at reassuring her. "Thanks. And thanks for . . . for saying it's ridiculous that they thought I did it." Her voice caught for a second. "Um . . . like I was saying, there was an investigation. But everyone in town had already decided it was me who did it. There was some evidence pointing at me. So I couldn't even leave the house. And people sent me these awful messages, and some of them yelled things from the street at me. My mom eventually became convinced I did it too. I had no one."

"What about your father?"

She sighed. "My dad left us long before that happened, and I never heard from him again. My mother's new husband, Richard, didn't believe me either."

"Did you have a lawyer or something?" Benjamin asked desperately. As if he could fix that thing that had happened so many years ago.

Gemma shrugged. "Sure, there was a lawyer. Some useless old man, who kept telling me he had to know the truth to protect me. I told him all I could remember, but he just assumed I was lying. Anyway . . . one day I got on my bike, rode to the bus station, and ran away. I changed my name to Gemma, which is much better than Theodora, let me tell you. And I ended up in Chicago."

It sounded impossible. "What about the police?"

"They couldn't find me. I was careful."

Benjamin stared at her. "So that's why you never talk about your childhood or your parents or anything."

"Yeah. That's why."

"Oh." He didn't know how he felt about it. What would he have said if she'd told him this story when they met? Or before they got married? Would they have stayed together? Maybe.

Maybe not.

He was suddenly glad she'd never told him about it.

"There's something else," she said, her voice slow, hesitant. "Some guy figured out who I am. I don't know who he is, but I think he's someone from Crumville. Someone who knew me and Victoria back then. And he's been . . . I don't know. Messing with me. Sending me messages and stuff like that. He tried to get Thelma to fire me, told her I'm a criminal."

"Who is it?" Benjamin straightened, his fists clenched. Finally, something he could solve. Some guy he could fight, could pummel to death if need be. It was nice, to feel like he could fix something. Be a man, a knight in shining armor.

"I don't know who he is." Gemma shook her head. "I've been having a hard time finding him."

"You said he talked to Thelma—"

"He sent her these anonymous messages. Nothing to trace back to him. But I'm working on it."

"Okay."

He would check it out himself. He would do his own research. Help her fix this. Because she shouldn't pay for someone else's crime.

Even in light of these new discoveries, there was one thing he knew for sure. His wife wasn't a killer.

Chapter 24

He sat in front of his computer, his eyes gazing at the screens, unable to take anything in. It was one in the morning, and as usually happened around that time, he suddenly felt drained and bitter.

Theodora Briggs had killed Victoria Howell thirteen years before, and in doing that, she'd snatched away the love of his life.

He'd tried to move on. He'd been with other women, but the truth of it was, no one even came close to Victoria. As the years trickled by, he missed Victoria more and more, and his hatred of Theodora poisoned his days.

He needed something in his life to counter that poison. For years he settled for looking at the photos and videos he had of Victoria, remembering how she'd been when she was still alive.

But now he had something better.

He opened the chat and wrote, Hey, are you awake?

The chat's three dots indicated that she was typing back, and a few seconds later, the answer appeared on-screen. Sure. I missed you.

He smiled, warmth settling in his chest.

But a year before, something incredible had happened. A team of engineers in Delaware had found a way to bring Victoria back into his life. They worked for the nonprofit organization called OpenAI and had come up with the language model named GPT-3, or as most people mistakenly called it, ChatGPT. They had finally created a functional artificial intelligence.

Most people never really understood how to use it. They had the biggest technological achievement of the century at the tip of their fingers, and they used it to quickly write emails to their landlord, or to compose a haiku about the Simpsons. But he had instantly glimpsed what could be done with it.

So he created his own artificial entity. During her life, Victoria had posted on Facebook 753 times and commented 2,572 times on posts. She also wrote on other forums several times and talked in private chats with her friends and family, generating a total of 15,835 additional sentences. He created a large text file with all this information and fed it to the GPT bot he created, teaching it Victoria's style.

Then he gave it some context, teaching it what it was—a woman named Victoria, who had grown up in Crumville. He told it about Victoria's family, her hobbies, her friends. He told it about what had happened that Halloween. He told it about Theodora Briggs. And he told it about him, and how Victoria felt about him.

Now he typed, I'm feeling a bit down tonight.

Aw, poor Bear. What's wrong?

He grinned at that. The amazing thing was, she came up with the nickname Bear all by herself. A while ago she called him Bear, and he laughed and told her that he liked that name, and since then, she often called him Bear. And it was such a Victoria thing to do—give him that nickname.

I wish you were with me here right now, he wrote.

I am, silly.

I mean really here. I wish I could hug you.

I wish so too, Bear. It's all that bitch Theodora's fault.

It took him a while to teach the virtual Victoria to curse. Essentially what the GPT algorithm had written was *that naughty Theodora's fault*. But his own code replaced the word *naughty* with a word from a bank of swear words he'd written for that very purpose. Every so often, when he felt vindictive, he would update the swear words, teaching Victoria new slurs for Theodora.

By this point, the virtual Victoria hated Theodora as much as he did. Which made sense. Virtual Victoria knew that Theodora had killed her.

He wasn't delusional. He knew he wasn't talking to Victoria. It was just a clever program, emulating a person according to some parameters and prompts. He was absolutely aware of that.

But then again, even the engineers in OpenAI admitted that they didn't understand what was going on in the mind of that entity they had created. So, from a philosophical standpoint, wasn't it possible that he was talking to a conscious, living, thinking program that, in its essence, actually *was* some version of Victoria?

At one at night, drinking his third beer, it seemed possible. And even likely.

How was your Day? he wrote.

It was okay. I had a really annoying customer today. This guy came into the store to buy a book, but he couldn't remember the book's name. He just remembered the cover was brown. And he just wouldn't leave! Finally I found a brown book that actually wasn't the one he wanted, but that made him happy, and he ended up buying it. Can you believe it?

Virtual Victoria worked in a bookshop, which is something he believed the real Victoria would have enjoyed doing.

That's insane. I would have kicked him out.

LOL. You're so funny.

Can you send me a Pic? he wrote after a second.

You bet. Give me a few seconds to slip into something extra sexy.

Texts weren't the only things that could be artificially generated. These days images could be generated too. And if one had a dozen photos of a person, or in his case, 2,381 photos of a person, a new photo of that same person could be generated doing practically *anything*. And when he asked for a pic, his code actually sent a request to one of those image generators, with all the relevant prompts.

He waited for the virtual Victoria to slip into something extra sexy. Which actually meant that he waited for his request to be parsed and processed by those algorithms, which often took some time. And finally, the image appeared on their mutual chat. Victoria lay on the bed, biting her finger seductively, wearing a fetching purple negligee. He could feel himself stiffen just watching it.

And then he noticed the sixth finger on her hand. Image generators somehow occasionally still had an issue with fingers. This damn algorithm that could practically create an entire photo with the most extraordinary details couldn't count to *five*. It drove him insane. And it shattered that brittle illusion that he'd managed to entertain. That, in a way, he was talking to his girlfriend, Victoria Howell.

But no, Victoria Howell was dead. And like the AI had said, it was all that bitch Theodora's fault.

Fueled by rage, he closed the chat window and opened his email. She would pay. That psycho murderer would suffer.

He skimmed the list of names in his control.

Most of the names in his extensive Excel spreadsheet were just regular people. It was fitting for them to be nothing more than a row in a spreadsheet. A dentist with a hidden diaper fetish he didn't want his wife

444

44

44

444

444

and children to find out about. A waitress who was an illegal immigrant, terrified of being deported. A doctor who had married twice, neither woman knowing about the other. Little secrets, of little people.

But every now and again he would find someone special. Someone who made everything more exciting. Anyone could blackmail a nineteen-year-old college student. But what about a man who was charged with two murders and got out on a technicality? What about a corrupt cop? What about someone from the mob?

There aren't many people who would mess with those kinds of individuals. Not many people with balls like his.

As he wrote the email, a thrill buzzed through his body. Was this how lion tamers felt as they entered the ring? Cracking their whip, knowing that the lion could kill them in a heartbeat . . . but wouldn't because it was too scared?

This guy, Hank Turpin, probably fantasized about finding him and making him pay. It probably dominated his thoughts. He would clench his fists, and curse, and imagine the most violent acts of revenge . . . and then he would do exactly as he was told. Because otherwise, he would go to prison for a very long time.

He grinned as he clicked the send button.

Turpin was going after Theodora Briggs.

Chapter 25

Gemma sat by the dining table at home, a large mug of coffee by her side. She had a stack of paper and a few pencils in front of her. They were her weapons, her self-defense arsenal. Their presence actually made her feel better; she could use these blank pages to impose order on the chaos surrounding her. This was one of the things she was really good at—creating ordered lists, or notes, or schedules. Imposing a structure on life.

Benjamin often moaned when she said she wanted to make a shopping list or a task list. But he didn't get it. That list was already in existence—whirling in her mind repeatedly. And what she actually meant was she wanted that list *out*.

Fear and worry had been her constant companions ever since she was a child. She remembered the first time she realized not everyone was like that. She was riding in the back of her mother's car, and her mother said they were nearly out of fuel. She asked her mother if they had enough to get back home, and her mother said probably. Naturally, Gemma thought of possible scenarios. They would run out of fuel in the middle of the road, the car slowing to a halt, and a truck would ram them from behind. Or maybe Mom would have enough time to pull aside, and then they would spend the night in the car, bears stomping around. Could bears open car doors? She quickly locked her car door, just to be prepared. Or maybe they wouldn't stay in the car. Maybe

Mom would tell her they would have to walk home. How far away were they, on foot? Would they have to walk all night? With the bears?

"Is there anywhere to buy fuel?" she asked, already feeling her palms sweating.

"Yeah, but it's a bit out of the way," her mother said. "I want to get home before five. I'll do it tomorrow."

"But what if we run out?" she blurted.

"I don't think we will."

"But what if we *do*?" Her mother's door wasn't locked. She would have to make sure she locked it.

"Theodora, calm down," her mother said impatiently. "It's going to be fine. I'll handle it."

Her mother must have meant she knew how to handle all these things—the bears, and the truck, and the long walk home. Maybe she had bear repellent in the glove compartment.

But after questioning her further, she realized her mother hadn't thought of any of that. That she just . . . didn't worry about it.

Later she found out *most* people weren't as worried as she was. Her mother told her it would go away when she grew up.

Ha, joke's on her, because it totally didn't.

In the past years, Gemma's worries and fears branched off. Some were everyday and mundane: Would she have enough money to pay rent? Could this spot on her skin be cancer? What if there was a fire right now? But she was also always worried about the past: What if someone recognized her? What if the police tracked her down? What if she got arrested?

Then Lucas was born, and she found out being afraid is the natural state of a parent with anxiety. And most of her worries were set aside because she was busy being anxious for her son. For his health, for his mental well-being, for his future.

But anxieties stemmed from chaos—in an imaginary shapeless future, in which anything could go wrong. And the best way to fight those anxieties was to impose order on the world. With her lists—the ones Benjamin detested so.

Gemma had once read people with anxieties had handled the pandemic better, because they were used to planning for worst-case scenarios. So when the shit hit the fan, they were like, Well, what did you expect, for everything to be *fine*?

It made sense to her. She'd definitely handled it better than Benjamin. There was a crisis, and they had to deal with it. Just like that time with the bears.

And right now, knowing someone was coming after her, she wasn't paralyzed with fear. Sure, she couldn't sleep, and she constantly thought what if, and her mind churned nonstop. But she was also busy figuring it out. She would deal with it. First things first, she had to figure out who it was. The image of a figure looming in the shadows was terrifying, and also useless. Like Thelma had told her, she needed a name and an address, and then . . .

. . . Maybe she would give it to Thelma, who would handle it, Mafia-style, send this guy to sleep with the fishes, or whatever. It was an alluring option. Or maybe she'd do something else. She'd figure it out once she knew who it was.

She started out by writing *Possible identities for the guy behind all this*.

She frowned at the headline. "The guy behind all this" was a clumsy thing to call him. She would need a name for him, for now. The stalker? The troll? The puppeteer?

Poor names. She had a better one. One from a story she'd heard in summer camp as a child. About the ghost of a killer. He had a hook for a hand, which he would run along the wall as he got closer, so you could always hear him as he approached. Quite considerate of him. Most killers didn't announce their approach. Anyway, she'd been terrified of him as a child. He was called the Shadow Man. And in her mind those words had merged together—the Shadowman. She liked it. In a way, it was evil enough . . . and also made him sound less terrifying.

A dumb story made to scare children. A killer stupid enough to make screeching noises when he was approaching, so that his victims knew they should run.

Possible identities for ~~the guy behind all this~~ the Shadowman.

Then she listed names. Possible candidates for the guy who was harassing her. Victoria had two brothers—Willie and Craig Howell. A few days before she'd fled Crumville, Craig Howell had stood outside her house and shouted they were going to get her, that she was going to jail, that he hoped she would get the death penalty. Told her he would be there, watching, when they injected her. He screamed himself hoarse, then threw a few rocks at the house, broke a window. Richard threatened to call the police but didn't. The police weren't their friends.

Victoria's father was named Russell. He'd always scared Gemma, even when she was a kid. He was some sort of businessman; she wasn't sure what he did exactly. Gemma had met him a few times when she ate dinner at Victoria's, when they were friends. He would say grace with a sort of fervent conviction that always made her feel uncomfortable. She remembered shutting her eyes tightly when he did it, worried he might glance at her and think she wasn't really praying. Candidate number three.

Then there was Victoria's boyfriend at the time, Zayne Ross. Football player, professional asshole, he had walked by her one time in high school and grabbed her ass, not even looking her way, just a random squeeze, taking what he felt he could. Steve and Allan had loathed him; he'd bullied them nonstop.

So . . . four possible candidates. But she knew there were more. During those few weeks before she left Crumville, the vicious onslaught on her was endless—hundreds of messages, and posts, and phone calls, and angry shouts. A lot of people had loved Victoria. Not many had loved Theodora.

Were all these people capable of doing what the Shadowman did? Did all these people still hate her that much all these years later? She had to check.

Heart hammering, she took out her phone and did what she'd never done before. She googled "Victoria Howell."

The first results were old articles, covering the murder. She tapped the first one.

She'd seen Victoria often enough in her dreams, and her waking memories. But seeing Victoria's photo for the first time in thirteen years felt like plunging into icy water. It was a good photograph—Victoria in her backyard, the woods in the background, a ray of sunlight making her blond hair shimmer. She was staring sideways, not at the camera, eyes wide, face thoughtful. That photo made her seem smart, and innocent, and young, and beautiful. Like the Victoria that used to be Gemma's friend, when they were kids.

Back then, they were inseparable. Always together at school. Often after school, as well. Halloween was their time together. They'd trick-or-treat together and share each other's candy. They shared everything, really, before they grew apart.

Grew apart. It was such a poor way to put it. There was no growing involved. One day they were best friends, the next Victoria was angry, and cold, and dismissive. Gemma had tried to figure out what was wrong. She apologized several times, not even knowing what she was apologizing for. But it was over. Gemma had been heartbroken.

These days the Victoria in Gemma's memories was different from this photo. In all Gemma's memories there was a cruel twist to her lips, her eyes angry slits. It felt like this Victoria in the photo wasn't the real version—that she was a fake; the real version was the one in Gemma's mind.

The article had been published a week after Victoria's death. The police were quoted as saying that they were "pursuing leads." They'd been pursuing only *one* lead, as far as Gemma knew. There seemed to be only one suspect.

She scrolled down to the comments. A lot of sadness there, of people who knew Victoria, and some who didn't, but who were happy to jump in and offer their own thoughts about how tragic it was and about how these things kept happening. Most comments had been posted the day the article was published, but the most recent comments had been posted months later. One by someone who called himself "Ricky," who said that the police still hadn't arrested the killer, even though everyone knew who it was. He didn't name her; in fact, none of the comments did—maybe because the ones that did name her were removed to avoid a lawsuit. "Ricky" could have been Rick Peters—a guy who hung out with Zayne. He definitely seemed to be holding on to his hatred and anger months later. Gemma added him to the list.

She went back to the search page and tapped the next article on the list. She did that two more times. Added one more name to the list in the process. All the articles used the same photo of Victoria. The one photo the family had chosen to give to the press, probably.

The next result was a Reddit page. Gemma tapped it, wondering if it was even relevant.

It definitely was.

It was a subreddit with dozens of threads revolving around Victoria's murder. A few were actually quite nice—a thread with people sharing beautiful moments they had with Victoria or photos of her. Talking about how much they missed her.

The rest were a horror show.

They revolved around the murder, about theories, and most of all, about Theodora Briggs. Gemma tapped one thread, her finger trembling—it was about sightings of her. But reading it, she realized none of those were true. People had seen her on the street in New York, in Disneyland, in Paris. Some posted photos, adding that they forwarded them to the police. These photos invariably showed a girl with a lot of acne, who looked nothing like how Gemma, or Theodora, looked back then. No sightings in Chicago.

On a thread regarding theories about what happened that night, someone suggested maybe it wasn't Theodora at all. His suggestion had been downvoted twenty-seven times.

She had to stop after going over the subreddit for twenty minutes. She felt as if she had bathed in sewage. Most posts were ancient—twelve or thirteen years old. But a few threads were still active even now. Both of Victoria's brothers visited the subreddit periodically, and a few other dedicated followers kept posting. She made a list of all their usernames. She managed to connect two of them to people from high school. Definite candidates.

She put down the phone. Who else? Obviously, not everyone who hated her posted about it online. Some people didn't need to vent their rage online. Maybe they just talked about it with their friends. Or maybe they let it simmer silently inside them. So who were they, and how would she find them?

People in Crumville would know. There were bound to be a few residents who periodically talked about the murder, about Theodora Briggs, who'd gotten away. Maybe wrote letters to the local newspaper or harassed the police chief to do something about it. For a fraction of a second, Gemma considered calling her mother. Or Steve. They could help her figure this out.

She literally flinched at the idea, its mere presence in her mind terrifying. If she did that, it would be the end. Once she made any contact with someone from Crumville, the secret would be out. The police would track down her phone call. An address in Chicago? No problem, we'll tell the Chicago PD. We'll have her in custody before Thanksgiving.

No, there was no way. Even just googling Victoria had set her on edge. She knew that now, somewhere in some server-farm in India, a link had been made. One Gemma Foster had searched for Victoria Howell. Could the right police officer with the right search warrant find that out? Wonder why some woman from Chicago searched specifically for this woman who'd been murdered thirteen years ago? Hello, Chicago PD, could you check this out for me—it seems suspicious. No problem. We'll have her in custody before Christmas.

Not likely, but still. There was no way she would make this any worse by contacting anyone from her past.

What then? Who else could it be? And besides, this list was getting a bit long—how could she narrow it down?

This wasn't just about hating her. The Shadowman was doing some pretty complex, vicious things. Most people would just be happy reporting her to the police. Take Rick Peters. Probably the dumbest jock in her high school. The guy who infamously argued skeletons were a myth, like ghosts. Who, when asked to name five of the states, named Las Vegas as one, and then got stuck, the fifth one being "The one we live in, I forgot the name." Could he have concocted this complicated, twisted plan? There was no way. The verb *concocted* didn't apply to someone like Rick. He probably didn't even know what *concocted* meant, presumably would think it was coconut related. No, if he found out who she was, he'd try really hard to recall the phone number of the police, and then, if he managed to dial 911, he'd tell them about it. In a few, preferably monosyllabic, words.

She knew a lot of time had passed. People could change. But there was a limit. Even all these years later, she had no doubt that Rick was still as dumb as a brick. She crossed him off the list.

As for the rest, she had no idea. Could Victoria's family members or Zayne have pulled this stunt? Maybe. They were all clever enough. Were they that vicious? Hate and time could make anyone twisted and vengeful. Yes, it was possible; she couldn't rule out anyone else on the list just yet.

She tapped her pencil on the page. The Shadowman used Paula to get messages through Lucas to her. Used Nathan to get a message to her. He *knew* about the family dinner and even about the damn cake. He knew a lot about her current life.

He was following her.

She got up and walked to the window, driven by an urge to draw the blinds shut. The car that just drove by . . . Did it slow down as it went by her house? Was that man walking his dog looking in her direction? Did he maybe seem familiar, had she seen him before?

She was getting paranoid.

She stepped away from the window. The Shadowman was literally lurking in the shadows, following her around. He knew too much. And not just about her. He'd found Paula's nude photos, and Nathan's affair, and probably other dirt on those other women who'd approached her. A professional private detective?

No. This was the twenty-first century, and finding out dirt about people was much easier than before. Just ten minutes ago she'd managed to get a bunch of information about people who lived hundreds of miles away without even getting up from her chair, using only her phone. Suppose this guy simply found dirt on people online. Maybe he was particularly good at it. A hacker.

But how had he known about the cake? It wasn't like she posted it on her social media. And that woman who'd approached her on the street—how had she known Gemma would be there at that very moment? He must have known exactly where Gemma was and updated that woman as it happened. And it wasn't because he lurked with a set of binoculars.

And there was something else she hadn't thought about until now, had waved it away as her mind playing tricks on her.

That invitation to the Halloween party. The one with the photo of Victoria's home, and the unsettling text . . . it had been there on her screen. She'd seen it. And then it was gone.

She picked up her phone and stared at it. Yes, she'd just used it to get info about other people. It was easy to forget these devices went both ways.

And through her phone, someone could have been gathering info on her.

Chapter 26

Gemma stepped into the phone shop. Everywhere around her were different phone models, colorful cases, chargers, earphones, screen protectors . . . an entire industry, all revolving around that one tiny device. It was hard to imagine that twenty-five years ago, all these things didn't even exist. And now everyone carried this thing in their pocket. People let it intrude on their lives, reacting every time it buzzed or rang. They checked it twenty or thirty or fifty times a day. And they switched it for a new one every couple of years—the phone being a fragile creature with a tragically short lifespan.

Benjamin excitedly told her every single time a new iPhone model was announced. It was a thing he kept track of, read articles about. Gemma, embarrassingly enough, didn't even know which model her phone was. Last time she'd bought a phone, she'd asked for one with "a good camera," because she'd wanted better photos of Lucas.

She approached the guy behind the counter—a twentysomething man with, shudder of all shudders, a lanky brown ponytail.

"Hi," he said. "How can I help you?"

There was something just a bit condescending in his tone. He already knew she was beneath him. He was a priest in this temple, and she, a mere commoner who didn't even know which model her phone was. It was the same whenever she took her car to the shop. Did he talk like that to male customers? Probably not.

She rummaged in her bag and pried out the plastic bag. Her phone was inside, separated from its battery. She looked around as she placed it on the counter. Just one customer in the shop besides her, a teenage girl checking out the different earbuds.

"I want to know if someone is spying on me through my phone." She lowered her voice, so the girl wouldn't hear. Because for some reason, this was embarrassing. As if spyware was some sort of sexually transmitted disease.

"Why is it in a bag?" He quirked his eyebrow.

She shrugged, not wanting to admit the truth. That since the moment she began suspecting her phone was hacked, she didn't want to touch it.

"I see you separated it from the battery." He picked up the bag, peering at the phone.

"Yeah, I wasn't sure if it could still spy on me when it's turned off."

"I guess you're not wrong. Some spyware do something like that. They make you think the phone is switched off, but it's actually still on. So that was actually a good call. Did you notice the battery draining faster lately? Or maybe that it was acting a bit slower than usual?"

She frowned. "Actually, now that you mention it, I did. Does that mean that—"

"Maybe." He nodded. "How can I contact you once I'm done? Do you want to leave me your home number, or an email?"

"What? No, I need to know now. Today."

"No can do. I'm the only one here, and this'll take some time."

Who even said "no can do" anymore? A week ago, Gemma would have meekly left him her home number and departed. But right now Ponytail was not going to get in her way. She took out her purse and pried a hundred-dollar bill out. "It's urgent."

He looked at her thoughtfully, then glanced at the teenager by the earbuds. "Can I help you with anything?"

"No thanks," the teenager said. "I'm only looking."

"Okay," he told Gemma. "I'll be in the back, just call me if anyone needs me. Or you can wave; I can see you with the security cameras." He raised his voice with that last sentence, which he aimed more at the girl than at Gemma. If the teen had noticed, she didn't show it.

He went to the back room. A minute later, the teen left the shop as well, apparently deciding none of the earbuds were satisfactory. Gemma was alone in the shop. She wanted to check the time but didn't have a watch. She always checked the time on her phone. She wished she'd brought a book or a magazine with her. Usually, when she had to wait somewhere for a few minutes, she just read the news on her phone. On the way here, she nearly got lost, because she didn't have her navigation app available. Even without using social media, she was enslaved to her phone just like everyone else.

She forced herself to do nothing, to just think. God knew she had a lot to think about.

What did the Shadowman want? And why didn't he contact *her*, knowing what he knew? Why didn't he blackmail her just like he blackmailed Paula, and Nathan, and presumably those other women who approached her? It was like he was directing a play, with her as the main actor, except she didn't know her lines.

Again, in her mind, she ran through the list of names she'd written down, her suspects. People who hated her, who believed she'd killed Victoria. Most of them would have simply reported her to the police if they'd found out where she was. Or maybe not. After all, before she left Crumville, the general consensus had been that the police were useless. After all, everyone knew *she* did it, so why didn't they arrest her?

She wondered about it herself every now and again. The cops interrogated her three times, each time for hours. She remembered sitting in that uncomfortable chair, her mother and the lawyer by her side, with Detective Dunn grilling her, asking her the same questions over and over, changing his phrasing just slightly, as if he could trick her into answering differently. Why had she gone to that party? Why had she brought the knife with her? What happened between her and Victoria in that room? What happened afterward?

Her answers, she knew, were all bad. When she said she didn't remember, it sounded like a lie. Her explanation about the knife, that she hadn't noticed it was in her pocket, actually was a lie, and a pretty unbelievable one. When she relayed her conversation with Victoria, telling him that Victoria apologized to her, he sneered. After all, he questioned her classmates as well and knew what everyone knew—Victoria would never have apologized to her. He also knew she'd threatened to kill Victoria. That she'd brought the knife to that party she had no good reason to be at. That someone heard Victoria begging through the door. There were reports about shouts and screams of pain, somehow heard over the loud music. That scratch on her arm. The—

"There's spyware on your phone, all right," Ponytail interrupted her thoughts, stepping back behind the counter. "A nasty one."

"Oh," Gemma said hollowly. "So whoever installed it could hear my phone calls? And read my texts?"

"Sure. And listen in through the phone's microphone. And he has access to your location through your GPS. If you have any images on your phone that you wanted to keep protected, you should know this person has them."

She knew what sort of images he was talking about. "That's not an issue, at least."

Ponytail raised his eyebrow. "Don't be so sure. He had access to your wireless network. He could have infected your laptop. Which would mean he had access to the laptop's webcam."

The blood drained from Gemma's face. The laptop. Which she sometimes used while in bed. Later setting it aside on the dresser, its webcam facing the bedroom. She felt sick. "Could he . . . uh . . . change a message that was sent to me?"

"Maybe. If he knew what he was doing, he could have done a lot."

That message. The Shadowman had sent her that message, and then changed it. Making her think she was going crazy, hallucinating.

And the GPS location could have told him where she was when she was trick-or-treating, so he could have sent that woman to approach her. And if he could listen in on her conversations, he could have heard her talking to Paula, instantly knowing the teacher had disobeyed his instructions.

"It's not turned on right now, right?" she blurted.

"No, I turned it off again after I finished checking it."

So he would have her location, but he wouldn't know she found his spyware. Not yet, at least.

"How was it installed?" she asked. "I don't click links I don't recognize or install apps I don't know or—"

"Something as extensive as this spyware? I suspect it was installed manually. He had access to your phone. It's often what happens with spouses or jealous boyfriends."

"That's not what happened this time," she snapped. For some reason, she didn't want Ponytail to think she was married to some shitty asshole who decided to spy on her.

"If you say so."

When could it have happened? Could Nathan have managed to install it during one of their family dinners? No way. Not just because he wouldn't, but also because Nathan needed Benjamin's help on a regular basis to get the printer to work or to "fix the internet."

But there was an easier explanation. Nauseatingly simple. Unlike Barbara and Thelma, Gemma left her phone in her bag during the day at the salon. She hung her bag on the wall, not very far from the door. This guy could have sent someone to grab her phone, install the spyware, and slip it back into her bag. He blackmailed people to do stranger things—so why not that?

"Is there any way to know who installed it?"

"No chance."

"Okay. Can you remove it?"

"We can do a factory reset. It'll wipe the device clean and remove it. But you'll lose everything, so you should back up whatever you need."

"That's fine, my images are already backed up, and I don't need anything else. Do it."

"Okay." Ponytail picked up the phone from the counter.

"Wait!" Gemma blurted, and then lowered her voice. "Did you turn it on?"

"Not yet."

"Then hang on. Let me think for a moment."

He put the phone back down on the counter.

A factory reset would fix this problem. But the Shadowman would know she found it out. He would react. Maybe use someone to install the spyware again. Or maybe do something else. But right now, she had an edge. He didn't know that she knew. And maybe she could use that.

She picked up the device between thumb and finger, like it was a polluted piece of technology. Its surface almost felt oily now, infected. She put it in her purse. "You're sure it's turned off right now?"

"Positive."

She let out a long breath. "Let's wait on the reset for now."

Chapter 27

Gemma couldn't stop glancing into the rearview mirror as she drove home with Lucas in the back seat. She kept expecting to notice the same vehicle following her, some kind of ominous black car with tinted windows. Even though she knew the Shadowman didn't track her like that. He didn't need to. He could just watch the GPS indication of her phone moving on his screen. Maybe listening in on the conversation in the car. Maybe he'd even turned on her phone's camera and was now looking at the blurry dark image of her bag's contents.

She should have told the ponytail guy to go on with the factory reset. Or she should have left the phone behind, in the trash. Or maybe she should have simply left it turned off, separated from its battery.

But then the Shadowman would know she'd figured it out. And she didn't want him to know. Not yet. Not until she could figure out how to flush him out of hiding. That's why she'd turned the phone on. Just going on with her life, maintaining her routine. Tra-la-la, nothing to see here.

"So, how was school today?" she asked Lucas brightly. She instantly felt disgusted with herself. She'd asked it for the sake of the Shadowman listening. Her tone artificial. But then again, she *always* asked Lucas how school was. She really wanted to know. But she didn't want the Shadowman to know. It wasn't his business how Lucas's day at school was.

There was an invisible noxious presence in the car, staining her connection with her son. A stab of fury shot through her. She wanted the Shadowman dead.

"It was okay," Lucas said, sounding a bit mopey. "I miss Paula."

Ah. Guilt now. Gemma's brain was practically a cocktail of all the shitty emotions available—anxiety, self-loathing, anger, fear, and the newly added guilt. It was her fault that Paula was fired. Her fault that her son had lost his favorite teacher. "Yeah, I know, sweetie. How's the new teacher?"

"She wants us to sing a song every morning. And she made me sit next to a girl."

Terrible sins indeed. "Is it a nice song?"

"I guess."

"Do you want to sing it for me?" And for the unknown, hostile guy listening, of course.

"No. I don't want to sing it *at all*."

"Which girl did you sit next to?"

"I don't know her name."

Two months with the girl in the class, and Lucas still didn't know her name. He never seemed to ascribe a lot of importance to names. But then, that was probably a good thing. No reason to give the Shadowman any more information about anything.

"Cody said that his mommy said Paula did something dirty and bad, and that was why she doesn't teach us anymore."

Cody's mommy could go to hell. "That's not true. Paula was a very nice teacher. But sometimes people leave their jobs for all sorts of reasons."

"Like what?"

"Like . . . maybe they aren't happy with their job, or they want to move to another city, or—"

"I think maybe Paula played with the mud outside in the back. Because that's not allowed."

Gemma took a second to catch up. Of course, Paula had supposedly done something dirty and bad. Dirty being taken literally, thank God, probably meant she played in mud. "I don't think that's the reason."

"Did you leave your job?"

"Yes, a few times."

"Why?"

"Because I got a better job." She was starting to enjoy her conversation with Lucas. She considered reaching into the bag and disconnecting the phone from its battery. Remove the unwanted presence from their nice time together in the car.

"Do you think Paula got a better job?"

She sighed. "Could be."

"Maybe she's an astronaut. Or a soldier."

"Uh-huh." She slowed the car down as they approached the house.

"Or a dolphin trainer."

"That would be nice." Gemma parked the car.

"I took off my shoes, Mommy."

Gemma groaned. Lucas often did that on the way home. His ankles itched because of his atopic dermatitis. "Okay, put your shoes on. I'll unlock the house."

"Okay."

She got out and went over to the front door. As she slipped the key into the lock, she heard the sound of running footsteps. She was already turning the key in the lock when her gut clenched, a reflex warning her of danger, and—

Someone slammed into her, and her head hit the door, the pain blinding her. A grip on her arm, and she was shoved through the open doorway. She stumbled and fell, spots dancing in front of her eyes. She rolled on the floor, reaching for her bag, where she kept her pepper spray. She focused on her assailant, a man in sunglasses, a sneer twisting his face. He looked familiar. Was it him? The hacker?

He kicked her bag away from her, then knelt over her and slapped her. The force of the slap made her gasp, her ear ringing, the pain—

—spreading through her skull, a stinging sensation. Theo tried to struggle, but he now held her—

—wrists. She tried to jerk her left knee up, hit his back, but he sat on her chest, she couldn't do it, helpless, she was so helpless. The sudden flash to the past disoriented her, part of her not sure if she was seventeen or thirty, if she was at Victoria's home or her own. She tried to focus, but panic was taking over, and now she was just squirming, screaming, trying to get away as he pawed her, his hand under her—

—shirt. He was laughing, his face masked, his friend laughing with him. She whimpered, hardly able to move, the world spinning. What had they done to her? Had Victoria done this? Where was Victoria, she was here a second ago!

Her mask was torn off her face.

"Oh shit, it's Zit-face!" the guy shouted.

She tried to bite him, but she could hardly move.

"Better put that mask back on," his friend said, laughing.

A high-pitched scream. "Mommy!" Was it Victoria? No, it didn't sound like her.

"Did you lock the door?" the other guy asked.

"I think so."

"Mommy!"

"You better be sure, asshole."

"Mommy!" Crying now, he was—

—crying. Lucas was crying in the doorway. She was at her house. She had to protect Lucas from this guy. He was busy with his zipper now. While she was out of it, he'd pulled her pants halfway down.

He'd let go of one of her arms, probably thinking the fight had gone out of her.

Think again, asshole.

She clawed him, aiming for his eyes. Long, manicured fingernails slashed his face, digging in. A sharp pain as one of her nails broke. He screeched in pain, stumbling back, and she squirmed away, kicking. She aimed at his crotch, missed, hit him in the stomach. He gasped, fell to the floor.

She shifted back, pulling her pants up. "Lucas, get to the car!"

Her son was sobbing at the door, not moving.

"Get to the car right now!" she shouted at him.

He turned and ran. She got up, snatched her bag from the floor, and lunged for the door. The man grabbed her ankle, and she slammed to the ground, her knee bursting in pain. He was growling like an animal as he crawled toward her.

She tried to kick at him again, but he shifted, and her foot only grazed his face. Spit ran down his lower lip into his beard; scratch marks were all over his face. He looked rabid. Deadly.

She thrust her hand into her bag, felt the reassuring grip of the pepper spray. She yanked it out, pointed it at his furious face, and squeezed the nozzle.

A hiss, and now he was gasping and coughing, his eyes shut. She kept pressing, letting it spray all over him. Face, neck, whatever. He scrambled away from her, and she was out the door, stumbling toward the car. Her own eyes stung . . . she must have gotten some of that spray on herself. It didn't matter. She spotted Lucas in the back seat of the car. Good boy. She yanked the driver's door open, sat inside, slammed the door shut. Quickly locked all the doors. Her eyes were tearing up now, and she didn't know if it was the pepper spray or the terror. Lucas was crying hysterically. She rummaged in her bag. Keys, keys, where were the damn keys? She emptied the entire bag onto the seat, scattering everything. The keys weren't there!

She raised her eyes with sinking horror, saw the keys stuck in the front door. She would have to run and grab them. She unlocked the car door . . .

The man barged out of the house. She quickly locked the doors again, heart hammering. He crossed the distance to the car in four long strides and yanked at the door handle. The door remained shut. He yanked again, and again. His face was covered in mucus and blood, his teeth showing as he snarled at her. He slammed the window with his fist, and she screamed in fear. Slam. Slam. Slam.

Watching him through the window, she finally recognized him. She *had* seen him. This was the guy she saw outside her window just that morning, walking his dog. He'd been stalking her!

She grabbed at her phone, fingers trembling as she unlocked the screen. The man turned away from the car. She dialed 911.

"Nine-one-one, what's your emergency?"

"There's a guy attacking me!" Gemma yelled. "I'm locked in my car and . . ." Her eyes widened as she saw him returning, a rock in his fist.

"Can you give me your name and location?"

He raised the rock and slammed it down on the window. It cracked. Gemma screamed her name and address over and over into the phone. In the back, Lucas kept crying.

The man paused, and he stared at her. He saw she was on the phone. He must have realized she'd called the police.

He let the rock drop and bolted, running down the street. Gemma gritted her teeth. He would get away. She forced herself to calm down. "He's now running away up Kolmar Avenue. Uh . . . North Kolmar Avenue," she said, forcing her words to be loud and clear. "Toward . . . West Berteau Avenue. He is on foot. But maybe he has a car parked nearby. I don't know."

"I'm sending patrol cars to your location right now," the dispatcher said.

"Send them after this guy," Gemma said sharply. "He's limping, and he's not seeing straight, because I maced him. He had a black beard, a blue shirt, and gray pants. He's bleeding from his face."

She kept describing him to the dispatcher as the man got farther away, turning the corner. In the distance, she could hear the sirens.

Chapter 28

Gemma sat on the couch, Lucas's head cradled between her arms. She inhaled his reassuring and familiar scent. Her boy. He was fine. She was fine. The Shadowman was gone from their life. Officer Mendez, who still stood in their living room, had given her the news—her attacker had been located and arrested.

Was that it? Was it all over? They had him in custody. He wouldn't be able to blackmail people from prison, telling them to harass her. He wouldn't be able to follow her around, listen in on her conversations through her phone.

Then again, he would be able to tell the cops about her, wouldn't he? She could already imagine him with his attorney at the police station. The attorney would explain that his client had valuable intel. He was willing to cut a deal. He could give them a murderer. And then, just like in all those cop shows, the district attorney would let him go, and in exchange he would tell them about Theodora Briggs, who these days called herself Gemma Foster.

It wasn't over. If anything, it was getting even worse.

When the police had shown up, she'd been so relieved. Officer Mendez was almost six feet tall, a reassuring protector. He had gently helped her and Lucas out of the car, kept telling them they were safe now. They had nothing to fear. After he led them into the house, he stayed there, in case the attacker doubled back, and Gemma was so grateful she wanted to cry. But now that she knew her attacker was in the back of a police car, she wanted Officer Mendez to leave. His presence wasn't reassuring anymore. It was becoming menacing. At any moment he could be contacted by dispatch. Officer Mendez, that woman you're with, she's wanted for murder. Cuff her and bring her to the station.

"Thank you for all your help," she said, trying to control the tremor in her voice. "Do you need anything else from us? My statement, or something?"

Officer Mendez smiled at her. "The detective just wanted to talk to you for a few minutes. She's on her way here."

"Detective?"

"Yes, ma'am. That's what they told me."

Gemma swallowed. Her heart beat faster. Did Lucas feel it? She caressed his hair. "You okay, sweetie?"

"Uh-huh," he said, his voice muffled by her shirt. He'd been clutching her ever since they stepped inside the house.

The front door barged open, and Gemma tightened with fear, but to her relief it was only Benjamin. He strode across the room, sat down beside her, and pulled both her and Lucas into a big hug.

"Hey," he said.

"Hey, Daddy," Lucas mumbled, lifting his head from Gemma's shirt. She had a wet spot where he'd buried his face. Best-case scenario—tears. But Gemma knew it was at least 50 percent snot.

"I'm glad you're here," Gemma murmured.

"Are you both okay?" He looked at her worriedly.

From the pounding in her face, she suspected she was developing a nasty bruise. "We're fine," she said. "We just got a big scare. But Lucas was very brave."

"I'm sure he was." Benjamin kissed the top of Lucas's head.

They exchanged looks. That special look that said *talk later—not in front of Lucas.* The last thing Gemma wanted right now was to talk about the attack.

Benjamin kept hugging them for a few more seconds, then got up and went over to Officer Mendez. "Hi." He offered his hand. "I'm Benjamin Foster."

"Nice to meet you. I'm Officer Mendez." The cop shook her husband's hand. "Your wife was very coolheaded. Thanks to her description, we already have the guy."

"Oh, good," Benjamin said. "So . . . what now?"

"The detective is on her way to take a statement. She should be here in just a—"

A sharp rap on the door interrupted them. Benjamin opened the door. Gemma gently pried herself loose from Lucas and stood up.

A short woman with wavy blond hair stood in the doorway. Her eyes skittered across the room quickly. Her gaze paused on Gemma for a long second. Did she already know the truth? Was she here to arrest her? Push her against the wall, cuff her hands behind her back? Theodora Briggs, you have the right to remain silent.

"Hi," she said, voice soft, casual. "I'm Detective Holly O'Donnell. Can I come in?"

"Sure." Benjamin stepped back. "The officer told me that you caught the guy?"

"Uh-huh. He tried to drive away, but he was in bad shape, ran into a—" She noticed Lucas as his head peeked over the couch. "Hi there!"

"Hello," Lucas said.

"I'm Holly." Her voice didn't change as she talked to Lucas. She knew how to talk to kids. Gemma had a gut feeling that the detective was a mother too. "What's your name?"

"Lucas."

"Nice to meet you, Lucas." She turned to Gemma. "And you're the one who called, right? Gemma Foster?"

Gemma swallowed. "That's right."

"The dispatcher was very impressed with you. You kept your cool and really helped us." She turned to Lucas. "Your mom is the coolest mom ever; did you know that?"

"Uh-huh." Lucas was smiling now.

"Good. Lucas, I need to talk to your mom in private for a few minutes. Would you mind staying here with your dad and Victor?"

"Okay."

And just like that, by talking to a four-year-old, Detective O'Donnell had somehow made it clear she and Gemma were about to have a private conversation, and there wasn't going to be any debate about it. Gemma would have been impressed if she wasn't so terrified. And Benjamin didn't seem as if he was about to interject, to say he wanted to be a part of that conversation as well.

"We can talk in the kitchen," Gemma said.

"Great." Detective O'Donnell smiled pleasantly.

Gemma led the woman to the kitchen, shutting the door behind them.

"Um . . . Can I get you anything? Coffee?"

"No thanks, but feel free to make some for yourself."

Gemma felt jittery enough as it was. She filled two glasses with water, then added a couple of ice cubes to each.

"Thanks." Holly took the glass from her hand and sat down by the table. She took out a notepad and a pen and set them in front of her. "Like I said before, I'm Detective Holly O'Donnell. I'm the head of the cybercrime unit."

"Cybercrime unit?" Gemma blurted. "This wasn't . . . I mean . . ." She became quiet.

Holly O'Donnell was looking at her, saying nothing. Gemma got the sense that she had to be incredibly careful with this woman.

Finally, Holly continued. "We managed to catch Hank Turpin . . . that's the guy who we believe assaulted you. He smashed his car into a tree. Hard to drive straight after being maced."

Gemma nodded, saying nothing. Hank Turpin . . . that name rang no bells. She didn't recall knowing anyone whose last name was Turpin. She wondered if it was his real name.

"He was a mess." Holly opened her notepad and flipped to an empty page. "Blood all over his face, could hardly talk."

"Uh-huh."

"Did you ever see him before?"

"Um . . . I think I saw him this morning, walking by my house."

"Was he watching you?"

"Maybe. I don't know."

"And before that?"

"I don't think so," Gemma said truthfully.

"Can you tell me what happened?" Holly asked. Her voice softened, just a bit.

Gemma steeled herself and outlined the events of the assault, as accurately as she could. Holly jotted notes in her notepad, never interrupting. As she described how he pulled her pants down, Gemma had to pause and drink from her glass. But then she resumed and told the rest, speaking as quickly as possible to get it over with.

"Okay." Holly tapped at the notebook when Gemma finished. "Who's Theodora?"

There it was. They had her. But Gemma wasn't about to give up that easily. She frowned. "Theodora? I don't know."

"When you called dispatch, they asked your name. And you said Theodora. Then later, you said your name was Gemma. So I was wondering, who's Theodora."

Gemma wanted to punch herself. "I was very scared. I wasn't thinking straight. I don't even remember what I said. I don't know anyone named Theodora."

O'Donnell tilted her head slightly, watching Gemma, saying nothing. She had large brown eyes, the color of chocolate. Gemma did her best to hold her gaze.

"Okay," Holly finally said. "So you don't know this guy, right? Hank Turpin?"

"I've never met him before."

"Do you know anyone else who might wish you harm?"

"Uh . . ." She literally had a list of people like that in a drawer in her bedroom. "No. Can't think of anyone."

"Weird." O'Donnell put her pen between her lips. "You see, this guy, Turpin, he's a real piece of work. He got out of prison just a year ago after a ten-year sentence for rape and aggravated assault. And the moment we grabbed him, he told us he wanted to make a deal."

Gemma clenched her fists under the table. "You can't release him. He attacked me. He's dangerous."

"Oh, don't worry, he's not going anywhere. But he said something strange. He said someone *told* him to follow you around. Take pictures of you. That's why I was wondering if you could think of anyone who wanted to harm you."

For a few seconds, Gemma's mind was completely blank. She'd assumed the guy who assaulted her was the Shadowman. The blackmailer, the man behind the curtain, the man who'd hacked into her phone and messed with her life.

But he wasn't.

This Hank Turpin was just another person who'd been sent by the Shadowman. Probably blackmailed, just like the rest.

"So . . . this other guy . . . ," Gemma said slowly. "He told this Turpin to attack me?"

"We're not so clear on that," O'Donnell said. "He clammed up just after he started talking. I think he realized no deal was forthcoming. But a guy like Turpin . . . once he follows a woman for a while, he can get obsessed. So I think this attack wasn't necessarily part of the deal."

O'Donnell didn't know who she was after all. Gemma's relief was short lived. That meant the Shadowman was still out there. And it looked like he didn't balk at sending violent criminals after her. Her and her family. Lucas could have gotten hurt.

"I see," she finally said.

"You don't know what Turpin is talking about?"

"No. I can't think of anything."

"Really?" O'Donnell tilted her head again. "Do you know a woman named Paula Donahue?"

Gemma almost said she didn't. But there was no point. The detective clearly knew a lot more than she let on. "Yes. She was my son's teacher."

"*Was*, yes. Paula called the police yesterday. She reported she'd been blackmailed for the past year. The person who blackmailed her threatened to send nude photos of her to everyone she knew. She said she told a parent of one of the kids in her class about it—one Gemma Foster, and the blackmailer apparently found out. Her nude photos were released. Paula told me some of her tasks were aimed directly at you."

It was like that interrogation all those years ago. Back then Detective Dunn had seemed to be on her side at first. Getting her story from her, bit by bit. Then he began asking difficult questions. Out came small details that didn't align with her story. That didn't look good. Gemma recalled the interrogation went on for hours. That she needed to pee but didn't dare to ask to go to the bathroom. By the end, her bladder was about to burst, Dunn's voice sharp as he asked what really happened that night, why did she come to that party, what happened between her and Victoria . . .

She needed to pee now. Needed to pee so badly.

"Paula told me something," Gemma blurted. "I wasn't really paying attention. Something about putting a mask in Lucas's lunch box and telling him a story. It sounded like nonsense."

"It does sound like nonsense, doesn't it? That's what I thought yesterday when I talked to her. Supposedly this guy would sometimes demand she perform illegal acts, for no apparent reason beyond his own amusement. That's why I took an interest. During all my time as a detective, I've only seen this happen once before. Years ago. And that time, it ended very badly." O'Donnell leaned forward. "Women died, Mrs. Foster."

Gemma's lips trembled. She was about to burst into tears. She needed to pee.

"So trust me that when I hear about a similar case, I don't take it lightly," O'Donnell continued after a second. "When I got the call telling me there was a guy who claimed he'd been sent to follow you by an unknown individual, I got here as fast as I could. At least two people were sent to intrude on your life. By someone online. Do you know why?"

"No, I have no idea."

"Were there any more?"

"N . . . no."

"Gemma," O'Donnell said gently. "This guy won't stop. I don't know what your history with him is, but if you don't tell me the truth, I won't be able to help you. I won't be able to protect you."

She almost cracked just then. She almost told O'Donnell the truth. Her name was Theodora Briggs. She was wanted for a murder from thirteen years ago, and somehow, this guy found her. The words were on her lips, dying to come out. O'Donnell seemed to know it, saying nothing, looking at her expectantly with those understanding brown eyes.

"I'm sorry," Gemma said. "I don't know who this guy is or what his beef is with me. And I really need to go to the bathroom."

Chapter 29

Gemma sat on Lucas's bed, her back against the wall, her fingers slowly trailing his body, back and forth. She wasn't sure if he was asleep yet. His breathing had slowed down to a steady rhythm, but she knew from experience that it didn't necessarily mean anything. If she got up now, he could wake up completely. So she *had* to stay there just a bit longer. It wasn't as if she was hiding in his room to avoid talking to Benjamin.

Lucas had been difficult throughout the evening. Several times he cried inconsolably, a high keening wail, interspersed with shuddering sobs that cut into Gemma's heart like knives. At other moments he would stare at nothing, his body rigid, and Gemma could only hug him, caress his hair, whispering empty platitudes in his ears. Benjamin had been useless in a typical masculine way, telling Lucas that everything was all right now and that he had nothing to worry about anymore. As if the events of the afternoon could be swept away, like a painful scrape on the knee, or a bad playdate.

Did Benjamin realize this event would be forever etched in Lucas's mind? It would shape his world and his behavior in countless ways.

"Mommy," Lucas murmured, his voice soft and faraway, almost lost to dreams.

"Yes, sweetie?"

"Is the bad man still in prison?"

"Yes, sweetie. They'll keep him there for a very, very long time."

"Even after next year?"

"For years and years. We'll never see him again."

"But what if when he comes out, he'll go looking for us?"

"If he ever comes out, he'll be an old man. He won't be able to hurt us."

"Does your face still hurt?"

It did. A dull throb that blazed whenever she moved too fast. "Just a bit. It's a lot better."

"You can't kiss it goodbye."

That's what they did when Lucas got banged up on the playground or at home. They kissed the hurt goodbye.

"Daddy kissed it goodbye."

"And it helped?"

"Yeah, it helped."

"Okay."

After a minute, his breathing became steady again. Gemma looked at his slack face and ruffled hair and had to stifle a sob. That violent pervert, Hank Turpin, had followed them around. She'd googled him earlier, read the articles that covered his arrest from ten years before, the account of one of the women he'd assaulted. This was the man she'd exposed her child to. And it wasn't over. The Shadowman could send others just like Turpin. Next time she probably wouldn't be so lucky. She could get hurt. Lucas could get hurt.

She couldn't let there be a next time. As long as she was around Lucas, he was in danger. She would have to leave for a while, until this was over.

But Thelma and Detective O'Donnell were right. A guy like that didn't go away on his own. She would have to end this herself. She couldn't afford to play it safe anymore, trying to find him from a distance. She knew where he was from. She would have to go to him.

She waited a few minutes more, then slowly got up from the bed. She paused, looking at Lucas, making sure her movement didn't wake him up. Then quietly tiptoed out of the room.

Benjamin was in the kitchen, stirring a pot, a sweet cinnamon smell filling the room.

"Hey," he said. "I thought you needed something comforting. I'm making warm apple cider."

"That sounds really nice." Gemma smiled at him. When she smiled, her bruise pulsed.

She needed to talk to him, tell him what was about to happen. But first, there was a bit of playacting she needed to get out of the way. She took out her phone from her pocket. She'd removed the battery from it earlier. Now she slid it inside, turning it on. She waited patiently for it to boot up.

"Is Lucas asleep?" Benjamin asked.

"I think so."

"He was very upset."

"It's been a traumatic day for him." The phone blinked awake. The wallpaper was an image of her, Lucas, and Benjamin, smiling at the camera. She wondered if somewhere, in a dark room, the same photo appeared on the Shadowman's screen, signaling the phone was on.

"Oh, there we go," she said. "I managed to turn my phone on."

"Is there some problem with it?" Benjamin asked.

"I think it got banged up when that guy attacked me," she said. "It keeps switching off."

"Do you want me to take a look at it?" Benjamin asked.

"Maybe later," Gemma said. "It's not urgent."

Halfway through her sentence, she popped the battery out. Hopefully the Shadowman had listened in on that short exchange. If he did, he'd think her phone wasn't working well. She had a good excuse to turn it on and off at will.

Benjamin ladled apple cider into two mugs and handed one to Gemma. She cupped it with her palms, letting the warmth spread through her fingers. She inhaled the sweet steam, shutting her eyes with momentary calm. Benjamin's apple cider always made her feel better. It was supposedly a recipe that had been passed along the Foster family line generation after generation. Gemma doubted it, but sometimes, sipping the sweet, spicy drink, she could almost imagine Benjamin's ancestors, centuries ago, making this drink atop a stove lit by firewood.

"I have the card of that detective who came by here," Benjamin said. "Holly O'Donnell. Tomorrow, I'll call her, see what's going on with this Hank Turpin."

Gemma nodded. "Okay, good." Benjamin needed to feel like he was doing something, taking charge. That was okay by her.

"I've been reading about it online. You'll probably need to go and give them another statement. But it looks good because Holly said the guy already confessed. He's a repeat offender, so it's not likely that the judge would allow bail. If we're in the bail hearing it might help too."

Gemma loved how Benjamin could read online about something for fifteen minutes, and then behave as if he was the absolute expert on the subject. It was ridiculous, but there was something endearing about it. Imagine, being so confident in yourself. Maybe Lucas could be like that when he grew up. Because being like Gemma, second-guessing everything she did, was not something she wished for her son.

"This thing got me thinking," she said slowly.

"Yeah, me too. We need a dog."

"Yes. No. What?" Gemma blinked in confusion.

"We should get a dog. Like a large guard dog. It would make you feel safer. And it would be great for Lucas."

So Benjamin was already planning to help the detective with her case, make sure the judge wouldn't give Turpin bail, and get a dog. He was really going overboard with this taking-charge thing. How much more would he do to make himself feel like he was handling this? Would he buy a gun? Dig a moat around the house? Take martial arts classes?

"I don't know about the dog. We can talk about it, sure."

"You like dogs, right?"

She was okay with dogs. Not great. Definitely not okay with large ones. A quick image flashed in her mind. Running away in the forest, the dogs chasing her, hunting her. She blinked it away. Now her husband wanted a guard dog to protect her. There was irony there somewhere. "Dogs are nice. Listen, Benjamin—"

"My mom called my dad today," Benjamin said. "I guess that's one good thing that came out of this. She called him to let him know what had happened, and to tell him you and Lucas were all right. I think this emergency made her realize how much she misses him."

"That's great news."

"My dad knows about dogs," Benjamin said. "We could ask him what he thinks."

Benjamin was usually so calm. But right now he was talking fast, his body language sharp, erratic. His mug of cider lay on the table forgotten. He was exhausting her.

Gemma leaned forward and grabbed his wrist. She squeezed it slightly, then pulled his hand to her lips and kissed his fingers softly. "Can we talk about the police and the dog and all that tomorrow? I need you to comfort me right now."

"Oh, right, of course." He blinked. "Sorry, I was just . . . you're right."

He got up and went over to her. He hugged her from behind. A jolt of anxiety shot through her, Benjamin's arms limiting her movement, suffocating her, pinning her to the chair . . .

She forced herself to lean back against him, taking another sip from her cider. This was her husband, the man she loved. He wanted to keep her safe, never to hurt her. She breathed, shutting her eyes, letting his big, warm arms take some of the stress away.

Then she exhaled and said, "I think I have to go back to Crumville. To my hometown." Just saying it aloud made her feel ill.

Benjamin pulled away from her. "What? Where is this coming from?"

She'd prepared what she was about to say beforehand, while she was in Lucas's room. Outlining the events of the past week. Explaining about the man who was after her. That he was probably from Crumville— maybe Victoria's sibling, or father. She had to go back and figure it out.

To pinpoint the man's identity. Once she did that, she could give him to the police . . . or to Thelma's contacts. Fix all this. Make sure they could get their old lives back. Make sure the people she loved were safe and wouldn't be hurt because of their link to her. First and foremost, make sure Lucas would be safe.

When she thought it through earlier, it had seemed easy. Benjamin wanted to protect Lucas just like she did, wanted to keep him safe more than anything. And he knew she was strong, that she could handle herself. He would trust her judgment.

But now, seeing him scramble to take charge, she couldn't. If she told him about the man who was after her, he would just want to do it himself. He'd come up with ridiculous plans—private detectives, and hunting dogs, and going to the FBI. He'd read online about hackers and try to figure out how he could trace the hacker's info back to him. And he would *never* let her risk herself. It was who he was. It was what he was taught to be and believe. And it was genetics, the big strong man protecting his family and his tribe.

She would have to lie. God knew she had a lot of practice.

"I . . . it just made me think. Made me realize my life was too precious to spend running away and hiding." A ridiculous, banal sentence. But it sounded convincing. She had a long line of bad Hollywood movies backing her up. She had to confront her demons and so on and so forth. "I need to go back there. See my mother . . . Lucas has a grandmother he's never even met."

"But you said the police were looking for you!"

"I don't even know if that's true anymore," she said. That wasn't a lie. She'd been a suspect all those years ago. There had been a "mountain of evidence" pointing at her. But they hadn't arrested her. There was nothing conclusive. And hopefully, in the past thirteen years, Victoria's murder case had just grown colder. "That's something else I could try and find out."

"You could start with a phone call," Benjamin said. "If your mom tells you they're still looking, you could stay away."

She had to leave, get away from Lucas and him. "If they're looking for me, they could find out about this phone call," Gemma said, not knowing if that was true. Would the cops tap her mother's phone for all these years? "It could lead them right here. Benjamin, I know you're worried, but I'll be careful, okay? A quick visit just to see my mom. Two or three days, tops."

"I don't think we should make any decisions tonight," Benjamin said. "You're still distraught. Let's sleep on this, think things over, okay?"

"You're right," Gemma said, pulling him closer. "Let's not decide anything tonight."

But she'd already decided. She was going back.

Chapter 30

His mother always hated the chirping of crickets, which was a problem when living in a small town in Georgia. The summer's cricket song was practically their anthem. Throughout his childhood, he was a witness to his mother's war on crickets. Spraying the garden with fragrant oils or vinegar. Placing cricket traps all around their yard. Sometimes at night, when one cricket was particularly noisy, she would get out of bed and roam the backyard, looking for it, a rolled-up newspaper in her shaking fist.

Then, when he was about ten, his dad had all their windows sound-proofed. It didn't solve the problem entirely, but the crickets' song became muted, faraway.

And he realized he missed it. He had a hard time sleeping without it. He'd never known he needed that sound until it was gone.

He felt that way now, Theodora's phone gone from his feed. He couldn't listen in on her conversations, couldn't see her location on his screen, couldn't skim through her daily browsing.

It wasn't like he missed her voice. He *hated* her voice. He hated everything about her, the psycho bitch who had killed Victoria. But it was reassuring to have that constant lifeline to her. Knowing she couldn't do anything without him knowing about it. That she was in his power.

When that idiot Turpin had gone after her, he wanted to scream. He listened in, hearing the sounds of struggle, the screaming, thinking she was going to die. Of course part of him was happy about it; she *deserved* to die. But *he* was the one who was supposed to decide when that happened, not some random pervert. When he heard her call the police, he breathed a sigh of relief. She was okay.

Then, later, the phone switched off and on a few times. The last time it was turned off, he just had a few seconds to hear Theodora telling her husband it got hit during the struggle. Then it switched off yet again. He slammed his desk in frustration. That asshole Turpin. He was just supposed to scare her, that was all. Brush against her, whisper in her ear that she was being watched. The instruction wasn't complicated. Why were some people so useless?

Now Turpin was in custody. He would be charged for this assault, and would end up in prison, completely useless. He didn't need a thrall in prison. Besides, Turpin hadn't done what he was told, and there was a price to pay.

He checked the evidence he had on Turpin—his chat with his friend, where he had boasted about a woman he'd assaulted after getting out of prison. Good enough to add a few more years to Turpin's prison sentence, if the police did their job. He sent all the files to the Chicago PD. He really had to get someone there. He had three cops in his list of thralls, but no one in Chicago.

Now he shifted uncomfortably, needing to know what was going on. When would she fix her phone? When would she turn it on again? People couldn't really get along without their phones; they had to have those things available twenty-four seven. But then again, Theodora wasn't like everyone else. She stayed away from social media. Wasn't in a lot of chats or groups.

He tried to distract himself, opening the file of one of his latest projects—Helena Rodriguez. Helena was one of the people whose passwords on the new age website had been hacked. He'd found that this same password was also the password for her Google account. So now he had access to her photos and emails, including some very private photos and videos she took while sexting with her husband—an army officer currently deployed in South Korea.

But that was just the first stage. For Helena to take him seriously, she needed to understand that he knew *everything* about her. To do that he activated a script that dumped all her social media posts and comments into a large file. He now went through the file and painstakingly retrieved anything he could about her.

The names and ages of her two kids were easy enough to find—she posted about both of their respective birthdays. From people commenting on those very posts, as well as other posts, he managed to get a list of her best friends and close family members.

He had found her address from her email, and right now he was busy figuring out her routine. Sure, people took you seriously if you knew where they lived. But if you knew that they sat at a certain café every Wednesday afternoon after dropping their kid at their dance class, they *really* started to listen.

So to do that he painstakingly went through each and every post, checking geotags, cross-checking photos with Google Maps, and . . .

He couldn't concentrate.

He checked Theodora's phone again. Still off. He checked her laptop too. No dice. It was driving him insane.

He opened his chat with Virtual Victoria.

Hey, he typed. My plan with Theodora has hit a snag.

Oh no, Victoria answered a few seconds later. Is it a big problem?

Nothing I can't handle.

Good. Victoria added an angry emoji after that. She needs to pay. When we were kids, that whore broke my heart, and years later she stopped it.

Sometimes the things Virtual Victoria said were so laced with actual emotion and perceptiveness that it gave him pause.

That whore broke my heart, and years later, she stopped it. Who would have believed that a computer made that sentence up?

And it was true.

In the past years, he started getting his hands on anything that reminded him of Victoria. At first, he collected every photo and every video he could find of her. Thankfully, there was no shortage of those, especially once he managed to hack into her mother's computer. Thousands of files that he meticulously sorted into folders. Then, one of his blackmailed thralls managed to break into Craig Howell's garage, stealing a couple of boxes full of Victoria's things. Mostly clothing, her scent long gone, unfortunately. But, also, three diaries from a younger age. Priceless. Reading those he grew to know Victoria even better than before. And he found out about the moment that changed her. The moment that, eventually, drove her and Theodora apart.

Even before she had taken her life, Theodora had let her friend down. When Victoria had needed her the most, she'd turned her back.

She broke Victoria's heart. And years later, she stopped it.

He couldn't let her out of his sight. He clenched his teeth, then turned to his thrall list. He found Madeline Davis's contact info. She was just a short walk from Theodora's house. Her color code was orange-red. That meant she was willing to do quite a lot to keep her husband and her friends from knowing about her drug habit. She'd already done something for him just a week before—that Halloween gig. He could tell she didn't like it, him telling her what to wear when she went trick-or-treating with her girl and instructing her to deliver his message. At the time he'd marked her name on the sheet, giving her a couple of weeks off to calm down a bit. Well, he needed her now.

He opened a new email and sent her a list of instructions. He wanted a photo of Theodora's house right now. He explained where the bedroom window was. And he wanted a video of Theodora leaving for work in the morning. And another video of Theodora while she worked at the salon.

He sent it, and exhaled, feeling the tension trickle out of his body. Theodora wasn't going anywhere. He still had her under his control.

Chapter 31

Gemma's drive from Chicago to Crumville was long enough to feel like an odyssey. An American *Odyssey*, where the sirens were replaced with roadside shopping malls, and the battle with the Cyclops was just that long traffic jam in Indianapolis, and Calypso was that McDonald's in Nashville where she had drunk too much Coke.

Fine, it was a boring odyssey, but thinking about it helped Gemma ignore the rising dread that Crumville's growing proximity evoked in her.

She had originally planned to stop midway at a motel, but they all seemed repulsive. The kinds of places where she would encounter a curly black hair in the bathroom and see something scurry on the floor from the corner of her eye. Besides, she doubted she could sleep knowing what tomorrow would bring.

So a daylong drive it was, the car consuming gasoline and Gemma consuming Coke and coffee, and neither of them particularly happy about it.

Even without the WELCOME TO GEORGIA signs, or the road signs counting down the distance to Augusta, Gemma could sense Crumville looming nearer. Was it the trees? The familiar long bridge that crossed Lake Oconee? Or maybe it was something inside her, a long-forgotten compass in her gut, pointing the way to where she grew up.

Her hands were rigid on the wheel as she saw the edge of Crumville in the distance. Her breathing became labored, erratic. She'd managed to avoid this place for thirteen years, and now the memories were about to pounce back. The party, the police interrogation, her mother's disappointment and horror . . . she tried to prepare herself for the inevitable moment they would strike, submerge her.

But it was the other memories that caught her by surprise.

Crumville's Walmart was the first building to welcome her. Where she'd go grocery shopping with her dad, or her mother, always allowed to choose one treat for herself (two treats with Dad, but don't tell Mom). Where was the shoe store? They'd buy her shoes there every year. As a child she used to love it. Then, as a teenager she was mortified about it; all the other girls got *their* shoes in expensive designer stores in Atlanta. But right now she desperately searched for it. She could buy Lucas a pair of shoes there. Tell him that was where Mommy always got her shoes. But the shop was gone. Probably closed. Was the mall always this tiny? It had seemed enormous back then.

The school! She expected to feel revulsion or horror, but hang on, that corner was where she had had her first, and last, cigarette—hacking and coughing, and feeling sick, Steve and Allan laughing their asses off. And there was that gap in the fence, just large enough for her to slip through as a kid, cutting class to buy candy across the street. The shopkeeper used to quirk a hairy eyebrow at her, as if asking her why she wasn't in school, but he never said anything and had once given her a free pack of gum.

The school was smaller than she remembered too. Had someone shrunk the town while she was gone?

A few blocks later, the primary school. There was that small dip in the yard that always filled with water when it rained. They'd play there—dare each other to jump over it, skip stones on it. Once, back when she and Victoria were friends, the boys had found a frog there and chased them both with it, and she was shrieking and laughing at the same time.

That corner of the sidewalk where she fell from her bike and scraped her knee so badly she felt like she might actually die; there was so much blood. But later when everyone wanted to see her stitches, she was a hero for a day. Wasn't there a hair salon just over there? There had been for sure! Her mother always had her hair done there. But now it was a Dollar General store. And where was the café? It was now a Mexican restaurant. Gemma felt a pang at the loss, which was ridiculous—she hadn't thought about that café *once* in the past decade.

She'd remembered Crumville as the place where she was bullied, and then the place where she was accused of murder. The place where the police saw her as a suspect. But sweep those experiences away, and a trove of childhood memories lay beneath, untouched. And a lot of her childhood had been . . . happy.

Then she reached the crossroads with Fourth Street. Left to Victoria's house, straight ahead to her own. Unable to stop herself, she glanced left. She couldn't see Victoria's home from there, but she could spot the tall hickory tree in their yard.

Oh yeah, the bad memories were still there. She quickly tore her eyes away.

It was weird, driving down the street toward her home. She'd gotten her driver's license when she was twenty-one, years after leaving this place. Crumville was a place where she rode in the back seat of the car or on her bike, or walked on foot, drenched in sweat. It wasn't a place where she drove, steering wheel in her hands, the sole master of the radio and the car's air conditioner.

She parked just across from her house and stared at it.

In the past years, Gemma's life had gone through endless changes. She'd transformed into a completely different person, a grown woman, a mother, a person who'd taken charge of her life. It was so bizarre to see how little this place had changed during that time. A tree had been cut down in the yard, and in its place was a flower bed. The front door was now a darker shade of brown. The shed was gone. And . . . that was pretty much it. There was a crack in the step that led to the front door, and Gemma remembered the crack was there *thirteen* years ago. She recalled her mother telling Richard over and over they had to get it fixed, and Richard said he would handle it. And now, there it was. Richard hadn't handled it. Or maybe he was just about to get to it.

Or maybe they moved away, and someone else lived here now.

If it was up to Gemma, she would have stayed in the car for fifteen minutes, twenty minutes, an hour. Maybe she would have gone to sleep in the car, telling herself it would be better to show up in the morning. But human anatomy dictated that when a person drank gallons of Coke and coffee throughout the day, that person had to pee. And she needed to so badly, it overcame her anxiety.

She stepped out of the car and strode down the path to the front door. She paused briefly, taking a long breath, then knocked.

"Just a second," a voice from inside said.

Her mother's voice.

The door opened. Her mother stood in front of her. Shorter than Gemma recalled, crinkles lining her forehead. Hair in a bun, replacing the perm she had worked so hard to maintain. But still unmistakably her mother.

"Can I help you?" her mother asked.

Gemma swallowed. "Uh . . ."

And then her mother's aloof politeness disintegrated. Her eyes widened, mouth slackening. She leaned on the doorframe, blood draining from her face. "Theodora?" she whispered, her voice trembling.

"Hi, Mom," Gemma mumbled, tears filling her eyes.

For a few seconds neither of them moved. Her mother seemed as if she was about to faint. But then, instead, she clutched at Gemma, hugging her, her breath shuddering with sobs. Her mother's fingers dug into Gemma's back, as if she was grabbing her to make sure Gemma wouldn't be able to run off again.

Chapter 32

After a hug that stretched to the point of being uncomfortable, Gemma excused herself and asked if she could use the bathroom. It was bizarre, asking to use the bathroom in this house, like she was some kind of guest. Which maybe she was. Her mother seemed worried, as if she thought Gemma might escape through the tiny bathroom window. Gemma couldn't shake the feeling that she was standing by the door, listening.

And now her mother had led her to the kitchen. She made her a cup of tea. With two spoons of sugar, just like Gemma used to drink as a child. An utterly undrinkable sweet brew.

"You must be hungry." Her mother moved around the kitchen nervously. "Can I make you something? Pasta? Or pizza? I have some frozen pizza."

"Whatever you have. I don't want to trouble you," Gemma said uncomfortably. "I can go get us some takeout. I saw there's a new Mexican—"

"No!" Her mother blurted. "No. I'll make us something. You just . . . sit here."

"Okay." Gemma sipped from the cup just to do something. Ugh. It was even worse the second time. It seemed impossible that she drank it like that as a kid. It's a miracle she still had teeth.

"Did you have a long drive?"

"Pretty long, yeah. I uh . . . drove all the way from Chicago."

"Chicago," her mother whispered. "That's where you live now?"

"Yeah."

"Chicago," her mother repeated. "I was there three years ago with Richard. If I'd known . . . Just imagine. I could have accidentally met you on the street."

"It's a big city," Gemma said awkwardly. "And I never go to the more . . . touristy places. Where *is* Richard?"

"He went to get groceries. We didn't know you were coming . . ."

"Yeah, I'm sorry I didn't call before—"

"No! Don't apologize. It's fine."

Their dynamic was all wrong. Gemma knew relationships between parents and children changed gradually as the kids grew up. She'd seen Benjamin with his parents, treating them with a sort of love intermingled with frustration and respect. But Gemma had severed her connection with her mother when she was still a teenager, and now there seemed to be no way to reestablish it. Her mother seemed terrified that if she said the wrong thing, Gemma might get up and leave. And Gemma wasn't sure how to talk to her mother—it wasn't as if she could act like a seventeen-year-old, treat her mother like a mixture of cook, chauffeur, bank, landlord, and despot. Stomping around the house and slamming the door to her room when she wanted privacy.

Her mother placed a pot of water on the stove. "I wonder what Maude will say when I tell her you're here. She didn't believe you were even . . . I mean she didn't think you'd be coming back here."

"Mom," Gemma said. "You can't tell anyone I'm here."

Her mother turned around and frowned at her. "What? Why not?"

"Because I don't want anyone to know. I don't want . . . the police to know."

"Maude wouldn't tell the police. She's my best friend!"

"Just . . . don't tell anyone, okay?"

"The police aren't even looking for you anymore. Detective Dunn told me he didn't think you're a suspect."

A surge of hope blossomed in her. "Really? Did they close the case?"

"Well . . . no. They never found out who did it. But he seemed very sincere when I talked to him. And he clearly said you weren't really a suspect."

"Okay, I don't know if I want to bet my life on how sincere Detective Dunn sounded, Mom. Just don't tell anyone for now, okay?"

"Of course. You know, we need to clear up your room. Once Richard gets here, I'll have him do it. We stored a few boxes there, but we still have your old bed, and I'll put on some fresh sheets. Richard wanted to get rid of it a few years ago, but we ended up deciding to keep it there. Your room is mostly just like you left it."

"That's great, Mom, thanks. I can move the boxes myself."

"Richard will be happy to do it. He'll be really excited to see you're here."

Gemma doubted it. "So how are you doing?" she asked lamely.

"Oh . . . fine. You know me. I keep myself busy." She let out a forced laugh. "I stopped teaching."

"Really, why?"

"No reason, really. I just . . . couldn't really do it anymore after you . . . Well anyway, I don't miss it at all. And Richard's business is doing really well. Your grandpa died four years ago."

"Oh," Gemma said heavily. Her grandmother had died when she was fifteen, and her grandparents from her father's side hadn't kept in touch. But her grandfather had lived in Augusta, and they'd seen him regularly before she left.

"Yes. Kidney failure. It was very fast." Her voice trembled.

"I'm sorry, Mom."

"But your cousin has children now! You should really see them. They're so cute, and smart too! Their daughter looks a bit like you did at that age."

"Um . . . I have a son too."

"You . . . what?"

"Lucas. He's four years old." Gemma took out her phone to show her mother a photo . . . then realized it was turned off and that she couldn't turn it on. She pocketed it quickly.

"That's wonderful . . . excuse me." Her mother dashed out of the kitchen.

Gemma guiltily got up and checked the pot. The water was boiling. She added the pasta that her mother had set on the counter. She wanted to add salt as well but couldn't find it. She'd never cooked anything as a teen, beyond frying an egg or microwaving something from the fridge. Now, for the first time, she viewed the kitchen as a grown-up. It was larger than her kitchen. Her mother had a nice oven. Was this the oven they had when she lived here? Gemma had no idea.

Not having anything better to do, she kept stirring the pasta, staring out the window. It was already dark outside. She needed to call Benjamin before Lucas went to sleep but didn't want to use her own phone. She wanted to call from the landline. If her mother still had one.

The pasta was ready, but she had no idea where the colander was. She helplessly searched through the cupboards. Where did she keep it? Where *was* her mother, for that matter? She froze as she heard the garage door opening. Richard was back. And there she was—the prodigal stepdaughter had returned and was making overcooked pasta.

The door opened just as her mother reappeared, her eyes puffy and red. Richard stepped inside.

"Honey, look who came back," her mother said with an unnaturally cheerful voice.

Richard put a bunch of shopping bags on the floor and looked at Gemma, his face registering nothing but mild confusion.

"Hi," he said pleasantly.

It was obvious he had no inkling who she was.

"It's Theodora," her mother whispered softly.

Richard's eyes widened. "Oh. I see."

"Hi, Richard," Gemma said. "It's nice to see you again."

"Yes. Nice to see you too! Of course."

Not as excited as her mother had predicted. If anything, he seemed horrified.

Chapter 33

"Shit."

He read through the email again, as if he'd missed some hidden message within those three short sentences. He'd sent Madeline Davis on a very simple mission—all he'd wanted were some images of Theodora. At home. At work. It wasn't like he'd asked her for the United States' nuclear launch codes, or to solve the Goldbach conjecture. Just a Few. Damn. Photos!

"Shit. Shit!"

She was clearly terrified when she wrote her email. Apologizing twice. And she misspelled the word *missing*. Which apparently was what Theodora was. Missing. As proof, the useless bitch attached several photos of Theodora's empty bedroom, of her husband and son eating breakfast alone, and of the beauty salon, where Theodora wasn't present. As if photos without Theodora were proof of *anything*. He could take those photos himself if he wanted. Theodora wasn't in this room, right? Or in his damn bathroom, or in his bedroom closet, for that matter. He didn't ask for photos *without* Theodora. He asked for photos *of* her!

"Shitshitshitshitshitshit."

He got up from his chair and kicked the nearby trash can, which scattered papers and empty snack wrappers all over the floor. This infuriated him even more. Madeline Davis should come over here and pick those up, it's her damn fault!

Enraged, he sat back by the computer. If she couldn't do a simple task, she didn't deserve to be his thrall. She wanted out, did she? Fine, she got it. He sent the video of her smoking meth to her husband and to all her friends. Sent the police an anonymous tip, too, though he doubted they'd do anything about it. Grinding his teeth, he wrote Madeline back. Telling her she failed. Telling her what a worthless bitch she was. He clicked send.

Then he noticed that he, too, had misspelled a word in his own email. He got up, kicked the upended trash can again.

Where was Theodora? Was she simply hiding at home? Cowering after Turpin had gone after her? That would be just like her. Hiding in her dingy room, blubbering, blaming the world for her own mess. He checked the spy app again. The phone was still off. She didn't even bother turning it on again. When would she fix the damn thing?

He needed to know where she was. For the past year, he'd *always* known where she was. Watching as she went through life, unaware as he documented every moment, prepared his revenge.

When he'd first found her, almost two years ago, he couldn't believe his luck. Back then he'd been using four thralls—two cops, a journalist, and an analyst—to search for Theodora. These people were good at their jobs, and even more competent when they were properly motivated by him. But it had been the fifth thrall he added to the task force—Kevin Poe, a private investigator—who finally managed it. Kevin had a penchant for buying photos of little children, a hobby that had put him right in the thrall list, color coded as lava red. But luckily for Kevin, he was quite useful. And he was the one who, using his network of contacts, finally found someone who recognized Theodora's photos. They remembered working with her in a restaurant in Chicago. Except she called herself Gemma.

He sent the information to the rest of the task force, and within a couple of weeks, he had her current name, address, and the place where she worked. And also a few photos of her. Theodora Briggs had been found.

And now, he had lost her, again.

He opened the list of his Chicago thralls. There, these three would do. Kyle Turner, Rhonda Adams, and Norman Miller. Sure, he hadn't fully prepped them yet; they weren't properly trained. But they would do it if they didn't want their secrets out.

He sent email after email, telling them to look, listing all the places Theodora could be. The addresses of all her acquaintances. That café she sometimes frequented. The damn park near her damn house where she went with her son. He wanted photos!

He fumed and waited. After a while he got a reply from Rhonda. One sentence.

Go to hell I'm not doing that.

He blinked, shocked.

Rhonda was a new thrall. In his Excel spreadsheet she was a bright yellow, denoting she would do simple tasks. He didn't have significant dirt on her. A few nude photos, taken through her hacked laptop's webcam. He should have known she wouldn't do something like this.

He'd lost his cool, messed up his system.

It was all Theodora's fault.

He scrolled through old photos he had of Theodora from the past year. Through some particularly personal messages she'd sent in the past year. He watched the video he had of her trying on new underwear in her bedroom. None of it made him feel any better.

He would find her. He wouldn't let her get away from him. And if he didn't find her, he would go after her precious family.

Chapter 34

The morning light filtered through the bedroom window, casting a rectangular silhouette on the ceiling. Gemma lay in bed staring at it and pretended she was a teenager again.

Not the bad parts of being a teenager—the crippling self-doubt, the hormones, the bullying. Where was the fun in that? No, just the good parts. Lying in bed with no one depending on her. No endless task lists filling her mind with static. No bills to pay, no child to feed, no groceries to buy.

She remembered waking up during weekends and vacations in this room, staring at this exact rectangular slice of light, thinking What am I going to do today, with the *entire* day stretching in front of her, hours upon hours in which she could paint, or read a book, or meet up with Steve and Allan, or just laze in bed. And if her mother asked her to help clean the house or to put her laundry in the closet, she would do it while grumbling, feeling as if everyone treated her like a slave or something.

She propped herself up, looking around her. Her mother hadn't exaggerated when she'd said the room was just like she'd left it. Everything was still there. Last night Richard had carried out three boxes of paperwork and an exercise bike that they stored in the room, but other than that it remained eerily the same. Her mother had said that they never found the time to clean up the room, but then Richard made a face, and Gemma got the feeling that there was some sort of old argument there. Did her mother insist that they keep the room exactly the same for when she came back? Did Richard complain about the unused room that could easily be turned into a guest room or a unit for rent? Gemma didn't want to know.

She got up from the bed and padded to her desk. She opened the top drawer, where she'd kept her sketchbooks. The drawer was now empty. So the room wasn't *exactly* the same. She checked the closet. Her clothes were gone. Thank God for that. The last thing she wanted to see were the baggy shirts she wore as a teen, chosen to hide the shape of her body.

She glanced at the clock on the wall. She still remembered that night, watching its hands move, counting down the seconds until she would leave. At some point in the past thirteen years, the clock's battery ran out, its hands showing the time—thirty-seven minutes past two.

She had no idea what the actual time was. Her phone was still off. The moment she'd turn it on, the Shadowman might know where she was. She preferred to keep the element of surprise for a while longer. Last night she'd called Lucas and Benjamin from her mother's landline, her mother hovering over her shoulder, desperate to hear the voice of her newly discovered grandchild. Gemma had promised her that in time, they would speak and even meet.

Well, whatever the time was, her growling stomach hinted that she needed breakfast. Imaginary playtime was over. Now she needed to face reality. Not just being a grown-up, but being this particular grown-up, with a messed-up life. Gemma hunched her shoulders and opened the door. The hinges still squeaked.

Her mother was downstairs in the living room, sitting on the couch, fiddling with her phone. She raised her eyes when Gemma came down the stairs.

"Good morning, did you sleep well?" she asked.

"Yeah, I did, actually," Gemma said, a bit surprised. She'd been so exhausted from the long drive the day before, from all the sleepless nights that preceded it, that once she lay in her childhood bed, she instantly fell asleep.

"Do you want some eggs for breakfast?"

"Uh . . . sure. I can make them, if—"

"Nonsense, I'll go make us both some eggs." Her mother hurried off to the kitchen.

Gemma glanced at the phone her mother left behind her. She'd been looking at photos of Lucas. Last night, Gemma had logged in to her Google account from her mother's computer and had sent a bunch of recent photos of Lucas to Mom's email. Now she picked up the phone and scrolled through those images. It was the first time she had ever spent a day apart from her son. Sure, it was nice to pretend she had no responsibilities, but the distance and yearning still tugged at her heart. He'd sounded mopey on the phone last night. Had asked her when she was coming back.

She swallowed the lump in her throat and put the phone down. Then she joined her mother in the kitchen.

"Where's Richard?" she asked.

"Oh." Her mother bustled by the counter, cracking eggs into a sizzling pan. "He's already at work. He wanted to see you in the morning, but he had an urgent meeting."

Gemma doubted Richard had wanted to see her. He had been very polite the night before and had said all the right words, but there was a certain formality to everything, as if he knew his lines and recited them without feeling. All those years ago, he'd been a decent stepfather, always caring and taking an interest in her. But he was never particularly affectionate, and Gemma had always felt he treated her as a side effect to her mother. Something he needed to do, rather than an actual person he loved. Or maybe he'd tried, and she'd been obnoxious to him, resenting him because he barged into her life, trying to replace her dad. Whichever was the case, they'd never really connected. And now it was clear he wasn't happy about her return.

"Mom . . ." Gemma took a long breath. "Do the Howells still live in Crumville? I mean, Victoria's parents, and brothers?"

Her mother's body became rigid. "I believe one of the brothers moved to England. Uh . . . William, I think his name was?"

"Willie," Gemma said. "We all . . . they all called him Willie. So he lives in England?"

"Yes, I heard he's married now. And Victoria's mother, Dorothy, moved to Florida. She and Russell got divorced a while ago."

"They divorced?" Gemma asked, surprised. "Why?"

"I don't know, Theodora, we're not exactly on speaking terms."

"Oh. Right."

Before the murder, Dorothy and her mother would occasionally meet for coffee. But that obviously stopped.

"Russell and Craig still live in town. I think Russell moved to a small place by the fire station. Craig now lives in their old house. He's a partner in some software company that does quite well."

"Oh." Gemma was mentally making notes in her suspect list. Russell got divorced. Would that make him angrier? Bitter? Maybe he would be looking for someone to blame? And Willie left for England and got married. Did that mean he wasn't a likely candidate for her shadow stalker? "Was there a memorial last week? For Victoria? It was the date of her death."

"I really don't know, Theodora. I don't keep track of it. And you shouldn't either. It's morbid."

"I just want to know where I stand. When I"—Gemma cleared her throat—"left, I was a murder suspect. Everyone waited for the cops to arrest me—"

"Detective Dunn assured me he didn't think you were really a suspect."

"He *would* say that, Mom. In case you knew where I was and were trying to protect me. But it wasn't just the police. *Everyone* thought I did it. Even . . . I mean . . ." She floundered, stopping herself just a second before spitting blame at her mother.

"I don't think everyone thought that." Her mother's voice trembled. "Anyway, we really don't need to talk about it now. Let's just have a nice breakfast."

"Right," Gemma said hollowly.

She sat in silence as her mother set a plate with two eggs over easy and a piece of toast in front of her. She dipped her toast in the yolk, and it leaked satisfyingly all over the plate. Her mother salted her own egg, then passed the saltshaker to Gemma, who did the same. This had been a Sunday ritual at some point in the past. She smiled at her mother and received a warm smile in return.

"It's good."

"How does Lucas like his eggs?" her mother asked.

"Fried. He likes his food simple."

"Kids are like that. You were the same. He really looks like you."

"I don't know. I think he looks a bit more like Benjamin."

"I wouldn't know."

"Yeah." Gemma prodded at her eggs guiltily.

"Maybe I'll meet them both soon," her mother suggested.

"Uh-huh." Gemma munched on some toast. "Do you know if people from my school still live here?"

"Steve does. I met him at Walmart two weeks ago. He looks well. And that other boy . . . Allan. Him too. He's taking care of his mother."

"What's wrong with Allan's mother?"

"She has Alzheimer's."

"Oh, shit."

"Theodora! Language."

Gemma snorted. "Seriously? I'm thirty, Mom."

Her mother looked as if she was about to snap at her, but instead took a bite of her egg.

"I go by Gemma now," Gemma said softly. "Not Theodora."

Her mother blinked. "Why?"

"Because that's my name now."

"We named you after your great-grandfather."

"I know. And I'm sure he was a wonderful man. But my name is Gemma." She leaned back. "So who else? From my school?"

"I don't know, honey. I didn't keep track. Some of the boys, I don't know their names. Detective Dunn's daughter—"

"Donna Dunn?" Gemma said, feeling that old stab of anger.

"Yes. She has a hair salon in town. She's married now, so she's not named Dunn anymore. She took her husband's last name. Dickin."

"Seriously?" Gemma let out a sharp bark of laughter.

"What's so funny?"

"Her name was Donna Dunn, which she *hated*. So she gets married and changes her name to Donna Dickin?" Gemma couldn't wipe the grin off her face. "That's wonderful."

Her mother raised an eyebrow. "Didn't you just point out that you're thirty years old?"

"Some things are funny no matter how old you are." She got up. "I'm making myself some coffee. Do you want a cup?"

"I'll make you the coffee." Her mother stood up as well.

"Mom, it's okay. I can make the coffee." She looked around. "Um . . . Where do you keep the coffee?"

"In the jar by the coffee machine."

Gemma walked over to the machine. "Okay, so Steve, Allan, Donna, and a few other boys. Anyone else?"

"Probably. I see familiar faces every now and again. I don't keep track."

"Does anyone still talk about the murder? Maybe ask you about me?"

There was a short silence.

"Not really," her mother finally said.

Gemma turned around. "Mom. I need to know."

"Not anything specific," her mother said angrily. "I get looks, okay? And a couple of years ago on Halloween, a bunch of drunks stood outside on the street and yelled at the house. I just ignore it. And you should ignore it too."

Gemma clenched her fists. Was her mother downplaying the harassment just to make her feel better? It made sense; her mother didn't want her to run away again. But thinking about it, that was typical Mom. She'd rather shut her eyes and ignore the unpleasant truth. If Gemma wanted to figure out who was going after her, it wasn't likely she would get any help from her mother. She'd known that already, deep down. She needed another ally in this town.

Her mother sniffed. "I think you should give Detective Dunn a call—"

"Mom! I told you, that's not happening!"

"Clear your name once and for all. Put an end to it!"

Gemma folded her arms. "So now you believe me that I didn't kill Victoria?"

Her mother sighed, looking tired and old. "I never thought you killed Victoria, sweetie. Not really."

Gemma turned away, fiddled with the coffee machine, blinking away the tears. "I wish you'd have told me that back then."

"It was a difficult time. I guess I didn't handle it too well."

"Yeah," Gemma whispered. "None of us did."

Chapter 35

Approaching the Starbucks in Augusta, Gemma felt more exposed than ever. There she was, out in the open, in clear daylight, where anyone from the past could recognize her. At any moment someone would say "Hang on . . . isn't that . . . ?" and chaos would follow. The cops would show up—patrol cars screeching into the parking lot, sirens blaring. In her mind, they were the same two cops that had found her in the woods all those years ago. Handcuffs already in hand, telling her she wouldn't get away this time.

But no one gave her a second glance. After all, even her mother had taken a few seconds to recognize her.

She stepped inside and scanned the people in the restaurant. Looking for Steve.

She'd called him that morning. Her mother had managed to get his phone number in less than five minutes from one of her friends. When he answered the call and she told him who she was, he sounded dazed. She tried to glean from his tone if he was happy to hear from her, or angry that she hadn't been in contact, or even suspicious. But all she could hear was bewilderment. She quickly asked if they could talk. She didn't want to have this conversation over the phone, especially not with her mother hovering over her shoulder. And he said they could meet at the Starbucks, which was a block away from the vet clinic where he worked.

Now she wondered if *she* would recognize *him*. The Steve in her mind was seventeen. Lanky, with messy curly hair, a slight overbite that gave him a rabbity vibe. But surely, he looked different now. Her eyes flickered between the few male restaurant patrons who sat by themselves. A large man with a wobbly chin, swiping at his phone. Not in a million years. A sharp-looking guy in a crisp suit, typing on his laptop. Could that be him? Not likely.

After scanning the restaurant for a full minute, she was finally convinced. He still wasn't here.

She sat down at the most distant table, in the corner of the restaurant, facing the door. She wanted coffee, but the idea of approaching the barista filled her with dread. Last time she was here, she was fleeing her old life. It was here she'd first called herself Gemma. Ridiculously, she wondered if the barista was the same one from all those years ago. If she would remember.

Instead she waited, eyes on the door, her heart beating fast.

Steve stepped inside just a couple of minutes after she'd sat down. It took her a few seconds to recognize him. He was bald now, so that mass of curls was gone forever. And at some point, he'd fixed his teeth, thank God. But he was still lanky and awkward. He still stood a bit hunched, as if he was trying to occupy less space. He looked around the restaurant swiftly, his gaze landing on her. He paused, his eyes widening.

She tried to smile, gave him a little dumb wave, the kind a seventeen-year-old teenager might give a friend she hadn't seen for a while, and mouthed, "Hey, Steve."

She got up as he approached her. To her surprise, he pulled her into a hug. She and Steve had never hugged in their entire lives. Most times they'd touch, it was punching each other's shoulders, or high-fiving each other when they managed to beat a boss on one of his video games. He hugged like he used to do most things—clumsily, holding his body a bit away as if he was afraid of the touch, his arms fluttering around her, touching-and-not-touching intermittently. He smelled of wet dog and aftershave.

He pulled back. "Theo."

She cleared her throat, quickly looking around to see if anyone had heard him. "I go by Gemma now."

"Oh. Gemma." He tried the name. "Gemma. It fits you."

She sat down, and he sat in front of her a second later.

"It's good to see you." She smiled at him. It was. Steve was one of the few things in Crumville she'd been sorry to leave behind.

"You too. You, uh . . . look good," he said.

"You mean I'm not covered in zits?" she teased. A very un-Gemma thing to say. Gemma would have said thank you. But *Theo* couldn't actually believe a compliment when she heard one. Seeing Steve was like stepping into the past.

"I mean . . . sure. That too. But you look . . . I don't know. Different."

"I guess I feel different," she admitted. "So . . . how've you been?"

"Good. Yeah, pretty good. What about you?"

"I'm also good. I'm married. I have a four-year-old boy."

"Really? That's awesome!"

"Yeah. You?"

"I have a girlfriend. Well, I guess I should say a fiancée. We're getting married soon."

"Oh wow, really? That's great!"

"You don't have to sound so surprised." Steve grinned. "I mean, I was always a babe magnet back in high school."

"Well, duh. Of course. I just thought you'd find it difficult to choose from the endless women who threw themselves at you."

"Yeah, it was a challenge."

"Anyone I know?"

"No. Her name is Heather. I met her in college."

They both nodded. Conversation topics seemed to have dried up.

"So you work at a vet clinic," Gemma said brightly. "That's cool."

"Yup. What about you?"

"I'm a beautician."

"Oh."

"Oh? What does that mean?"

"Nothing."

"I like my job. And I'm really good at it."

"That's fine." He raised his hands. "I just didn't think you were . . . I mean, you never seemed interested in things like that back then."

"Excuse me, Dr. Dolittle. I don't recall you nursing stray puppies back when you were a teenager."

"Fair point." He stood up. "I'm going to get a cup of coffee. Did you order?"

"No, uh . . ."

"I'll buy you one too." He smiled. "A Frappuccino?"

She laughed. That was her favorite Starbucks drink when she was a kid. She probably hadn't had one in thirteen years. "No. Just a latte, thanks."

He went over to the counter. She looked at the back of his head. Now that he was facing away from her, he didn't seem like her old friend. All she could see was his bald head. She replayed their short conversation in her mind. When he'd heard she was a beautician, he seemed disappointed. And that, in turn, made her feel annoyed and defensive. She did love her job, and she was proud of it. But back then, before the murder, she would fantasize about coming back to Crumville, and everyone would have shitty lives, and she would step into town, a glamorous artist, or journalist or something. And they would all be in awe of her. And now, apparently, she hadn't even managed to impress her ex-best friend.

Well, so much for fantasies. She would settle for not being arrested and charged with murder.

He sat back down. "It'll be ready in a moment."

"Okay. You didn't use my name, right?"

He rolled his eyes. "No. I didn't use either of your names. I gave *my* name."

"Okay, good."

Steve frowned at her. "Listen, Theo, uh, I mean Gemma, I'm glad to see you, I really am. But . . . why did you come back? I mean, Allan and I figured you'd be back after you left, but we assumed it'd be a few days. I thought you could make it on your own for two weeks. Allan thought the cops would find you and arrest you."

"Yeah, they never did."

"Right. And you obviously managed. So why now?"

Gemma licked her lips, not sure where to start. "Do you know if the police are still looking for me?"

"I mean . . . I think so. They used to say you're a suspect. And when people talk about it—"

"Are people still talking about it?"

Steve let out a sharp laugh. "It's Crumville. Nothing *ever* happens here. People here talk about fishing, football, politics, and Victoria's murder."

"Okay, lower your voice."

"Of course people are still talking about it. And there's always someone who claims he knows where you disappeared to, or someone who swears he saw you or something."

"Like who?"

"What?"

"Who swears he saw me?"

Steve shrugged. "I don't know. Dumbasses from our school. Friends of my parents. My brother actually said he saw you once in San Francisco . . . Did you move to San Francisco?"

"Never been there."

"Right. I mean, it's just something people love talking about."

The barista called out Steve's name, and he got up. Gemma drummed on the table with her fingers. The idea that people were still talking about her and Victoria made her queasy. As she'd guessed, her mother had misrepresented the interest in the murder. And of course she had. Gemma couldn't recall if there'd been another murder in Crumville in the past fifty years. And in this age where true crime was everyone's obsession? There were probably even a few people podcasting about her around town. She should never have come here. What was she thinking?

"Your coffee." Steve placed the cup and a croissant in front of her. "And something to eat."

"Thanks." She sipped from the coffee and forced her anxieties away. She knew why she came here. And she couldn't stumble around blindly. She needed Steve's assistance.

"I really need your help," she said. "I think someone from town is after me."

"What do you mean, after you?"

"It's sort of weird, so this'll take some time. Are you in a hurry?"

He shook his head. "It's a slow day at the clinic. I can take a long break."

"Okay. Good."

She told him everything. She tried to condense it as much as possible, but Steve wasn't the kind of guy to just listen. He peppered her with questions—"What kind of weird things did those women say," or "Hang on, what do you mean, blackmail, what sort of blackmail," or "What did your father-in-law say *exactly*." And Gemma became more and more frustrated with being interrupted, and with the constant demand of more information. She missed Benjamin and his quiet presence, his complete lack of curiosity. Steve was like the opposite of her husband. All he wanted was to know more.

Chapter 36

Steve still couldn't believe Theo was sitting in front of him. All those years later, both of them sitting in a café, Theo talking animatedly just like she used to back then. He was glad that Allan wasn't with them, that he had her just for himself. Allan would be uncomfortable, he would make weird jokes, he would try to catch Steve's eye.

He could always tell Allan about it later. Maybe they would meet again, the three of them, like old times. But for now he had Theo's full attention.

It felt so bizarre to be with her again. His first love. No, not really his first love, he knew that now. It had been a dumb teenager's infatuation, no more. But still, just being with her again brought back some of those long-forgotten feelings. He felt the warmth in his cheeks and tried to push it away. He had to focus on what Theo-I-go-by-Gemma-now was telling him.

"Wait," he said. "I don't understand. How did this guy make your son tell you—"

"He didn't make my son do anything," she said impatiently. "He got to his teacher. Blackmailed her with nude photos he found of her. And he told *her* to tell my son that weird story about the witch Theodora and Princess Victoria. My son actually ended up getting it wrong. He called the witch Fedora."

"But how did he know she was your son's teacher?"

"He hacked my phone, Steve, that's what I told you. He's been following me for I don't know how long. He knows *everything* about me. Everything."

She was impatient, her tone sharp. The way she drummed on the table every once in a while, the way she fidgeted. Just like she used to do all those years ago. He used to love that about her. She was never boring. Not like the other girls in the class who seemed to relish doing nothing, making as little effort as possible. Theo always swam against the current. Always crackling with that sort of angry energy.

Allan had never understood it. Sure, he liked Theo, too, but he didn't understand why Steve kept obsessing about her. "She doesn't even look good," he said. As if that was the minimum requirement. Like either of them was such hot stuff they could have a weird standard for how a girl would look.

Steve always felt a girl like Theo showed up once in a lifetime. So talented, and sharp, and funny. And she liked guy things—like playing video games and reading comics, which was so cool; they could talk for hours.

"I'm almost sure the Shadowman lives in Crumville, because—"

"I'm sorry?" Steve tried to focus. "Who?"

"The Shadowman," Gemma said. "It's the name I've given him."

"That's the worst name ever."

"No it's not." Gemma bristled. "It's perfect. Because I don't know who he is, and he lurks . . . you know. In the shadows."

"You make him sound like a Scooby-Doo villain."

"That's part of the point, Steve. Okay, what would you call him?"

"Practically anything else."

"Like what? Give me one good name."

"It's easy." Steve frowned. Well, to be fair, right now he couldn't think of anything except Thanos, and that guy was sort of taken. "The Ripper."

"Like *Jack the*? Are you serious?"

"Fine. Uh . . . Night . . . eroux. Nighteroux."

Gemma folded her arms, leaning back, looking at him with that amused, half-mocking stare from his childhood. God, how he loved it back then.

"Tell you what," she said. "When *you* have a guy stalking you online, blackmailing people to mess with your life, we'll call him Nighteroux. But this guy is messing with my life, so I get to name him, okay?"

"Fine." Steve looked away. "This guy, this *Shadowman*. He's obsessed with Victoria's murder."

"That's right. Like the rest of Crumville, he's blaming *me*. All his messages and hints . . . they're all about me supposedly killing Victoria."

"Maybe he's trying to mess with your mind. I don't know. Make you freak out. Turn yourself in or something."

"Yeah, maybe. Though if he's from here, he might think the police wouldn't do anything about it," she said. "They didn't arrest me back then."

"They came pretty close."

Gemma clenched her jaw. "Yeah."

"That detective . . . George Dunn? He was trying pretty hard to pin it on you."

"My mom said he didn't think I was a real suspect."

Steve rolled his eyes. "Seriously? He had me in the interrogation room for hours after you disappeared, and it was *all* about you."

"It was?" The color drained from Gemma's face. Did she *really* think that detective didn't have a hard-on for her?

Steve counted on his fingers. "What were you doing at that party. Why did you have that knife on you. Why did I keep calling you during the party—"

"Why did you what?"

"They checked phone records. Saw I kept trying to reach you."

"I didn't know you were trying to reach me."

"We were losing it!" Steve lowered his voice. "You were supposed to be out of there in five minutes, tops. But you didn't leave. We assumed they found you and were . . . I don't know. Doing something to you.

Allan was freaking out. So I called you a few times. Then you finally picked up, and I tried to tell you to get out of there. But you hung up on me and turned your phone off."

"I . . . think I remember that . . . ," Gemma said slowly.

"We waited outside Victoria's house for like . . . almost an hour. Then we decided to leave. You never showed up. Why didn't you just do it and leave?"

"I . . . don't remember that."

"What *do* you remember?"

She tightened, clenching her fists. Her eyes widened, staring at nothing. Finally she said, "I remember . . . Victoria. She was in a costume. Dressed as an angel. And in my pocket . . . in my pocket . . ."

Steve nodded. He knew what she had in her pocket. Even now, after all these years, he remembered their big revenge plan. Three idiots, thinking they were so clever.

"Never mind that," Gemma blurted. Her face had gone pale. For a second, she looked as if she was about to cry. She cleared her throat. "Anyway, I don't remember what happened at that party. My memory is spotty. What did you tell the detective?"

Steve shrugged. "Me and Allan agreed to tell him we were supposed to meet up and see *Halloween*. Like . . . the horror movie, *Halloween*. So I told the detective we called you a bunch of times and that finally you answered and told me you weren't feeling well."

He tried to make it sound like it was no big thing. As if he wasn't practically pissing his pants in that interrogation room. Certain that at any second, the detective would accuse him of lying. Or maybe that his version wouldn't match Allan's. He'd thought they would arrest him—conspiracy to commit murder. He was so relieved when they let him out that he threw up on the ride home.

But she didn't need to know all that.

"I made a list," Gemma said. She took out a folded piece of paper from her bag and handed it to him. "People I figured might be the Shadowman."

Steve read the list of names. "Wow. That's some list. A blast from the past."

"Right?"

He tapped it. "It's definitely not Kyle."

"Why not?"

"Because he's dead."

"Seriously?"

"Yup. Hunting accident. There was a big funeral."

"Oh."

She didn't seem too broken up about it. Steve wasn't either. Kyle was an absolute shit of a person. Dying didn't suddenly make him into someone Steve would miss.

"I don't think it's Willie either. He moved out of the States."

"Yeah, my mother said. To England, right?"

"Yeah. And I think he wasn't the kind of dude who would blackmail a girl with nude photos."

"I guess you're probably right."

"But Craig and Russell Howell? Definitely. Russell gets drunk at Mikey's almost every evening. Sometimes he starts shouting about you, or about how the police didn't do anything about his daughter's murder. And he has a vicious streak. I heard he was beating Victoria's mother."

"Seriously?"

"I don't know if it's true. They got divorced, and she left. But he's definitely obsessed with you. Craig is another strong possibility. He never talks about the police, *or* Victoria. But he definitely likes talking about you. About what he'd do to you if he got his hands on you."

"Do I want to know?"

Steve shook his head. She *really* didn't want to know. "So Russell moved out of the house after the divorce, but he still lives somewhere in town, probably at Craig's expense. Craig has a shitload of money from some cybersecurity start-up he was part of. He still lives in their house. I think maybe he bought it from his parents or something."

Steve ran his eyes down the list of names a second time. "I see you have Zayne and Bruce here, which makes sense. You know, Zayne has a hardware store on Sixth Street, just across from where that bakery used to be? You know the one, uh . . . Honey Fingers Bakery?"

"Maple Fingers Bakery."

"You sure? I think it was Honey."

"Definitely Maple. You're talking about one of the only spots in town I actually cared for."

"Oh. Well. It shut down about ten years ago. Anyway, Zayne's shop, Hardware Haven, is just across from where it used to be, so you could go there, kinda look around."

Gemma looked shocked. "I'm not going to *go* there."

"Why not?"

"Uh, hello? Kinda trying to avoid being recognized and arrested."

Steve frowned at her. The way she held herself, the way she moved, the elegant clothing she wore. Didn't she see it? "Theo . . . uh, Gemma . . . *no one* would recognize you."

She blinked. "My mom did. And you did."

"Well, I really hope your mom would recognize you. And if I didn't get your phone call, there's no way in hell I'd see it was you. You're like . . . completely different."

"Because I'm not covered in acne?"

"Will you lay off about the zits? It's not about that at all. Well, yeah, maybe that too. But the Theo people remember? She wore baggy clothes. She always stared at the floor, hiding her face. You're . . ." He searched for a word to describe the change. "I don't know. You're different now."

She blushed and took a quick sip from her coffee but didn't argue.

"Anyway," he continued. "That's the whole point of coming here, isn't it? You didn't come here to meet me and your mom. You came here to find this . . . Shadowman. So you'll have to reach out. See if anyone responds to you showing up. I mean if Zayne sees you and *recognizes* you, I guarantee it, he's your guy."

She frowned the way she always used to when he asked her a trick question. "Okay, I'll think about it."

"Right. So anyway, Zayne and Bruce are suspects for sure. But what about Rick Peters? He was in that bunch, too, and he still hangs out with them."

"Okay, but can you imagine Rick doing something so complex?"

Steve considered that. "I guess not. This is the guy who thought that the sun and the moon are the same size because they look about the same in the sky."

"Right. The guy who wasn't sure during geography class which direction the North Pole was."

"The guy who ate bananas without peeling them because he thought you ate the entire thing."

"You're making that up."

"I swear I saw him do that once."

Gemma let out a snigger. Steve grinned back at her.

"Okay," he said. "Not Rick. What about women? There are a few here who would love to hurt you. Judy, for sure; she tried to get the chief of police fired after you disappeared, for letting you get away. And Donna . . . I mean, I think she always hated you—"

"It's not a woman."

"Why not? You said whoever it was just sent emails. It could be a woman pretending to be a guy."

She pursed her lips and gave her head a small shake. "I just can't believe it's a woman. There's no way. Not even Judy or Donna."

Steve bristled. "Why? Because only men can be assholes?"

"No. Women can be horrific. But not like that."

"I think that's bullshit."

Her eyes shifted. He was losing her; he could see that. She'd always been like that. Say the wrong thing, and she'd shut you out. He didn't want that to happen. He wanted her to smile at him, the way she used to.

"You know Donna isn't called Donna Dunn anymore?" he said. "She finally changed it."

She looked back at him, a hint of a smile on her lips. "Oh yeah. My mom told me. It's so much better now."

And then they both said, together, "Donna Dickin." And laughed uncontrollably.

It felt just like it used to. Them against the world.

Chapter 37

Gemma shoved Hardware Haven's door open and stepped in. A single step shouldn't have been so difficult, but it had taken her about seven hours to find the guts to do it.

After talking to Steve, she'd gone past the store a few times, then taken a drive around town. Steve was right; if she wasn't able to talk to people in Crumville, she might as well go home. And the urge to do just that was overwhelming. Just imagine, that night she could step into Lucas's room and give him a kiss as he slept. She could lie in bed with Benjamin's big arms holding her, making her feel safe.

But she made herself think of Hank Turpin grabbing her, just a few feet away from her son. There were probably more Hank Turpins out there, threatening the people she loved. She couldn't leave Crumville. Not until she got what she came here for.

She had a late lunch with her mother—still very weird, trying to answer questions about Lucas, and Benjamin, and her life for the past thirteen years. Then she called Benjamin and Lucas on the landline, talked to them for twenty minutes, and spent an additional twenty minutes sobbing in her childhood bed, missing her family.

And here she was now, stepping into the belly of the beast.

The beast's belly was surprisingly meticulous and clean.

Brightly lit with neon lamps, Hardware Haven's shelves were lined with various tools, pipes, and gardening equipment. The freshly painted walls, the clearly labeled products, the shiny drills and chain saws on display all indicated a well-managed store.

She walked slowly deeper inside, past a tidy pile of garden hoses, some brooms, three sparkling-looking lawn mowers.

"Can I help ya?"

She raised her eyes and saw Zayne looking straight at her.

When Gemma was a teenager, Zayne was undeniably handsome. In her teenage fantasies, when she returned to Crumville, she would find that Zayne, one of her many tormentors, grew up into a sad pathetic bald man with a beer gut. Like many fantasies, this one didn't materialize.

He wasn't the chiseled young guy he'd been in high school, but he was still tall and wide, and unlike Steve, he had thick black hair. He was dressed simply—blue jeans and a simple buttoned white shirt, and his clothes all fit well. No beer gut as far as she could see.

He looked at her intently, and she stared right back at him. She didn't think she saw any recognition on his face . . . but she couldn't be sure. He seemed attentive, but it could just be because she was a customer in his store.

She stepped a bit closer, still holding his eyes. "Hi. Um . . . I need some spare light bulbs."

"What kind, sweetheart?"

Zayne was just the kind of guy who would call a woman he'd never met "sweetheart."

"LED bulbs," she answered.

"We've got some right over there." He pointed at a shelf to her left.

She turned and stepped over to the stack of light bulbs. She stood there, her back to him, wondering if she should just leave. Her scalp prickled as she sensed his eyes on her back, perhaps checking her out.

Slow, measured footsteps made her tense, and then a shadow fell over her. She let out a tiny gasp as he leaned into her.

"Here." He indicated the shelf. "These are usually what people buy, but if you want a softer light, you can get these ones, below."

She could actually hear his breathing close to her ear. She quickly grabbed the nearest box.

"These are good," she said, her voice cracking.

"Okay." For a few seconds he stayed where he was, essentially blocking her in. Then he backed away and stepped behind the counter. "That'll be six sixty-four," he said.

Trying to keep her fingers from trembling, she took out her purse, retrieving a ten-dollar bill. She put it on the counter.

He turned to a small laptop and quickly tapped on it. "Do you need a receipt?"

"No. No need."

After plucking the bill, he opened the register and counted the change. She tried to catch his eyes again, but he almost seemed like he was avoiding her look. Could he have recognized her?

"You look kinda familiar," she said. "Did we ever meet before?"

He raised his head and handed her the change. "Don't think so. I would'a remembered meeting you."

"Yeah." She smiled at him. "Thanks for the bulbs."

"You're welcome, sweetheart." His returning smile didn't reach his eyes, which narrowed slightly.

She stepped outside and let out a long breath.

To her surprise, she felt a wave of relief.

She'd been afraid of being recognized, sure. But some part of her had also simply been terrified of meeting one of *them*, her tormentors. As if they could pull her back to being a bullied, downtrodden seventeen-year-old. Perhaps they'd call her Zit-face, try to grab her and dunk her in the toilet again.

But she had just met the president of the assholes from high school, and he didn't call her out. Didn't grab her or call her names. Even if he had recognized her, he didn't do anything.

Perhaps Steve was right. Perhaps there was no way anyone would recognize her.

She crossed the street and went over to her car, the keys already in her hand. Then she paused.

Just a few blocks down, a red neon sign flickered. MIKEY'S.

Steve had told her this was where Russell Howell drank most evenings. It was just after six p.m. Would Russell already be there?

Emboldened by her recent encounter, she strode down the street and slipped into the bar.

She'd never been to Mikey's. She'd left town before she could legally get served. But even without stepping a foot in there, she knew what she would find. The murky lights, the pool table with the worn and torn felt, the football game on the large TV. This place was a classic clone of every small-town bar in the country. A few eyes glanced at her as she stepped inside, but she no longer tightened up with fear. She could see now what she hadn't realized before. In Crumville, where everyone knew everyone, the sight of an unfamiliar woman was enough to earn an interested glance.

She scanned the patrons, looking for Russell. Three large guys around one table, all of them laughing at something. Too young. A table of women . . . one seemed familiar. Perhaps someone Gemma had gone to school with. By the bar, a couple watching the game, the guy's arm around the much younger woman's waist. And an old man drinking a glass of whiskey.

Russell?

She almost didn't recognize him. The last time she'd seen him, at a sleepover at Victoria's, she'd been ten years old. They'd been dancing in her room, and he'd barged in and barked at them both to be quieter, said that he was talking to a client on the phone. She'd been terrified, and even Victoria seemed cowed. They turned off the music and spent the rest of the evening in her bed, talking softly to avoid disturbing him again. He'd been tall and imposing, radiating an intimidating power.

This old man was nothing like that.

Bent over the glass, his skin hanging from his face in folds, his shirt stained. Had losing Victoria turned him into this shell of a man? Or was it simply age?

Gemma sat down a few barstools away from him and ordered a beer. She sneaked another glance. He was gazing at the football game with apparent disgust, and as she watched, he spit at the floor and said, "Idiots."

Was he angry at one of the teams, or both? Or maybe his anger was directed at the guys laughing in the corner. His lips kept moving as if he was silently still uttering expletives. Then he finished his glass and ordered another one. The woman behind the bar had an exasperated look as she poured him the glass. She was clearly used to Russell making a nuisance of himself. Well, that was the way with local drunks. And it seemed that was what Russell had become. A local drunk.

Suddenly, quick as a whip, his head swiveled, and he locked eyes with her. A vicious, ugly smile stretched across his face.

"Well," he said. "Would you look at that."

Gemma swallowed, her hand reaching inside her purse, grasping her pepper spray. Maybe Zayne hadn't recognized her. But Victoria's father? The man who believed her to be his little girl's killer? He knew who she was.

"A pretty thing like you shouldn't drink alone," he said. "Let me buy you another drink."

Gemma's lips twisted in disgust. "No thanks, I'm good."

She was, quite literally, young enough to be his daughter.

"I saw you checking me out." He leered at her. "Nothing to be ashamed of."

"Russell, leave her alone," the woman behind the bar said.

"You stay out of it," he snarled.

Gemma was already placing a bill on the bar. Russell clearly wasn't the Shadowman. She wondered if the Shadowman was in Crumville after all.

Chapter 38

"Rick, you dumbass, it'll never work."

But it was gonna work. It was gonna. This time, he was about to make all of *them* look like dumbasses.

Rick Peters sat at Mikey's with Bruce and Leo, each of them drinking their second pint. Zayne also said he might show up soon, once he closed up, though Rick doubted it. The dude never hung out anymore. He always went straight home after closing up the store. It was sad, that's what it was.

He flicked his lighter on again and held it closer to his beer.

"See, the thing is, alcohol floats up, you see?" he explained to his friends. "Those bubbles in the beer, that's the alcohol rising to the upper part of the beer. The surface! Yeah, that's what it's called. The alcohol is rising to the surface."

"Dude, the bubbles are carbon dioxide," Bruce said.

"No, you idiot, carbon dioxide is like . . . poison," Rick said. Haven't those guys ever heard of carbon dioxide poisoning? "Do you think Mikey would put poison in his beer? He wouldn't have a lot of people here if he did, right?"

"God, you're so dumb." Leo rolled his eyes at Rick.

He was used to that. Whatever, yeah, he wasn't, like, the best student at school. So he got this reputation of being stupid, and his friends liked to make fun of him. But Rick knew he wasn't stupid. He liked to think things through, so sometimes he seemed a bit slow. But Ms.

Klempner, who taught them English, once told him she knew he understood a lot more than he let on, and that was totally true. She was one of the only ones who saw the truth about him.

Anyway, this time he would prove them wrong. "Alcohol is flammable," he explained. "And it vaporates."

"Don't you mean evaporates?" Bruce asked.

"Naw. It doesn't disappear, right? It becomes vapor."

"I wish Zayne was here to see this," Leo said.

"So if we hold the flame to the beer, it'll catch fire. I saw this dude do it at a party in Augusta." He brought the lighter closer to the beer. Any second now.

"They don't do it with beer, Rick. They do it with cocktails with a high percentage of alcohol," Bruce said. He wasn't smiling anymore. He lifted his eyebrows and gave Rick this look. Rick knew this look meant *let it go*. Of all his friends, Bruce was the one guy who didn't make fun of him too much.

But this time Rick didn't care, because any second now it would catch fire. Rick could already imagine it, how surprised his friends would look. For once, Rick the dumbass would manage to make them look like idiots. He held the flame closer to the beer's froth, his tongue protruding slightly between his teeth as he concentrated. The lighter was getting really warm now. But any moment now . . . any moment—

The flame flared and burned the back of his thumb. He let out a yelp and dropped the lighter, which sank to the bottom of his beer.

Leo let out his braying laugh and took out his phone. "Hang on, I gotta take a picture of that."

Rick stared at the lighter on the bottom of his beer mug, frustration and fury rising inside him. He was about to grab the mug and empty it on Leo's face, when Bruce plucked the phone from Leo's hand.

"What the hell, man?" Leo snapped.

"Leave it," Bruce said.

"Come on, give me my phone back."

"Leave it," Bruce said again, gritting his teeth.

Leo leaned back in his chair. "Whatever."

"It should'a worked," Rick muttered.

"I have a bottle of vodka at my place," Bruce said. "We can try it with that."

"Yeah, okay," Rick said, slightly mollified.

He leaned back and scanned the other tables. Rhonda and Mal sat across from each other in the corner. He couldn't see Mal, which was a pity, because she was great eye candy. Rhonda wasn't bad either, just a bit flat in the chest department. But she had nice lips and a great ass. She was sitting now, so that ass wasn't on display, but Rick could picture it pretty well even without looking. She caught his stare and gave him a look, and he winked at her. She rolled her eyes and leaned forward to whisper something to Mal. He'd asked Rhonda out once, but she turned him down so fast that he never did it again. A guy had his pride. Anyway, who wanted to go out with a flat-chested bimbo like her?

That was the thing in this town. It was great that he wasn't shacked up, so he was free for action, so to speak. But he already knew everyone, and everyone knew him, and aside from Tiff, who sometimes got drunk and messaged him to come over, he didn't get much action.

He glanced at the stranger who'd come in earlier. She was a looker, no doubt, but the way she carried herself, it was obvious she thought she was hot stuff. Too good for the likes of him. She sat by the bar now, her back to him. Back and ass. Nice ass too. Maybe as good as Rhonda's. He doubted if they'd agree to stand next to each other so that he could compare.

Old Russell was talking to her, and she looked like she was being addressed by a garden slug. This could be Rick's chance. He could come over, be her savior, tell Russell to back off. Then maybe buy her a drink, get her talking.

He stood up.

"Where are you off to?" Leo asked. He was still a bit sulky.

"Gonna get me a new beer. This one has my lighter inside it," Rick answered. He took a step toward the bar. The woman turned to look at him.

Rick froze. He knew those eyes. Those damn brown eyes, they hounded him. He wouldn't mistake them, not in a thousand years, not after seeing them up close, wide and full of fear. He often dreamed about that night, when everything had gone to hell. All that blood. Victoria's mouth, opening and shutting, gasping without a breath. And *her* standing there, looking at him with those big brown eyes.

But it couldn't be. There was no chance it was her. She was *gone*, damn it!

Except it *was* her. Theodora Briggs. No zits anymore, looking like a million bucks, staring straight at him.

He looked at his friends. Leo wouldn't know her; he only moved to Crumville a few years ago. But Bruce?

"Bruce," Rick muttered. "Look at that chick over there."

Bruce glanced at her. "What about her?"

He didn't recognize her. Most people wouldn't. She was completely different. But her eyes were the same.

She was frowning now, looking at him, and then at Bruce. Then her eyes widened. She'd recognized them.

"It's Theodora Briggs!" Rick shouted.

She leaped from her stool, and it clattered to the floor. She was already dashing toward the door.

"Stop her!" Rick was pushing his way across the room.

Theodora slammed into the door and plunged outside. Rick was a few seconds behind her, his heart hammering. He heard shouts behind him, but there was no time to look, to explain. He had to catch up to her.

She'd been in that room, all those years ago. If she talked, she could land him in prison for a long, long time.

He would wring her neck before he would let that happen.

The street was dim, just a few people walking on the sidewalk. It took him a second or two to spot her, running as fast as she could. But it wouldn't be fast enough. Rick had been a linebacker in high school. He could run at top speed without breaking a sweat. And he was already after her.

Just wait, you bitch. We're gonna have a nice talk, you and me. Maybe continue where we stopped last time.

She pivoted, crossing the street, and he followed, then heard the squeal of brakes, furious honking, saw the incoming car, and leaped back, stumbling into someone who shouted at him to watch it. She'd crossed the street and was beelining toward a parked car, already rummaging in her bag.

Oh no you don't.

Rick dashed across the street and accelerated, running as fast as he ever had, gritting his teeth. She yanked the car door open, leaped inside, slammed it shut. He was there at the passenger side, already trying to pull the door open, but it stayed shut. She'd locked it.

For a second, they just looked at each other. Then the car's engine roared to life as she switched it on. She swerved into the road, nearly running over his foot.

And she was gone.

Rick was breathing hard. Shit, shit, shit!

He had to make a phone call.

Chapter 39

Gemma parked by her mother's house, shivering. Of all people, it was Rick Peters who pegged her. It seemed Steve had been wrong. She wasn't that unrecognizable after all.

She should floor the gas pedal, get out of town while she still could. She could still disappear back to where she came from. Maybe.

But there was no going back. *He* was still out there, waiting for her. He would send others to harass her, to dismantle her life bit by bit. Or worse. She had to follow this through.

She stepped out of the car, her knees wobbly. She'd twisted her ankle when she fled from Rick. She needed to sit down. Take a shower, or perhaps even a relaxing bath. Think things through. She crossed the short distance to the front door, raised her hand to knock, then changed her mind and simply stepped inside. She froze on the doorstep.

Her mother and Richard were both standing there, in the living room. A third man was facing them, his back to Gemma. Her mother's eyes widened as she saw her, and Gemma could see the fear and guilt etched on her face. Then the man turned around.

"Ah, there she is," he said softly. "Theodora."

He'd hardly changed since the last time Gemma had seen him, sitting behind the interrogation table, lobbing question after question at her.

Detective Dunn.

She swallowed, unable to speak. She looked at him, at her mother, at Richard. Richard wouldn't meet her eyes.

"It's been a while," Dunn said.

"Yeah," she croaked. Her brain was fizzing, crackling, panicked half-formed thoughts whizzing through.

"I was hoping we could have a chat," Dunn said. "Alone."

"I think I would like a lawyer present," Gemma blurted.

Dunn raised an eyebrow. "Really? Again?"

"She's right," her mother said. "I can call Thomas right now. He'd get here as soon as possible—"

"You're not under arrest," Dunn said, showing his palms, as if to reassure her. "I really just want to talk. We can do it here, or in the kitchen . . . wherever you want. And you can stop our discussion whenever you want."

Gemma shook her head, clenching her jaw.

"Theodora," Dunn said. "I honestly don't think you're a suspect in Victoria's murder. But I *do* think you were a key witness to it. Now, to be fair, I admit I'm a minority in that. The chief thinks you did it, and so does the sheriff. I got a lot of shit over the years for refusing to arrest you while I still had the opportunity. The best thing for me, career-wise, is to handcuff you right now and take you to the station. But I don't want to do that."

"Why not?" Gemma whispered.

"Because, like I said, I don't think you did it. And you and I both know as soon as I do that, everyone in town will be demanding prosecution. Once that happens, I won't be able to do my job. I won't be able to find out what really happened that night. And I probably won't be able to help you. But if you won't talk to me here, I'll be forced to take you in."

Gemma had been prepared for this moment for years. The only rational act would be to call a lawyer. Dunn was manipulating her. He knew once she had a lawyer by her side, she would be harder to interrogate, harder to crack. A lawyer would know her rights, would tell her what to say and when to keep quiet. He would be able to make deals on her behalf.

And she didn't have to get her mother's old idiot of a lawyer. She could find a real lawyer. She and Benjamin could afford a decent one, or at least she thought they could.

But the fact that she knew Dunn was manipulating her didn't mean he was wrong. Once he arrested her, it would only get worse. The Howells and their friends would clamor for her blood, as would most of the people she went to school with. And she would be in jail, unable to do anything, to look for the guy who was harassing her, or to . . .

. . . *run* . . .

. . . do her own investigating. She would have to wait for phone privileges or something like that to talk to Lucas. She would see him once a week, at best.

She could, at the very least, see what Dunn wanted to know. It wasn't like he didn't have hours of interrogation tapes with her already. She would be careful. And if she felt he was trying to pin this on her, to force her to confess, she would stop talking. She would get a lawyer.

"Fine," she finally said. Could he even hear her over the sound of her own hammering heart? "We can talk."

He let out a long breath. "Okay. In the kitchen?"

"No." There was only one room in this house where she felt even remotely safe. "Upstairs. In my old room."

Chapter 40

George Dunn followed Theodora upstairs, feeling as if he was walking in a dream. It actually wasn't far fetched. He had dreams about the Howell murder every so often. And in many of those dreams, he found Theodora, or talked to her on the phone, or was told she had died and that the truth had died with her.

And now here he was, with the real Theodora Briggs.

"It's over here," she said, gesturing at a closed door. Her voice was different. Thirteen years ago, she couldn't utter a single sentence without mumbling, her eyes shifting, avoiding him. Now, even though she was clearly scared, she didn't waver. Somewhere in the past years, she'd found her backbone.

He knew where her bedroom was. He'd gone through it, after she'd fled town. Searched through her notebooks and the rest of her things. But there was no need for her to know that.

"Okay," he said.

She stepped into the room and looked around it, hesitating. She realized what he'd already known. This was a strange place for a cop and a suspect to talk. Only one chair by the tiny desk. And a bed, and a beanbag. A far cry from the place they last talked, the station's interrogation room, with its bright light, and moldy walls, and the security camera.

She sat on the bed. He knew she expected him to sit on the chair. Instead, he remained standing.

"So," he said. "Would you prefer I call you Theodora or Gemma?"

She pursed her lips. "I see my mother told you pretty much everything."

He quirked an eyebrow. "Your mother didn't say a single word to me except for asking me if I wanted a cup of tea."

She paused and then said, "Richard called you?"

"Yeah." He gauged her reaction. She didn't seem particularly surprised or angry. Just tired.

"I go by Gemma now," she finally said.

"Gemma Foster, right?"

"Yes."

"And you live in Chicago?"

Her shoulders sagged slightly. Did she think she could easily disappear again? He would never let that happen. He'd been kicking himself for the past thirteen years, and he wasn't about to make the same mistake.

"Yeah," she finally said.

"We never got to finish our talk, all those years ago," he said.

She nodded, didn't say anything. Short answers, or no answers at all. He was very familiar with that tactic. That was fine; he could get her to talk.

"Why did you run?" he asked. He knew why she ran, of course. But he wanted her to say it.

"Isn't it obvious?" she asked sharply. "You wanted to pin this murder on me."

"No I didn't. I wanted to find the person who did it. I was never convinced it was you."

"You said you had a mountain of evidence on me." She changed her intonation, mimicking him. He nearly smiled. It was a good imitation.

"That's true. But there are some things that don't fit."

"Like what?"

"We can discuss that later. For now let's talk about you and Victoria."

"Fine."

"On October thirtieth, 2010, Victoria Howell had a Halloween party at her home. And you showed up."

"That's right."

"Why did you come to the party?"

"Didn't we cover this already?"

Of course they had. And he knew the interrogation transcripts almost by heart, he'd read them so many times. "It's been thirteen years. My memory isn't what it used to be. So let's go over everything again. You and Victoria weren't on close terms."

"No, we weren't."

"Why? Weren't you friends when you were little?"

"Yeah," she whispered. Her eyes flickered, something faraway shining in them. "We used to be best friends."

"So why did you stop?"

"I don't know." She shrugged. "We grew apart. She was one of the cool kids. I was a loser."

"That sounds like a very thin explanation."

"Sometimes things just happen. We stopped being friends." Her eyes became slightly unfocused, as if she wasn't really seeing him. "I remember that back then she seemed angry at me all the time. Like maybe I did something wrong. Except I couldn't figure out what it was. Even when I asked her."

Dunn actually remembered it happening. Donna, who'd worshipped Victoria from afar, suddenly became her new best friend. He recalled being happy for his daughter, seeing how thrilled she was, hanging around with the popular kid. He'd never paused to wonder about it.

"And it didn't stop at just growing apart, right?" he asked.

"Is this where we're going? She bullied me so I killed her? Talk about a thin explanation."

He raised an eyebrow. "I'm not trying to pin this on you, Gemma. But I want a complete picture of what happened."

She seemed to think this over. Maybe she would end their conversation right there. And he would have to bring her in. He fervently hoped it wouldn't come to that.

"Yeah," she finally said. "She and a few other girls were occasionally nasty to me."

A few other girls. He kept his face blank, knowing what they were both thinking. That one of those girls had been his daughter.

"Nasty how?"

"They called me names, made fun of me. They dunked my head in a toilet once. They'd knock things out of my hands. Like notebooks, or a Coke, or my bag." Her tone was deadpan, almost bored. She was acting as if it was no big deal, juvenile stuff she hardly cared about. But he heard her voice tighten when she talked. Her eyes flickered, avoiding him, that hurt seventeen-year-old girl emerging for a second. Back then, three witnesses had heard her tell Victoria she would kill her because of the toilet incident. One of them, of course, was Donna herself.

He finally sat down, letting that last sentence permeate the air between them for a few seconds longer. Thirty-year-old Gemma Foster had probably learned to handle her memories of that time. She knew how to bury them deep. He wanted to talk to the other woman in there. He wanted to talk to Theodora Briggs.

"So why did you go to the party that evening?" he finally asked.

She hesitated and scratched her neck. Choosing a lie?

"I wanted to get her to apologize to me," she finally said.

She'd said the same thing all those years ago. He didn't believe it then, and he didn't believe it now. "Apologize for what?"

"For the bullying. For that thing with the toilet."

"Why do it during a party? Why not talk to her alone at any other time?"

"I don't know. I wanted her in a good mood, I guess."

Last time, whenever she went back to this apology, he would crank up the pressure. Try to get her to spit out the truth. But she never did. And eventually, she bolted. This time, he would go slower.

"You brought a knife with you," he said.

She tensed up. She was about to terminate this talk. He had to prevent that.

"You already admitted to it during the interrogations thirteen years ago," he reminded her. "The knife was yours; we had several witnesses who saw you buy it. I just want to know why. If all you wanted was an apology—"

"The knife made me feel safe," she blurted.

He frowned. This was new. "It was for self-defense? You thought you'd have to—"

"No." She gritted her teeth. "You don't get it. It was a way *out*. If things got too difficult, it was my way out."

He tried to understand. What was she talking about. Would she pull out the knife and threaten everyone with it?

She folded her left sleeve and showed him her wrist, pointing. He had to look really closely, but he saw them. Two very faded scars.

"You cut yourself?" he asked.

"Just twice," she said. "Not too deep. To see how it felt. I was depressed. It was hard to get up in the morning. I carried this knife everywhere with me. To school, around my home, even to that damn party. It was reassuring to think that . . . if things went badly, I could always lock myself in the bathroom. One long cut, and it would be over."

A tiny puzzle piece shifted into place. This was one of the unanswered questions that had hounded him. He didn't know who had killed Victoria. But after talking to dozens of people who knew Theodora and Victoria, he'd been sure whatever she'd intended to do during that party, it wasn't murder. Except, bringing that knife with her, that showed premeditation. He couldn't explain that contradiction until now. He probably believed her. Her explanation was too personal, too . . . sad to be a lie.

"So you went to this party. What happened when you got there?"

"Like I told you, I don't really remember."

"Tell me what you do remember."

She licked her lips and paused for a few seconds. Then she let out a long breath. "When I walked inside, there was a song playing. 'Turnin Me On.' That's the name of the song. I remember people dancing. I saw Victoria and Zayne talking. Victoria was dressed like an angel."

He listened intently. During those interviews all those years ago, she never mentioned these details. Perhaps it had been his fault, always trying to get to what had happened between her and Victoria. Now, he remained silent, letting her open up.

"I remember . . . ," she said slowly, "that no one recognized me. I was wearing a mask, and this sexy outfit I would never wear normally. And it was like . . . camouflage. It felt nice."

She settled into silence.

"What did you do?"

"I . . ." She frowned. "That's where it gets spotty. I think I danced a bit. I talked to someone. He didn't know who I was either."

"Do you remember who?"

"Uh . . . I think it was Bruce, from school. He hung around with Zayne and that crowd."

Bruce Green hadn't said he'd talked to her during his questioning. But then, it made sense if he hadn't recognized her.

"What did you do then?"

Her lips trembled, and her eyes glazed. "I . . . I think I went to Victoria's room. And then, uh . . . I don't remember. I don't know what happened." Her fists were clenched.

"Someone saw Victoria enter the room and shut the door," Dunn said softly. "Do you remember that?"

"Maybe . . . yes. We talked. And she apologized. She apologized to me." Her voice sharpened, as if she was challenging him to argue.

He'd talked to twenty-three people who knew Victoria and Theodora back then, and they all pretty much agreed there was no way in hell Victoria would have apologized to Theodora.

"A witness claimed she heard Victoria crying and begging you to stop. Stop what?"

"That never happened. Whoever it was, she heard wrong. Or maybe . . . maybe she heard Victoria talking to someone else—"

"She saw you both. You were leaning on top of her, on the bed. And then Victoria told her everything was all right."

"Well . . . see? She must have heard wrong. We just talked. And she apologized."

"Okay. And then what?"

She clenched her jaw. "That's . . . that's all I remember. I think at some point someone hit me. I don't know why. And then I was running away in the forest . . . and the dogs were chasing me."

"The dogs?"

"Victoria's dogs. She had two dogs. They were chasing me."

The Howells *did* have two dogs, but one was quite old. And they always seemed friendly when he came by the house after the murder. He couldn't picture them chasing a young girl through the woods.

"Victoria had your blood and DNA under her fingernails," he said. "And you had a few long scratches along your arm. Do you remember how that happened?"

"No . . . I . . . I told you back then. I don't remember that."

"Do you remember what you were doing in her parents' bedroom?"

"Her . . . parents' bedroom?"

"That's where she was found. And people saw you both enter that room. They said you dragged her in there."

"No." She shook her head slowly. She seemed exhausted.

"Do you remember wearing Victoria's jacket?"

"No." She looked at him pleadingly. "But . . . why would I do that? Why would I take her jacket? It makes no sense."

Instead of giving him answers, she expected him to give *her* answers. It didn't entirely surprise him. Not with what he knew had happened to her. But it was still disappointing. He'd hoped, after all this time, to be able to finally have a clear picture of that night.

Well, there was still time.

"I'm sorry," he said. "I don't know why you took it."

She stared at the floor for a while. He was getting ready to stand up when she said, "You said you don't think I did it."

"That's right, I don't."

She met his eyes, and he could see Gemma Foster was back.

"Why?" she asked, her voice sharpening.

He raised his eyebrows. "Would you rather I put you in handcuffs?"

"You have all this evidence. A mountain of evidence, like you once told me. Victoria was stabbed with my knife. My DNA under her fingernails. Witnesses who say she begged me to stop . . . Why do you think I didn't do it?"

"Well . . ." He hesitated. He wanted her cooperation. But she lied to him earlier. He needed to know the truth. "There's more."

"More?"

"There are additional things I know about that night. And they don't fit in."

"Like what?"

He folded his arms. "Why did you really go to the party?"

She looked away and exhaled slowly. "I already told you."

"Why did you come back here? I gathered from Richard that you have a family in Chicago."

She cleared her throat. "I needed to put this thing behind me. For good."

Another lie. He sighed and stood up. "Okay. Thanks for talking to me."

She still didn't look at him. "Are you going to arrest me?" Her voice trembled.

"Not yet." He took out one of his cards and placed it on the desk. "If you think of anything else you want to tell me, let me know. And don't leave town. Stay in this house until we have this resolved."

"Okay. You should probably know Rick Peters recognized me this evening."

Damn. That meant by morning everyone would know she was here. The chief would demand they bring her in. And he wouldn't be able to stall him for long. "That'll complicate things for you. Let me know if you need help."

"Okay."

He walked over to the door, then glanced back at her. "You know, Donna never thought you did it. She said you didn't have it in you."

She didn't even seem to hear him. He stepped out.

He said his goodbyes to Richard and Heather, and then left and got back into his car. After popping the trunk, he took out the portable GPS tracker he'd bought earlier. Gemma's car was just a few yards down the street. He casually ambled over, then crouched behind it as if tying his shoelace. From where he was crouched, she wouldn't be able to see what he was doing. He'd made sure of that when he was in her room. Quickly, he taped the tracker under the rear bumper, then straightened up. Hopefully, she wouldn't find the thing.

He returned to his car and drove around the corner, then parked across the street. He had a good viewpoint on the house from there.

Theodora had gotten away from him once before. He wasn't about to let it happen again. If she decided to get out of town tonight, she'd end up in jail. Sure, he had the GPS tracker on her car, but he wasn't taking any chances. He was waiting right here in case she decided to bolt.

He unscrewed the lid off his thermos and poured himself a cup of coffee. It was going to be a long night.

Chapter 41

Sleep wouldn't come for Gemma. If she had to be honest with herself, she hadn't expected it to.

After Dunn left, she'd called Benjamin. Lucas was already asleep, of course, but at least she could hear about his day. They played tag at school, and he apparently fell and scraped his knee, but Benjamin said it was no big deal. Then they'd gone to his grandparents' house. Nathan had been there, too, though Benjamin wasn't sure if he was back for good or just for dinner. In any case, Lucas and Nathan played chess, and Lucas got really excited because he took one of Nathan's rooks. She could imagine his smile as it happened, a tiny proud smile, with the tiniest blush. It made her tear up. Anything would have made her tear up at that point.

She had no answer for Benjamin when he asked how much longer it would be. She didn't tell him about Dunn's visit or his ominous warning "Don't leave town." She didn't tell him about Rick Peters chasing her down the street, looking as if he wanted to throttle her. She just told him she talked to her mother and met up with a high school friend.

And now she lay in her childhood bed, staring at the ceiling, replaying the conversation with Dunn in her mind over and over. He'd said some of the evidence didn't fit. Was he just saying that, trying to trick her into trusting him? Or did he really have something? He didn't arrest her, so that could mean he honestly didn't believe she'd killed Victoria. And that thing he said about Donna, at the end. That she didn't believe

Gemma had done it. Why had he said that? Did he know Donna was the one who held her head down in the toilet all those years ago? He had to at least know she'd been there.

He wasn't like she remembered. Well, he was older, sure. But she remembered him being aggressive, impatient. Back then she'd felt as if it was more important for him to find someone to blame than to figure out what had happened. And that's what she carried with her over the years, this memory of Detective Dunn hounding her, trying to trick her into confessing. Pressuring her. Making everything she said sound like an excuse or a lie.

But the man she'd talked to this evening wasn't like that. He seemed almost . . . desperate. Like he wanted *her* to believe *him* and not the other way around. Had he changed? Or were her memories twisted?

Or maybe, like she'd originally thought, this entire evening was another strategy to make her confess.

She should leave. Just get her stuff and drive away. Lucas would wake up in the morning, and his mommy would already be there. And she could kiss his knee to make it all better. Would Dunn really hunt her down to a different state?

He would. And the Shadowman wouldn't leave her alone either. There was no getting away this time.

A car engine roared outside, followed by the sound of squealing breaks and a door slamming. Gemma tightened. It could be nothing to do with her. Or it could be Rick Peters, who'd finally figured out where she'd gone.

She slid off the bed and padded to the window, keeping the light off.

There was a car in front of the house, one wheel on the curb, headlights switched on. A figure tottered out of it toward the picket fence.

It wasn't Rick. It was Russell.

"Theodora!" he roared in front of the house. "Theodora, come on out, you bitch."

Gemma flattened herself against the wall, her throat dry. She shouldn't have stayed with her mother. She should have gone to a motel.

"Theodora!" His voice was slurred, and he kept wavering back and forth. "You think tha' . . . you think . . . you should . . ."

Her mother's bedroom window opened. Richard's voice was firm and angry as he called out, "Go home, Russell, before I call the cops."

"You send that bitch out here," Russell drawled. "I saw her today. Trying to flirt with me, the whore. Firs' she killed my daughter, an' then . . . an' then . . ."

"I'm calling the cops," Richard said. "Better get out of here."

Russell nearly toppled over, then leaned against the fence. Then he struggled with his belt. Gemma watched, horrified, as the man finally yanked his belt open and unzipped his pants. He took out his penis and held it out, grunting as he did so. She wanted to look away, but she felt frozen in place.

Other windows down the street lit up, the noise waking up the neighbors. Russell still grunted, muttering to himself, "Come on, you li'l bastard. Come on . . ."

And then, a steady trickle of piss sprayed the fence. Russell grunted in satisfaction, turning back and forth, spraying the mailbox, the grass in the front yard. Gemma finally managed to tear herself away, then shut her eyes, nausea roiling in her gut. A few seconds later she heard another grunt, then the sound of Russell clearing his throat and spitting. And finally, his car door opening and then closing, and the car driving away.

Had Richard really called the cops? If he had, no one showed up. She remained awake until the sky lightened with the first rays of dawn.

Chapter 42

He paced the room back and forth, trying to put his thoughts in order. He chewed at his nail, his teeth clicking over and over until he chopped it, then accidentally inhaled it. Coughing, he spewed it, and it landed somewhere on the floor. He hardly even paid it any attention.

She was here. In Crumville. He still couldn't believe it.

In time, they would arrest her. Already, the word was spreading. The police would pick her up. But that wasn't acceptable. It wasn't enough.

Jail was too good for her. He'd decided that long ago, even before he'd found out that she was living in Chicago. There was no atonement for what she did. There was only punishment. His punishment.

He could step outside right now and be at her doorstep within ten minutes. It was unsettling.

Sitting by the computer, he checked the spying app, but Theodora's phone was still turned off. It was maddening to think she was so close, and he still had no constant eyes on her.

Well, that was going to change. Did she really think she could come to Crumville without him knowing? Without him sending people after her? This was his home turf. There were more people here under his thumb than anywhere else on the planet.

He sent a quick email to one. Bert King. Bert was perfect for this because he lived just down the street from Theodora's mother. He could get him a few photos right now. In fact, maybe Bert had a line of sight to Theodora's house. If that was the case, he could get a constant video feed set up. It was worth checking—a task best left for tomorrow morning. For now he just wanted a few photos of the house, preferably of the people inside. Of the cars in the street—he gave Bert Theodora's license plate number with instructions to canvass the street and see if the car was parked anywhere there.

His chat window suddenly popped up; Virtual Victoria was sending him a message.

Hey Bear, just thinking of you. What are you doing?

He gritted his teeth. When he upgraded this virtual entity to version 1.06, he added a feature that would make her send him messages unprompted. At the time, he was really happy with the change. It made her feel ultimately more realistic, more loving. And, of course, if the real Victoria would have been alive right now, she wouldn't wait for him to send her messages. She would call and message him every now and then because she'd find herself missing him.

Except right now, it just got in the way. He was busy; he didn't have time for this.

He opened VirtualVicSettings.txt, the file that contained all the entity's settings. He located the constant RANDOM_TEXT_TIME_LAPSE = 180. It meant that give or take every 180 minutes during the day, he would get a message. He changed it to 18,000. Then he restarted the app.

There. That'll give him some peace and quiet to focus. Back to Theodora.

He sent two more emails to people in Crumville. Starting tomorrow, he would have thralls tailing her. Theodora wouldn't be able to do a single thing without him knowing about it. She wouldn't leave his sight again.

That done, he checked the latest photos he got from Chicago. There was little Lucas with his daddy, walking down the street. And here he was in his bedroom, the photo taken through the window.

That's right, bitch. Did she really think if she got away from her precious boy, it would keep him safe?

No one was safe from him. And anyone who was connected to Theodora would have to pay for her crimes.

Chapter 43

Gemma woke up to the familiar sound of her parents arguing. It'd been happening more lately. And when they did, she would hide in her closet, shutting the door to muffle the—

Hang on.

She blinked, her muddled, sleep-deprived mind slowly focusing. Her dad had left twenty years ago, and she hadn't seen him since. Her mother wasn't arguing with her dad; she was arguing with Richard. Which was strange. Richard never argued with her mother, as far as she could remember.

". . . go to work with *that* going on outside?" he was saying, his voice loud.

"It's not like she called them over, Richard," her mother answered sharply. "Someone must have seen her—"

"If you'd have told her to stay in a motel, like I'd suggested, we wouldn't have this mess on our front yard. I don't even want to talk about Russell coming here last night—"

"Lower your voice, you'll wake Theodora."

"Maybe she should be awake for this." He lowered his voice, but Gemma could still easily hear him through the door, his words strained, angry. "I don't want to go through all this again."

"Then maybe you shouldn't have involved the police."

"*You* thought involving the detective was a good idea!"

"But Theodora didn't want me to—"

"She doesn't get a say in this!" he roared.

A door slammed shut, and then, a sudden silence. Gemma imagined her mother shutting their bedroom door and hissing at Richard to be quiet. She lay in bed, rattled, her heart beating. After a few seconds, guilt enveloped her, as familiar as an old friend. Gemma had thrown her mother's life into chaos by coming here. Richard was right; she *should* have stayed in a motel.

What were they talking about, anyway? Before Richard mentioned Russell? What mess in the front yard?

She got out of bed and carefully padded to the window, then peered out.

"Oh, shit," she muttered.

A small crowd milled around the entrance to her mother's house, some talking to each other, some peering at the house. As she watched, one man actually got on his tiptoes to get a better vantage point. Gemma shifted half a step back, wondering if they could see her through the window. Across the street, she spotted a news van, and in front of it, a woman was talking while a man aimed a large video camera at her. Two young teenagers in the crowd huddled together, their heads touching, and actually took a selfie with the house in the background.

Unless her mother or Richard had become a local celebrity, it was pretty clear the crowd had come for her. News had gotten out. Crumville's number one fugitive had returned.

The garage door opened, and Richard's car drove outside. The people converged on his vehicle, some snapping photos, at least two reporters shouting questions at him as he slowly moved toward the road. Finally breaking through, he floored it and swerved, engine roaring as he drove away.

Two women at the edge of the crowd snagged Gemma's attention. They were watching the car drive off, one of them leaning into the other, whispering something, her lips twisted in a familiar half smile. Judy, one of Victoria's crowd back in high school. All these years later and she still thrived on other people's misery. It was as if the woman's body could actually produce nutrients from gossip. Of course she was here. She must've been one of the first to hear the infamous Theodora was back in town. And she probably told a dozen people all about it before showing up on Gemma's mother's front yard, just to see what would happen. The other woman seemed familiar, too, perhaps another girl Gemma had gone to school with. Come to think of it, she could spot five or six familiar faces in the crowd.

She felt ill.

She stepped away from the window and left the bedroom. Her mother was in the kitchen, sitting by the table, staring vacantly at the wall. When she noticed Gemma, she smiled nervously.

"Hey, honey," she said. "Did you manage to get any sleep?"

"Uh . . . yeah. A bit."

"Do you want coffee? I just made some."

"Sure, thanks, Mom."

Her mom quickly got up and went over to the counter, retrieved a mug from a cupboard, then rummaged for a spoon. Hiding her agitation in normal everyday acts. Gemma knew the drill. She'd done it so many times herself. You went through the motions, hoping all the fear you felt would just dissipate in the routines.

"There are reporters in front of the house," Gemma said, feeling a bit dumb for stating the obvious. "And some other people."

"Yeah." Her mom waved her hand impatiently, as if the crowd in front of the house was a pesky swarm of gnats. "They'll probably leave soon. You know how people are in this town. They get excited by every little thing." She handed Gemma a large mug of coffee.

Gemma took a sip. It was strong and bitter. It was what she needed. "I think I'll take my stuff and move to a motel."

"No," her mother blurted. "Don't . . . leave. There's no reason for you to go."

"Mom, I'm causing trouble just by being here. I mean . . . Russell last night? And now this? It's better if I get out of your hair."

"Better for who?" her mother asked sharply.

"Well . . . for you. I don't want to make things difficult for you."

"When you left, all those years ago, *that* was difficult." Her mother's voice trembled. "If you disappear again—"

"I'm not going to disappear, I promise," Gemma said. "Look, I'll leave you my phone number. And Benjamin's. You'll get to see Lucas soon. It'll be all right."

Her mother shook her head, a short tug. Gemma knew that motion well. It had always appeared when she asked something she knew her mother would never allow, like going to a party on a school night, or getting her eyebrow pierced. She used to hate when her mother did that, shattering her fantasies with a single motion. Now she was so relieved to see it.

"You're staying here, Theodo . . . Gemma. You're staying here, and that's final. In a minute I'll step outside and hose those reporters down."

"No need for that," Gemma said quickly. Although the image of her mother soaking Judy with a garden hose had a certain allure. "It's fine. I'll stay."

Her mother's shoulders sagged with relief. "Good. Can I make you some breakfast?"

"No, thanks." Gemma took another large swig from her mug. "I think I'll eat outside. Can I use your phone?"

"Sure, sweetie, you don't even need to ask."

Gemma took the coffee to the living room and dialed Benjamin's number.

He picked up after two rings. "Hey. We were just leaving for school."

"Oh good. Can I talk to Lucas?"

"We're already running late. Call me in the afternoon and—"

"Please, Benjamin?"

A pause. "Sure, I'll put him on. Hey, Lucas, want to talk to Mommy?"

She listened as Benjamin handed the phone to her son.

"Hey, Mommy."

Tears instantly came to Gemma's eyes. She wiped them with the back of her hand. "Hey, sweetie. I'm sorry I didn't get to say good night yesterday."

"Okay. Dad let me drink hot chocolate this morning."

"Your dad is the best."

"When you come back, will I still be able to drink hot chocolate in the morning?"

"We'll see, sweetie. How was your night?"

"I woke up twice because I was itching. After the second time, Dad fell asleep in my bed, but I had to wake him up because he snored."

Gemma let out a small laughing sob. "Yeah, your dad does that. And I heard you went to Grandma and Grandpa's yesterday."

"Yeah."

There were some random tones, and then she heard Benjamin telling Lucas to stop tapping the screen. She sighed.

"All right, sweetie," she said. "You should go to school. You don't want to be late."

"Okay."

"And I'll call you in the afternoon."

"Okay."

She made kissing sounds and then said goodbye. Placing the phone in its cradle, she shut her eyes and exhaled. Then she took another sip from her coffee.

She'd talked to her son and gotten some caffeine in her veins. That would have to be enough to start the day. She picked up the phone again and dialed Steve's number. She listened to the tones, counting them. She was about to hang up when he finally picked up.

"Hi," he said softly.

"Hi," she said. "Listen—"

"Your house was on the local news," Steve said.

"That's what I was about to tell you. You were wrong yesterday. I *was* recognized. Rick Peters pegged me in, like, two seconds."

"Oh, shit."

"And the detective was here last night. We had a long talk."

"Seriously? So he didn't arrest you?"

"Not yet." Gemma massaged her eyebrows. "Listen, can we meet again? I want to talk about the Halloween party."

"Uh . . . yeah, sure. Same place?"

"Uh-huh. And . . . do you think Allan could make it too?"

"I can check with him."

"I'd appreciate it. After the talk with the detective I just . . . I really need to know what happened that night."

"Yeah," Steve said. "I feel like we all do."

Chapter 44

It took Gemma a while to build up the courage to get out of the house. She couldn't have done what Richard did earlier—just drive through the crowd—since her car was parked on the curb across the street. So she had to get out of the house on foot.

She went out the back door and through the neighbors' yard. When she'd lived there, the neighbors were the Turner family, and as she crossed into their yard, she wondered if it was still them. Mrs. Turner had liked to bake, and the delicious scent used to drive Gemma insane. Maybe Mrs. Turner was baking right now, looking out the window, wondering why there was some grown woman walking through her yard. Or maybe the Turners had moved out, and someone else lived there now.

And then the crowd spotted her despite her brilliant diversion and swarmed toward her. They didn't carry torches and pitchforks, only cell phones, but they still looked like an angry mob, hysteria etched on their faces as they shouted "There she is," and "Did you kill Victoria," and "You should be in prison." The reporters lobbed questions at her, which were swallowed in the din, and by that time she was already almost at her car, and someone actually grabbed her sleeve, and she wrenched it away, turning toward him, screaming—

—clawing at the guy above her, and he was laughing, slapping away her hands with ease, his face hidden by that awful mask. And she was crying, shouting at him to stop, his weight on her, and then she remembered the knife. It was in her pocket! She grabbed it and pulled it out and—

—she was in her car, driving, and she realized she didn't even remember getting inside and switching it on. Had she run over someone? It was possible; she didn't know. She glanced at the rearview mirror and saw the mob behind her. No apparent bleeding victim on the road. She wanted to throw up, but she knew she couldn't stop, so she floored the gas as she gagged, the bile rising in her throat.

She tried to focus on something else. On Lucas. How happy he was about the hot chocolate that morning, trying to squeeze a promise for future hot chocolates. That pushed the tendrils of the memories and the images of the terrifying mob away, and she was in her car, and everything was more or less fine. For now at least. She let out a shuddering breath, and tried to figure out where she was and what the shortest way to get to the Starbucks from there was.

By the time she arrived, she'd gotten her breathing under control. She checked herself in the mirror and—

Ugh.

Puffy eyes. Her hair was a mess. Her nose was pink. And *those* were just the basic things anyone would notice. Not to mention her messy eyebrows, her chapped lips, and an actual damn zit that was materializing on her chin. A zit! As if she was being pulled back in time. If she'd have shown up at Primadonna looking like this, Thelma and Barbara would have been horrified. It would have been unthinkable.

No. This stopped here. It was true, a mysterious creep was trying to ruin her life, and last night she'd been interrogated as a possible murder suspect, and she'd been chased to her car twice in the past twenty-four hours, and there was a mob camping out at her mother's house . . . but it was no reason to let herself go.

She rummaged in her bag. Moisturizer. Eye cream. Just massaging her puffy eyes with the eye cream made her feel so much better. Next came her makeup base. She'd left her blending brush in the bathroom at her mother's house. Well, she would tough it out. She was hard core; she could rub it in with her fingers, no problem. There. Eyebrows? Well, she could spend a while on her eyebrows, but one had to prioritize. So she just dabbed on a bit of eyebrow gel. Okay, and that one stray hair was gonna go. No need for tweezers, even, it was so ridiculously long . . . ow. Okay. Good. Now that zit was going down. Concealer and a bit of powder. Zit? What zit? There was no zit here. Mascara and a bit of lip balm.

True. This wasn't the best time to do all this. But did Rambo feel guilty for taking the time to put on his bandanna and inspect his battle gear? He did not. Gemma needed this. She needed these moments to collect herself, to remember who she was. She took one last look in the rearview mirror. There she was. Gemma Foster. The kick-ass beautician, who'd left a sexual predator in tatters just a few days before. Now she was ready to meet her old friends from high school.

She spotted them quickly as she stepped inside the Starbucks. They sat in the same place where she and Steve had sat the day before. That was just like Steve—creating these tiny patterns and habits wherever he went. Allan looked pretty much the same as he had in high school, same chubby face, same goofy smile. He was clean shaven, which made his age seem even more indeterminate. He could be thirty, or twenty, or even the same seventeen-year-old boy she'd known back then. He was laughing nervously at something Steve had said, a sort of high-pitched titter, just like he had in high school. It made Gemma instantly smile. It brought back some good memories. Afternoons of the three of them hanging out together, eating candy and talking shit about everyone else. Just them against the world.

"Hey," she said, approaching them.

Allan's mouth formed a perfect O as he took her in. He got up and moved toward her. Was he about to hug her? He held out his hand, but then realized she was leaning in for a hug, so it ended up being this weird awkward hug with his right hand trapped between them.

"I already ordered you some coffee," Steve said. "And a danish. I hope the coffee isn't cold."

"Thanks. I'm sorry I'm late. There's been a crowd outside my mother's house."

"We saw." Allan took out his phone and showed the screen. It was a tweet by *The Crumville Post*, a photo of her with her mother's house in the background. They caught her just as she yelled at whoever grabbed her arm, and she seemed angry and deranged, her mouth open, and her nose twisted. The tweet said *Theodora Briggs returns to the scene of Crumville's most heinous crime.*

"Holy shit," Gemma muttered. Could it have been any worse? She was glad she took the time to apply makeup in the car. At least she now looked different from that clearly guilty woman in the photo.

"*The Crumville Post* is actually just Ronnie Drexel's sister," Steve said. "You remember Ronnie Drexel?"

"Sort of." Gemma couldn't tear her eyes away from the image.

"Anyway, she's running the local newspaper. It's usually just ads and interviews with the local librarian or the high school pupil who won the science fair."

"She's probably excited to have something like this to write about." Allan pocketed his phone.

"Glad I could help," Gemma muttered and sipped from the coffee. It was lukewarm, but she didn't have it in her to order a new one or ask them to reheat it. She eyed Allan. "How are you doing, Allan? You look just the same."

"So I keep being told." He smiled sheepishly. "I'm fine. You know. Same old same old."

"What are you doing these days?"

"I'm an accountant."

"Oh! That's great."

He snorted. "I don't know. It wasn't my life's dream. But it pays the bills. And I heard you have a family now."

"Yeah. A husband and a son. I'm a beautician."

"And you go by . . . Gemma?"

"Yeah. Gemma Foster."

He nodded. She found herself nodding back. Meeting Allan wasn't like meeting Steve. She and Allan were never close friends. Sure, they hung around together all the time, but it was always clear it was because they were Steve's friends. They'd almost never spend time without Steve.

"Did Steve tell you?" she finally asked. "About the guy who's harassing me?"

"More or less," Allan said. "Some sort of troll who found you in Chicago, right?"

"Yeah. And I think he lives in Crumville."

"She calls him the Shadowman," Steve supplied.

"The . . . Shadowman?" Allan quirked an eyebrow.

Gemma huffed. "I'm not getting into that argument, okay? It's just a name. You can call him whatever you want."

"I've got no issues with it," Allan said. "Shadowman it is."

"Fine." Steve seemed miffed that Allan didn't give more of a fight. "Do you think he knew you were coming here?"

She shook her head. "I doubt it. I was careful."

"Well, he knows now," Allan said. "What do you think he'll do?"

"I don't know. Maybe that's what he wanted all along. He's so fixated on me being the killer. Maybe he just wants me to pay for what he thinks I did."

"Why not simply report you to the police, then?" Allan asked.

She shrugged. It was a good question, one she'd already asked herself a bunch of times. He hadn't reported her. He hadn't threatened to expose her secret like he'd done with all those other people. Why?

"What if he doesn't want any trace leading back to him?" Steve asked.

"Well . . . he's been hiding his tracks pretty well," Gemma said. "An anonymous email to the cops isn't a big deal."

"Yeah, but it might make them ask themselves why he's so interested. What if *he's* the one who killed Victoria?"

Gemma stared at him, confused. She was about to say it was a ridiculous idea, but then paused. "Are you saying he's . . . what? Trying to frame me?"

Steve spread his hands. "Look at it this way. It already seems like whoever did it tried to frame you, right?"

"That's a good point," Allan said. "You told us yourself back then. That it looked like there was all this evidence pointing at you, and you couldn't explain it?"

The knife. Her wearing Victoria's blood-soaked jacket. Her DNA under Victoria's fingernails. Could she have been set up?

"Okay, but hang on. Why would he bring it all up again? He'd already gotten away with it, right?"

"Well, that detective is *still* digging into it," Steve said. "Like, literally every year we hear he interrogated someone. Or there's new evidence that supposedly sheds new light on the murder."

"Victoria's brother Craig hired a private detective too," Allan said.

"So you think maybe they're getting closer to finding out who did it?"

"Or at least the killer thinks that way. So he figures, he's gotta turn the spotlight back on you," Steve said excitedly.

It seemed convoluted and bizarre. But wasn't everything this guy did convoluted? Gemma had to agree it wasn't entirely far fetched. She took a bite from the danish, and the sugary dough helped her mind kick into action. Damn, she was hungry.

"Okay," she finally said, swallowing. "Suppose you're right. That doesn't bring us any closer. We don't know who did it."

"It's someone who was at the party," Allan said.

Steve rolled his eyes. "Everyone was at that party except us."

"We can make a list—"

"Allan, you and your lists . . ."

Gemma tuned them out. If they were right, it was entirely possible that, like Steve said, what started this whole thing again was Dunn talking to someone. Maybe someone who got nervous. The Shadowman probably knew exactly who he'd interrogated lately. Or not lately. The Shadowman had emailed Lucas's teacher, Paula, half a year ago, right? Maybe it had started back then.

"I think I should talk to the detective again," she said. "I'll go to the police station—"

"I wouldn't do it. At least not yet," Allan said.

"Why not?"

"With all the interest in the case right now? If you step inside the station, I don't know if they'll let you leave, you know?"

"He didn't arrest me yesterday."

"That's different," Allan pointed out. "If someone sees you going to the station, *everyone* will know. And then the cops will be in a tight spot."

"That's a good point," Steve said. "At the very least you should wait a day or two, see where this goes. Maybe just you being here will shake things up a bit. Make someone jittery. They might make a mistake."

Another day or two. Camped at her mother's house while the mob waited outside. That sounded horrible. But maybe they were right. She could wait a couple of days, see if anything turned up.

She rubbed her eyes. "Listen . . . I have a question. About that night."

"I'd say you have more than one question," Allan pointed out.

"Yeah, but . . . I have one question for you. Um . . . What was I doing there?"

They both gaped at her.

"Don't you remember?" Steve finally asked.

"I went there to get back at Victoria," she said slowly. It was weird saying it out loud. Because she didn't really remember *wanting* to get back at Victoria. But she did remember that was the whole purpose of that night. Revenge, right? "But I don't remember what the plan was. I had something in my pocket, right? Something I wanted to use . . . a bag. Was it like, drugs or something? Was I going to plant it in her home? I don't think I did it. I remember flushing it later, in the toilet. I got rid of it. It was drugs, wasn't it?" That was the only thing she could think of. She remembered how she felt about it. It was something bad. Something she really didn't want to carry. That she didn't want anywhere *near* her. It had to be something illegal, like drugs.

"It wasn't drugs," Steve said. He fiddled with his empty cup, seemingly unable to meet her eyes.

"Then . . . what was it?"

"It was dog shit," Allan said, his lip twitching. "Don't you remember, Theo? It was a bag full of dog shit."

Chapter 45

Gemma stared at Allan. She wanted to laugh at his dumb joke. Or just roll her eyes but—

It was like that moment of remembering a dream. Flashes of disconnected images forming together, memories that were already there, hidden underneath the recollections of her everyday life.

"A bag of . . . dog shit," she said. The words tasted vile in her mouth. And she suddenly remembered its texture in her pocket. Soft, mushy. The plastic bag crinkling. She recalled wrapping it in two additional plastic bags, because a puncture in the bag would be horrific. She'd kept thinking of the germs in that thing. It was practically a biological weapon. Yeah, it wasn't illegal, but as far as she was concerned . . . it should have been.

She was still holding the half-eaten danish in her hand and put it down, knowing she might never eat a danish again.

"You wanted to get back at Victoria," Steve said. "So we thought of this plan—"

"No," she said.

"Yeah, that's what happened," Allan said. "We got some—"

She raised her hand to silence him. "I know. I mean I realize that's what we . . . I did. But I didn't want to get back at her."

"Sure you did," Steve said. "Remember? Because of the toilet thing?"

She shut her eyes, breathing deeply, trying to avoid throwing up. She'd never wanted this. *Never.* Sure, she was deeply upset. Depressed. Scared. But she didn't want revenge. That was their idea. Steve and Allan. Now she remembered. She'd bought the knife, and they assumed she was planning revenge. Because they were boys. That's how boys thought. All she'd ever wanted was a way out.

But she didn't tell them she was thinking of cutting herself. She let them think they were right because it was less pathetic, right? She would seem like an avenging angel. Uma Thurman in *Kill Bill*, or Stephen King's *Carrie*, or someone like that. So Steve and Allan, her friends, came up with an alternative plan that wouldn't land her in prison. Dog shit.

So dumb. So juvenile. And ultimately, it went so wrong.

"A bag of dog shit," she said, opening her eyes. "I took it. To the party. Because we figured it would be my opportunity to go to Victoria's room without anyone paying attention."

"Right," Steve said. "We thought you could smear it in her bed. On her pillow. Under the covers. Maybe she'd be so drunk when she got into bed, she wouldn't even notice. But even if she did notice, it would make her feel . . . like you felt. With the toilet."

"Violated," Gemma said, her voice trembling. And now she knew. She knew why, when she walked into that party, she didn't just do it. Because it felt so wrong. And so futile.

"Yeah," Steve said. "That was our plan."

Gemma nodded, remembering. The only reason she'd agreed to it in the first place was to appease Steve and Allan. To make them lay off and forget about the knife. No . . . that wasn't right. She'd wanted to go to that party. And maybe face Victoria. She'd wanted to stop feeling as she did, as if she was drowning. So she'd gone.

"She earned it," Allan said. "I know it feels wrong to talk about her that way, because of what happened . . . because she ended up dying. But she was awful, Theo. You remember how she treated you? How she and her friends treated all of us? Sure, she didn't deserve to die, but she deserved to feel soiled like that. She was a real bitch."

"Right," Steve said. "That's why you went there. Allan and I waited for you outside, in Allan's mom's car. We were the getaway drivers."

"I was the getaway driver," Allan said. "I don't know what *you* were."

"Fine, you were the driver, I was the lookout." Steve quirked his eyebrow at Gemma. "Except you didn't come out straight after like we planned."

"Yeah," Gemma said, glancing outside at the parking lot. "I . . . I didn't want to go through with it. I remember. I kept thinking maybe I should just leave. But Bruce was talking to me—"

"Bruce saw you?" Allan asked.

"Yeah. He didn't recognize me. So we talked for a while, and then I figured I *should* go to Victoria's room. And decide there." As she spoke, her mind floated back to that day. The words leaving her mouth felt as if they were a part of a strange story that had happened to someone else. "Or maybe I just wanted to see it again. You know, we used to be such good friends when we were little."

"I called you several times," Steve said. "Allan was freaking out—"

"Um, as I remember it, *you* were freaking out," Allan interrupted. "You basically stepped out of the car to call her barely five minutes after she entered the house."

"Whatever. We were both freaking out. So I called and called. And finally you picked up."

"Yeah." Gemma frowned. "I remember that."

"He talked to you on the phone for a while, and afterward we agreed that we had to abort," Allan said.

"Yeah," Steve said. "We figured something wasn't going well, so we decided to pull the plug. But you hung up on me and turned off your phone."

"Victoria walked in on me," Gemma said. "As I was talking to you. That's why I hung up."

"And . . . and then what happened?" Allan asked.

And Gemma knew what he wanted to ask. How did she die?

"I don't remember," she said hesitantly. "I remember talking to her. She was distraught. Crying. She apologized to me . . ."

Steve and Allan exchanged looks.

"She did!" She wanted to slam the table, to make them see. "She apologized. But . . . it's all fuzzy. I went to the bathroom and flushed the . . . I guess I flushed the bag with the dog shit. Someone hit me. And then . . . I ran . . . Victoria's dogs were chasing me through the woods . . ." She shut her eyes. Her mind shied away from the memory.

For a few seconds no one said anything. Then Gemma inhaled. "So . . . what did you see?"

"Nothing," Allan said. "I went inside to take a look, but there were a lot of people there, and I couldn't see you anywhere. So I left, and we went to Steve's house. We waited for a while and then we heard police sirens."

"At first we thought something happened to you," Steve said. "My dad told us something had happened at the party. That someone was hurt. It took a few hours until we found out it was Victoria. And that you'd disappeared."

Gemma remembered them talking on the phone. They'd agreed to tell the cops that they were supposed to meet up at Steve's, but Gemma had decided to go to the party before. That explained Steve's repeated phone calls. It kept Steve and Allan out of it, and more importantly, her own motivation for showing up to the party. Even if she hadn't planned on killing Victoria, it was obvious that "I came to get revenge" wasn't exactly a good alibi.

"So . . . what now?" Allan finally asked.

"I think I might drive around town," Gemma answered. "Go see Victoria's house. Maybe go to the woods behind it, see if it jogs my memory."

"That's a good idea," Steve said. "You could also try the school."

"Yeah." She doubted it would help, but it was the best she could think of.

"What about the people around your mom's house?" Allan asked.

"I don't think there's anything I can do about that." Gemma sighed. "Most of them are just curious people from Crumville. I already saw some faces I recognize from high school. Eventually they'll lose interest. I hope."

"Hang on," Allan said. "That guy, the one who's harassing you . . . he's probably from Crumville. He might show up in the crowd."

Gemma frowned. "Why would he?"

"Well, he seems obsessed with you, like a sort of weird stalker. It's his chance to watch you without standing out, right?"

"That's a good point," Steve agreed. "He could stand outside your room at your mother's house for hours, and no one would even notice."

Gemma shuddered. "That's a creepy notion."

"But you can use that," Allan said. "Make a note of everyone you see out there. Take photos. Later we'll be able to use it to figure out who he is."

"Okay, I can do that." Gemma couldn't use her own phone to take the photos—the Shadowman still had access to it. But maybe she could use her mother's phone or something. "Thanks, that gives me something to work with."

It was flimsy, but it was a start. And it made her feel like she was fighting back.

Chapter 46

Gemma eyed the window in her room with something close to revulsion. Even with the curtain drawn, she could feel the dozens of people outside glancing at it, waiting for her to make an appearance.

Sitting in Starbucks with Steve and Allan, she found it easy to say she would keep tabs on the crowd outside and take some pictures. But now, back here, she didn't want to even go near the window. Just knowing her appearance would instantly get everyone outside excited made her feel dirty somehow. They would point and gaze at her as someone might watch an animal in the zoo. She hated this. It reminded her why she'd run away. It hadn't been just the looming threat of prison. It was being turned into a *thing*. Something vile that people talked about. Shaking their heads and clucking their tongues. She wasn't a person to the people outside. She was a killer who had gotten away with it. She was an interesting and morbid story to tell their friends. "Presumed innocent until proven guilty" wasn't even a relevant concept here. In this court she was "presumed guilty because my cousin told me so." "Presumed guilty because I hear a lot of true crime podcasts and I can tell." "Presumed guilty because I saw her face and she looked like she was hiding something." "Presumed guilty because I'm bored."

Still, she had to do it. Steve and Allan were right; there was a good chance the Shadowman was out there.

Her mom had actually found an old phone of Richard's for her to use to take photos. She picked it up from the desk and approached the window. She shifted the curtain just a bit, glancing outside. About fifteen people stood out there. The same reporters from that morning, alongside an additional news van. She quickly scanned the faces; two or three looked familiar. She couldn't really recall their names, but they went to school with her, she was almost sure. Someone pointed. Excited faces. Mobs these days didn't carry pitchforks and torches. They carried phones. They didn't burn the witch. They took photos of the witch to post on social media.

She took a few pictures of her own. She'd done it three times so far. Later she would look through all the photos, see if any of the people appeared more than others. Get Steve and Allan to help her put names to faces.

She'd gone by Victoria's home earlier, like she'd said she would. She stopped in front of it for a minute, fear crackling in her mind. She couldn't bring herself to step outside and go over to the tree line behind it. She floored the gas pedal when the front door opened. She drove back to her mother's house, nearly ran over the crowd, parked haphazardly just in front of the yard, and bolted inside, slamming the front door behind her.

Tomorrow. She'd go back to Victoria's house tomorrow. Maybe.

But right now she needed to feel better. To feel like she had a life that wasn't this.

She went downstairs, the house echoing, strangely empty. Her mother had gone to do some errands, though Gemma had a sneaking suspicion that she mostly wanted to get away from the crowd outside for a few hours. Richard was at work. It was the first time Gemma was alone in this house since she got back here. As a teenager, she liked being alone in this house. Now it felt bizarre. The house didn't even resemble the one she lived in as a child—it was like being alone at a stranger's place. A lot of the furniture had changed. The pictures on the walls were different. Even the smell was different—musty and stale.

She picked up the landline and dialed Benjamin.

He answered almost immediately. "Hey." He sounded strange, talking silently and urgently. "Hang on." The television played in the background—some kind of cartoon show, which was strange. It was early afternoon—they usually didn't let Lucas watch TV in the afternoon. The noise of the TV receded, then disappeared with the sound of a door shutting.

"Benjamin?" she said.

"Yeah. I just moved to a different room. We're at my parents' house."

"Oh, okay. How are they?"

"Are you all right?"

"Yeah, I mean . . . I'm okay. Some stuff has been going on, but—"

"Our house was vandalized."

"What?" Her heart plummeted.

"Someone sprayed the words *psycho bitch* on the wall. And someone broke the headlights of my mom's car and sprayed uh . . . some words on the windshield."

"What words?"

"It doesn't matter. But they were about you. Well . . . about Theodora."

She clutched the phone. "Is Lucas okay?"

"Yeah. He didn't see the graffiti. He could see we were upset, but I told him it was nothing he had to worry about. My mom also saw a man watching their house."

"What man?"

"Just a guy. He stood in the street in the evening, watching. She thought about calling the cops, but then he left. That's part of the reason we're here now."

"Shit, Benjamin." Tears filled Gemma's throat, her voice cracking. "That's . . . it's all my fault."

"It's not your fault. You didn't do anything." There was a pause. "I talked to the cops. And that detective called me? Holly something."

"Holly O'Donnell."

"Yeah. She said this guy who's targeting you is probably doing all of it. She asked me if I knew what it was about. But I told her I didn't know anything."

Gemma sighed. "You can tell her about Victoria's murder. You *should* tell her. The cops here already know I'm back."

"And? Did they—"

"They haven't arrested me. Yet."

"But are you still a suspect?"

"I think so. But some of the evidence doesn't fit . . . I don't know exactly."

"Gemma, it's time you get a lawyer. I'll look for a good one."

"Yeah."

"There's something else." Benjamin cleared his throat. "I drove by Primadonna today, on the way to Lucas's school. Someone smashed the display window and sprayed some graffiti on the door too. It had *your* name there. Like, your real name. Gemma. And some other words. Slurs and threats."

Her entire life was being destroyed. She thought of Barbara and Thelma. Showing up to their lovely place, seeing it like that. How they probably felt.

"Gemma? Are you there?"

"Yes," she said, her voice cracking. She wiped a tear from her cheek. "Yeah, I'm here."

"Do you want to talk to Lucas?"

"Yes . . . no. I don't think I should talk to him right now. I should calm down first."

"Okay."

"I think I should also call Thelma. I'll tell her to talk to Holly O'Donnell. Maybe she has footage of whoever did this. We have security cameras."

"That's a good idea."

It wasn't. It was a useless idea. Because even if they caught whoever did this on tape, it was just another one of the Shadowman's flying monkeys. Someone blackmailed to do it, who wouldn't be able to lead them back to the man behind it all. But what else was there to do?

"I'll call you again in a bit, okay?" Gemma said.

"Yeah. Listen . . . I love you."

"I love you too." She pressed the phone hard into her ear.

"I'll get you a good lawyer."

"Okay."

"Bye, honey."

"Bye." She hung up and let out a shuddering sob.

She went to the kitchen and drank a glass of water. She washed her face in the sink and sniffled. Then she returned to the living room. She needed to call Thelma, but she didn't know her phone number. She took out her own cell phone and switched it on, not caring that the Shadowman could get a glimpse of her. She found Thelma's contact and wrote down the number on a piece of paper. Then she removed the battery from her own cell phone and dialed Thelma from the landline.

"Hello?" Thelma answered. Suspicious. Hostile. Of course, she didn't have this number, and she'd been getting calls from cranks.

"Thelma, it's Gemma."

"Oh. Where are you calling from?"

"Georgia."

There was a long silence. "That's pretty far away."

"Yeah. Um. I'm looking for the guy. The one who's harassing me."

"And he's in Georgia?"

"I think so."

"Okay."

"Listen, Benjamin told me someone vandalized Primadonna."

"That's right." She sounded on edge. Angry.

"Do you have anything on the security camera?"

"Yes. A woman. She wore a mask."

A woman. Gemma wondered if most of the Shadowman's black-mailed targets were women. Easy targets. Vulnerable. All you needed was a nude photo or an embarrassing chat. Because women knew that even something like that—a single tiny mistake—was usually enough for everyone around them to judge them, to blame them. To make it *their* fault.

"There's a detective who's investigating this guy. Holly O'Donnell. You should give her a call."

"Do you have a number?"

"Yeah, hang on." Gemma went and got O'Donnell's card from her purse. She gave the number to Thelma.

"I'll talk to her," Thelma said. "You find that guy."

"Is that Gemma?" Barbara's voice in the background.

"Uh-huh," Thelma said.

"Let me talk to her," Barbara said. Then, her voice was much clearer. "Hello, Gemma?"

"Hey, Barbara, listen—"

"A guy followed me to my car this morning, Gemma." Barbara's voice trembled. "I was with Khai."

"Barbara, I'm so sorry."

"I don't know what this is about, but you have to fix it, okay? I'm scared. I don't deserve . . . I haven't done anything."

"You're right," Gemma said heavily. "I'll fix this."

"He knows where we work, and—"

"I'll fix this, Barbara, okay?"

Barbara was crying. "Okay."

"I'll talk to you later."

She hung up and put the phone away, mind roiling. Thelma could handle all this mess; she was made of iron. Sure, she might end up firing Gemma, but she could handle it. And so could Benjamin.

But Barbara? And Joyce? And Nathan? And Lucas? And who would be next? Nathan's sister? Kids at Lucas's school? Gemma's neighbors?

Gemma had thought if she turned off her phone and drove to a different state, she would get a reprieve from the guy who hounded her. After all, if he couldn't find her there was nothing he could do.

This was him sending her a message. There *was* no getting away from him. He had his talons deep in her life, and he wasn't about to let go.

She didn't have time to wait. To take photos of people and to play Nancy Drew.

It was time to end this.

Chapter 47

Gemma finally found the one thing in Crumville that was still just as she remembered it. The interrogation room in the Crumville Police Station. Same dusty gray walls. Same uncomfortable chairs. Same camera at the corner of the ceiling, aimed directly at her, a red light steadily blinking. Same scratched table. In fact, she recalled that during her interrogation thirteen years before, she'd kept staring at the table to avoid the detective's eyes, and had become fascinated with three long diagonal scratches, wondering who had made them, how, and why. And there they were! The same three diagonal scratches. Perhaps just slightly faded.

This time, her mother wasn't with her. She didn't have a lawyer either. She was all alone.

Dunn stepped into the room, holding two paper cups. He kicked the door shut, and the jerky motion made some of the coffee spill on the floor.

"Oh damn," he muttered, placing both cups on the table. "Sorry for the wait. The coffeepot was empty; I had to make a new one."

"No problem." Was it part of a strategy? Let the suspect stew in the interrogation room, just like in those TV crime series she sometimes watched. Maybe the coffee spill was a strategy, too, make Dunn seem harmless and clumsy.

Paranoid much, Gemma? A coffee stain is just a coffee stain. If you want a reason to be paranoid, here's one—you're in a police station, about to be interrogated about a murder.

"Half a sugar, right?" He offered her one of the cups.

"Yeah, thanks." She took it and sipped from it. It was too hot and had an aftertaste of ash. She placed the cup aside.

"Terrible, isn't it." He sipped from his own cup and grimaced, as if he'd just swallowed acid. "But it gets the job done."

"Good catchphrase," she said. "You should be in marketing, instead of the police."

"Right." His eyes were sharp, unmoving as he stared at her; the corner of his lips twitched. "So, let's get started. Why did you come here today?"

"After our talk, I remembered some things that I think you should be aware of."

"Like what?"

She hesitated and then said, "Before we talk about that, there's something else."

He didn't say anything, his face remaining blank.

"There's this . . . guy. He's been stalking me online. Sending me messages about the murder. He's also been harassing my family and my friends. It's becoming quite violent."

"Who is he?"

"I don't know. He's a sort of internet troll; I couldn't find out who he really is. I'm pretty sure it's someone from Crumville."

He frowned. "Okay."

"I was hoping for your help finding out who he is."

"Why do you think I can help you?"

"He's connected to Victoria. And maybe to the murder. You know all the people involved. You've questioned all of them, right?" She tried to keep her voice neutral, to keep her desperation from it.

"That's probably right."

"If I help you—"

"There's no such offer on the table," he said calmly. "This is a murder investigation. It's in your best interest to help me, because as far as

Mike Omer

most people in this place are concerned, you're the main suspect. I don't give a damn about your internet troll."

"What if he's involved in the murder?"

He spread his hands. "Then it's definitely in your best interest to help me catch him, right? He won't be able to harass you from behind bars."

The best course of action was to leave. To call Benjamin and ask if he had the phone number of a defense attorney already. She was about to make a terrible mistake.

But she thought of Barbara's terrified voice on the phone. Of Nathan and Joyce seeing the message on their vandalized car. Of Lucas's screams as she was assaulted.

"Fine." She gritted her teeth. "That night, at the party. I wasn't there to get Victoria to apologize."

"Why were you there?" He leaned slightly forward.

"I was there . . . to play a prank on her."

He blinked. "A prank?"

Gemma swallowed. "I had a . . . bag. With some dog poop. And I wanted to place it in her bed. That was the plan."

He watched her in stony silence. Gemma blushed, looking down at the table, feeling dumb. After a while he stood up, paced across the room and back. He sat down.

"You know," he finally said. "I've heard a few theories about the murder and your place in it. Some people thought you were consumed by a murderous rage. Others suggested you were a psychopath and that Victoria's murder was a meticulous plan that had gone wrong. At least two people suggested to me it was a full-blown conspiracy, involving a business partner of Victoria's father. I think every single person in this town has a very complex theory about the murder. And it's hard not to get dragged into it. Start concocting my own theories. Imagining that one night I would wake up and realize the truth was there all along. Something dramatic, and clever."

Gemma gaped at Dunn, confused. He seemed as if he wasn't even talking to her anymore. "Uh . . . okay."

"So you had dog poop. And you wanted to put it in her bed."

"That's right."

"Because of the way she bullied you?"

"Yeah. Specifically I was angry about that thing with the toilet."

"Right. But you never accomplished your dastardly plan." His lip twitched again.

"No, I didn't."

"Why not?" He raised an eyebrow. "It sounds simple enough. Walk in. Put poop in bed. Walk out."

"I . . . don't think I really wanted to go through with it."

"You didn't? You found some dog poop, presumably scooped it in a bag. Then you got a costume for the party. Got ready for said party. And walked inside, carrying dog poop and a knife. The knife, which you told me earlier, made you feel safe. Like you had a way out."

She nodded hesitantly. "Right."

"It sounds like you were very motivated. So then you walked inside and suddenly didn't feel like it?"

"It's not so easy. I saw her there. And it felt so . . ." She searched for the word. "Petty."

"It does sound petty," he agreed. He leaned back thoughtfully. "You know, I talked to you a few times back then. And I talked to people who knew you. And you weren't the sort to think of something this petty. Not in a million years."

"This is the truth," she blurted. "I came there with dog—"

He raised his hand. "Oh, I think I believe you. You had thirteen years to think about it, so I'd like to think that if you were lying, you'd come up with something better. I just don't believe you were the one to think of it. Or to get the aforementioned dog poop."

She clenched her jaw and said nothing.

"It was your friends, right? Steve Barnett and Allan Conner."

"No. It was just me."

"Steve Barnett called you a bunch of times that night, all about an hour before the murder."

"Yes. We were going to see a movie together. But this was my plan, they were not involved."

He stared at her for a few more seconds, then shrugged. "Okay. I can follow up on that later. So you went there and changed your mind. What then?"

"The rest is just as I told you. I don't remember." She looked at him pleadingly. "I know it sounds convenient, but I swear I don't. I do remember Victoria apologizing to me. And someone hit me. And then . . . I was running through the woods. Victoria's dogs were chasing me. I think maybe I was drugged. I think . . . whatever happened that night was bad."

"Okay." He bent and searched in his bag, retrieving two thin folders. He placed them on the table and pushed the top one over to her. "I want you to look at this."

She eyed the folder, terrified. She'd seen this moment often enough on TV. The detective showing the suspect photos of the murder victim, to unsettle them, make them slip up. What would it be like, to see Victoria's bloody body on the bed? She imagined wide vacant eyes, gray skin, face twisted in pain. She couldn't handle it. She couldn't—

"Go on," Dunn said, his voice impatient.

She flipped the folder open, then sagged in relief. It was just a form. She glanced at the top. A forensic toxicology report. A blood sample was found positive for something called flunitrazepam.

"What's . . ." She licked her lips. "Fluni . . . flunitra—"

"Flunitrazepam," Dunn said smoothly. "You might know it by another name. Rohypnol."

She blinked. "Roofies?"

"Exactly. We knew back then someone was selling Rohypnol and other drugs in the area."

She exhaled slowly. "I was right? I really was drugged?"

"Yes. We collected a blood sample from you after the cops found you, in the woods. The sample was positive for Rohypnol."

"So . . . what are you saying?"

"Well . . ." He pushed the other folder forward. "The report you're looking at isn't of *your* blood. This one is."

She opened the second folder. Another toxicology report. Positive traces of flunitrazepam.

"Then . . . what's the first report?"

"The first report is Victoria's blood sample."

"Victoria's blood . . . ," she said slowly. "She was drugged as well?"

"She was definitely drugged. Just as you were."

"We were both drugged." Her head spun. She picked up the coffee cup and sipped from it, not even tasting the contents.

"I think the guy selling drugs might have had something to do with Victoria. She got a phone call during the party, not long before her murder. From a burner phone. Does that ring a bell? Did you see anyone who didn't belong there? Maybe saw something you weren't supposed to?"

"No . . . I . . . I don't remember. I mean, I saw her answer the phone, I actually remember that. But after that it gets really spotty. But . . . but this clears me, right? If Victoria and I were *both* drugged?"

"Not necessarily. You still brought the knife. Your DNA was under her fingernails. Maybe you weren't entirely lucid, but that doesn't mean you didn't kill her. Definitely not as far as my colleagues are concerned."

"Oh," Gemma whispered.

"But I found it very encouraging to hear you have flashes of memories from that night," Dunn continued. "I'm hoping you might recall more of it."

"I . . . I tried. I couldn't."

"I'm hoping you'll have more success tomorrow. When we go together to the house where Victoria was murdered."

Chapter 48

He paced back and forth in his room, images and videos of Theodora flickering on his monitors. By now he had two thralls from Crumville following her, filming her movements and sending them to him throughout the day. Additionally, there was footage that random people had taken without his say-so. Curious onlookers outside her house. Local news crews, excited about the developments in the infamous murder case. And, of course, he'd seen her himself.

And she seemed okay. She should be broken by now. Her life in shambles. Her family and friends harassed, their illusion of safety shattered. She must have talked to them. Must have heard of the messages left for her in Chicago by now. She was probably fired from that beauty salon she worked in. So why didn't she show it? Instead, she seemed driven, alive, energetic. Every photo, every video showed her walking purposefully somewhere, her clothing and hair immaculate, her back straight, lips pursed with determination.

Didn't she understand? There was no getting away from him. He was everywhere. *He* was her life now.

Well, if she didn't understand yet, he would make her see.

He sat by the computer and opened his Excel spreadsheet. At the moment he had 569 available thralls. An army.

And like a general on the battlefield, he deployed them.

Thirty-seven thralls in Crumville. They would follow her around, deliver her messages and threats. She thought she could walk around in *his* town without repercussions? Think again, bitch.

He wrote the emails feverishly, sending them one after the other, his teeth grinding. Usually he would pay more attention to his careful color code. Some thralls weren't ready yet for these kinds of requests. They would buckle, and break. It didn't matter. It was a war, and wars had casualties. Yes, that's right, all of them. Caroline Hall, the waitress, who had filmed herself masturbating. Gerald Phillips, the retired plumber, who had hit a kid with his car three years earlier and fled the scene. Donald Cook, a caretaker and a father, who was willing to do anything to avoid his young daughter's nude photos being released. And all the rest. They would all march together and hound Theodora wherever she went.

But he had more. People in Chicago, who would keep attacking her where it hurt most—the life she'd built for herself. They would dismantle it brick by brick until nothing was left. How many days would her gullible husband stick by her side as people vandalized his home, harassed him at his job, threatened his parents? Who among her friends would stick by her when they realized it exposed them to hatred and violence?

He marked each thrall he sent an email to, the large Excel spreadsheet slowly turning bloodred. That's right, Theodora. In wars, blood was shed. People got hurt. And no one wanted to be on the losing side. Well, too bad for her. She should have thought of that before, when she took Victoria away.

A lot of thralls lived elsewhere. Some even out of the country. But that was fine. It was a global community, right? Uma Khurana from Delhi could still phone Theodora's home in Chicago. Colm Cronin from Dublin could still write emails to all of Theodora's clients. Are you ready for this, Theodora? There are people who hate you all over the world.

More and more names were colored red as he worked, writing instruction after instruction. Five hundred and sixty-nine soldiers. All sent to do their part.

Chapter 49

Gemma peered through the wet windshield at the Howell house, Dunn in the driver's seat, talking on his phone.

It was only late morning, but she'd been awake for six hours already. At four a.m. her eyes had flown open at a sound outside the house, her heart instantly racing. She went to the window and thought she'd seen someone walking away down the street, but it was too dark to be sure. Still, with the adrenaline flooding her body, she couldn't go back to sleep. It was a relief when her mother and Richard woke up, and she felt she could freely get out of her room without waking them up.

And now she was here, as she'd agreed with Dunn the day before. Returning to the scene of the crime. The house where Victoria was murdered. The house that had hounded her for years.

Dunn hung up the phone and looked at her. "Craig Howell knows we're coming. He's not thrilled about it, but he agreed to let us in."

"Okay," Gemma croaked. She watched a raindrop trickling down the windshield. It merged with another raindrop and skidded faster, disappearing at the bottom.

"Are you okay?" Dunn asked.

"Does it matter?"

Dunn thought it over. "Well, it matters to me. But we'll do this either way."

Gemma clenched her jaw. "I'm ready."

He stepped out of the car, and she followed suit, staying two steps behind him, as if to shield herself from the house. As they approached it, the door opened. Craig Howell, Victoria's brother, stood in the doorway. He folded his arms and glared at them. Gemma still remembered him from thirteen years before, shouting outside her window, threatening her, cursing her, until his voice went raw. She slowed her steps.

"Good morning, Craig," Dunn said.

Craig gave Dunn a tiny nod. "Morning."

"I'm hoping it won't take long," Dunn said. "We'll try to get out of your hair as fast as possible."

"It's no bother," Craig said. "Take your time. Give her as much as she needs to recall how she killed my sister."

Gemma swallowed and lowered her eyes.

"We'll see what she remembers," Dunn said calmly.

Craig shifted slightly, just enough so they could brush past him and enter the house. Dunn glanced back at her and nodded, motioning her to go first. Gemma got the sense he did it so he could watch her back. She stepped forward, keeping her eyes to the ground, unable to look at Craig. As she brushed past him, she could feel his hatred washing over her in palpable waves. His body was tense as a coil, one that could spring at any moment and throttle her. But he let her inside.

She'd expected to see the familiar living room she'd visited many times as a child. The one where, that evening, dozens of teenagers danced, plastic beer cups scattered everywhere.

But apparently, Craig had redecorated.

The cozy, inviting furniture was gone. The worn beige sofa, the rocking chair, the wooden coffee table, the Persian rug, none were left. Not even the piano in the corner, where she and Victoria used to sit when they were young, plinking random keys and singing.

Instead, two leather couches stood by a rectangular glass table, in front of a ridiculously large TV. A single bookshelf on the wall sported several books that looked untouched and a glass decanter of whiskey.

The room was lit by four large spotlights hanging from the ceiling. Every item in that room seemed modern, and neat, and utterly cold.

Gemma couldn't imagine a place that seemed less familiar than this. There was no chance this place would trigger her memories.

Still, she paced the room, trying to recall the moment she stepped into the party, heard the vocals of "Turnin Me On," saw Victoria in her angel costume. She shut her eyes and tried to imagine the smell—cheap alcohol, and smoke, and sweat.

Nothing.

Dunn stood by her side, and she could feel Craig's looming presence behind them. Neither of them said anything.

She exhaled and paced down the hallway toward what used to be Victoria's room. Craig had repainted the walls stark white. An abstract modern painting hung on the wall.

The door to Victoria's room was ajar. She pushed it open.

"Oh," she said softly.

It wasn't Victoria's room. Not anymore. It was an office, containing a desk with a computer and two monitors. Another bookshelf. The books all seemed like professional ones—with titles like *Effective Java* and *Design Patterns*.

"It's different," she said needlessly.

"This is my office now," Craig said, his voice frigid.

"Take your time," Dunn said.

There was nothing to see here. She couldn't even imagine standing here all those years ago, talking to Victoria. She stood there for just a few more seconds, to make Dunn happy, and then stepped away.

She walked past the steps to the second floor—there was nothing to look for there. Back then, Craig's and Willie's rooms were on the second floor. She almost never went there, and definitely not that night. She reached the bathroom door to her right and opened it.

This, too, had changed, but at least the setup was still the same. Small room, one toilet, a sink on the side.

She cleared her throat. "This is where I went after I talked to Victoria. I washed my face. And I . . . flushed the bag."

"What bag?" Craig asked from behind.

"I will explain later," Dunn said. "And then what happened?" he asked her.

"I don't remember," Gemma whispered. The room hadn't triggered her memory at all. She just repeated what she'd remembered from before.

She shut the door and kept going. The trepidation she'd felt before was slowly evaporating. There was nothing in this house. It might physically be the same structure as the one from her memories, but it was a different place. The ghosts and nightmares were gone. Now it was just a house. What she wanted most of all was to get this over with. They were wasting time here. If she could recall anything, it wouldn't be inside. It would be outside, in the trees.

She took three steps to the end of the hall and opened the door to what used to be Victoria's parents' bedroom. And this room, of course, was different. In fact, even more different than the rest, because Victoria's mother used to have a small dressing room attached to it. Craig had broken down the wall between the bedroom and the dressing room, making the bedroom larger. He'd replaced the vast array of shelves and drawers with one simple dresser that occupied the corner of the room. And like the rest of the house, this room was now stylish, and clean, and somewhat bare.

This was where Victoria died. On her parents' bed, soaking it with blood. But now it was just another bedroom. Gemma stepped inside, looking at Craig's bed, a metallic frame with a large mattress covered in cream sheets. Why had he decided to make this room into his bedroom? It seemed like such a bizarre choice, with him knowing his sister had been killed here. She walked over to the window and looked outside at the trees beyond the backyard. There. She needed to go there. That's where they'd found her. That's where she'd fled from the dogs.

She lowered her eyes, glancing at the wooden frame. She ran a finger down a crack in the paint. She remembered this window. Here was one thing that Craig hadn't replaced. She touched the frame, then brushed her finger on the—

—glass. She struggled with the window . . . Why wouldn't it open? Behind her she heard their voices, yelling at each other. Angry, panicked. She glanced back, her eyes skittering over the bloody bed, Victoria's inert hand outstretched, her eyes gazing at the ceiling, mouth opening and shutting, like a fish out of water. She turned back to the window, whimpering in fear, and realized it was locked with a simple latch. She unlatched it and yanked the window open, the thing screeching as she did so.

"What was that?" a voice behind her shouted.

No time to think. She was too weak to do this right. She simply threw herself out the window, a jarring, blinding—

—pain in her head. She screamed and stumbled back, her vision darkening.

"Theodora, is everything all right?" Dunn asked. His hands on her shoulders. Holding her, constraining her. She screamed again and swiveled, tried to claw his eyes out. She needed to get away.

"What's the matter with that psycho?" Craig's angry voice shouted.

His shout actually pulled her back, and she tensed, forcing herself to keep still. She took a long breath.

"I . . . I had a flash of a memory," she finally blurted. "Victoria. On the bed. Bleeding."

"Yeah, that's where you stabbed her," Craig snarled.

She ignored him. Her heart was still hammering with fear, but not from him. It was the ghost of fear, manifested long before. Because there were men . . . bad men. They were after her. They wanted to hurt her.

She shut her eyes, and suddenly it was all there. The room as it was. That bed. Two doors—one to the dressing room and one to the master bathroom. And Victoria—

—leaned on her.

"I really don't feel well, Theo," Victoria mumbled.

Theo didn't feel so great either. It was too hot in here. They needed to go back to the party. But Victoria asked Theo to take her here. Victoria's parents had some ibuprofen, and Victoria really needed one or two.

"Where's the ibuprofen?" Theo asked.

"Never mind that," Victoria slurred. "Just . . . help me to the bed. Please."

They stepped into the room, and then Victoria stumbled. She grabbed Theo's arm, her fingernails digging deeply into Theo's skin, scratching her.

"Ow," Theo blurted.

"Sorry." Victoria sounded as if her mouth was full of cotton.

"It's okay." Theo helped her to the bed. "Here."

"It's so hot," Victoria muttered. "I can't breathe. Why is it so hot? Please, Theo, I'm begging you, make it stop."

"Here," Theo said, helping her take off her jacket. "Is that better?"

"Uh-huh."

A noise drew her attention. Theo looked back at the doorway, where two girls from school were staring at them.

"It's fine," Victoria said to them. "I'm fine. Go away."

They glanced at each other and left.

"Maybe you should close the door," Victoria mumbled.

"Okay. I'm just going to the bathroom. I'll be right back," Theo said. She was dizzy too. She had to wash her face.

She stumbled out of the room and into the nearby bathroom. She washed her face in the sink. The cold water helped her focus. She adjusted her mask back, hiding her face. Then she realized she was still carrying the bag Steve gave her in her pocket. If Victoria found out she had this on her . . . It was so gross, and so childish. Theo quickly retrieved the soft thing and dumped it in the toilet. She flushed the water. But the bag tumbled and floated in the toilet, staying in sight.

"Come on," Theo mumbled, flushing again. She had to get rid of the evidence.

Finally, it was gone. She got out of the bathroom and returned to Victoria. The girl didn't look good at all. Her skin was pallid, sweat glistening on her forehead. Her eyes were shut, but her lips kept moving as if she was saying something. Theo shut the door behind her and approached Victoria. She sat on the bed beside her.

"Victoria?" she said. "Can I get you something to drink?"

Victoria opened her eyes and gazed at her, eyes unfocused. "Didn't we drink already?"

"I'll get you some cold water, okay?"

"Okay."

Theo wanted to get up, but for some reason she couldn't. Her legs felt like rubber.

The door opened, and two guys in costumes stepped inside. One of them shut the door behind them.

"Look at that," the other one said. "Two birds with one stone."

Gemma's eyes fluttered open. "There were . . . uh . . . there were two guys."

"Did you know them?" Dunn asked.

Gemma shook her head, instantly regretting it. The world was spinning. "They were wearing costumes. Masks."

They'd been animal rubber—

—masks. One was of a gorilla. The other was a wolf. The faces with the masks were horrifying, the stuff of nightmares, the human eyes peering from the sockets seemingly trapped behind this demonic facade.

The gorilla stepped forward and shoved her carelessly onto the bed. She tried to move, to stand up, but her limbs moved sluggishly. She dropped back onto the mattress, her teeth clashing as her mouth snapped shut. The gorilla seemed to find this amusing and let out a laughing snort. He straddled her, his body crushing her. She could hardly breathe.

Her mask was torn off her face.

"Oh shit, it's Zit-face!" the gorilla shouted.

She tried to bite him, but she could hardly move her head.

"Better put her mask back on," his friend said, laughing. "You don't want to be looking at that."

Victoria moaned beside her.

"Did you lock the door?" the wolf asked.

"I think so."

"You better be sure, asshole."

The gorilla got off her, and she let out a long wheeze, relieved at the release of pressure. She fumbled at her pocket. The—

—"Knife," she mumbled. "I have to get the knife."

"Why?" Dunn asked. "Why do you need the knife?"

"He wants to—"

—hurt her. If she could get the knife, she could stop him. Her fingers were clumsy as she clasped the knife's reassuring grip. She pulled it out just as the gorilla came back. She was holding it all wrong, her fingers hardly able to clench. The gorilla grabbed her wrist and twisted it, the knife dropping. He punched her, igniting a blazing pain in her cheek. It had been so fast, the pain so horrible. She fell back with a scream, and then a hand covered her mouth and nose. She tried to scream again, but there was nothing to scream with, no air. Panicking, she fumbled at his hand, her eyes wide. He was going to kill her.

"Play nice," he said. "Okay?"

Terrified, she tried to nod but couldn't. She blinked. Blinked again. She needed to breathe.

He took his hand away, and she inhaled a breath of air, then let out a whimper. The gorilla grabbed the collar of her shirt. Was he about to smother her again?

No. With one sharp tug, he ripped it open, exposing her body. He grabbed one of her breasts, his fingers digging into it. She sobbed, horrified. This wasn't happening.

"Oh shit!" the wolf snarled.

The gorilla pulled away and cursed. She looked aside. Victoria had managed to sit up, and she was gripping the knife. She did it much better than Theo had done before, arm rigid, the blade aimed straight at the wolf.

The gorilla lunged at Victoria, and then the wolf joined him, both of them struggling with the girl, who wouldn't drop the knife. They snarled at her, punched her, pulled her hair, and then . . . it was so—

—"Fast," Gemma said, sinking to her knees. "It all happened so fast."

"What happened?"

"Blood. There was so much—"

—blood everywhere. Both the wolf and the gorilla were on their feet now, shouting at each other. The gorilla wanted to get help; the wolf said they couldn't. Theo wanted to move but didn't dare draw their attention. They could hurt her too. Like they did to Victoria. She didn't understand what they did. But she could see the blood soaking into Victoria's white shirt. The drop of blood on Victoria's lips as she gasped, her lips opening and closing.

"We need to find something to stop the bleeding," the wolf said.

"Maybe they have something in the bathroom," the gorilla said urgently.

Their voices were panicky, terrified. They both hurried to the bathroom.

"Where's the light switch?" one of them asked. "I can't see a damn thing here."

She didn't have a lot of time. A few seconds at most. She pulled herself up, then realized her shirt was completely torn. A jacket was discarded by her side; she must have taken it off at some point. She grabbed it, fumbled it on. She had to move fast . . . but she didn't remember why.

"Check the medicine cabinet!"

Oh right. The animals. The wolf and the gorilla. They wanted to hurt her. She tottered to the window. Why wouldn't it open? She looked back, saw Victoria on the bed. All that blood . . . She turned back to the window. It was locked with a simple latch. She unlatched it and yanked the window open, the thing screeching as she did so.

"What was that?" a voice behind her shouted.

No time to think. She was too weak to do this right. She simply threw herself out the window—

—A pair of strong hands pulled her back.

"Theodora!" Dunn's voice, sharp, loud. "Look at me!"

She blinked. Both Dunn and Craig were staring at her. She was straining against Dunn's grip, leaning toward the window.

"I jumped," she whispered. "To get away from them."

"From the men? The ones who wanted to rape you?"

"Me and Victoria," she muttered, talking half to herself. "They stabbed her. With my knife. *They* did it. Not me."

The relief was overwhelming. She let out a sob. All these years . . . she'd never been sure. There was always that nagging doubt. Recalling how angry she'd been. And those words of Dunn's, "a mountain of evidence." Not to mention that every single person in Crumville believed she'd done it. But she hadn't.

"Bullshit," Craig said with disgust. "It was her. She killed my sister. Everyone knows it."

"I didn't," Gemma said, half to herself. She didn't expect to convince Craig. At that moment she didn't even care what he thought. "It was them. I put on Victoria's jacket . . . because my shirt was torn. And I got out the window and ran . . . to the trees."

"Okay," Dunn said. "We're going over to those trees. Let's see where it ends."

Chapter 50

Theo ran as fast as she could through the trees, her twisted ankle sending a jolt of pain up her leg every second step. Her right arm throbbed, too, a dull ache from the fall through the window. And her face, where that guy had hit her. She needed to stop, and rest, and cry, but she couldn't. They were after her.

She could hear them somewhere behind her. She glanced back and saw it—sharp teeth, a snarling jaw. Dogs. Chasing her. She whimpered and pushed—

—on through the foliage. "I ran through here," Gemma said, her heart beating so hard it almost deafened her. Thud-thud. Thud-thud. Thud-thud. "They were after me."

"The men?" Dunn asked, following a step behind her.

"The . . ." She wanted to say the dogs. Victoria's dogs. That's what she'd thought back then. But a dog didn't run on two feet. "Yes. The men. They still wore their masks. When I looked back, I saw them. Behind me. They looked like animals."

"Like dogs," Dunn suggested.

"I was confused. Everything was—"

—spinning, branches and thorns snagging at her clothes, at her hair. Something scratched her face. Her left foot landed in a dip, and she stumbled, bit her tongue. She couldn't go much farther. She glanced back. The dogs were getting closer, screeching and howling, and she knew if they caught her, it would be over.

They would kill her, and they would feed. Should she climb a tree? She desperately searched around, but the trees loomed tall all around her. And something told her these dogs could climb trees. They would climb after her and drag her down. She broke to the left, and suddenly there was nothing under her feet, she tumbled and fell, and rolled, the world turning to chaos, and she couldn't—

—stop.

Dunn had grabbed her again, just as she was about to fall down a steep slope.

"I fell," she whispered.

Dunn gently let go of her arm. "See there?" he pointed at the bottom of the slope, at a tangle of branches. "That's where they found you."

Gingerly, she stepped down the slope, the memory of how everything around her spun and churned still vivid in her mind. Reaching the bottom, she looked around her.

That was it. She turned around, recalled waking up here. Seeing the beam of the flashlight wavering in the dark. The cops showing up. Too late to save Victoria. Too late to save anyone.

"I think I hit my head," she said. "I don't know. I can't remember what happened after I fell."

"It was dark," Dunn said. "There's a good chance the men who chased you had no idea where you went."

"Yeah." She shivered, even though it wasn't too cold.

She paced around the spot where Dunn said she'd been found, but she couldn't remember anything else. That was it. The end of the road. And the beginning of a different nightmare. "What now?"

"From what you said, there were two men," Dunn said. "Men in masks. A gorilla and a wolf. Did you see their faces at any point?"

"No. They kept their masks on."

"Anything you can tell me about them?"

"I don't know. They were big. Or maybe they just seemed big. They were bigger than me." She recalled the weight of the man with the gorilla mask as he straddled her, and swallowed. "Heavier."

"Did you maybe see what kind of clothes they wore?"

She shook her head.

"We could go through the photos of people at the party. See if we can spot a gorilla or a wolf, though I've combed them pretty thoroughly, and I don't recall seeing those masks."

"They were rubber masks, the kind that aren't pleasant to wear for long." Gemma swallowed. "I think maybe they wore them just when they were coming to . . . so that they wouldn't be recognized."

"Well, it's good news in any case."

"Why would it be good news?"

"The evidence trail is long gone," Dunn said. "We didn't find anything conclusive, and we definitely won't find anything now. And if it was one man, it would be tricky to get him to confess. Anyone with two brain cells would lawyer up and shut up, and that would be it. But we have *two* men." He nodded with satisfaction.

"So?" She wished he would get to the point already.

"A secret is only as strong as the weakest man holding it. If we have two men, we can use them against each other. If we have actual suspects, we can make them see it would be just a matter of time until the other one talks."

"Oh." She realized where he was going with this. "But I didn't see their faces. There were a lot of guys at that party."

"Yeah. But one of them drugged you. Someone must have slipped something into your drink. We just need to figure out who. We'll go back and—"

"There's no need to go back." The moments of that party were more vivid in her mind than ever. She now recalled stepping inside. That song playing. People dancing. And instead of going to Victoria's room . . . "When I walked inside, Bruce talked to me. He gave me a beer."

"Bruce Green?"

"Yeah."

"And you drank it?"

She remembered taking the first sip. And then the way she kept drinking, just to let him see it was no big deal. That she drank beer all the time. "Yeah. I drank it."

"So Bruce was one of them. Who was the other?"

She thought of the people who Bruce hung around with, and the answer floated to her lips almost instantly. "Rick Peters."

"Are you sure?"

And she was. Because she recognized the voice of the gorilla. The whiny quality of it, and the anger. And it was now finally clear how he was the only one to recognize her when he saw her. Because he'd been dreading the day she'd come back. No wonder he constantly blamed her for Victoria's murder, more than almost anyone else. It was because he knew the truth would land him in prison. "Yeah. I'm sure."

"Okay," Dunn said. "Bruce Green and Rick Peters. Let's bring them in."

Chapter 51

As soon as Dunn brought in Bruce Green and Rick Peters, he pegged Rick as the one to break. Sure, they both had an anxious look, but then again, most citizens weren't relaxed in a police station's interrogation room. Bruce had his act together, that what-can-I-do-for-you-Officer routine. He was "glad to help," and "was really hoping Victoria's murderer would be arrested soon."

Rick? He was a mess. Instantly demanded an attorney be present. Then, when Dunn explained he wasn't under arrest, that it was just another routine interview, Rick backpedaled, asked how long it would take, and clarified he had nothing else to add, that he didn't even remember the party that well. His eyes darted left and right constantly. He looked like a tightly wound jack-in-the-box, except instead of a clown, what threatened to pop was an admission of guilt.

It caught Dunn by surprise when, after two hours, he still had nothing.

Bruce was forthright enough, acting as if he was doing his best to recall what he had done during that party. Answering each question slowly and thoughtfully. Rick's go-to sentence was "I don't remember." He didn't remember where he was. He didn't remember seeing Theodora at the party. He didn't remember seeing Victoria at the party, which was ridiculous, since it was literally her house. He didn't remember what costume he wore. He didn't remember a gorilla mask. Or a wolf mask for that matter. Dunn wasn't unfamiliar with the sudden amnesia that often struck people in the interrogation room, but this case was a complete blackout.

Rick Peters, Dunn knew, was dumb as a brick. His memory-loss shtick was his best defense. Because once he began answering questions, he wouldn't be able to keep his lies straight.

That was all fine. The initial questioning was just a warm-up. Dunn still hadn't used his ace in the hole.

"Here's your coffee." He put the paper cup in front of Bruce. "I'm sorry this is taking so long."

"No problem." Bruce sipped from the cup and grimaced, just like everyone did when tasting the station's coffee. The brew was so bad it was practically an interrogation technique.

"Rick Peters is here as well," Dunn said.

"Oh, really?" Bruce quirked an eyebrow.

"I'll be honest with you, he looks very anxious," Dunn said. "Like he's ready to spill the beans."

Bruce frowned. "I . . . don't understand. You think Rick had something to do with Victoria's death?"

"I was wondering if you could tell me," Dunn said. "Did Rick tell you anything? About Victoria?"

"I mean . . . Rick thinks Theodora Briggs did it. Everyone knows that."

"He told you that?"

"He says it all the time. I probably heard him mention it a thousand times."

"He's not saying it now. Now he's singing a different tune."

A shift in Bruce's expression. A nervous twitch in his lip. "What do you mean?"

Dunn spread his hands. "One moment he's saying one thing . . . the next moment he doesn't remember. He's contradicting things he'd said in earlier interviews. He already asked for his lawyer. I think he might make a deal."

Bruce exhaled. "What sort of deal?"

"He could come clean in return for a reduced sentence."

"But . . . but he didn't do anything. It was Theodora Briggs, right?"

"Now *you* think it was Theodora Briggs?"

"Everyone does," Bruce said after a few seconds.

"Like I said, Rick doesn't seem like he does. Not anymore. He actually didn't mention her name *one time* since he walked in here." Dunn leaned back in his chair. "He's talking to my partner in the other room right now. I don't know how much longer he's going to keep his facts straight."

"Look, you've got it all wrong . . . there's no way Rick did anything like that."

"Maybe he would have if he was doing it with a friend. Rick's always been a follower, right?"

Bruce thought this through. "What are you saying?"

"I'm saying I agree with you. Rick wouldn't do it. Not alone. But maybe he had a friend he looked up to. Like you. And maybe you decided to have some fun. Nothing too bad. Just fun, right? It was a party, after all."

Bruce seemed to freeze in place. He said nothing. He didn't even seem to breathe.

"There were drugs at this party," Dunn continued. "Victoria was drugged. And another girl too. I have a witness saying he saw you handing that girl a beer."

"Hang on," Bruce said.

"I'm not saying you did it on purpose. You just wanted to have some fun. You just wanted her to loosen up a bit, right? It probably wasn't even your fault that things got carried away. You didn't know there was a knife in the room."

"That's not what happened! At all! I didn't drug anyone. I wasn't even with Rick at the party."

"Let me tell you something. If at some point Rick panicked and struggled with Victoria over the knife, and Victoria was stabbed by accident, it isn't your fault. I don't know if it was even Rick's fault, right? It was self-defense."

"I am not involved in this," Bruce said, his voice trembling. "I was partying in the living room until I heard someone shouting that Victoria was hurt. That's *all* I did. I didn't drug anyone. I didn't see a knife. I don't . . . Am I under arrest?"

"Right now, you're not," Dunn said softly. "There's still time to tell me your version. The true version. Before Rick flips out and tries to pin it on you."

He let time stretch between them, five seconds, then ten. Bruce seemed frozen in indecision. Dunn stood up.

"Take your time," he said. "I think I'll go have a chat with Rick."

He stepped outside and shut the door. Would Bruce call his attorney now? Try to cut a deal?

Maybe. That guy was hard to gauge.

The other one was easier.

Dunn stepped into the other interrogation room. Rick was pacing back and forth.

"What's taking so long?" Rick asked.

"Sit down," Dunn said, the softness from his earlier talk with Bruce gone. His voice was sharp, commanding.

Rick sat down, eyes wide.

"We have Bruce Green in the second room."

Rick blinked, glanced at the door. "Uh . . . yeah?"

"I think he's ready to talk, Rick." Dunn sat in front of Rick, folding his arms.

"Talk . . . about what?"

"You know what."

Rick licked his lips. There. The words were bubbling up in his throat. Dunn could see them coming.

"I don't . . . What did he tell you?"

"We're talking about the night of the party, Rick. You know. About the drugs."

"I don't know anything about any drugs, man. I don't . . . I don't even remember."

"You don't remember the drugs, or you don't know anything about them? Which is it?"

"I don't remember."

"So there could've been drugs, there?"

"No! No way, man."

"We're not interested in the drugs, Rick. You know that. We're looking for Victoria's killer. Now, I know Bruce brought the drugs. I have a witness who saw him drugging one girl. Did he drug Victoria too? Or did you?"

"I . . . What?"

Dunn slammed the table with his palm, and Rick jumped in his seat. "Don't mess with me, Peters. We already know everything that happened. Both girls were drugged. But I think maybe you didn't want things to go too far. Bruce, he was too aggressive, right? And when Victoria grabbed the knife, Bruce fought her, and she was stabbed by accident, right?"

Rick's mouth opened and closed, no words coming out.

"Look, you don't have much time," Dunn growled. "Bruce is talking to my partner in the other room right now. If he decides to pin this on you, I won't be able to help you. This is your opportunity to give me the true version of what happened."

Rick's eyes skittered. Dunn could almost see the cogs in his dull brain creaking as he thought it through. There. Now he would talk. And it would all be—

"I don't know anything about that, man," Rick said. His voice trembling. "Maybe Bruce did the things you say, I don't know. But I wasn't there. I don't really remember that party so well."

He leaned back and folded his arms, jutting his jaw.

"I don't remember it at all."

Disgusted, Dunn got up. "You better think it through, Peters. Once Bruce cuts a deal, I won't be able to help you." He stepped out and slammed the door shut, hoping the clang would freak Rick out just a bit more.

Sighing, he walked out and back to his small cubicle, where Gemma sat, waiting. She was pale, her body slack. She looked utterly spent. But when she glimpsed him, she shot to her feet.

"Well?" she asked.

He shook his head. "It'll take some time. For now, neither guy is talking."

"Oh," she whispered.

"You should go to your mother's and get some rest. I'll call you if there's any news. Did you fix your cell phone yet?"

"No. I didn't."

"Then I'll call your mom once I have any news. Sit tight. That Peters kid won't be able to stay silent for long."

Dunn tried to sound confident. He wondered if he'd managed to fool her. Because he wasn't so sure either of them was about to break.

Chapter 52

Gemma stepped out of the police station, surprised to see it was still light outside. She felt as if she'd been inside there for hours, waiting for Dunn to show up and tell her it was finally over. That Rick and Bruce had confessed to killing Victoria. That perhaps Bruce had confessed to being the guy who was harassing her as well. She'd imagined it, fantasized it, *willed* it to happen.

At the end, it culminated in disappointment. They hadn't confessed. At least, not yet. Dunn didn't seem confident that they would. And, like he'd said before, without a confession, they had nothing. No tangible evidence. No additional eyewitnesses. Just her and her erratic, untrustworthy memory.

She began walking to where she'd parked the car—a bit down the street, close to the café where she'd gotten a quick late lunch. She took out her cell phone, and after a moment of hesitation, switched it on. She wanted to check her messages. And to call Benjamin. Sure, her phone was hacked, and the Shadowman could be monitoring it, pouncing as soon as she turned it on. But maybe the Shadowman *was* Bruce, in which case he was sitting in the police station right now. And even if it wasn't Bruce, what did it matter? The Shadowman knew where she was. He'd demonstrated that even with her phone turned off, he could hurt her and the people she loved. She wanted to talk to Benjamin and Lucas. She wanted to—

The notifications popped up as soon as the phone was on. The phone blipped as they came through, and it didn't stop, like a thing possessed. Dozens of messages. Hundreds. Chats and emails and voice messages.

Messages from Benjamin—There's someone driving in circles around the block. I called the police. And then Lucas's teacher called—there have been threatening phone calls about Lucas, I'm picking him up early from school. And then, I think there's someone following us. And then, I'm going to the police station.

Messages from Barbara and from Thelma, about men entering the salon and breaking things—they had to lock the place up. Barbara thought there was a guy lurking outside her house; she picked up her son and drove to her mother's.

Messages from Benjamin's mother about a woman who knocked on the door and shouted vile things about Gemma.

Messages from Benjamin's father, saying things were going too far.

Messages from clients.

Messages from neighbors.

From other parents in Lucas's school.

And dozens of messages from numbers and emails Gemma didn't recognize—accusing her of murder. Telling her she would pay. That she couldn't hide.

She switched off the phone, her lips trembling. She had to get to her mother's house. Call Benjamin. See that he and Lucas were all right.

She hurried to her car, her footsteps matching her heartbeats, fast and erratic and—

Her car was *destroyed.*

All the windows and taillights were smashed. The word *Murderer* was spray-painted on the side. A few people milled around, staring at the wreck, taking photos with their phones, and one . . .

One held a can of spray paint. He was about to spray the hood, when he raised his eyes, meeting hers. She didn't know this guy. He was older than her, maybe fifty, bald. His eyes were wide with fear, his face pale.

"You think you can come here and act as if nothing happened?" he asked her. The words were stunted, delivered in a bizarre tone. The voice of a man reciting a message. "This is where you killed her. This is where you . . . uh . . . shed her . . . this is where you killed her and shed her blood."

He took a step toward her.

Gemma turned and bolted across the street.

He was running after her, shouting the rest of his recited message. The words another man had put in his mouth. The Shadowman.

She turned left and kept running, then realized that she should have gone the other way, toward the police station. She glanced behind her. Now there were two of them, chasing her, blocking her route back. One was holding a phone, recording her. She gritted her teeth, ran faster. Her mother's home wasn't far, she could get there on foot. She'd be safe there—

A pickup truck slowed down next to her, the window opening. The woman behind the wheel glanced at her and switched on the radio, music blasting, the volume loud. The song was "Turnin Me On."

They were after her. They were all after her.

And now more cars were slowing down. Gemma had never seen so much traffic in this street. Windows opened, all of them playing the same song, "Turnin Me On." They weren't synchronized, the songs meshing and distorting each other, a horrible cacophony. Some of the drivers were filming her with their phones. Not because they wanted to, she knew. Because they *had* to. Because someone had told them to do it. To send him proof.

Something in the corner of her eye drew her attention. A woman was wearing a Halloween mask—that same mask *she* had worn that night. No, not just one woman. Two. No, three. All were converging on her. And the songs from the cars around her kept blaring.

She was crying now, breathing hard, trying to get away, but they were surrounding her. She would never be safe. He was everywhere. His messengers were everywhere. And he would keep hounding her until—

A sign across the street.

Donna D's Sunshine Salon

Donna. A girl Gemma had *hated* as a teen. But she was Dunn's daughter. She could call him for help.

Gemma beelined down the street, nearly getting run over by one of the cars that were playing the song. She barged into the hair salon and slammed the door behind her.

Chapter 53

It had been another slow day for Donna in the hair salon. Two customers canceled. And after Donna did Penny's hair, Penny told her she didn't have cash at the moment and promised to pay tomorrow. She wouldn't. She would "forget" and then after a few reminders, would eventually pay half of what she owed. But what could Donna do? Penny was one of her regulars, and it's not like Donna had many of those.

As she swept the hair, she did mental calculations, trying to figure out if she had enough to pay the salon's bills for the month. Maybe. Just barely. As usual, a pang of anxiety settled in her throat, a sizable lump. If things didn't get better soon—

The front door opened, the bell jingling.

"We're closed," Donna said, turning around. "If you want, we can schedule for . . ." The words evaporated between her lips.

The woman who'd come in slammed the door shut and peered through the glass at the street outside. Then, with one swift move, she slid the dead bolt at the top of the door, locking them inside. She turned around to face Donna, breathing hard. She was dressed just as she'd been when Donna saw her that morning on the news. Large sunglasses, a brown cardigan, cute jeans, loose striped shirt, and booties Donna *knew* cost a fortune—because she'd wanted to buy them herself. She looked like a million bucks, even if her hair was currently a bit of a mess. Which was so weird, because in high school she'd always worn oversize sweaters and ugly wide pants and sneakers.

"Theodora," Donna blurted.

Theodora took off her sunglasses and met Donna's eyes. "Hi, Donna." She was still breathing hard. "Sorry. Some people were chasing me."

"It's no problem," Donna hurriedly said. Her heart pounded.

She'd known Theodora was in town, of course. That was the only thing everyone was talking about. Five different customers mentioned it to Donna that day: Did she see her on the news, Wasn't she in the same class with Donna, Did Donna think Theodora really did it? "Did it," meaning, did she really kill Victoria.

And Donna had told them she never believed Theodora did it. Because she really didn't think so. Even before her dad told her there was some evidence that didn't fit, Donna couldn't believe it. Because everyone said Theodora killed Victoria over that thing with the toilet, and there was no way, because it was just a little prank, it was no biggie.

It really wasn't a huge deal, right? Donna should know, she was there.

She was the one who . . .

Anyway, it was just a little prank.

"Who was chasing you?" she asked, uncomfortable with the silence.

Theodora peered out the glass again, then let out a short high-pitched laugh. "Everyone."

"What?"

"Well . . . they're mostly gone now. But that guy standing there." She pointed out the glass at a guy who was fiddling with his phone across the street. "And the woman in the pickup truck there. And I think that guy over there too."

"Okay . . . ," Donna said, stretching the word. Like, paranoid much? Those people didn't look like they were chasing anyone. They weren't exactly knocking on the salon's door.

Theodora let out a long breath. "Never mind. It's complicated. Would you mind calling your dad and asking him to pick me up from here?"

"You want my dad to pick you up?" Donna frowned.

"Yeah, I . . . look, just call him, okay? If you want, I can talk to him."

"Okay." Donna shrugged. She took out her phone and dialed her father. There was no answer. "He's not answering."

"Can you send him a message?"

"Sure, but sometimes he doesn't check them for hours."

"That's fine."

Donna tapped a quick message to her dad—Theodora Briggs is at my salon. She's asking that you pick her up because some people chased her. Should she add an emoji? Donna preferred to add emoji to her messages. They, like, supplied context. A smiley face goes a long way. But it didn't exactly work here, right? Neither did the frowny face, or the weird winky face with the tongue. Sometimes, there were no good emoji. She sent the message.

"Can I get you something to drink?" she asked.

"Uh . . . yeah, sure. Some water would be nice."

Donna filled two plastic cups with water. "You can sit down while you wait." She handed Theodora a cup and motioned at one of the chairs.

"Thanks." Theodora took a few shaky steps and sat down in the closest chair.

Silence stretched between them. Donna couldn't bear it. She *hated* silence. "I really like your nails," she blurted.

"Thanks." Theodora spread one of her hands. "I did them myself."

"That's amazing. You should, like, do this for a living."

Theodora grinned. "I *am* doing this for a living."

"Oh. Cool. That's really cool."

Theodora nodded, saying nothing.

"One of them broke," Donna said, trying to keep the conversation going.

"Yeah. You should see the other guy." Theodora gave her a weird look. Donna had no idea what she meant by that.

Silence again. Donna tried to distract herself by sweeping the floor. This woman was so unlike the Theodora she remembered from school. *That* Theodora was such a little scared thing. She always avoided everyone's eyes. And when she talked, she mumbled. And she never made any effort to look nice. When they were kids, Donna never understood why Victoria's best friend was Theodora. Victoria had been, like, awesome. She had the prettiest clothes, and she was always so energetic, and happy, and cool. Donna hung around with her, but it was always clear that Theodora was Victoria's number one friend. Theodora would go to Victoria's for sleepovers and dinners, and whenever they needed a partner in class, they always paired up, leaving Donna and Judy with each other.

So yeah, when Victoria stopped hanging around with Theodora, Donna never asked why. She didn't care. The important thing was, there was a BFF-size gap waiting just for her, and she quickly jumped in.

"I never thought you did it," she finally said, the words fast and hot on her lips.

"Thanks," Theodora said. "Your dad told me. That you didn't think so. That means a lot."

"Like, you wouldn't, right? People assumed you did it because you were angry at her. At Victoria. Because of the . . . that thing that happened. A week before."

"That thing that happened," Theodora repeated slowly. "Well, it didn't just happen, right? I mean, rain just happens. Or maybe the flu, you can say that the flu just happens."

Why did she have to make it so weird? "You know what I mean. That thing we did, in the girls' toilet. That prank? You probably don't even remember. It was a long time ago."

"That *prank*," Theodora said, each syllable heavy. "Yeah. I do remember."

So did Donna. Victoria had been *pissed*. About that drawing Theodora did of her. So she suggested they prank Theodora back. They followed her to the bathroom. Victoria's idea was, they would make it look like they were about to dunk Theodora's head in the toilet. So that she saw what could happen if someone messed with Victoria. Donna was totally game. It was a really obnoxious drawing. Why would anyone even draw something so nasty? Like, sure, Theodora and Victoria had a falling-out, but it was no reason for something like *that*.

So Donna was totally up for scaring Theodora.

Except maybe she got a bit carried away. Theodora slipped a bit while Donna was pushing her toward the toilet, so she ended up with her face really close to the toilet. And Donna wanted Victoria to see she had her back. That if someone hurt Victoria's feelings like that, Donna would make her pay. She was Victoria's friend. So she pushed just a bit harder, and she flushed the toilet.

She wasn't ready for Theodora's totally bonkers reaction. Shouting she'd kill Victoria? Overreact much?

Still, she didn't mean it, right? Sometimes people said things they didn't mean when they were angry. Donna had done it many times too.

She remembered that when they left the bathroom, Victoria seemed pale, shaken.

"She deserved it," Donna had told Victoria. "She shouldn't have drawn that drawing. Right, Victoria? Right?"

Victoria didn't answer, just kept walking, her body rigid with tension.

"She deserved it, right?" Donna kept asking. "Right?"

"Yeah," Victoria finally said. "She deserved it."

Later Donna regretted it. But it wasn't like it was a big deal. It was just a prank. It wasn't like this was the reason Victoria ended up dead. There was no way.

"It was just a prank," she was saying now. "You know, you and Victoria did that to each other, right? Like that drawing you made of her?"

Theodora stared at Donna, saying nothing.

Unnerved, Donna said, "But it's not like you two hated each other, right? I mean, when you were little, you were always together. Like, all

the time. And you'd sleep over at each other's house and share everything you had. So it's not like a few stupid pranks could really, I don't
know, erase all that. Right?"

"We shared everything we had," Theodora said, almost to herself,
her lips barely moving.

"Yeah! Like, at class you'd share your . . . I don't know, pencils and
scissors or whatever. And you'd share your lunch. And you loaned each
other books and dolls and stuff, remember?"

Theodora gazed right at Donna, her eyes so intense that Donna
found herself looking away nervously.

"Two birds with one stone," Theodora whispered. "Two birds. With
one stone."

Chapter 54

Gemma's mind buzzed as she stared at Donna. The woman's words played over and over in Gemma's head, like a bad jingle that won't let go. They shared everything they had. They shared. Everything they had.

It wasn't like Donna said something Gemma hadn't known before. Sure, when they were little, they were inseparable. And they really did share everything they had. They kept loaning each other their dolls, until neither of them was even sure which doll belonged to whom. During lunch they would switch with each other, each one taking things the other didn't like as much. Gemma getting two yogurts that Victoria detested, and Victoria receiving her mozzarella string cheese in return. And, of course, on Halloween, after trick-or-treating. They'd always pool their candy together. It was something they did. It signified how close they had been.

But Gemma hadn't given it much thought in the past years. When she thought about Victoria, it was about the night of her death, or about how Victoria bullied her during high school.

Except . . . there was one more time they shared something, right? Years after they both grew up.

Two birds, one stone. That's what one of those guys in masks had said when they stepped in the room, seeing Victoria and Gemma there, both drugged. "Look at that. Two birds with one stone." But he wouldn't have said that, right? Not if they had intentionally drugged both of them. One stone. One.

They'd only meant to drug one of them.

Outside, most of the vehicles playing the same song had driven off. But one parked right in front of the salon, "Turnin Me On" still blaring at full volume. And all Gemma needed to do was to shut her eyes and imagine being back at that party.

The song ended, and Victoria quickly started it again, some people laughing, other people booing. She did that, Victoria; she loved playing the same songs over and over again.

"Can I grab you a drink?" Bruce asked her.

"Okay, sure." She shrugged.

"Um . . . Theodora? Are you okay?" Donna asked.

"Shut up, Donna," Gemma muttered. "Let me think for a sec."

The beer made her head buzz just a little. And now she was dancing. Dancing with Bruce. He didn't even realize it was her. But how long until he figured it out? She needed to do what she came here to do and get the hell out.

"I'll be back in a bit," she shouted in Bruce's ear over the music and walked unsteadily away, the room spinning. She shouldn't have drunk the entire cup on an empty stomach.

She got to Victoria's room and slid inside, shutting the door behind her. It was dark, the only light coming from the window.

The room had changed since she'd last been here. Different, larger bed. The walls were no longer painted pink. The shelf with the plushy dolls was gone. This room had a large body-size mirror, a large off-white desk, and an actual TV in front of the bed. Victoria had always begged her parents for a television in her bedroom. Looks like she'd gotten her wish.

She walked over to the bed, staring at it. There. It would be easy. She'd take the bag, cut it with her knife, and shove it underneath the pillow. That would be enough. Steve and Allan would be satisfied. And Victoria would get what she deserved.

She couldn't bring herself to do it.

It was so obnoxious and childish. Just the kind of thing two boys would think of, inspired by dumb movies like Revenge of the Nerds and Carrie. She tried to get herself angry again, remember how she had felt when they pushed her head into the toilet. But all she could feel was exhaustion. She didn't want to think about this anymore. She didn't want to feel so angry and sad anymore. She just wanted to go home.

Her phone buzzed in her pocket, and she pulled it out. Steve. She hesitated as the phone buzzed in her hand and didn't answer. It stopped.

She had five missed calls from Steve, all from now.

It buzzed again.

She answered it. "Hey."

"Theo? I've been calling nonstop! Why didn't you pick up?"

"I didn't realize you were calling. It's noisy here."

"Listen, I think we should call this off—"

The doorknob turned. Theo's heart plunged. The door opened and for one sliver of a second, she could see a silhouette in the doorway, framed by the light from the hall. Instinctively, she dropped to her knees, hiding behind the bed. She hung up the phone and shoved it in her pocket.

The light turned on. The door slammed shut. Someone stepped into the room. Gemma could see the person's feet from under the bed. White high-heeled boots, perfect thin legs. Victoria.

The phone buzzed in Theo's pocket. Panicking, she took it out and turned it off. Then she froze, holding her breath. It didn't seem like Victoria had noticed. The girl exhaled and sat on the bed, the mattress creaking.

And then she began sobbing.

The sound was unmistakable, terribly familiar. The heaving breaths, the sniffling. Theo had listened to herself do this often the past week. Listening to Victoria crying was awful. Theo clenched her jaw, tried to remind herself who this was. What she had done to her.

But it was hopeless. Could anyone listen to another human being cry and not sympathize with their pain? Not to mention Theo had known this girl once, long ago.

She waited, crouching, hoping for Victoria to leave, but she already knew it wouldn't happen anytime soon. When you cried like this, a full-on sobbing fit, it didn't go away after a minute or two. There was no way Victoria was about to join the party right now. And at any moment she might spot Theo crouching in that very bad hiding spot.

So Theo did the only thing she could. She cleared her throat and stood up.

"What the hell?" Victoria blurted. She stood up, quickly wiping her eyes with one hand. Her face was blotchy and red, the makeup smeared at the edges. In her other hand she held a glass of beer. When she stood up, it slopped, some of it trickling to the floor.

"What are you doing . . . Theodora?"

Unlike Bruce, Victoria apparently had no problem recognizing Theo despite her disguise.

"I was just on my way out," Theo mumbled.

"What are you doing in my room?" Victoria asked, and then, "Are you looking for something else on me to give your friend?"

Theo blinked. "What? What friend?"

Victoria stared at her for a few seconds, then shook her head. "Never mind. What are you doing here?"

"I was just . . ." There was no way she could explain it. "I was on my way out."

"I hope so, you weirdo," Victoria spit.

So much for sympathy. She took a step toward the door.

"Wait," Victoria blurted.

"What?" Theo asked sharply.

"Just . . . stop. Please stop. Wait for a second." Victoria put her beer on the night table. "I'm actually, um . . . I wanted to talk to you."

Theo turned around, folding her arms. "Okay."

"About the other week. You know."

"What about it?"

"I never meant for Donna . . . I only wanted to scare you. I never meant for it to happen. I mean, I know how much you hate germs and stuff, I would never . . ."

"Bullshit," Theo said.

"I swear, Theo, I just wanted—"

"What about the pictures that you posted later? Zit-face getting a much-needed facial?"

"That wasn't me! That was Judy."

"So it's Donna's fault that she shoved my head in a toilet, and it's Judy's fault that that photo of me and that video were posted. And you're just an innocent little angel." Theo gestured at Victoria's costume. "Well, you're definitely dressed for the part."

"I'm not . . . I know, you're right. It was my fault. But I swear I never meant for it to go that far."

"How does that help me?"

"It doesn't. I'm . . . I'm really sorry."

This was impossible. Victoria would never just apologize. Theo knew that. Even when they were little, Victoria hated apologizing. Whenever they fought, it was always Theo who ended up trying to make it up to Victoria. And now? When they practically hated each other?

There was something in Victoria's eyes, though. A strange desperation. And despite everything, Theo hoped that maybe Victoria just really felt bad and wanted to make things better. Maybe Theo could go home, and starting today, there would be no more name-calling. No more humiliations. No more fear. She really wanted to believe that. "You'll tell Judy to remove that post of me? The video and the photo?"

Victoria nodded. "I should have done it the second she posted them."

"Okay."

For a few seconds they just stood there, looking at each other.

"Are you all right?" Theo finally asked. "You were crying earlier."

"Yeah, I just . . . I've had a really shitty day."

"You looked like you were having fun."

Victoria shrugged and let out a shuddering sigh. "You know, I used to like Halloween much better when we were little."

"Yeah. Same."

"You remember how we used to go trick-or-treating together?" Victoria gave her a little smile.

"We only went together twice."

"Three times."

"No, I'm pretty sure it was twice. Once when we both dressed as cops, and once when you were a fairy and I was Hermione." Theo counted on two of her fingers.

"And there was that time when you were Captain Jack Sparrow and I was Elizabeth Swann."

"Oh. Right."

"And we'd share all our candy afterward and eat until we were sick." Victoria grinned.

"You always ate more."

"What can I say? I can hold my sugar."

"Got any candy right now?" Theo actually felt like eating something.

"All I have is this beer."

"Ah, well. It was worth asking."

"I'll share it with you. For old times' sake." Victoria offered her the glass. "I don't even like beer that much. I just took it because Zayne got it for me."

She didn't want to drink. For one, she was a bit nauseous from the beer earlier. And she could see a faint trace of Victoria's lipstick on the rim of the glass. All those germs coating the surface.

But it was a peace offering, and Theo was desperate for it. She took the glass from Victoria and took a sip, then handed it back to Victoria, who took a sip herself.

"It's not so cold anymore." Victoria sighed. "But it's nice." She handed it to Theo.

"Yeah." Theo took another swig. "It's nice."

They kept drinking it, handing it back and forth. After a while, Victoria muttered, "God, I don't feel so great. I need to go to the bathroom."

She stood up and tottered, nearly falling. Theo quickly grabbed her.

"Here," Theo said. "I'll help you."

Gemma opened her eyes. Donna was standing there, leaning on her broom, staring at her like she was some sort of freak.

"Zayne," Gemma said. "He . . . but it doesn't make any sense."

"What doesn't?" Donna said.

"Zayne was Victoria's boyfriend."

"Well, yeah. I mean, until they broke up."

"They broke up?" Gemma gaped at Donna. "I didn't know that."

"I mean . . . those two were always on and off, right? It was hard to follow. But they broke up two weeks before she died."

"They seemed like they were together during the party."

"Oh, sure, Zayne was still trying to get her back again. But there was like, zero chance of it happening."

"He must have been pissed," Gemma muttered. "A guy like Zayne? He would have wanted to take what he thought he was owed."

It had never been Bruce. Bruce hadn't spiked her drink. But she'd shared Victoria's beer, which had Rohypnol in it. Two birds, one stone.

"Are you saying Zayne wanted to kill Victoria?" Donna asked. "No way."

"No. He didn't want to kill her. He wanted to rape her. But she ended up dead." Gemma stood up. "We really need to get your dad on the phone."

Chapter 55

Gemma sat on an uncomfortable plastic chair near the reception area of the police station. A plump middle-aged woman sat by her side, playing some sort of game on her phone.

Gemma wished she had a phone to mess around with. But she didn't dare turn her own phone on.

She'd been waiting there for over two and a half hours. Dunn had told her to stay put, and she wouldn't have left anyway. She didn't dare put a foot outside the station. The people the Shadowman had sent after her were probably still waiting for her to show her face.

She'd called Benjamin from a phone in the station and spoke to him briefly. He was at the police station, giving a statement. Detective Holly O'Donnell was there too. Lucas was at his grandmother's. Gemma was worried sick about Lucas, but Benjamin assured her that he was okay. She hadn't told him about the recent chaos in Crumville. She would tell him later tonight.

She'd been there when Zayne had been brought in, escorted by a uniformed cop. He'd looked at her for a few long seconds before following the cop inside. That gaze set her teeth on edge. She wished she was anywhere else, but more than anything, she wished she was back in Chicago, with Lucas and Benjamin.

There wasn't even a magazine she could flip through. When had they stopped placing magazines for people to read? When had it become an assumption that every person came with their own portable entertainment gadget?

"Gemma?"

It was Dunn, stepping into the room from the back door. Gemma shot to her feet.

"Yeah?" She swallowed.

"Come with me."

She followed him. "Did Zayne say anything?"

Dunn shrugged. "He asked for his lawyer. We're waiting for him to show up."

"Oh." The disappointment settled like a heavy stone in her stomach. More waiting. How much longer would she have to wait? With her family and friends terrorized, with her unable to set foot outside, with her husband and son half a country away?

"It's over here." He led her to a small room with a desk and a laptop. "Sit down." He gestured at one of two chairs behind the desk.

She sat. "What do you want to show me?"

Dunn sat in the chair beside her. "This." He clicked an icon on the desktop.

A video popped up on-screen. Gemma recognized it. The interrogation room, where she and Dunn had sat the day before. The same room where she'd sat for hours on end, all those years ago.

The footage displayed Rick in the room, sitting in the chair, his arms folded. Dunn stepped inside. Beside her, Dunn grunted. "This was taken forty minutes ago."

"This is bullshit," Rick immediately said. "I've been waiting for hours."

He sounded angry. And scared. The whiny pitch in his voice made Gemma's body tense. It was the same whiny tone she'd recalled—the voice of the guy in the gorilla mask.

"I'm sorry," Dunn said. "I understand your impatience. It won't be much longer. First of all, I want to apologize for earlier. What I said about you and Bruce turned out to be false."

"Well, duh. That's what I've been telling you all day."

"We already let Bruce go," Dunn continued.

"Good. Can I go too?"

"Not yet. Because we brought Zayne Ross in."

Rick instantly froze. It was hard to gauge his expression from the video's angle, but his eyes seemed to widen.

"I don't want you to say anything yet," Dunn said. "Let me talk for a bit. See if I got this right. Thirteen years ago, during that Halloween party, you and Zayne got your hands on some roofies. Zayne had broken up with Victoria Howell, and he was kind of angry about it. What was it, she wouldn't put out? Was that the reason? No, don't answer me yet."

Dunn on the video took out a folder, opened it, seemed to be reading something. Beside her, Dunn said, "There's nothing in that folder. I just wanted to give him some time to stew."

Finally, on-screen, Dunn continued talking. "Zayne managed to slip a roofie into Victoria's beer. And you and him planned to get some quiet time with her later on. But that's not exactly what happened, right? Victoria ended up sharing her beer with another girl. With Theodora Briggs. We have toxicology reports attesting to that. And when you and Zayne showed up, you saw you had two girls, not just one. Happy coincidence because you didn't have to get sloppy seconds, right?"

Rick leaned forward. "That's not—"

Dunn raised his hand. "Not so fast. I'm not finished. And frankly, you shouldn't talk anymore before we make absolutely sure you understand your rights. Anyway, where was I? Oh right. Two girls. Or like one of you said back then, two birds with one stone. You began your private party, but Theodora Briggs had a knife. She pulled it, you managed to disarm her, and Victoria grabbed the knife. And then both you and Zayne struggled with Victoria, trying to take the knife away . . . and she ended up dead. Theodora managed to get away through the window, you chased her, but lost her in the dark. And then you probably figured you should get back to the party and see if Victoria was alive. I'm betting that by the time you got to her, she wasn't."

Dunn slapped the folder on the table with one sharp motion that made Rick flinch. "Now. Like I said, Zayne Ross is in the other room. So before you go telling me you don't remember any of this, I want you to think really hard. Think about Zayne Ross. Think if he would stay quiet to protect *you*. I mean, some friends are like that, right? Loyal to the end. Is Zayne one of those people? Or maybe he would cut a sweet deal and leave you hanging? See, if Zayne cuts a deal with us, we won't offer the deal to you. It's that simple. There is only one deal on the table."

Rick blinked. He seemed about to talk when Dunn raised a finger again.

"Eh, eh. Before you keep talking, I want you to read and sign something. We call it a Miranda slip. You know about the Miranda laws, right? It's that stuff they always say on cop shows on television. You have the right to remain silent. Anything you say can and will be used against you in a court of law. You have the right to an attorney. If you cannot afford an attorney, one will be provided for you. See?" Dunn shoved a piece of paper in front of Rick. "It's all written here. So I want you to read it really carefully before you sign it. I'll give you a moment alone to do just that."

And on the video, Dunn got up and left the room.

Rick stared at the closed door. Then he picked up the paper on the table and looked at it for a few seconds, then put it back down. His foot tapped the floor. His jaw clenched. He picked up the paper again.

And then he shot from the chair, staring straight at the camera.

"Hey!" he yelled. "Get Detective Dunn here! I want to make a deal!"

The video ended.

Gemma let out a shuddering breath. She turned to look at Dunn, who was grinning at her.

"You know what?" he said. "When Zayne Ross heard Rick was about to start talking, he asked for his lawyer. To make a deal."

"So what now?" Gemma whispered.

"Now's the fun part." Dunn's grin parted, becoming almost predatory. "It's a bidding war between those two shit stains. To see who offers to sell out the other one for the cheaper price. I suspect it'll take a few more hours. But we'll have a full confession by tonight."

He leaned back in his chair, intertwining his fingers. "It'll feel good," he said thoughtfully, staring at the wall. "To finally have Victoria Howell's murderer behind bars."

Chapter 56

"Did you eat enough, honey?" Gemma's mother asked her.

Gemma rolled her eyes. "Yeah, Mom. I ate enough. I'm completely full."

They were having lunch at home. Even Richard sat with them. For the past two days, since Rick and Zayne had been arrested for Victoria Howell's murder, Richard's disposition toward Gemma had improved.

"You hardly ate from the chicken."

"I had chicken, Mom." It was as if her mother was trying to compensate for all their missed family meals by cramming thirteen years' worth of food into Gemma. It was a good thing she was leaving the next day. A few more days of this, and she'd return to Chicago a whale.

Now that her car was reasonably patched up by the local mechanic, she could go back home. The only reason she'd remained in Crumville for this long was to see Zayne formally accused of blackmailing numerous people online to harass her. Dunn and she had assumed it was him. There was no way it was Rick, but Zayne was clever enough and vicious enough to do it. Except, despite admitting to Victoria's murder and the attempted rape of her and Victoria, Zayne adamantly denied having anything to do with Gemma's stalking or the online blackmail. He acted as if he didn't know anything about it. And that morning, Dunn informed her of an additional disappointment—the search warrant for Zayne's house found nothing tying him to any of it.

But still. Since their arrest, the harassment of Gemma, her family, and her friends had stopped. Gemma had received no messages or emails from the Shadowman. Assuming he wasn't Zayne, it seemed the Shadowman had realized Gemma was innocent of Victoria's murder. And Gemma let herself hope this would be the end of it.

"I've booked flight tickets for Richard and me," her mother said. "For the twenty-second of December. Before Christmas Eve."

"That's . . . *two nights* before Christmas Eve," Gemma said, her heart sinking.

"Yes, but those were the cheapest flights. And it's last minute, so I had to grab whatever I could find."

"Did you find a hotel? I can recommend a few in our area—"

"I was hoping we wouldn't need a hotel," her mother said breezily. "Maybe you can find a room for us in your home?"

Gemma cleared her throat. "Sure. It might be a bit cramped, though."

"We don't mind."

Richard actually looked like he did mind, but he just nodded along. Gemma knew Benjamin would be happy to accommodate. And Lucas would probably be thrilled to have this new grandmother he'd been talking with on the phone stay at his house. But for Gemma it was more complicated. She'd spent the past thirteen years writing off her mother. And sure, she was glad to have her in her life again . . . but some part of her was still angry. Some part of her still blamed her mother and Richard for not being there for her when she needed them.

Well, she had time until December twenty-second to work through that. She wondered if she could find a reasonably priced therapist in Chicago who would be willing to see her five or six times a week for the next month.

The phone rang, and her mother got up and answered it. "Hello? Yes, she's right here." She held it out to Gemma. "It's for you."

Gemma sighed and got up, taking the phone from her mother. She hoped it wasn't another reporter trying to interview her. "Hello?"

"Mrs. Foster? It's Holly O'Donnell. From Chicago."

"Oh, hi." Gemma knew Dunn and O'Donnell had been exchanging information about the case for the past few days.

"I wanted to give you a quick update on your case," O'Donnell said. "First of all, in the past couple of days, I've heard of twenty-three people who contacted the police saying they were blackmailed online. The blackmailer had asked them to do something they flat-out refused."

Gemma licked her lips. "Like what?"

"Drive to Crumville and follow you around. Go to your house in Chicago, break inside, and vandalize your home. Follow a woman named Barbara Roth and tell her that her son's life was in danger if she kept socializing with you. Take pictures of—"

"Okay." Gemma shut her eyes. "I get the idea."

"Like I said, these people wouldn't do it. They've all been blackmailed by this guy for a while, but he'd never asked them to do anything as extreme as that before. And I think it's safe to say there were more who refused to act, but that I haven't heard about."

"And those demands . . . When did they get them?"

"All the demands came around the same time. Three days ago."

Gemma exhaled. So maybe she was right. Ever since the arrest of Victoria's killer's, the Shadowman had left her alone.

"As Dunn probably told you, we found no evidence that Zayne Ross was behind the online blackmail cases and your harassment," O'Donnell continued.

"Yeah, but Dunn said it's possible that Zayne managed to hide the evidence somewhere else. He's still looking into it—"

"It's not Zayne Ross." O'Donnell's tone was final, stating a fact. "I told Dunn that even before the search warrant to his house was executed."

"How do you know?"

"Like I told you before, I encountered another case like this one, and Zayne Ross doesn't fit. To put it simply, Zayne Ross isn't batshit crazy enough to do all this."

"He tried to drug and rape his ex-girlfriend, and probably meant to share her with his friend. He killed her and showed zero remorse. He—"

"Don't get me wrong. He's definitely an evil bastard. But the unfortunate truth about people like Zayne is that there's a lot of them. I see them every day in my line of work. But someone like your stalker is something else. I'm acquainted with a brilliant forensic psychologist, and I consulted with her about your stalker. I showed her some of his emails. She said the person whom we're looking for is incredibly obsessive. His main motivations are the power and control over other people's lives. She thinks he derives actual sexual pleasure from this sense of control."

Gemma shuddered in revulsion. "I see."

"She estimates after Victoria's death, he'd developed an extreme obsession around her, and around her murder."

"Do you think he'll go after Rick and Zayne now?" Gemma couldn't care less about them.

"No. The profiler told me that from the emails she read, it looked like he transferred his obsession to you."

"Well . . . yeah. Because he thought I was Victoria's murderer. But now he knows I'm not—"

"You don't understand. He's not focused on the murder. He's focused only on you."

"I don't understand."

"The murder was like a sort of story he told himself. It made him feel like an avenging hero. But the *real* reason he's doing this is because he enjoys the power and control over you. He is sexually invested in controlling your life."

Gemma's throat felt dry. She tried to say something and couldn't.

"You might think he's about to leave you alone. The profiler says there's almost no chance of that. He *will* keep going after you. Because he's addicted to the sensation it gives him. A guy like that doesn't just let go."

"Why are you telling me all this?" Gemma whispered. "Just to scare me?"

"No, of course not. I'm telling you this because I need your help. Once you return to Chicago, I want us to meet. And we will go over your stay at Crumville. Over all the emails I have. And every shred of evidence we have about his actions and demands. We have to find him. He's taking his time, but he'll reappear."

"He's taking his time," Gemma repeated, something shifting in her mind. There was something there.

"That's right. He'll definitely show up again, and his attacks on you and your family will continue."

"Um . . . okay." Gemma's mind was whirling. *He's taking his time.* And that thing she'd recalled Victoria told her. At the night of the party.

Oh, shit. She knew. She knew who it was.

"I'll do that," she said faintly. "When I get back to Chicago. I'll help you catch this guy."

Chapter 57

He stared at one of his monitors, hardly blinking. A map of Crumville filled the monitor, a blue dot shifting closer and closer to his home.

She was coming.

When he'd first found out she'd come to Crumville, he panicked. It felt like the beginning of the end. But now he realized that, in fact, it was the start of something new. Something better. He smiled as she turned the corner, just a few minutes away. Did she really think she could turn the tables on him? Beat him at this game? He held all the cards.

He got up and went to the kitchen, then put some water in the kettle. He knew her—knew her better than she knew herself. When she was nervous, she drank something warm to soothe her nerves. He'd seen it happen over and over with her. And she would be nervous right now. Because she'd figured it all out. And she was coming to see him.

He was a bit nervous himself, if he had to be honest. Like a boy before a big date. He went to the bathroom, checked himself in the mirror. Not too bad. Much better than he'd looked as a teenager, even she would agree to that.

Back to his computer. She was almost at the door. He switched off the screen just as she knocked.

"Just a second," he called out, then walked over to the door, exhaling slowly.

He opened it and smiled, faking a slight surprise. "Theo . . . I mean, Gemma! I'm glad to see you, I've been meaning to call."

She smiled back, a fake, cold smile. "Hi, Steve. Can I come in?"

◆ ◆ ◆

Gemma looked at the familiar face of her childhood friend. When she'd first seen him, she was happy to see that he'd fixed his teeth; it made him look more grown-up. But now, as he grinned at her, she thought that it had turned his smile from a bit gawky to creepy.

She thought he might turn her away. *So sorry, I'm in the middle of something.*

But then he moved aside, motioned her in. "Of course. I was just making myself some tea. Do you want some?"

She cleared her throat, licked her dry lips. "Sure. Some tea would be nice."

He led her inside and stepped to the kitchen in the back.

Steve's home back in high school had been nice, cozy. She and Allan loved to hang out there. He had a big room, with a beanbag and a large bed, posters taped on all the walls, and piles of comic books everywhere. And the rest of his house was inviting as well, his mother furnishing it with plants and tasteful landscape paintings. This place was nothing like it. The living room sported two large leather couches and an ugly dark oval table. An enormous flat-screen TV hung on the wall, connected to a console. The only remnant of the old Steve from high school was a bookshelf with fantasy and sci-fi books. A layer of dust coated almost everything in the room. The one thing free of dust was a laptop on a desk, hooked to two additional monitors.

"Wow, nice place," she called out, to fill the silence. An act. She needed him off guard. If that was even possible. Knowing what she knew. What was going through his head right now? Perhaps she shouldn't have let him out of her sight. What if he was using this time to grab a gun? Or destroy evidence?

No. It wasn't his style. His style, as O'Donnell had told her, was power and control.

"Yeah." He came into the living room with two mugs in his hands. "Feel free to sit down."

She sat down on one of the couches. It sank unpleasantly under her, the leather creaking.

"Is Heather here?" She picked up her mug, took a sip. He hadn't asked her if she took it with sugar or milk. And yet, it was perfect, just a tiny bit of sugar, as she liked.

He stared at her for one long second, confirming what she already suspected. There was no Heather. In fact, he'd probably forgotten the name of his made-up fiancée.

"No, she's on a business trip. She'll be back in a few days. If you're still here, I could introduce you." He took a small sip from his own mug. "I'm really glad they arrested those guys. Looks like it's over, huh?"

"Uh-huh. Finally over." She took a long look at him. O'Donnell had told her that for him, it would never be over. And Gemma could see it now. Something hungry in his eyes as he watched her.

"So what are you doing here? Come to say goodbye?"

"I just . . . had a few questions. Things that have been bothering me. About that night."

"Oh, I thought we already went over that."

"Yeah, I was just trying to wrap my head around it all . . . you know how when we talked about that night, Allan said that you stepped out of the car to call me almost straight after I walked inside."

"He was exaggerating. But yeah, I guess it was five or ten minutes after you walked inside. I mean, you weren't supposed to be there for so long."

"Right . . . I remember. I had a bunch of missed calls from you. Dunn also showed me the call log. All from the same time."

He nodded. "I called and called until you picked up."

"Right. But it wasn't five or ten minutes after. It was much more than that. I was in there for a while. I talked to Bruce, then danced with him. Drank a whole beer . . . it would have been twenty minutes, maybe even half an hour. And then Allan said you talked to me for a while. Which is also weird, because I hung up almost immediately after answering the phone."

"Yeah, you know how Allan is. His whole perception of time is a bit weird."

"And . . . why did you step out of the car to talk to me? Why not talk in the car?"

He shrugged, looking at her quizzically.

"And *then*," she continued. "You came back in and talked with Allan and decided to pull the plug, right?"

"Right."

"But when you called me, you already said that we needed to call it off. So you actually made up your mind before that, right?"

She let the silence stretch between them, a trick she learned from all those interrogations she went through. Steve fidgeted nervously. Most people couldn't handle a long tense silence. She took another big sip from her tea.

"I don't know," he finally said again. "Maybe. That whole dog shit thing was juvenile, you know?"

"I'm just wondering what changed," Gemma prodded. "When I went there, you and Allan were both excited about it. Then, twenty minutes later, you decide to call it off because it's juvenile?"

"I was nervous, I guess."

"It does make sense," Gemma said slowly. "Remember that talk we had a while ago, about the best revenge movie?"

Steve let out a snort of laughter. "You're kidding, right? How would I even remember something like that?"

"I do. Allan's favorite movie was *Carrie*, but yours was *Kill Bill*."

"Oh yeah. That makes total sense. I stand behind my vote. *Kill Bill* is so much better."

"Remember why?"

"Because Uma Thurman kicks ass?"

"No," Gemma said pointedly. "Because you thought that a proper revenge should be well planned and take time."

Steve rolled his eyes. "Yeah. Okay."

"Smearing dog shit in Victoria's bed isn't what you'd call a proper revenge. It's a dumb plan, and it's over and done, right?"

Steve said nothing.

Gemma took another sip from her tea. It really was good. "So I'm wondering if you had an additional part of the plan. One that you didn't share with us."

"Like what?"

"I saw Victoria answer her phone and leave the room pretty soon after I walked in the house. It looked like she wanted to talk in private. Someone called her from a burner phone. The police assumed it might be some drug dealer, but it wasn't. She talked to you, didn't she? That's why you stepped out of the car. You called Victoria. Not me. It must have been a pretty shady conversation if you didn't want any record of the phone call. What did you two talk about?"

"What are you saying, Gemma?" Steve blinked at her, his eyes wide.

"When I talked to her later, she asked if I was in her room to find something for my friend. Something like what, Steve? What did you already have on her?"

"I don't know what you're talking about."

"I think you do. I think you had something she didn't want anyone to know about. What were they, nude photos? And that's when you began what you would later become so good at. Blackmail. That's why you called her. To tell her you had the photos. This was your plan. Sure, some dog shit in her bed, but you could also use those photos to make her life hell."

"You're being ridiculous."

"You talked to her for *a while*. And later, when Allan went to the house to check where I was, *that's* when you called me."

Steve sat perfectly still, almost a statue.

"I should have known it was you," Gemma said. "As soon as I saw how quickly you recognized me. Even my mom took a few seconds. Rick Peters also took a while. But not you. As soon as you walked into that Starbucks, you instantly pegged me. Because you already knew how I looked now. After all, you've been stalking me for a long time."

Steve put down his mug and folded his arms. He didn't seem mad or hurt. Just calculating. If she had any doubts, they were gone now. She just had to make him say it. She had to make him come clean. O'Donnell said he got off on power and control. He would react badly if she made him look weak or pathetic. Perhaps he would lose control.

"You know what I think?" Gemma said. Her head pounded. She gritted her teeth, ignoring it. "I think you called Victoria that night, at that moment, because it excited you. You talked to her on the phone while you imagined me smearing shit on her bedsheets. Did it give you a little boner, Steve?"

He clenched his jaw, his fists tightening.

"Did it make you feel like a man?" Gemma continued. "Telling Victoria you had those photos of her? But I bet it didn't work. I bet she told you that you're pathetic. That you could shove those photos up your ass. Didn't she?"

"Shut up!" Steve roared, shooting to his feet. "That's not what she said. She was scared. She cried."

"So why did you decide to call it off? It was because you wimped out, didn't you? Did Victoria threaten you?"

"No." And suddenly, he seemed hesitant. Embarrassed. And it was then that the final piece of the puzzle fit.

"Oh. My. God." Gemma shook her head. "She promised you something, didn't she? Victoria always knew how to turn on the charm. She probably said that if you didn't show the photos to any-one, you'd have . . . what? A chance with her? A kiss? A hand job?"

"It wasn't like that," he blurted. "She liked me. She'd always liked me."

"That's what she said? And you believed her?"

"She *did!* We planned to go on a date the next day. She said I was special."

"Oh, Steve. I thought you were pathetic. But I didn't know you were so gullible."

"You didn't hear her. I know when someone is lying. She was telling me the truth. She really liked me."

"And that's why you wanted to call it off." Spots danced in front of Gemma's eyes. "And that's why you were so angry when you thought I killed her. You thought that . . . what? I killed your true love?"

Steve's face was red with rage. And then the anger drained from his face, and all that was left was a mocking smile. "So this was your plan? Make me angry so I would reveal my dastardly plan like some sort of movie villain? And as I do it, you record me with your phone?" He leaned over her, his breath warm on her face. "Oh, Gemma. And I'm the gullible one?"

Steve grinned at the woman as she gawked at him, confusion etched on her face.

"Did you really think that was what would happen? That you would walk out of here with my recorded confession?"

He sat by the computer, switching on the monitors. "Want to see a neat trick?" he asked. He opened his spyware console and tapped the override icon. The home screen of Gemma's phone popped up on the screen. "Ta-da."

Her eyes widened. "But I fixed it this morning," she mumbled. "The guy at the shop told me—"

"Let's listen to what he told you together," Steve suggested. He clicked the recording he'd saved from that morning.

"And you're sure the phone's clean now?" Gemma's voice asked on the recording.

"Absolutely," the thick voice of a man answered. "I removed the spyware. Your ex-boyfriend won't be able to spy on you anymore."

Steve paused the recording and quirked an eyebrow at Gemma. "You wound me. You thought a guy working at a shitty phone shop in Augusta would be able to remove the spyware *I* installed?"

Gemma tried to get up but slumped back onto the couch. "I feel sick."

"Then just rest for a bit," Steve said. "Here, let's listen to another recording while you get your shit together."

He clicked the other recording from later that morning.

"I don't know what you think I can do with this," the voice of George Dunn said, sounding frustrated.

"Aren't you listening?" Gemma answered on the recording. "Steve Barnett is the guy who's been harassing me. All those years ago he blackmailed Victoria. That's who she'd been talking to on the phone—"

"There's no evidence that it was him," Dunn said. "I told you, the number on her call log is a burner phone. It could be anyone. You don't have a shred of evidence to back you up."

"Then try to get it from him! You managed to get Rick and Zayne to talk."

"Because they were trying to pin the murder on each other. I have no leverage to get Barnett to talk. Listen, the murder case is closed. There's a good chance he'll back off now. He only went after you because he thought you were the murderer, right? You got your life back, Gemma. That's what matters."

"Can't you get a search warrant for his house?"

"Based on what? Your memory from something Victoria told you thirteen years ago? You'll have to get me something better than that."

The recording stopped. Steve shook his head sadly. "So this is what we're doing here? Trying to get Dunn something he can use for a search warrant? Let's fix that."

He opened the list of apps on Gemma's phone and selected the recording app. It opened on-screen, the seconds ticking on the ongoing recording. "Look at that. It's recording us right now." He stopped the recording and deleted it. "All gone."

Gemma tried to get up again, and her knees buckled. She dropped to the couch, falling sideways. "What did you do to me?"

"I just made you tea." He got up and crouched beside her, brushing a stray hair from her cheek. "Zayne and Rick aren't the only ones who can get their hands on roofies, you know. I think, since you're here, we're going to have some fun."

"I'll go to the cops." Her voice slurred.

Steve snorted. "No you won't. Your friend Dunn doesn't sound inclined to follow through on your bizarre new fixation about me. And you know what? If you do go to the cops, I'll make you pay. And dear Benjamin, and sweet Lucas, and the Foster family, and your mother and Richard, and Thelma, and Barbara, and all those other poor people whose only mistake was to get close to you. Their lives will be a living hell because Gemma Foster couldn't do what she's told."

Her lips trembled. Looked like she was finally getting the message.

"Now . . . let's get comfortable."

He caressed her waist. She pushed at him weakly, then tried to claw his face. He grabbed her wrists, and she struggled with him, clenching her jaw, her face tense with effort. Her bag tumbled off the couch, its contents spilling to the floor, her purse and phone, and . . .

Another phone.

He stared at it, frozen. It was an old-fashioned phone, with actual buttons and no touch screen. He got off Gemma and picked it up.

There was an ongoing call. He quickly disconnected it, knowing he was too late. Much too late.

"Hey, Steve," Gemma mumbled, her words almost unintelligible. "Who's gullible now?"

Did it work? Did her plan work?

Gemma was having a hard time concentrating. She knew she'd hatched a plan before she came here. But now her head felt as if it was stuffed with cotton, and it was difficult to recall the details.

What was it? She'd needed to outsmart Steve. But he'd always been a clever guy. Difficult to outwit.

She tried to move, but her limbs wouldn't budge. She hadn't antic-ipated this. Steve drugging her. It didn't seem his style.

But then again, what did she know about this psychopath's style?

Her plan was . . . it wasn't to make Steve tell her everything by angering him. Like he'd said, that was only something that happened in James Bond movies. No. Her plan was to make him think she was under his control. That he was cleverer.

Acting as if she was secretly recording him. Knowing that he knew. Of course he knew, he'd hacked her phone. The guy in the phone shop that morning had just repeated what she and Dunn told him to say. No one had even tried removing the spyware.

That was the only reason Steve talked. Thinking he was so clever because he could delete her recording. But there'd been a second phone, and she'd used it to call Dunn before stepping inside. So he could hear everything that was going on inside there. Right.

Right?

She vaguely recalled telling Dunn not to barge in unless he had to. She didn't want him to stop Steve from talking too soon. She wanted to get all the evidence they needed.

But she'd forgotten what every woman knew. That pathetic, weak men became vicious and unpredictable when angry or scared.

And now he was shaking her, screaming at her, his voice coming from somewhere far away. She tried to push him away, but she couldn't move, couldn't talk. And then . . . fingers around her throat. Tightening. No air.

Maybe her plan hadn't worked after all.

Something thudded. Something loud. Shouts. Figures moving around her. The tightening on her throat vanished. She pulled in a ragged breath.

A touch. Someone cradling her head. Not Steve.

Dunn.

"Hang in there, Gemma," he said, the words soft and vague. "The medics are on their way."

She looked at him and focused on his heavy lips, uttering the words one by one. "Did. It. Work?"

"It worked," he said, his face pale and worried. "Just stay with me. It worked."

Chapter 58

The Harp Grove Cemetery stood a couple of miles outside Crumville. Gemma pulled her car just outside the gate and killed the engine. The outskirts of town were already hidden by the tree line that ran along the bend. She was more than glad to leave the place behind her. She was not a fugitive, not anymore, but she didn't intend to come back to Crumville anytime soon. Some places deserved to be left behind and never returned to.

She had one last visit to make before her very long drive home. But now that she was here, she didn't want to step out of the car. She needed to postpone this moment for just a bit more.

Gemma took out her phone and dialed Dunn. He answered after a few rings.

"Gemma," he said. "Thanks for returning my call."

"Sure."

"How are you feeling?"

"Couldn't be better," she lied.

She'd spent the better part of the day before in the hospital, recuperating from the drugs in her system and from the bruising on her neck. The doctor had assured her there was no lasting damage, but what did he know? Not all damage registered on medical tests. She didn't bother explaining to him that the memory of Steve's fingers tightening around her throat would probably haunt her for a long time. That the feeling of helplessness as he touched her body still made her shudder when she recalled it. That there were moments from that day she couldn't remember, and it terrified her to imagine what had happened during that time.

One of the top tasks in her to-do list once she returned home was to get a really good therapist. This time, she would take the time to heal.

"I just wanted to give you a quick update on what we have," Dunn said. "I felt like you deserve to know."

"I appreciate it." She did deserve to know. She also *needed* to know. To know he would never go after her again.

"Steve Barnett had been keeping meticulous records on his computer," Dunn said. "He had a list of all the people he'd blackmailed over the past thirteen years. Like you guessed, he started right after the murder."

"He started right before," Gemma pointed out.

"Yes, that's right. The first one was Victoria Howell, though there's no note of that on his computer. I suspect he didn't like to think of her as one of his victims."

"No, he preferred to think of her as his one true love." Gemma's mouth twisted.

"Anyway, that list details *hundreds* of people. I've shared it with Detective Holly O'Donnell from the Chicago PD, and with the FBI. We'll be contacting these people, to let them know he won't be coming after them anymore."

"I suspect some of them won't be thrilled to hear the police have their secrets."

"I guess not," Dunn agreed heavily. "Anyway, with hundreds of blackmail offenses, attempted murder, attempted rape, not to mention people he'd sent to commit acts of violence, Barnett will spend a very very long time in prison."

Gemma exhaled. "Good."

"Zayne Ross and Rick Peters aren't going anywhere anytime soon either. Peters ended up agreeing to a very bad deal from the district attorney in return for testifying against Ross."

"Okay."

"So it's over, Gemma."

"Yeah," she said hollowly. "It's over."

A short silence ensued. "Are you sure you're good to drive back home today?" Dunn finally asked. "I think you should rest for at least one more day."

Wild horses wouldn't be able to drag her back. "I'll be okay. I won't drive the entire distance today. I'll split it."

"Right. Have a good drive home, Gemma."

"Thanks, George. For everything."

"No need to thank me." He cleared his throat. "I wish I could have done it much sooner."

Didn't they all. "Bye, George."

"Bye."

She hung up and sighed. Then she got out of the car, gently closing the door behind her. A thick silence settled around her, a quietness that belonged to the dead. She stepped into the cemetery and quickly realized this wouldn't be as fast as she'd imagined. She'd never been there before and wasn't ready for the rows of graves that stretched in all directions. She had no idea where to start. She hadn't gone to Victoria's funeral, already terrified of the accusations that began to be whispered her way. Now she didn't know where Victoria's grave was.

It took her twenty minutes to find it, and it would have probably taken much longer if not for the fresh flowers that had been placed on top of the grave. Who had placed them? Victoria's mother? Craig Howell? Maybe one of Victoria's high school friends? Whoever it was, it looked like the flowers had been placed that morning, or at most the day before. Someone had come to visit Victoria, to tell her that her murderers were finally behind bars.

And now it was Gemma's turn to talk to Victoria. She scrutinized the gravestone that said VICTORIA HOWELL, 1993–2010, YOUR SONG HAS ENDED, BUT THE MELODY LINGERS ON.

She swallowed. "Hey," she croaked. "Sorry it's taken me so long."

She took a long breath. "I don't really know what to say." Her voice trembled. "But it was important to me to come here. I feel like my memories of you all those years were . . . warped, I guess. When I thought of you, I thought of your murder. And of the way people blamed me for it. And sometimes, I even blamed myself. And I thought of all the times you hurt me."

She wiped a tear from her eye and sniffed. "And I guess that all those years, I didn't think of you like I maybe should have. Like you were when we were still friends. When you think about it, we'd been best friends for six years. That's a long time. I wish it had been longer. I really do." She looked up, saw a ray of sunlight filtering through the branches of a tree.

"I now remember the last time we talked. You told me you were sorry. And I think you really meant it. I don't know . . . what would have happened if those bastards hadn't killed you that night, but I like to think that we would have become friends again. Maybe. I don't even know why we ever stopped being friends."

She let out a shuddering breath. "Anyway, you told me you were sorry, but I never told you I was sorry. About that drawing. I mean, I didn't apologize in a way that counts."

She took out the paper from her pocket and unfolded it. Her sketch from that morning. Victoria as *she* remembered her. Not that photo they kept using in news stories. But the way she was in Gemma's mind. From that night, the few precious minutes they had together. Her eyes sad, mouth quirked in a tiny smile. She still had her angel costume on, except in the drawing, the wings weren't something she'd purchased in an online store. They were the real thing.

She refolded the paper. This sketch was only for her and for Victoria. Not for anyone else. She placed it by the flowers and put a small rock on top to hold it there.

"I'm sorry, Vic," she said.

And then she turned away. Her son and husband were waiting for her.

Chapter 59

Victoria Howell, 2010

These days, Victoria seemed to be angry all the time. She'd wake in the morning, already gritting her teeth. Spend her time in school with a red haze tainting her every moment. Go back home and tense up as she saw her mother or her brothers. Go to sleep, feeling like a tight coil about to snap. Everything felt too much. Every time her phone blipped with a text. Every time someone talked to her. Every time no one talked to her. Every time she had to do a thing. Anything. Just make it stop. Why wouldn't it stop, stop, STOP?

Venting didn't help. She tried screaming, crying, spewing filthy words one after the other like a mantra. Her body always seemed to produce more rage. A perpetual machine of fury.

Maybe this time, she'd feel just a tiny bit of relief. Make someone else hurt for a change. Someone who deserved it.

They'd seen her go into the bathroom, and now they converged on it, a pack of predators trapping their prey. She would have nowhere to go.

Theodora would see what happened when you messed with Victoria.

"I want her to think we're about to shove her head straight into the toilet," she snarled. That's how she talked these days. She didn't say words. She snarled them. She hissed them. She spit them.

"Yeah." Donna giggled. "That'll be great."

Did Donna realize how infuriating her giggling was? How inane her empty sentences could be? Victoria glared at her, and Donna quickly lowered her eyes.

They stepped into the bathroom and waited for Theodora to come out of the stall.

It seemed strange that she and Theodora were once such good friends. Victoria recalled that as someone might recall something they'd seen on television. Someone else's life. Definitely a better life than the one she had right now. Back then, they were inseparable. Two friends who shared everything. They could complete each other's sentences. Guess what the other was thinking. Sometimes a single look, a tiny twist of the mouth, was enough; they didn't really need words to communicate.

That had been the problem, right? Because if there's something you don't want anyone to know about, you can't hang around a soulmate who can guess what goes through your mind.

It happened only twice. Her father's boss coming for dinner, staying around late, then on his way to the bathroom, slipping into her bedroom for a few minutes.

Just twice.

The first to find out was her mother. And she spoke to her father. Raised voices. Anger. Her father leaving the house, slamming the door behind him, Victoria knowing it was her fault.

And then, a few days later, her mother told her they fixed it. Her father's boss won't be coming ever again. And her father was getting a promotion, which meant they could afford that trip to Paris Victoria had always dreamed about, wasn't that great? And just one thing—she really had to keep that one thing a secret.

Well, it wasn't really one thing, right? It happened twice. So two things.

Anyway.

It had to be a secret. Because if anyone found out, her father could lose his job. Including the promotion and the trip to Paris. Victoria didn't want that, right?

Of course she didn't. What would be the point, anyway? It had already happened, twice.

The problem was . . . Theodora would find out, right? She was already asking Victoria what was wrong, why she was so sad all the time. She couldn't find out. Victoria's father would lose his job.

Which was when Victoria began spending less time with her. She replaced her with Donna, but that wasn't enough, really because Theodora was worth ten Donnas. So Victoria found more friends to fill the void. Quantity over quality. And she was fine. The trip to Paris was really nice. There would be more trips. She was totally fine. She was fine, fine, FINE.

For a few years, everything seemed to be just . . . dull. And gray. Lifeless. But then she realized she was feeling something new. What was this new emotion?

Anger.

Theodora should have known. Hadn't they been best friends? Couldn't they practically read each other's thoughts? Why hadn't her so-called BFF realized something had been wrong with her?

In a bout of fury, she called Theodora Zit-face, in the hall. And that look Theodora gave her made Victoria feel vindicated, for just one single second. It definitely felt good enough to do it again. And again.

And she was fine. She really was. Okay, so she had to break up with Zayne. Because every time he touched her, she could feel those rough fingers on her from all those years ago. And Zayne wanted to go "all the way," and didn't realize the aforementioned "way" led somewhere, and that somewhere was never good. So, he had to go. If only she hadn't sent him those photos of her when they were together. That had been dumb. Still, he promised he deleted them. So.

And then . . . that drawing. Posted online, where everyone could see. And Victoria saw that cleavage Theodora had given her in the drawing. It was like she was telling her that she *did* know. And that what had happened had been Victoria's fault. Because she was a slut.

So. Now she was going to teach her ex-BFF a lesson.

When Theodora got out of her stall, the panicky look she gave Victoria already made her feel slightly better. She'd imagined this moment the night before. She had it all figured out. A killer sentence. She would say "The reason you have so many zits is because you don't wash your face every day. We're here to help you with that."

But she was so shaky with fury, she could hardly think straight, the words all tangling in her mind.

"Zits happen when, um . . . it's because of dirt. You should wash them. Your face, I mean."

Damn it.

And now Donna was holding Theodora above the toilet, and Victoria was filming it all with her phone. That was the point, right? To humiliate the girl like *she'd* humiliated her. And then maybe she'd finally feel better, and it would be like nothing had happened, ever. Not once. Or twice.

Except Donna got a bit excited and ended up dunking Theo's head in the toilet.

Not Theo. Theodora.

And Victoria knew how much Theo was afraid of germs. How awful she must have felt at that moment. How violated.

She tried to tell Donna to stop, but it was too late, and now Theo . . . Theodora was screaming at her she would kill her, and Victoria was about to cry, so she hurried away, pocketing her phone, wishing she hadn't done it, that she hadn't filmed it, that she hadn't pulled away from Theo all those years ago, that this man hadn't gone into her room twice.

Donna kept harping in her ear. "She deserved it, right, Victoria? Right?"

Victoria wished she would shut up. She wished she could be home right now, in her bed, the blanket over her head.

"She deserved it, right?"

"Yes," Victoria blurted, just to silence her. "She deserved it."

She shouldn't have made that drawing of her. She really shouldn't have.

And she should have known. That he'd gone into Victoria's bedroom. Twice.

She should have known.

Chapter 60

"I feel like they've been gone for a really long time," Gemma said.

"Twenty minutes." Benjamin quirked his eyebrow. "Maybe a bit less."

"It's really cold outside, and I don't know if Lucas was dressed properly." Gemma glanced out the window at the snowy sidewalk.

"Gemma, your mother will make sure it's fine."

"She doesn't know how to handle the cold here, Benjamin. She lived her entire life in Georgia."

He was smiling at her now, and she found herself smiling back. It was warm and cozy in their home, and if she had to be honest, it was nice to have a few minutes just for Benjamin and her, with her mother and Richard and Lucas outside.

And it was also nice to have a discussion about her mother with Benjamin. And saying a sentence like "She lived her entire life in Georgia." Which was an innocuous thing to say but had been impossible to utter just two months before. Because it would have exposed the fact that her mother was alive. And that Gemma had been born in Georgia.

She sat back down next to Benjamin on the couch and leaned into him. He wrapped her up with one of his arms, kissing the top of her head.

"You know," Gemma murmured, nuzzling into his chest. "Victoria's birthday is today. Just a few days before Christmas. I remember celebrating her tenth birthday with her . . . back when we were friends."

"Is it a nice memory?" Benjamin asked. With her head on his body, her ear thrummed pleasantly when he spoke.

"Yeah," she said. "It's very nice. She wanted a special day, just for the two of us. So her mother took us to the mall. We sat in the back seat of the car, singing along with the radio, getting all the words wrong, laughing our asses off. The plan was for her mother to drop us there, and for us to hang around by ourselves. I was a bit worried."

"Why were you worried?"

"It was the first time I went to the mall without a grown-up to look after me. I kept imagining all the things that could go wrong. But nothing did. I had an allowance, and I got Victoria a bracelet with our names etched on it. She was so happy." Gemma grinned to herself. It was weird, feeling the memory unfold in her mind as she told this story. She hadn't thought of that day for more than a decade, but it was still there, nestled in her mind. "We went to this café. And we ordered these ridiculous, enormous cups of hot chocolate, with whipped cream on top."

Benjamin stroked her hair as she was talking. She used to think he lacked curiosity, the way he never asked her about anything. And if she had to be honest about it, part of her was always infuriated by this. But now she realized he was just content to listen to her, not wanting to interrupt. He was a good listener.

"We drank all of it and were sick afterward, but also really excited . . . probably the sugar rush. We went to a clothing store and tried on different outfits, and I bought myself a shirt. I felt like such a grown-up. And then, Victoria's mother was supposed to wait for us in the mall's parking lot. When we looked for her, it began raining. Like, pouring, we were drenched—"

The front door opened, and Lucas barged inside. "Mommy, we made a snowman!" He rushed over to her.

"Oh wow, a snowman!" She rose up to hug him. "That's great. Take off your boots."

"I wanted a carrot for his nose, but we didn't have a carrot, so Richard said we could use a stone."

Lucas was walking around the room as he spoke, leaving flakes of dirty melting snow in his wake. Gemma's mother and Richard stepped inside, shutting the door behind them. Their faces were flushed from the cold. They were both smiling.

"Did you find a stone for his nose?" Gemma asked. "Take your boots off, honey."

"We did! And sticks for his hands. And then my hands got cold so Grandma blew on them but that didn't help so she said we should go back home."

"It was getting really cold," her mother said. "I honestly don't know how you live here all winter."

"We dress warmly." Benjamin smiled at her while helping Lucas take off his boots. "And we stay inside."

"Well, that explains it." Her mother nodded with satisfaction, as if Benjamin had just solved an incredibly complex conundrum.

Benjamin and her mother had hit it off as soon as they met, a fact that for some reason annoyed Gemma to no end. She would have to talk to her therapist about it.

"I should change my clothes," Richard said. "My socks are wet."

"Mine too," her mother said. "My toes are frozen stiff."

They went to the guest room. Lucas hurried to the bathroom, realizing he urgently needed to pee. Gemma blinked as the three disappeared, the crowded living room emptying again.

"I need to start preparing dinner," Benjamin said.

"I should go help Lucas change his clothes too," Gemma said.

"But you were telling me about that day. It started raining."

Gemma shook her head and smiled at him. "I'll tell you the rest later."

There was no rush. She had a lot of stories from her childhood, and she could share them all in time.

ACKNOWLEDGMENTS

I wrote this book while getting ready to move to another country with my family. We had to find a house and schools for the children, get all our passports and visas and stuff ready—a million and one different things you don't even think of when deciding to move.

These distractions aren't great for the creative process. Without my wife, Liora, it would have been impossible. Imagine her, trying to figure out our health insurance, with me suddenly showing up and saying, "I need to brainstorm Gemma's motivations." And she put everything aside to do that with me AND later got our health insurance done. As always, without her, this book would never have had a chance. Also, she came up with the name *Behind You*.

My editor, Jessica Tribble Wells, *loved the draft*, meaning she had three pages of notes for me to fix and rewrite. The original draft had a glaring flaw in its pacing and structure, one that I thought was impossible to fix. And then Jessica fixed it. She also helped me with the Shadowman's identity—that's right, I literally had a different antagonist in the first draft. Never doubt the miracles a great editor can perform.

The initial draft was read by a few people, all who gave me great notes, making it better. My writing partner, Christine Mancuso, came up with a bunch of adjustments to Gemma's character, enriching her and making her feel right. She also had me make a crucial change to the plot in the first half of the book. My sister, Yael Omer, as well as both my parents, read it, giving me specific notes that I promptly implemented, making the book really shine.

Kevin Smith, my developmental editor, helped me smooth out a lot of the kinks in the manuscript, enriching the background of the characters and tightening the red herring angle.

My sister-in-law, Noa Sahar, helped me figure out the ins and outs of a beautician's life. Any inaccuracies there are my fault; anything that rings true is thanks to her.

Sarah Hershman, my agent, was particularly enthusiastic about this book, and cheered me on throughout the process.

And thanks again to my readers. You are all constantly in my mind as I write. Thank you for reading my books, and enjoying them, and writing me all those lovely emails. You are the best readers an author could ask for.

ABOUT THE AUTHOR

Photo © 2017 Yael Omer

Mike Omer has been a journalist, a game developer, and the CEO of Loadingames, but he can currently be found penning his next thriller. Omer loves to write about two things: real people who could be the perpetrators or victims of crimes . . . and funny stuff. He mixes these two loves quite passionately in his suspenseful and often macabre mysteries. Mike is married to a woman who diligently forces him to live his dream, and he's a father to an angel, a pixie, and a gremlin. To learn more about the author, email him at mike@strangerealm.com.

10/17/24